my LITTLE PONY The MOVIE

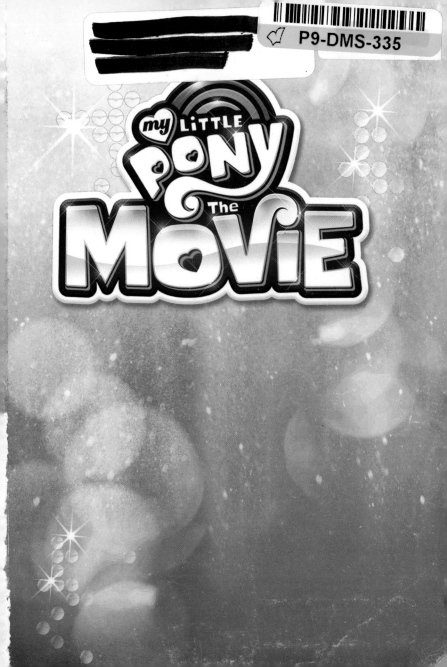

Special thanks to Meghan McCarthy, Eliza Hart, Ed Lane,
Beth Artale, Heather Hopkins, and Michael Kelly.

ISBN: 978-1-68405-116-8
20 19 18 17   2 3 4 5

www.IDWPUBLISHING.com

Licensed By:

my Little PONY the MOVIE

Screenplay by
**Meghan McCarthy, Rita Hsiao,
and Michael Vogel**

Adaptation by
Justin Eisinger

Edits by
Alonzo Simon

Lettering and Design by
**Tom B. Long, Robbie Robbins,
& Gilberto Lazcano**

Publisher
Ted Adams

MEET THE PONIES

Twilight Sparkle

TWILIGHT SPARKLE TRIES TO FIND THE ANSWER TO EVERY QUESTION! WHETHER STUDYING A BOOK OR SPENDING TIME WITH PONY FRIENDS, SHE ALWAYS LEARNS SOMETHING NEW!

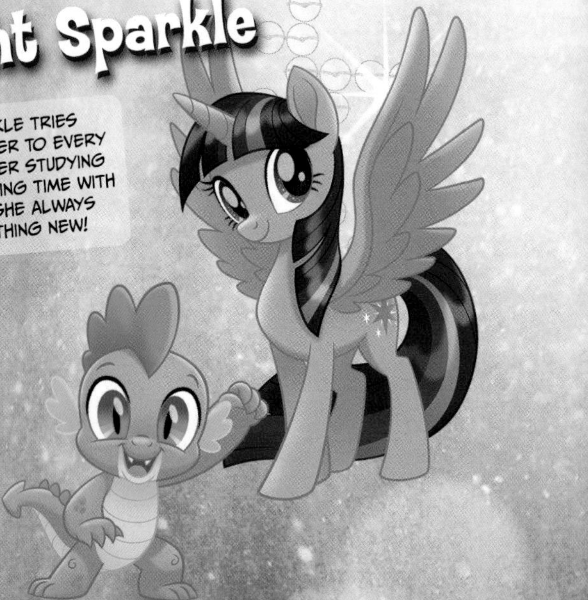

Spike

SPIKE IS TWILIGHT SPARKLE'S BEST FRIEND AND NUMBER ONE ASSISTANT. HIS FIRE BREATH CAN DELIVER SCROLLS DIRECTLY TO PRINCESS CELESTIA!

Applejack

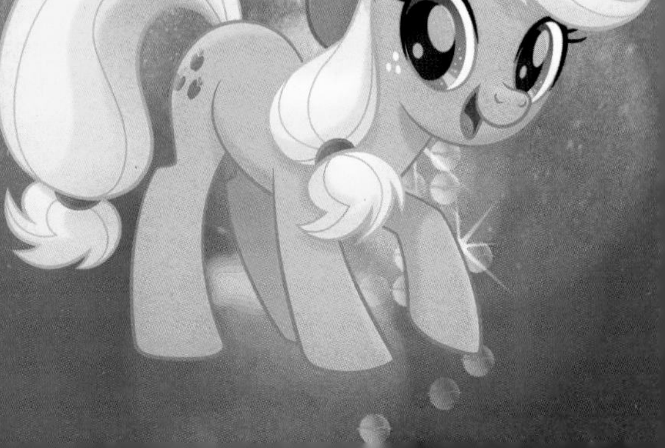

APPLEJACK IS HONEST, FRIENDLY, AND SWEET TO THE CORE! SHE LOVES TO BE OUTSIDE, AND HER PONY FRIENDS KNOW THEY CAN ALWAYS COUNT ON HER.

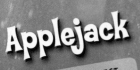

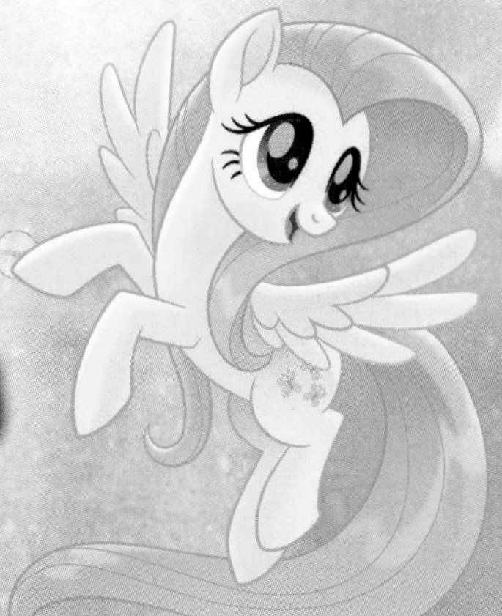

Fluttershy

FLUTTERSHY IS A KIND AND GENTLE PONY WITH A BIG HEART. SHE LIKES TO TAKE CARE OF THE OTHERS, ESPECIALLY HER LITTLE ANIMAL FRIENDS.

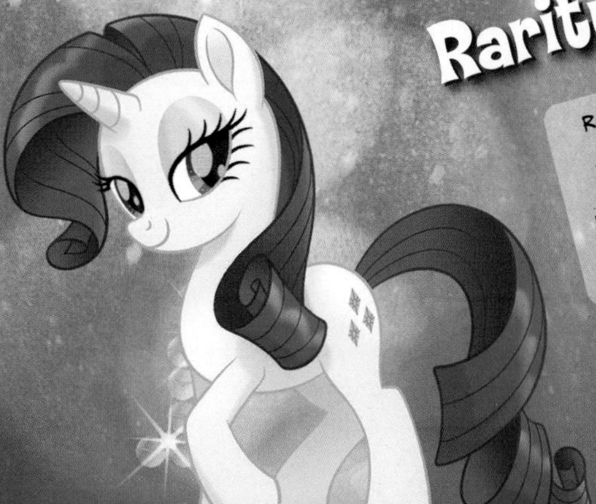

Rarity

RARITY KNOWS HOW TO ADD SPARKLE TO ANY OUTFIT! HER GENEROUS NATURE INSPIRES HER TO HELP OTHERS LOOK AND FEEL THEIR BEST.

Pinkie Pie

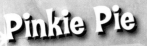

PINKIE PIE KEEPS HER PONY FRIENDS LAUGHING AND SMILING ALL DAY! CHEERFUL AND PLAYFUL, SHE ALWAYS LOOKS ON THE BRIGHT SIDE.

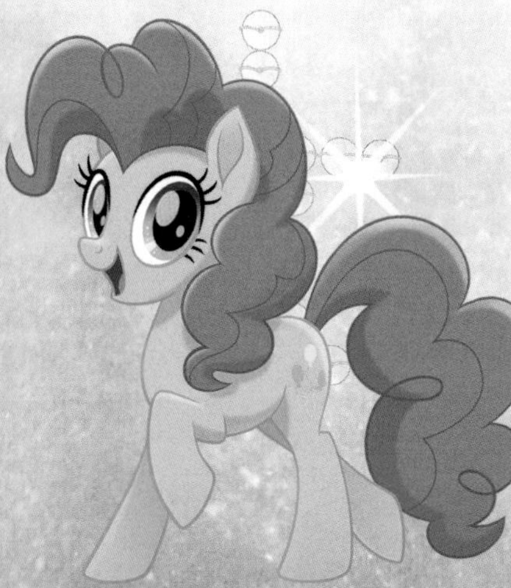

Rainbow Dash

RAINBOW DASH LOVES TO FLY AS FAST AS SHE CAN! SHE IS ALWAYS READY TO PLAY A GAME, GO ON AN ADVENTURE, OR HELP OUT ONE OF HER PONY FRIENDS.

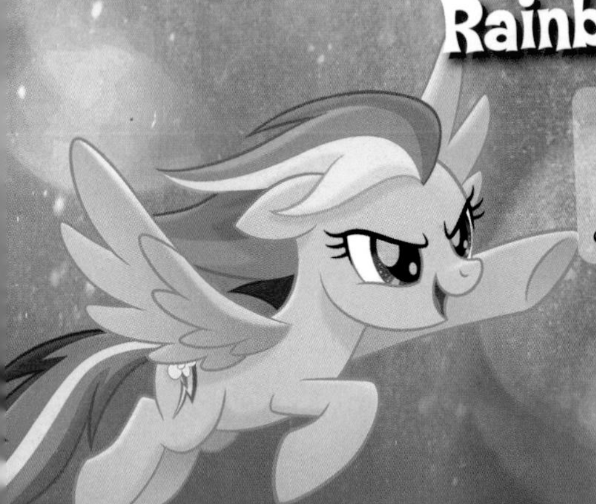

Princess Celestia

PRINCESS CELESTIA IS A MAGICAL AND BEAUTIFUL PONY WHO RULES THE LAND OF EQUESTRIA. ALL OF THE PONIES IN PONYVILLE LOOK UP TO HER!

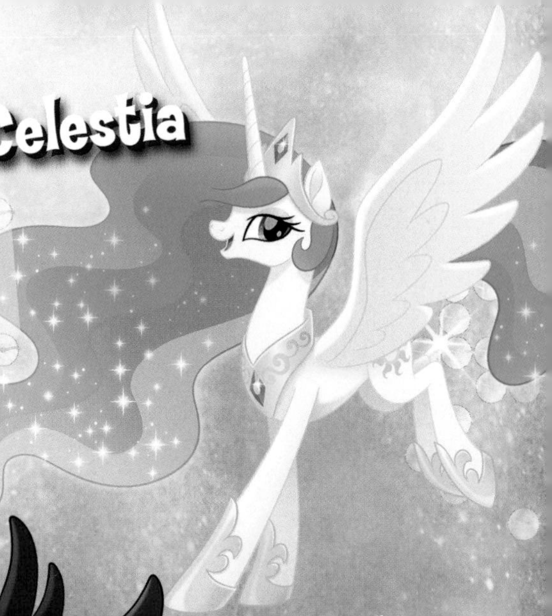

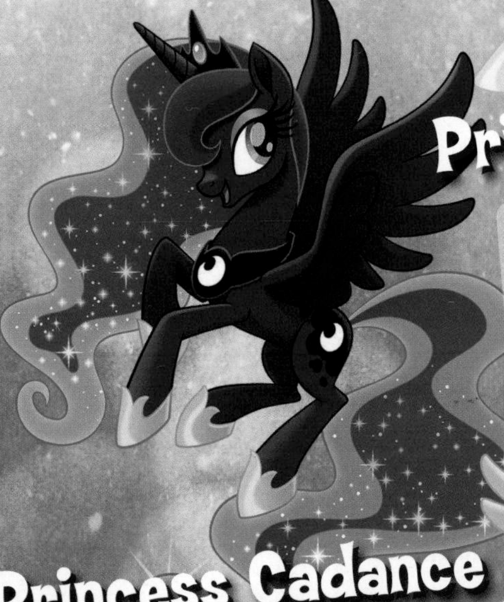

Princess Luna

PRINCESS LUNA IS THE YOUNGER SISTER OF PRINCESS CELESTIA AND THE GUARDIAN OF THE NIGHT. SHE CONTROLS THE MOON!

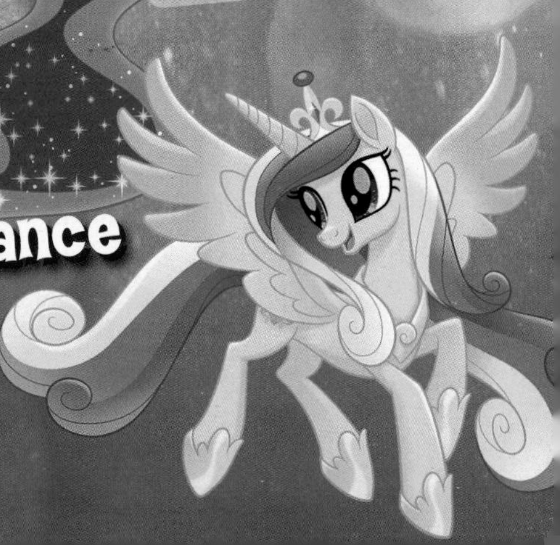

Princess Cadance

PRINCESS CADANCE, FULL NAME PRINCESS MI AMORE CADENZA, USED TO FOAL-SIT FOR TWILIGHT SPARKLE WHEN SHE WAS YOUNG. NOW SHE RULES THE CRYSTAL EMPIRE ALONGSIDE TWILIGHT'S BROTHER, SHINING ARMOR.

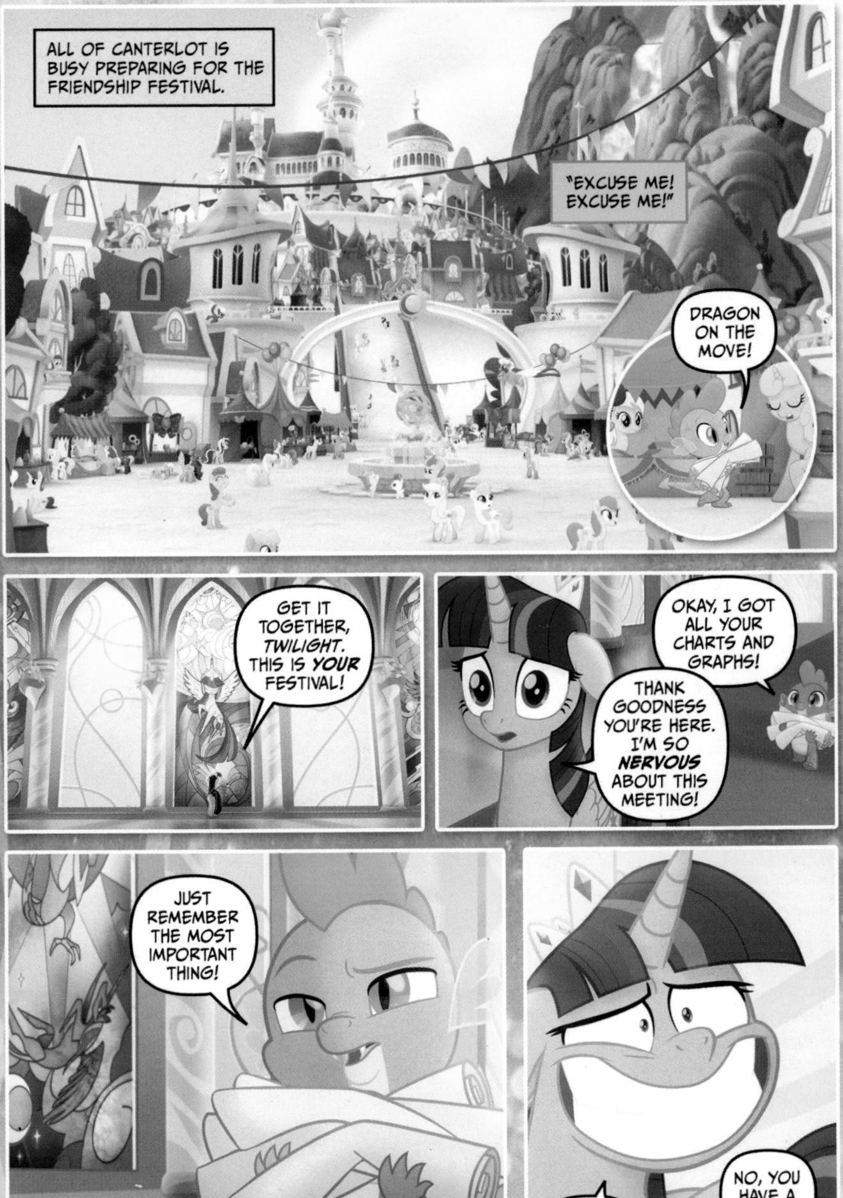
ALL OF CANTERLOT IS BUSY PREPARING FOR THE FRIENDSHIP FESTIVAL.
"EXCUSE ME! EXCUSE ME!"
DRAGON ON THE MOVE!
GET IT TOGETHER, TWILIGHT. THIS IS YOUR FESTIVAL!
OKAY, I GOT ALL YOUR CHARTS AND GRAPHS!
THANK GOODNESS YOU'RE HERE. I'M SO NERVOUS ABOUT THIS MEETING!
JUST REMEMBER THE MOST IMPORTANT THING!
SMILE?!
NO, YOU HAVE A PLAN.

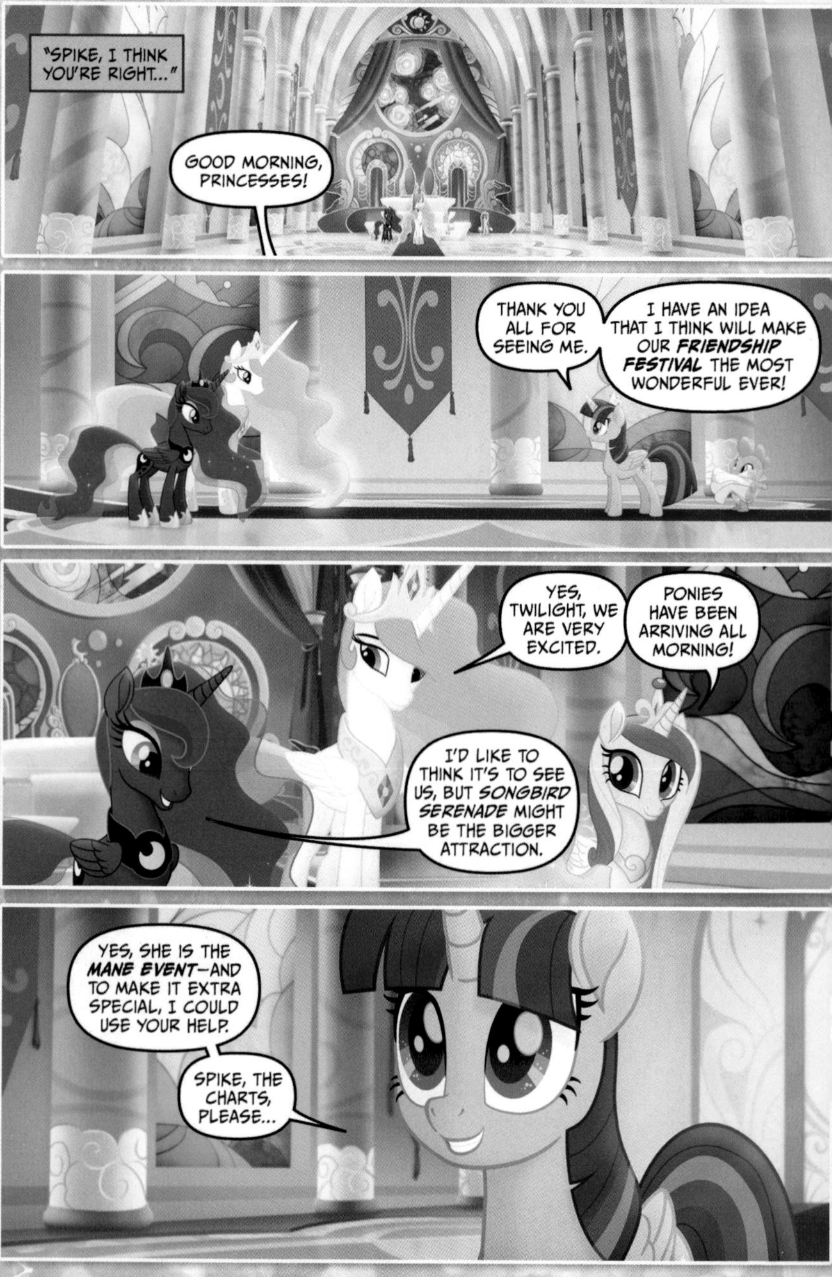
"SPIKE, I THINK YOU'RE RIGHT..."
GOOD MORNING, PRINCESSES!
THANK YOU ALL FOR SEEING ME.
I HAVE AN IDEA THAT I THINK WILL MAKE OUR FRIENDSHIP FESTIVAL THE MOST WONDERFUL EVER!
YES, TWILIGHT, WE ARE VERY EXCITED.
PONIES HAVE BEEN ARRIVING ALL MORNING!
I'D LIKE TO THINK IT'S TO SEE US, BUT SONGBIRD SERENADE MIGHT BE THE BIGGER ATTRACTION.
YES, SHE IS THE MANE EVENT—AND TO MAKE IT EXTRA SPECIAL, I COULD USE YOUR HELP.
SPIKE, THE CHARTS, PLEASE...

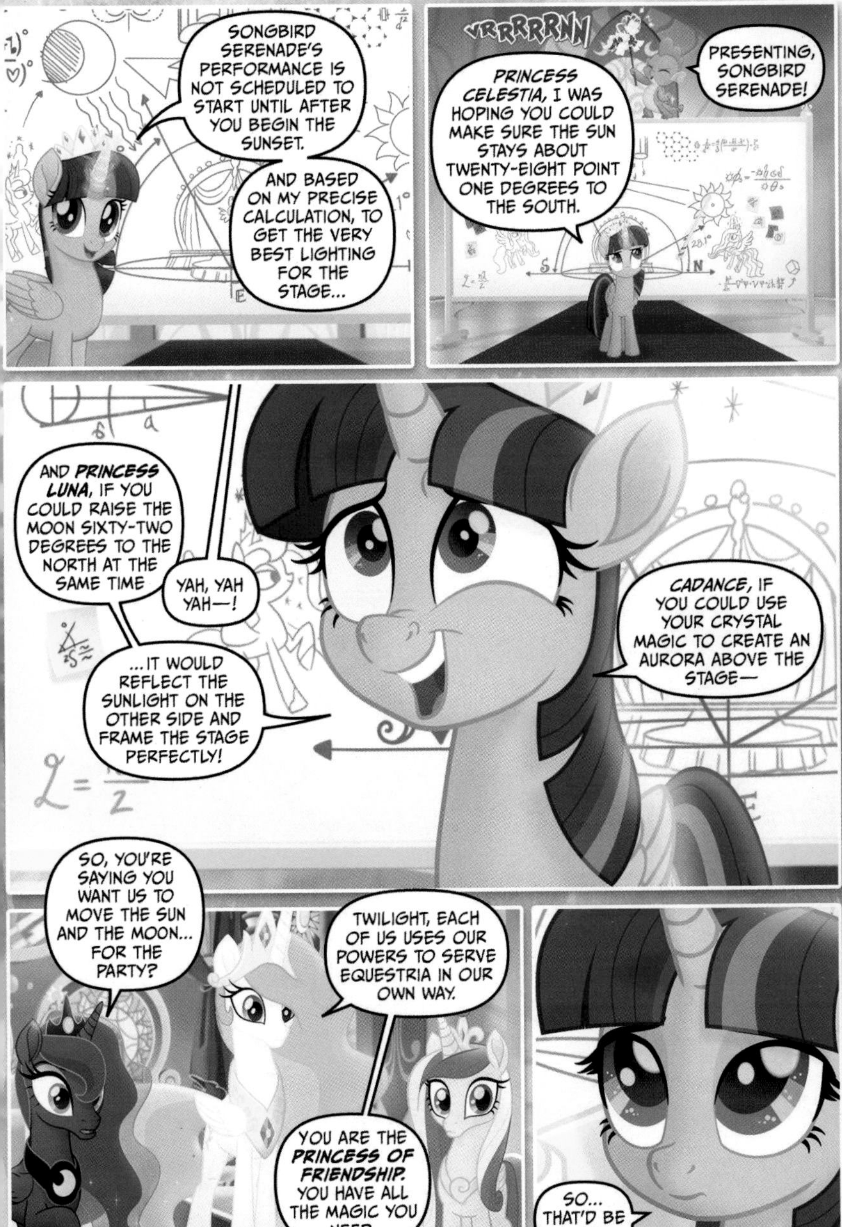
SONGBIRD SERENADE'S PERFORMANCE IS NOT SCHEDULED TO START UNTIL AFTER YOU BEGIN THE SUNSET.
AND BASED ON MY PRECISE CALCULATION, TO GET THE VERY BEST LIGHTING FOR THE STAGE...
VRRRRRNN
PRESENTING, SONGBIRD SERENADE!
PRINCESS CELESTIA, I WAS HOPING YOU COULD MAKE SURE THE SUN STAYS ABOUT TWENTY-EIGHT POINT ONE DEGREES TO THE SOUTH.
AND PRINCESS LUNA, IF YOU COULD RAISE THE MOON SIXTY-TWO DEGREES TO THE NORTH AT THE SAME TIME
YAH, YAH YAH—!
...IT WOULD REFLECT THE SUNLIGHT ON THE OTHER SIDE AND FRAME THE STAGE PERFECTLY!
CADANCE, IF YOU COULD USE YOUR CRYSTAL MAGIC TO CREATE AN AURORA ABOVE THE STAGE—
SO, YOU'RE SAYING YOU WANT US TO MOVE THE SUN AND THE MOON... FOR THE PARTY?
TWILIGHT, EACH OF US USES OUR POWERS TO SERVE EQUESTRIA IN OUR OWN WAY.
YOU ARE THE PRINCESS OF FRIENDSHIP. YOU HAVE ALL THE MAGIC YOU NEED.
SO... THAT'D BE A NO?

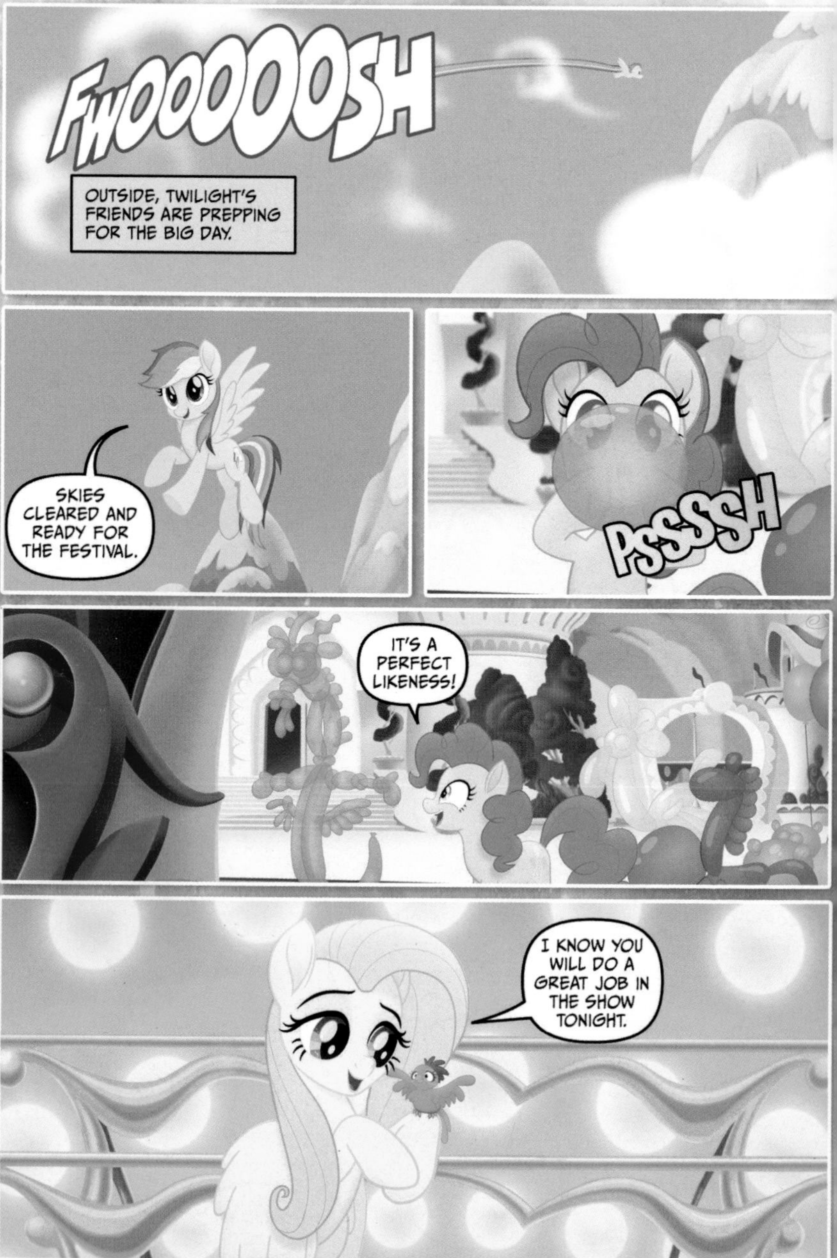
FWOOOOOOSH
OUTSIDE, TWILIGHT'S FRIENDS ARE PREPPING FOR THE BIG DAY.
SKIES CLEARED AND READY FOR THE FESTIVAL.
PSSSSH
IT'S A PERFECT LIKENESS!
I KNOW YOU WILL DO A GREAT JOB IN THE SHOW TONIGHT.

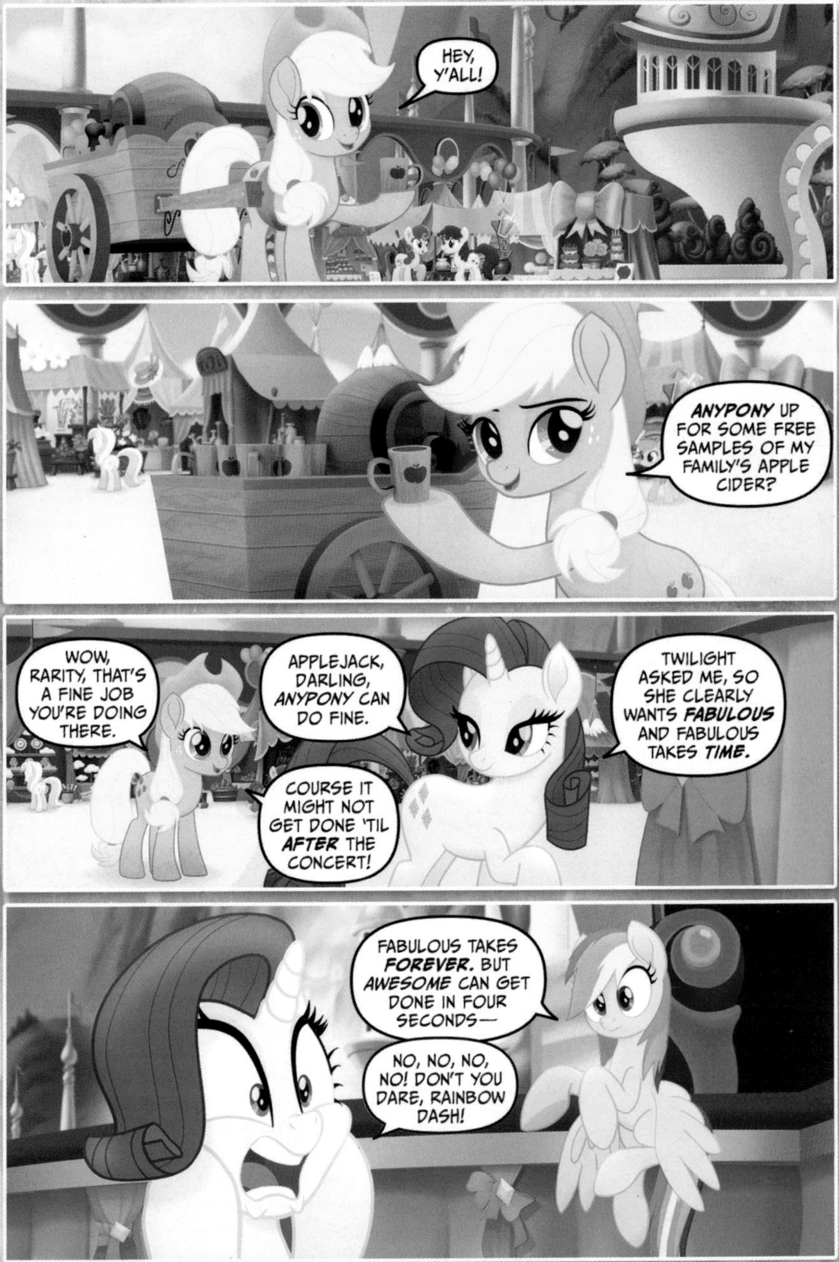
HEY, Y'ALL!
ANYPONY UP FOR SOME FREE SAMPLES OF MY FAMILY'S APPLE CIDER?
WOW, RARITY, THAT'S A FINE JOB YOU'RE DOING THERE.
APPLEJACK, DARLING, ANYPONY CAN DO FINE.
COURSE IT MIGHT NOT GET DONE 'TIL AFTER THE CONCERT!
TWILIGHT ASKED ME, SO SHE CLEARLY WANTS FABULOUS AND FABULOUS TAKES TIME.
FABULOUS TAKES FOREVER. BUT AWESOME CAN GET DONE IN FOUR SECONDS—
NO, NO, NO, NO! DON'T YOU DARE, RAINBOW DASH!

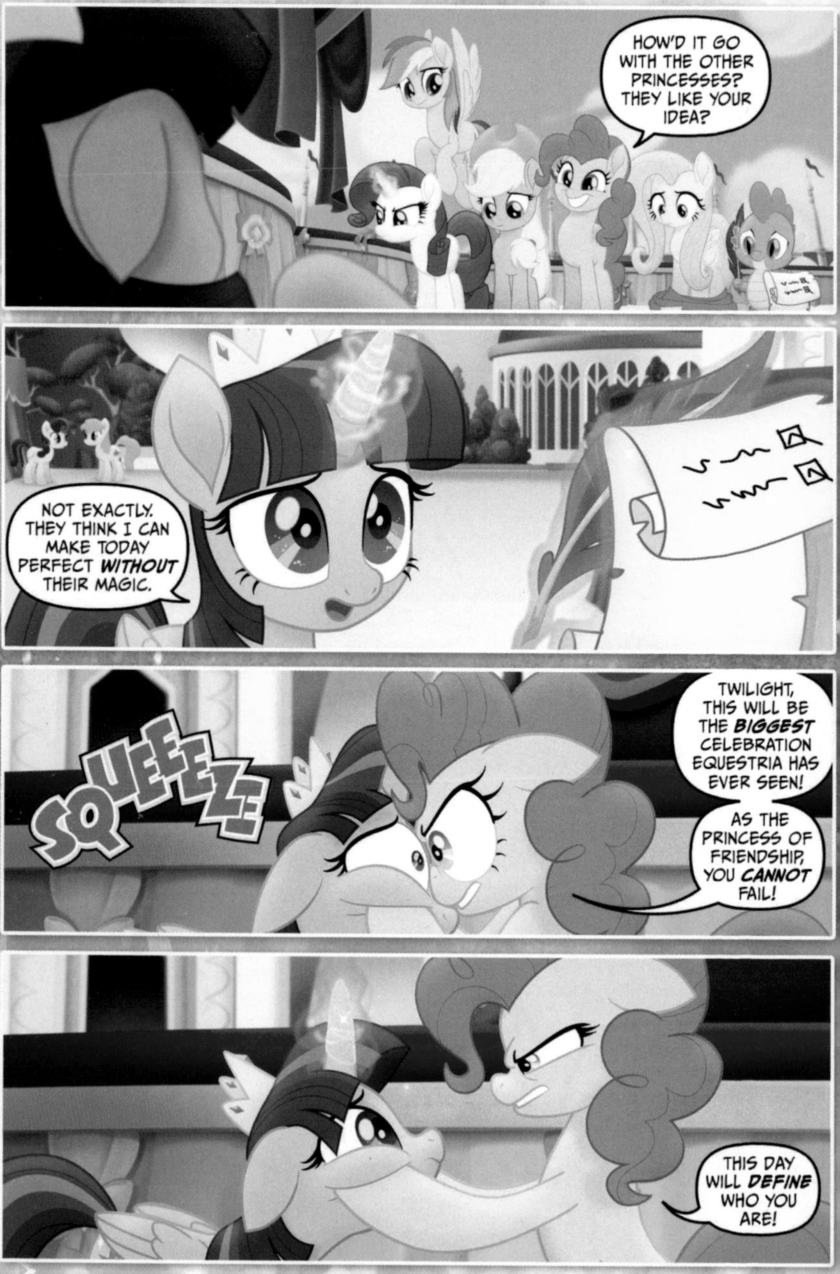

HOW'D IT GO WITH THE OTHER PRINCESSES? THEY LIKE YOUR IDEA?
NOT EXACTLY. THEY THINK I CAN MAKE TODAY PERFECT *WITHOUT* THEIR MAGIC.
SQUEEEZE
TWILIGHT, THIS WILL BE THE *BIGGEST* CELEBRATION EQUESTRIA HAS EVER SEEN!
AS THE PRINCESS OF FRIENDSHIP, YOU *CANNOT* FAIL!
THIS DAY WILL *DEFINE* WHO YOU ARE!

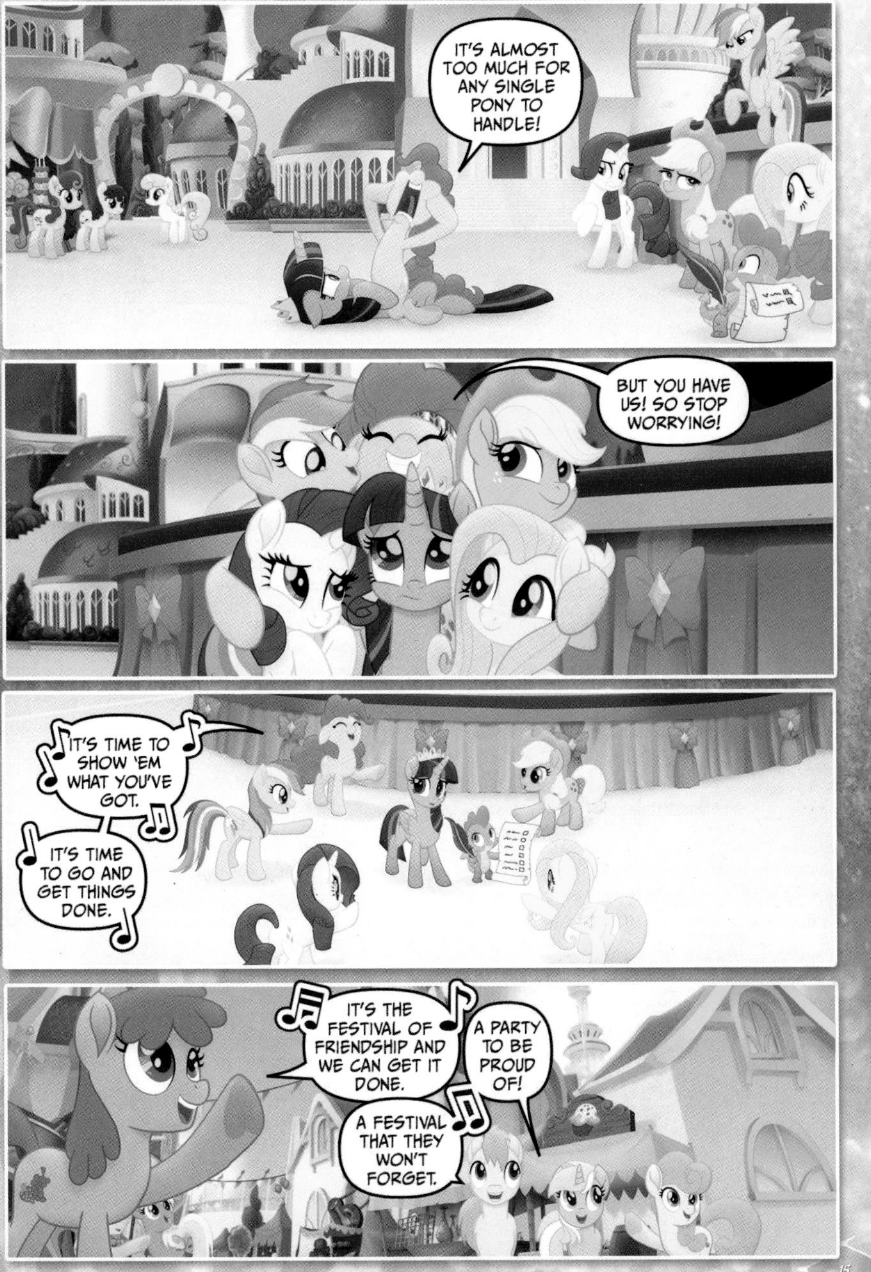
IT'S ALMOST TOO MUCH FOR ANY SINGLE PONY TO HANDLE!
BUT YOU HAVE US! SO STOP WORRYING!
IT'S TIME TO SHOW 'EM WHAT YOU'VE GOT.
IT'S TIME TO GO AND GET THINGS DONE.
IT'S THE FESTIVAL OF FRIENDSHIP AND WE CAN GET IT DONE.
A PARTY TO BE PROUD OF!
A FESTIVAL THAT THEY WON'T FORGET.

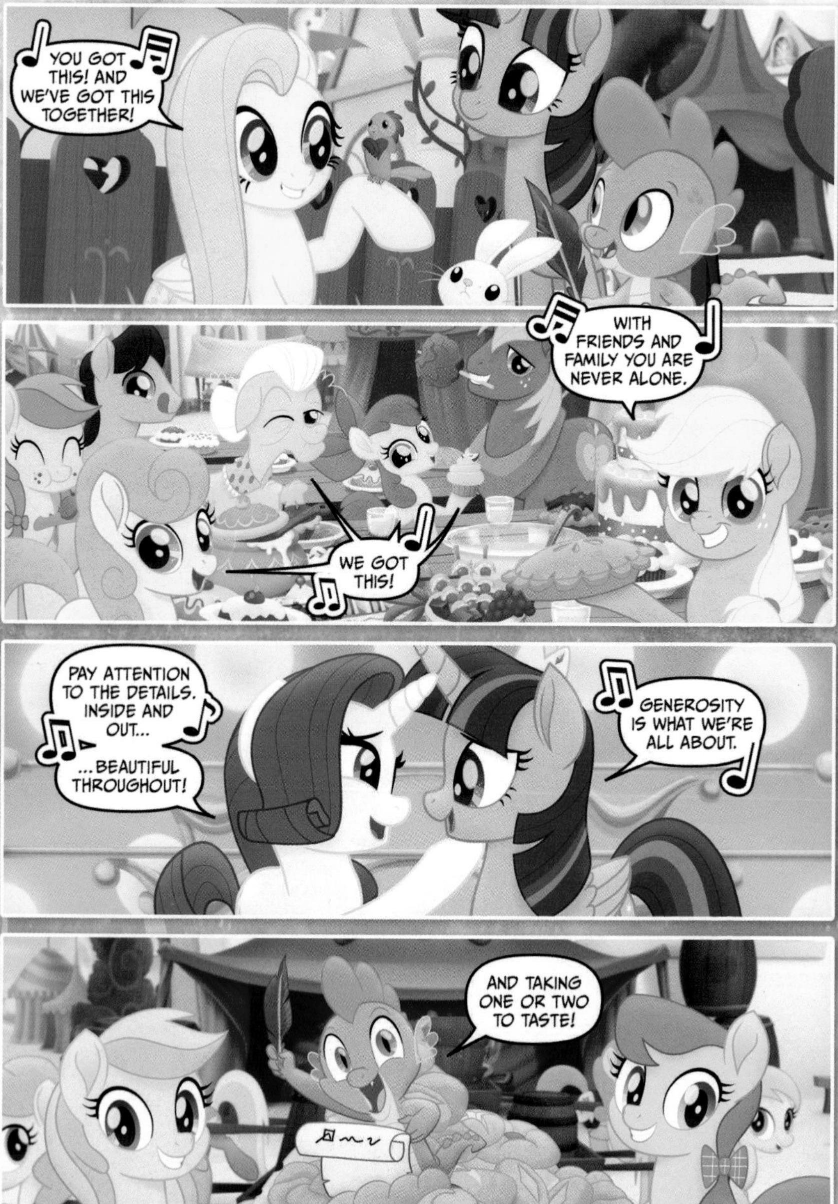
YOU GOT THIS! AND WE'VE GOT THIS TOGETHER!
WITH FRIENDS AND FAMILY YOU ARE NEVER ALONE.
WE GOT THIS!
PAY ATTENTION TO THE DETAILS. INSIDE AND OUT...
...BEAUTIFUL THROUGHOUT!
GENEROSITY IS WHAT WE'RE ALL ABOUT.
AND TAKING ONE OR TWO TO TASTE!

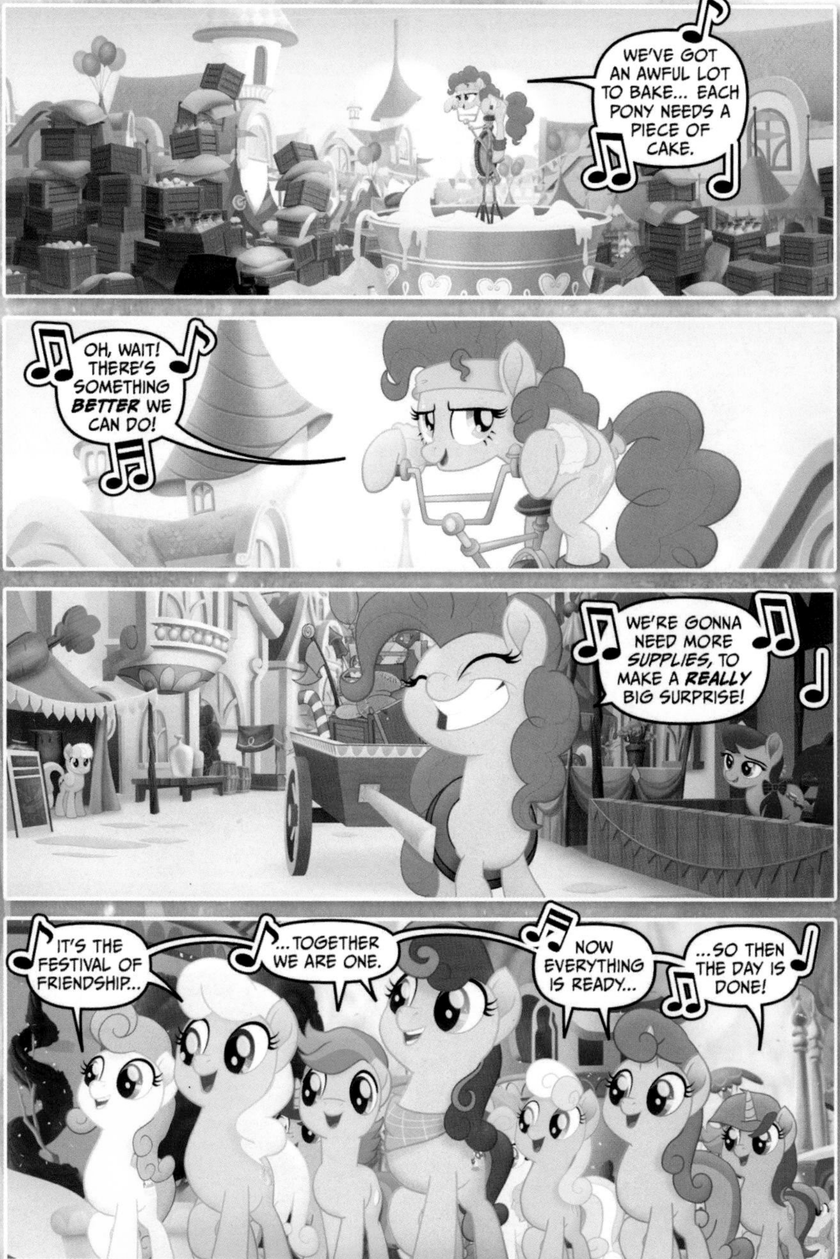
WE'VE GOT AN AWFUL LOT TO BAKE... EACH PONY NEEDS A PIECE OF CAKE.
OH, WAIT! THERE'S SOMETHING **BETTER** WE CAN DO!
WE'RE GONNA NEED MORE **SUPPLIES,** TO MAKE A **REALLY** BIG SURPRISE!
IT'S THE FESTIVAL OF FRIENDSHIP...
...TOGETHER WE ARE ONE.
NOW EVERYTHING IS READY...
...SO THEN THE DAY IS DONE!

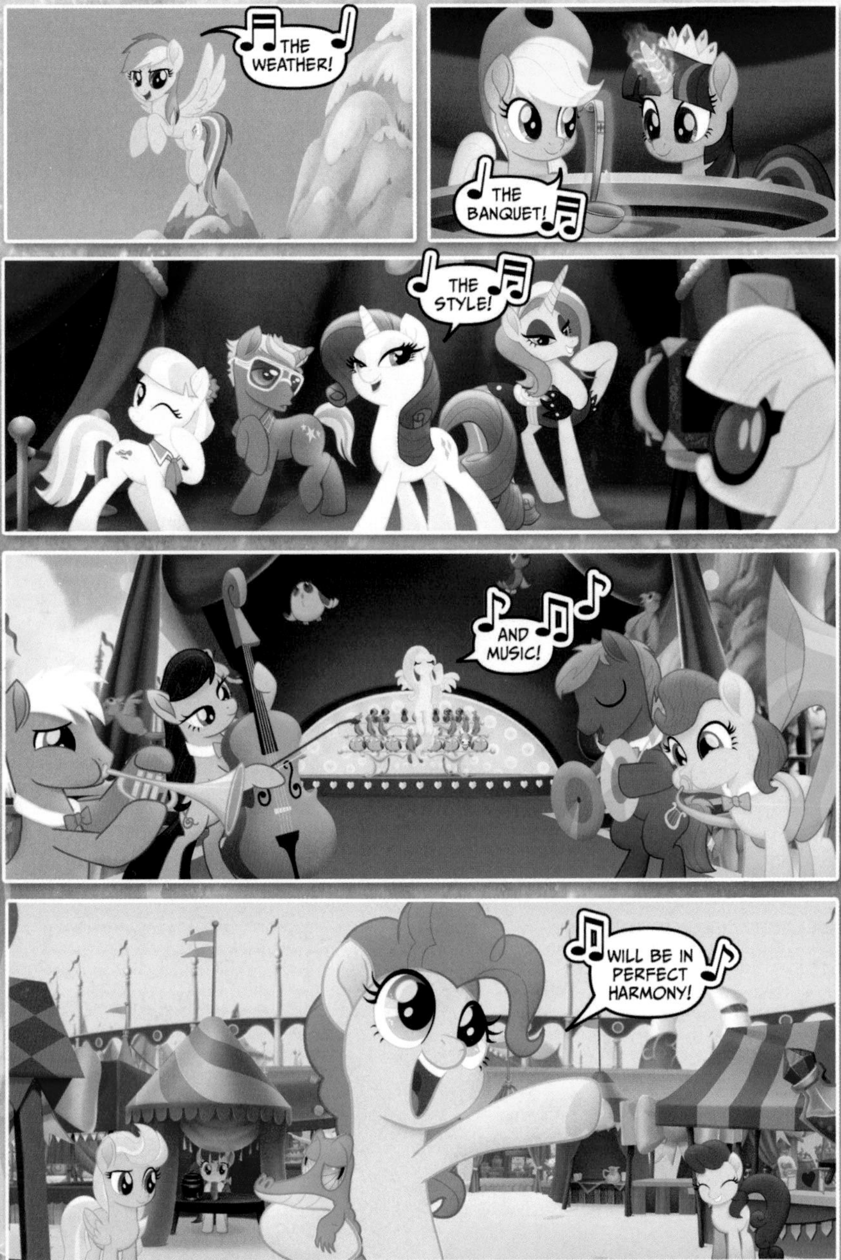
THE WEATHER!
THE BANQUET!
THE STYLE!
AND MUSIC!
WILL BE IN PERFECT HARMONY!

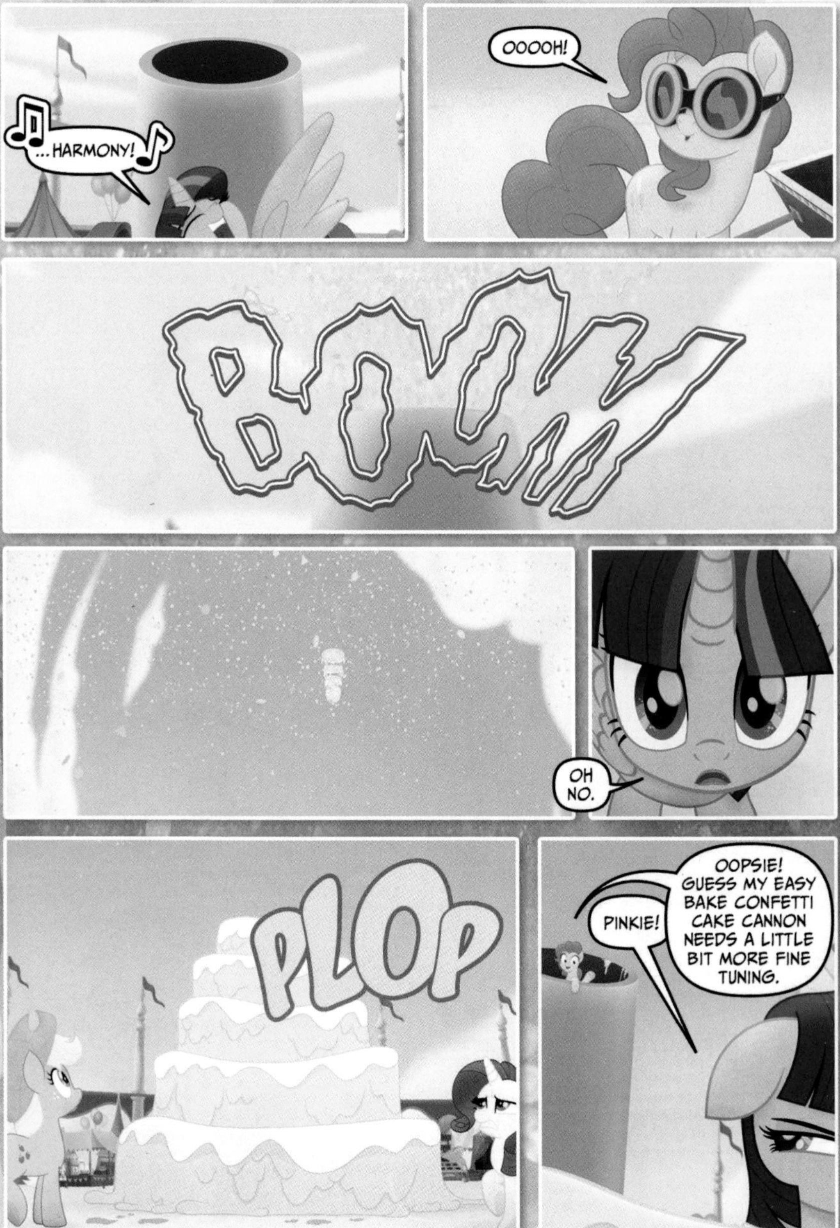
...HARMONY!
OOOOH!
BOOM
OH NO.
PLOP
PINKIE!
OOPSIE! GUESS MY EASY BAKE CONFETTI CAKE CANNON NEEDS A LITTLE BIT MORE FINE TUNING.

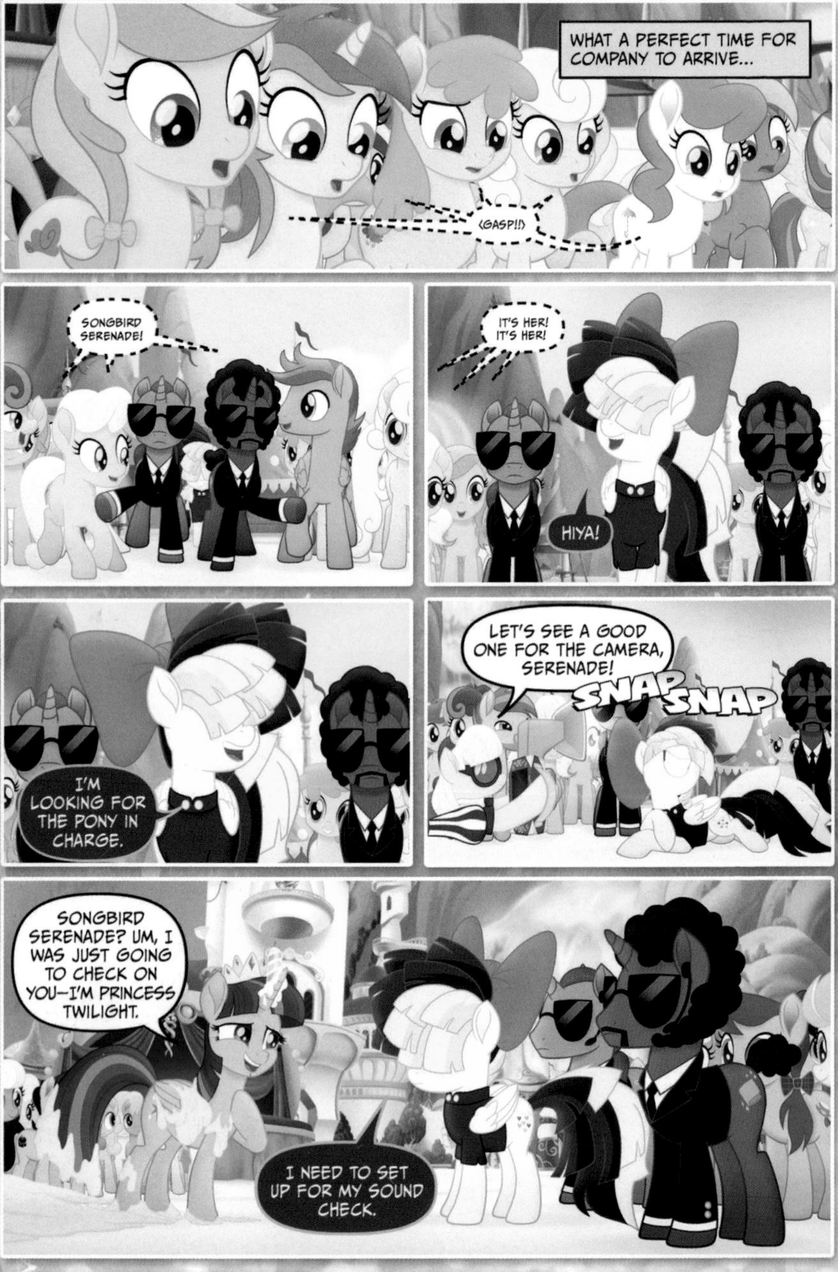
WHAT A PERFECT TIME FOR COMPANY TO ARRIVE...
(GASP!!)
SONGBIRD SERENADE!
IT'S HER! IT'S HER!
HIYA!
I'M LOOKING FOR THE PONY IN CHARGE.
LET'S SEE A GOOD ONE FOR THE CAMERA, SERENADE!
SNAP SNAP
SONGBIRD SERENADE? UM, I WAS JUST GOING TO CHECK ON YOU—I'M PRINCESS TWILIGHT.
I NEED TO SET UP FOR MY SOUND CHECK.

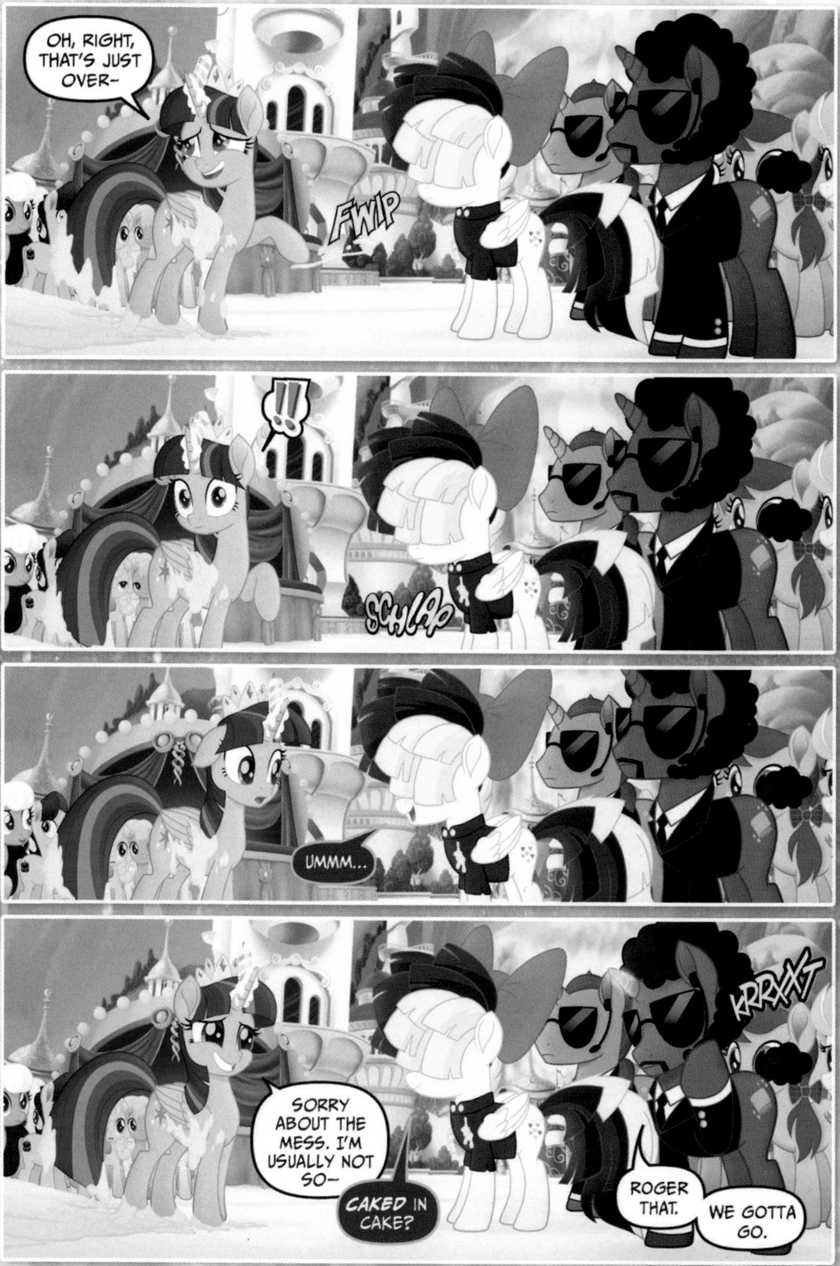
OH, RIGHT, THAT'S JUST OVER–
FWIP
!!
SCHLAP
UMMM...
SORRY ABOUT THE MESS. I'M USUALLY NOT SO–
CAKED IN CAKE?
KRRXXT
ROGER THAT.
WE GOTTA GO.

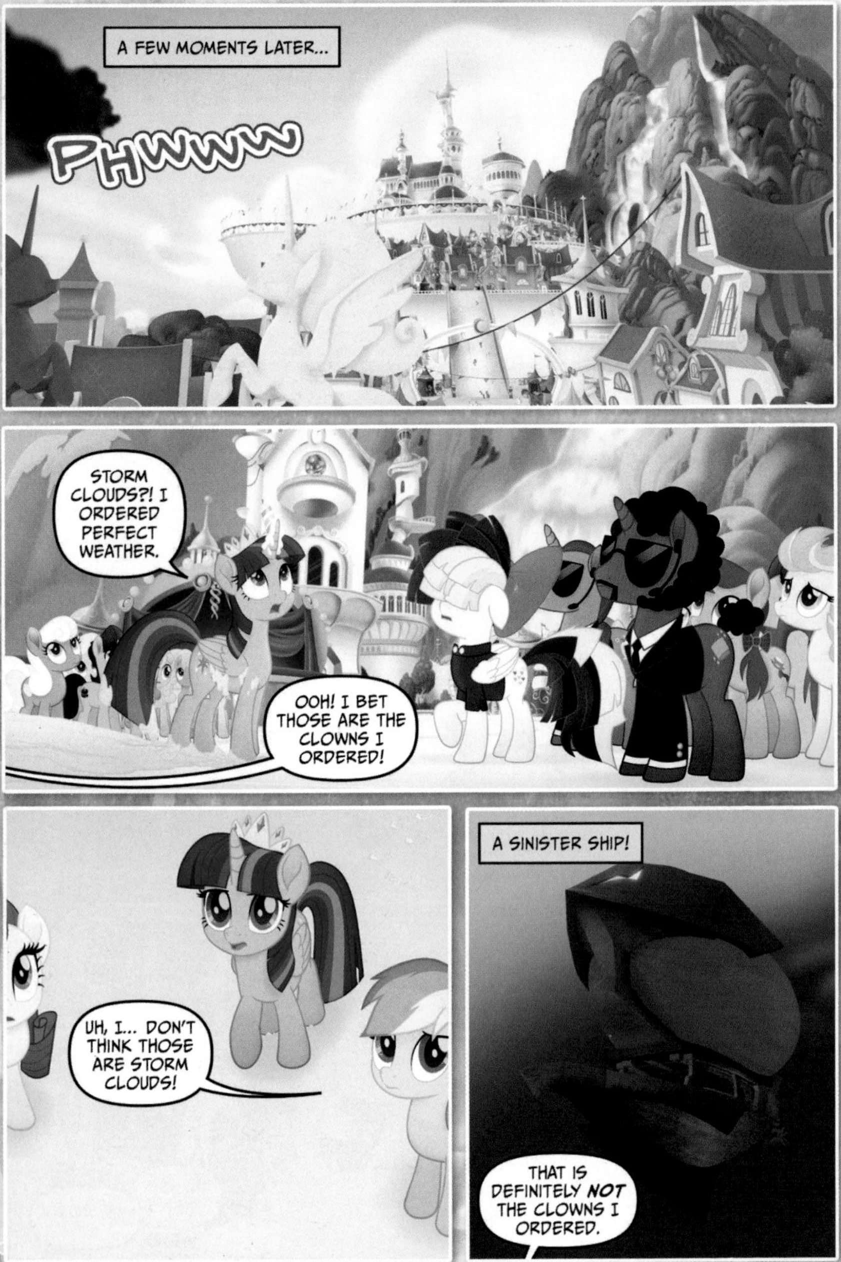
A FEW MOMENTS LATER...
PHWWW
STORM CLOUDS?! I ORDERED PERFECT WEATHER.
OOH! I BET THOSE ARE THE CLOWNS I ORDERED!
UH, I... DON'T THINK THOSE ARE STORM CLOUDS!
A SINISTER SHIP!
THAT IS DEFINITELY ***NOT*** THE CLOWNS I ORDERED.

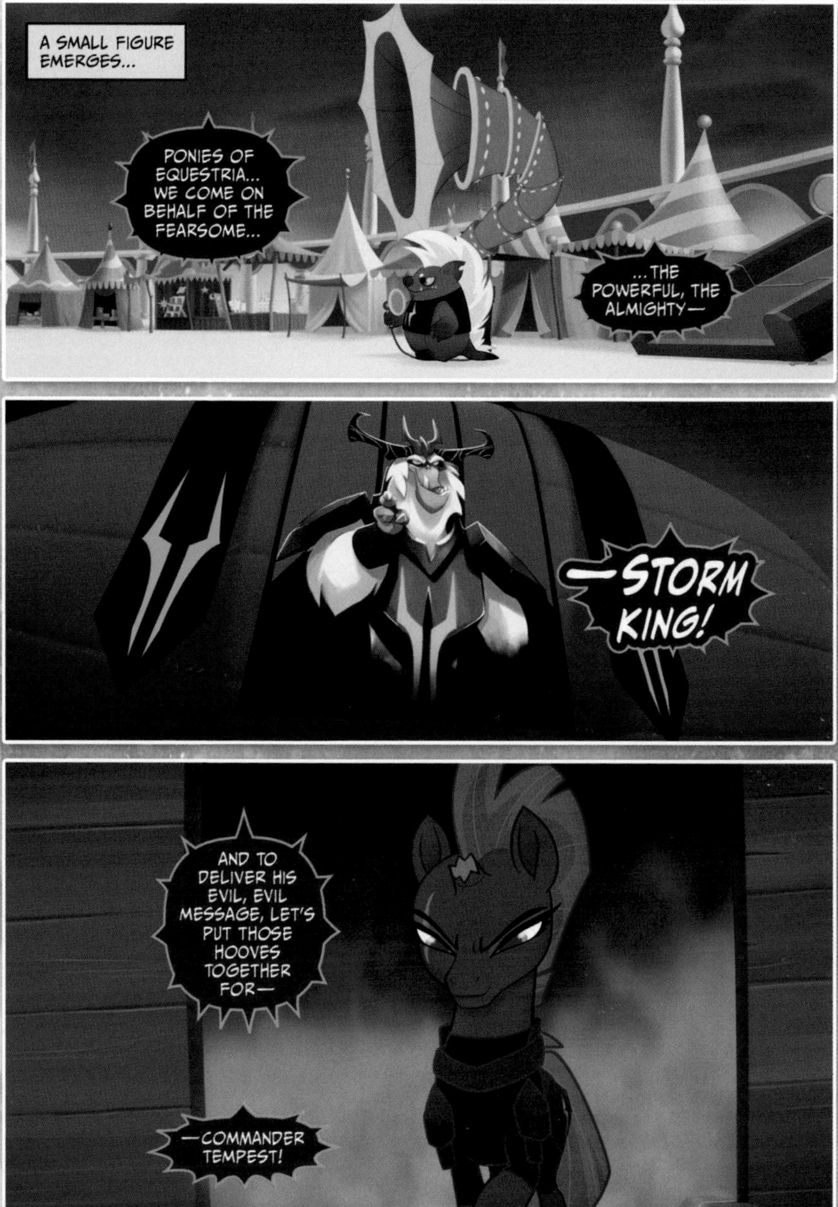
A SMALL FIGURE EMERGES...
PONIES OF EQUESTRIA... WE COME ON BEHALF OF THE FEARSOME...
...THE POWERFUL, THE ALMIGHTY—
—STORM KING!
AND TO DELIVER HIS EVIL, EVIL MESSAGE, LET'S PUT THOSE HOOVES TOGETHER FOR—
—COMMANDER TEMPEST!

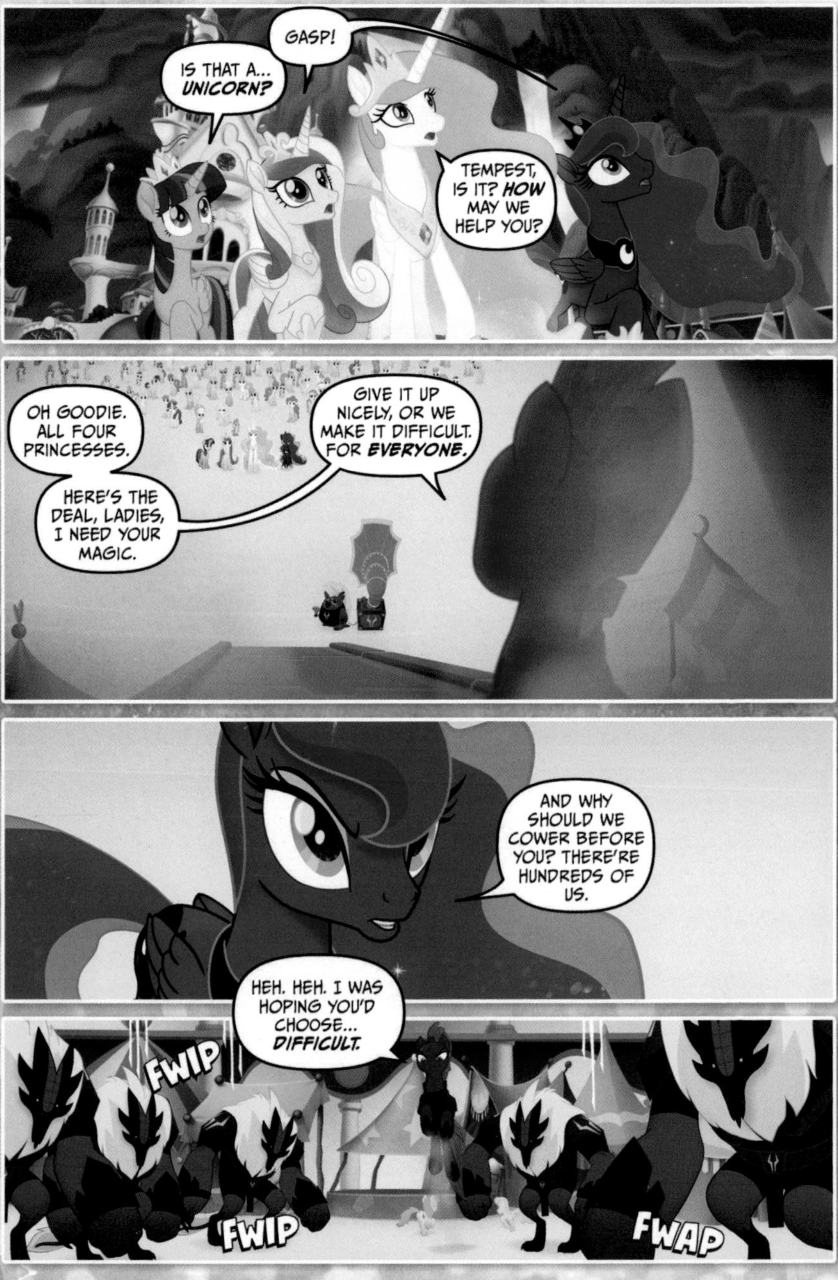

IS THAT A... UNICORN?
GASP!
TEMPEST, IS IT? HOW MAY WE HELP YOU?
OH GOODIE. ALL FOUR PRINCESSES.
HERE'S THE DEAL, LADIES, I NEED YOUR MAGIC.
GIVE IT UP NICELY, OR WE MAKE IT DIFFICULT. FOR EVERYONE.
AND WHY SHOULD WE COWER BEFORE YOU? THERE'RE HUNDREDS OF US.
HEH. HEH. I WAS HOPING YOU'D CHOOSE... DIFFICULT.
FWIP
FWIP
FWAP

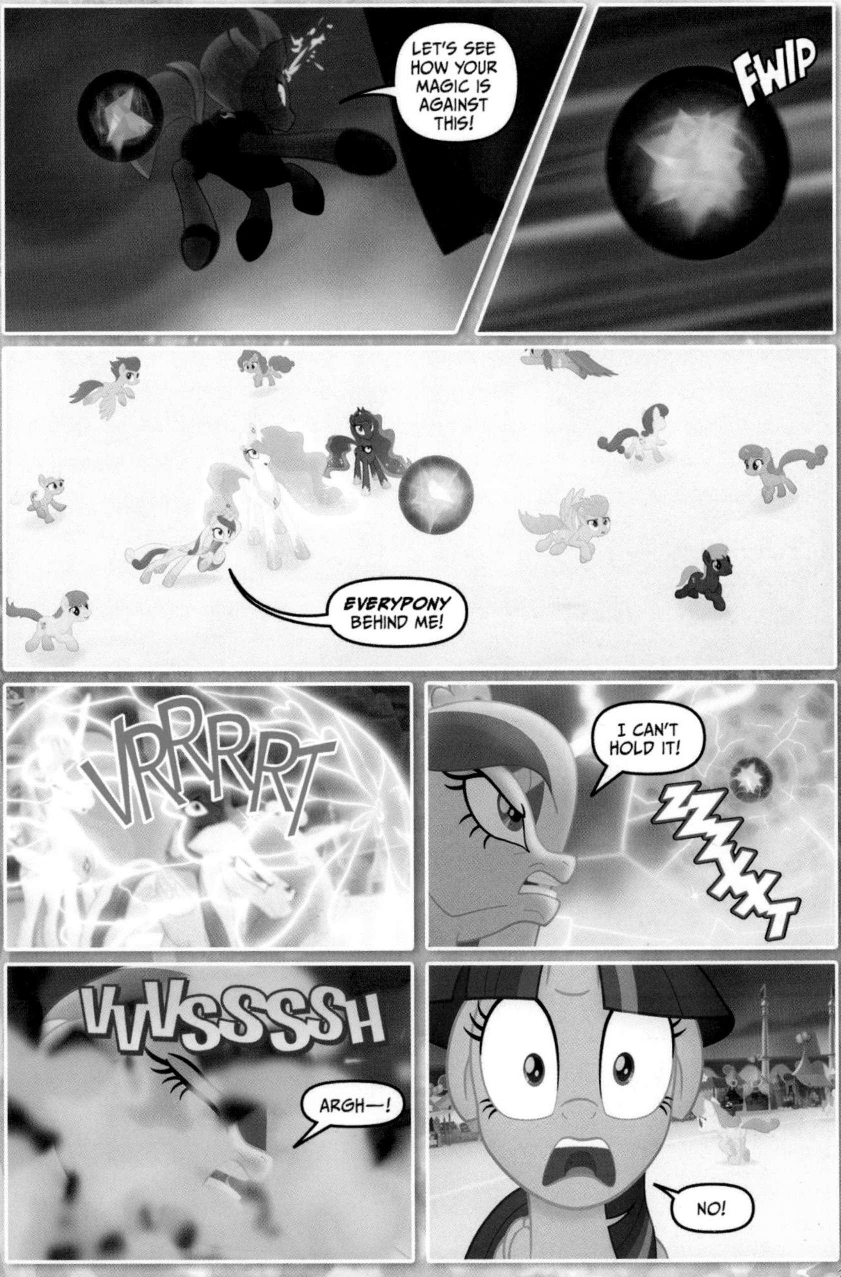
LET'S SEE HOW YOUR MAGIC IS AGAINST THIS!
FWIP
EVERYPONY BEHIND ME!
VRRRRRT
I CAN'T HOLD IT!
ZZZXXT
VVVSSSSSH
ARGH—!
NO!

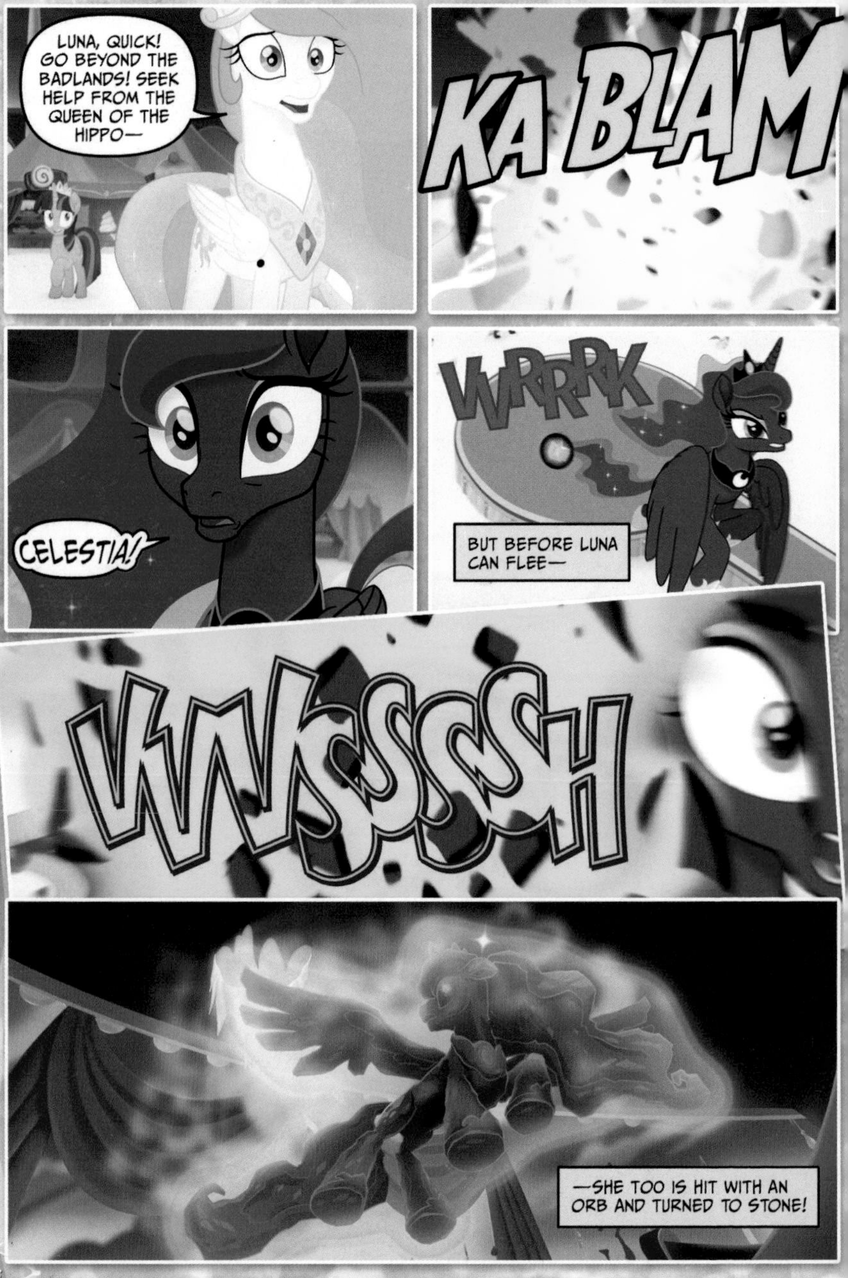

LUNA, QUICK! GO BEYOND THE BADLANDS! SEEK HELP FROM THE QUEEN OF THE HIPPO—
KA BLAM
CELESTIA!
WRRRK
BUT BEFORE LUNA CAN FLEE—
WSSSCH
—SHE TOO IS HIT WITH AN ORB AND TURNED TO STONE!

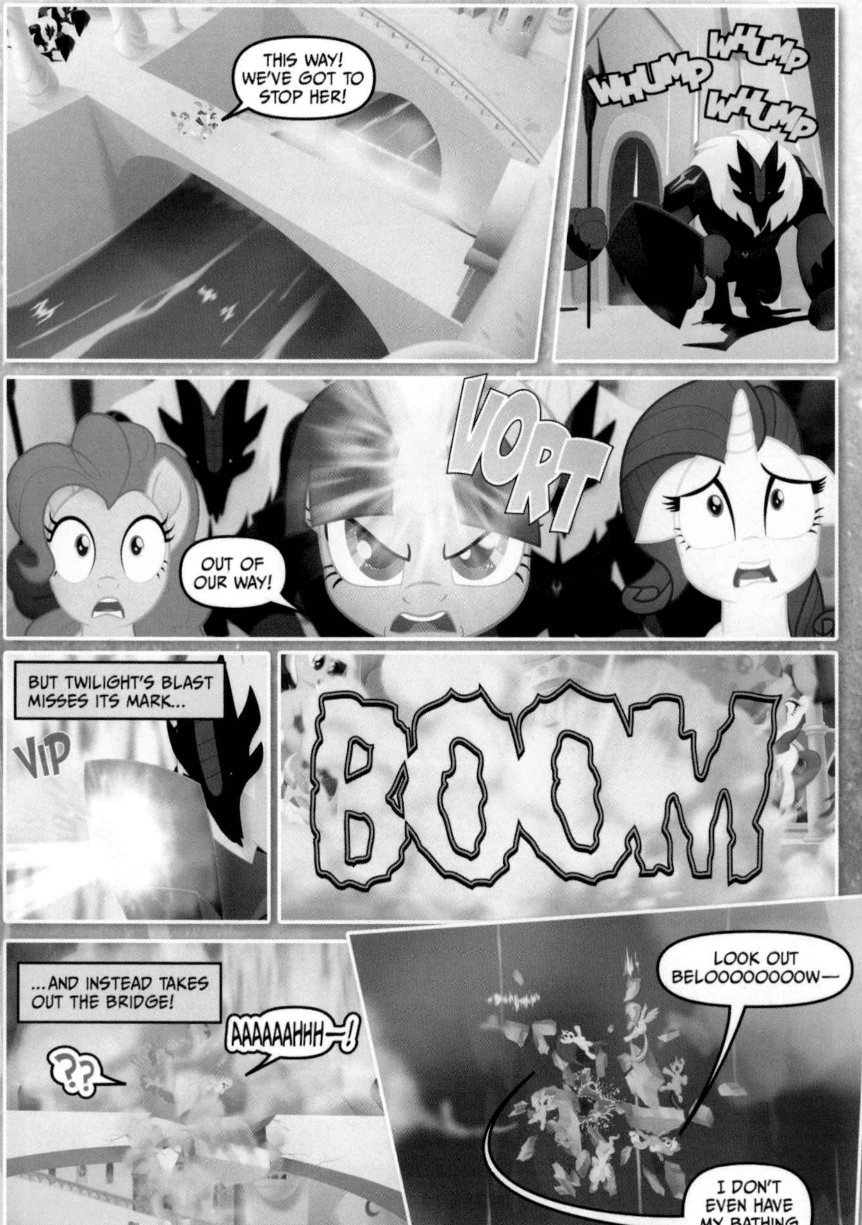
THIS WAY! WE'VE GOT TO STOP HER!
WHUMP WHUMP
WHUMP
WHUMP
VORT
OUT OF OUR WAY!
BUT TWILIGHT'S BLAST MISSES ITS MARK...
VIP
BOOM
...AND INSTEAD TAKES OUT THE BRIDGE!
??
AAAAAAHHH—!
LOOK OUT BELOOOOOOOOW—
I DON'T EVEN HAVE MY BATHING SUIT!

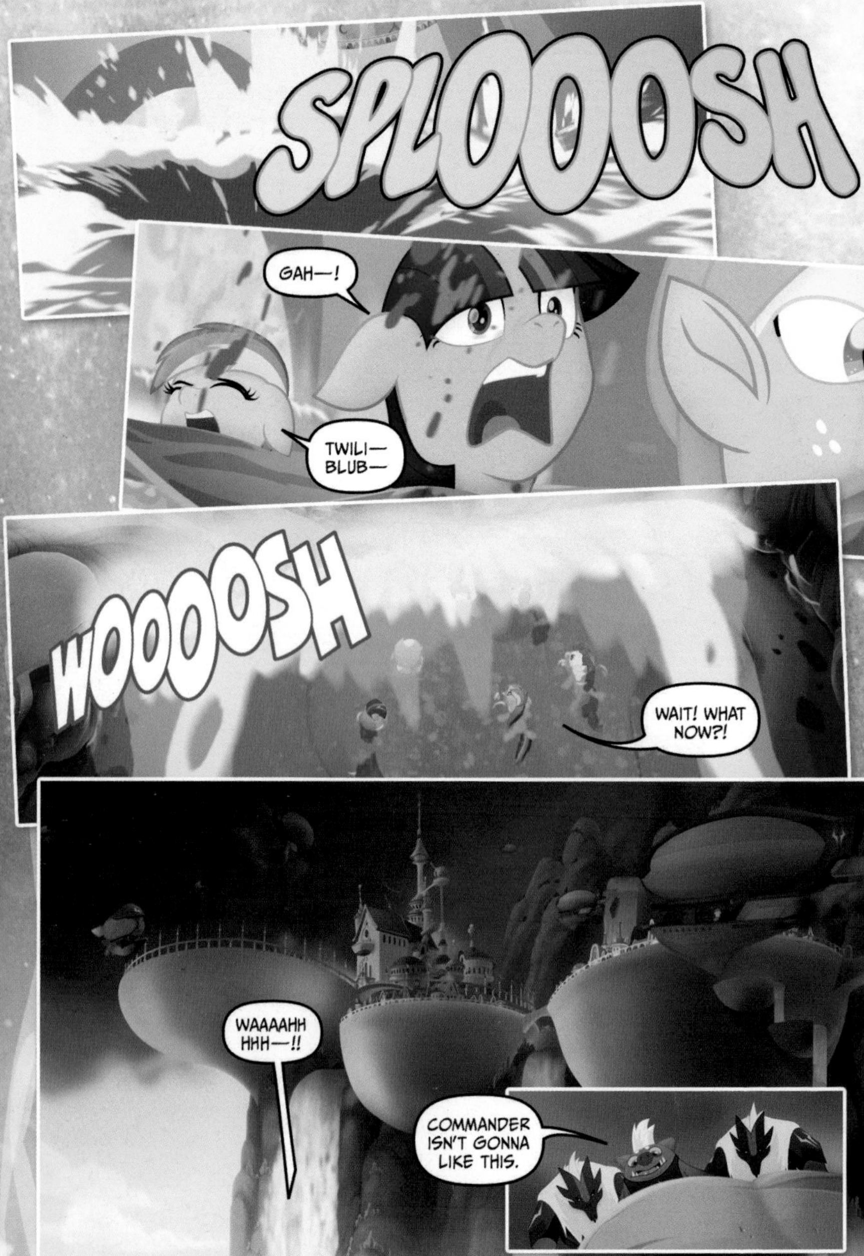
SPLOOOSH
GAH—!
TWILI— BLUB—
WOOOOSH
WAIT! WHAT NOW?!
WAAAAHH HHH—!!
COMMANDER ISN'T GONNA LIKE THIS.

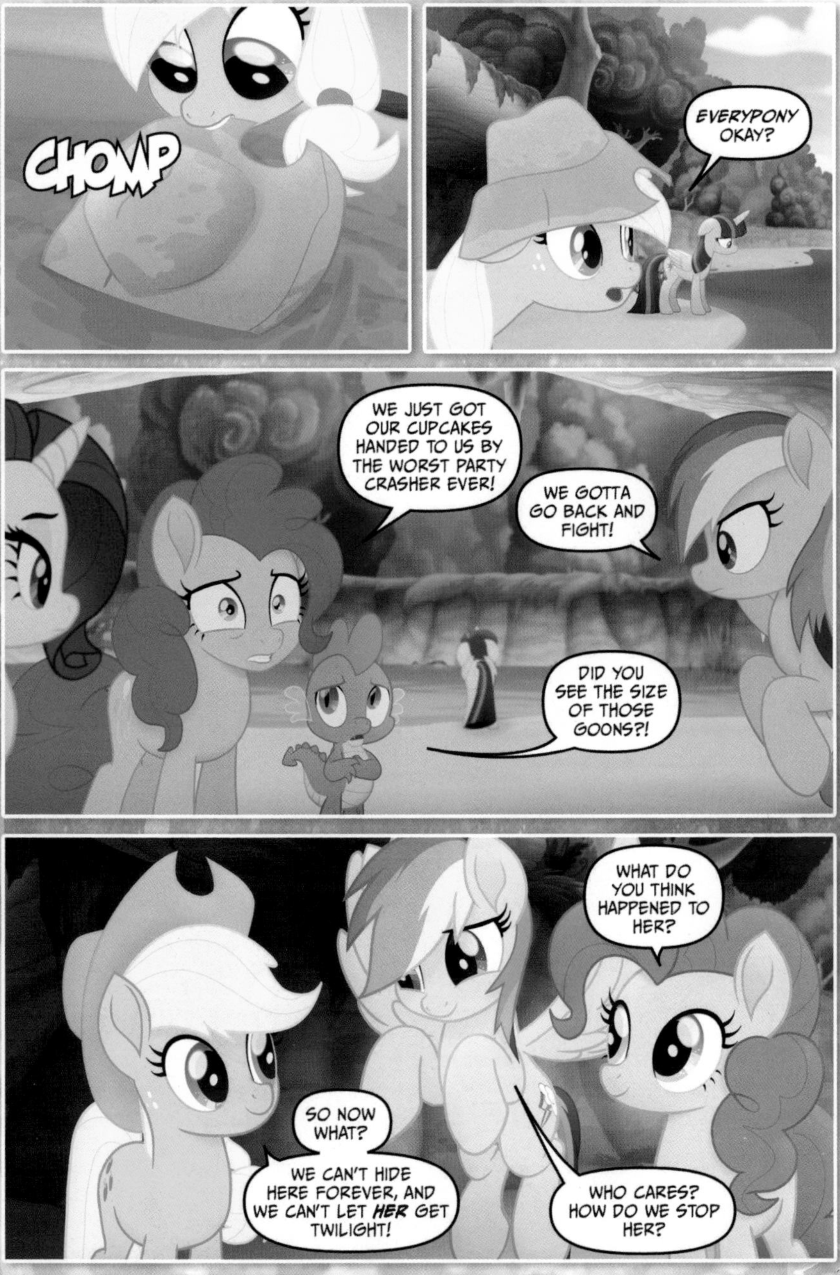
CHOMP
EVERYPONY OKAY?
WE JUST GOT OUR CUPCAKES HANDED TO US BY THE WORST PARTY CRASHER EVER!
WE GOTTA GO BACK AND FIGHT!
DID YOU SEE THE SIZE OF THOSE GOONS?!
WHAT DO YOU THINK HAPPENED TO HER?
SO NOW WHAT?
WE CAN'T HIDE HERE FOREVER, AND WE CAN'T LET **HER** GET TWILIGHT!
WHO CARES? HOW DO WE STOP HER?

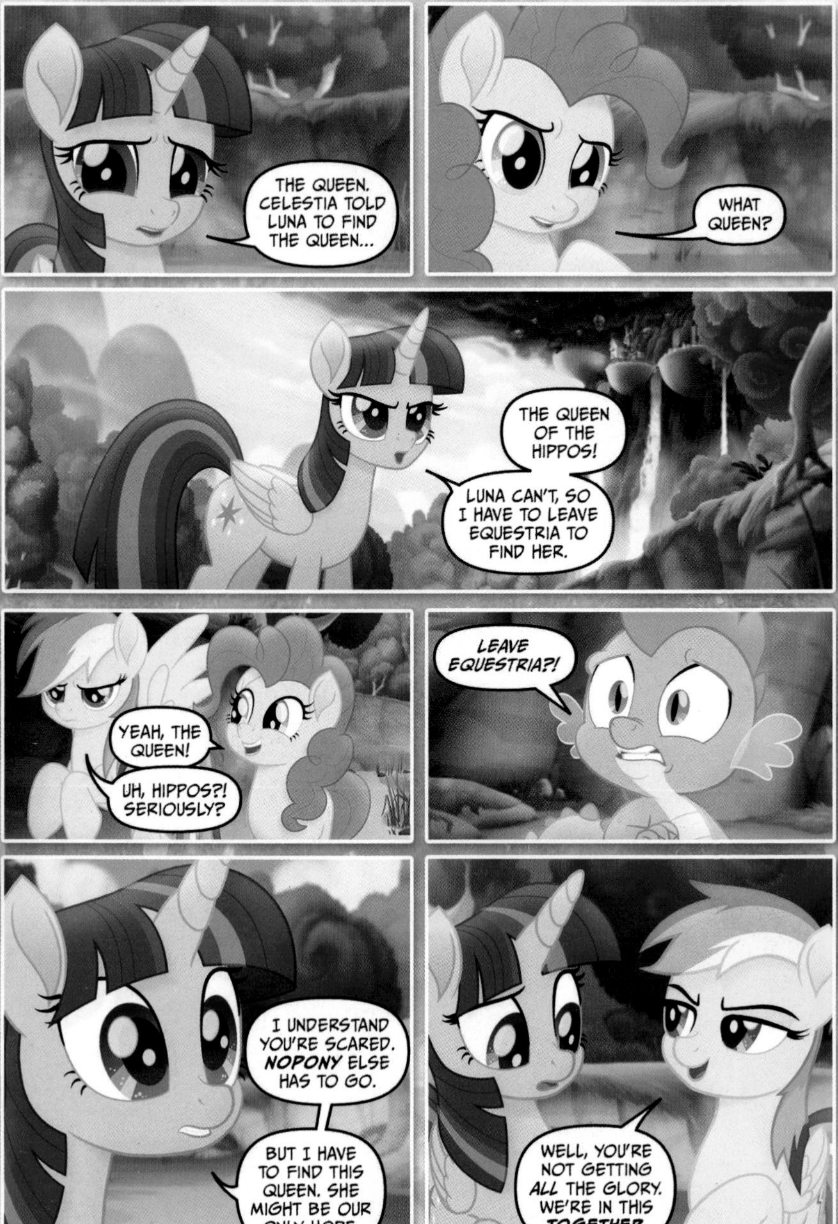
THE QUEEN. CELESTIA TOLD LUNA TO FIND THE QUEEN...
WHAT QUEEN?
THE QUEEN OF THE HIPPOS!
LUNA CAN'T, SO I HAVE TO LEAVE EQUESTRIA TO FIND HER.
YEAH, THE QUEEN!
UH, HIPPOS?! SERIOUSLY?
LEAVE EQUESTRIA?!
I UNDERSTAND YOU'RE SCARED. NOPONY ELSE HAS TO GO.
BUT I HAVE TO FIND THIS QUEEN. SHE MIGHT BE OUR ONLY HOPE.
WELL, YOU'RE NOT GETTING ALL THE GLORY. WE'RE IN THIS TOGETHER.

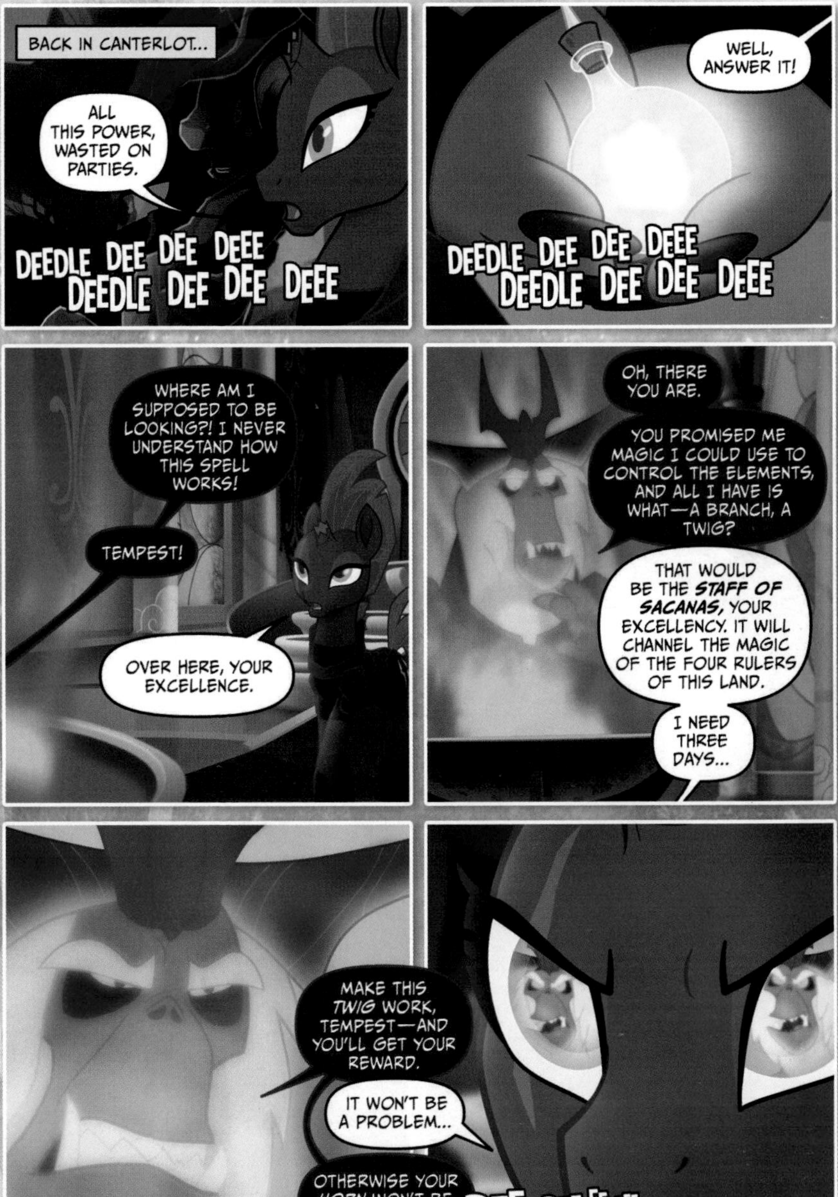
BACK IN CANTERLOT...
ALL THIS POWER, WASTED ON PARTIES.
DEEDLE DEE DEE DEEE DEEDLE DEE DEE DEEE
WELL, ANSWER IT!
DEEDLE DEE DEE DEEE DEEDLE DEE DEE DEEE
WHERE AM I SUPPOSED TO BE LOOKING?! I NEVER UNDERSTAND HOW THIS SPELL WORKS!
TEMPEST!
OVER HERE, YOUR EXCELLENCE.
OH, THERE YOU ARE.
YOU PROMISED ME MAGIC I COULD USE TO CONTROL THE ELEMENTS, AND ALL I HAVE IS WHAT—A BRANCH, A TWIG?
THAT WOULD BE THE *STAFF OF SACANAS,* YOUR EXCELLENCY. IT WILL CHANNEL THE MAGIC OF THE FOUR RULERS OF THIS LAND.
I NEED THREE DAYS...
MAKE THIS *TWIG* WORK, TEMPEST—AND YOU'LL GET YOUR REWARD.
IT WON'T BE A PROBLEM...
OTHERWISE YOUR *HORN* WON'T BE THE ONLY THING *BROKEN*—
DEE DEE EE EEE

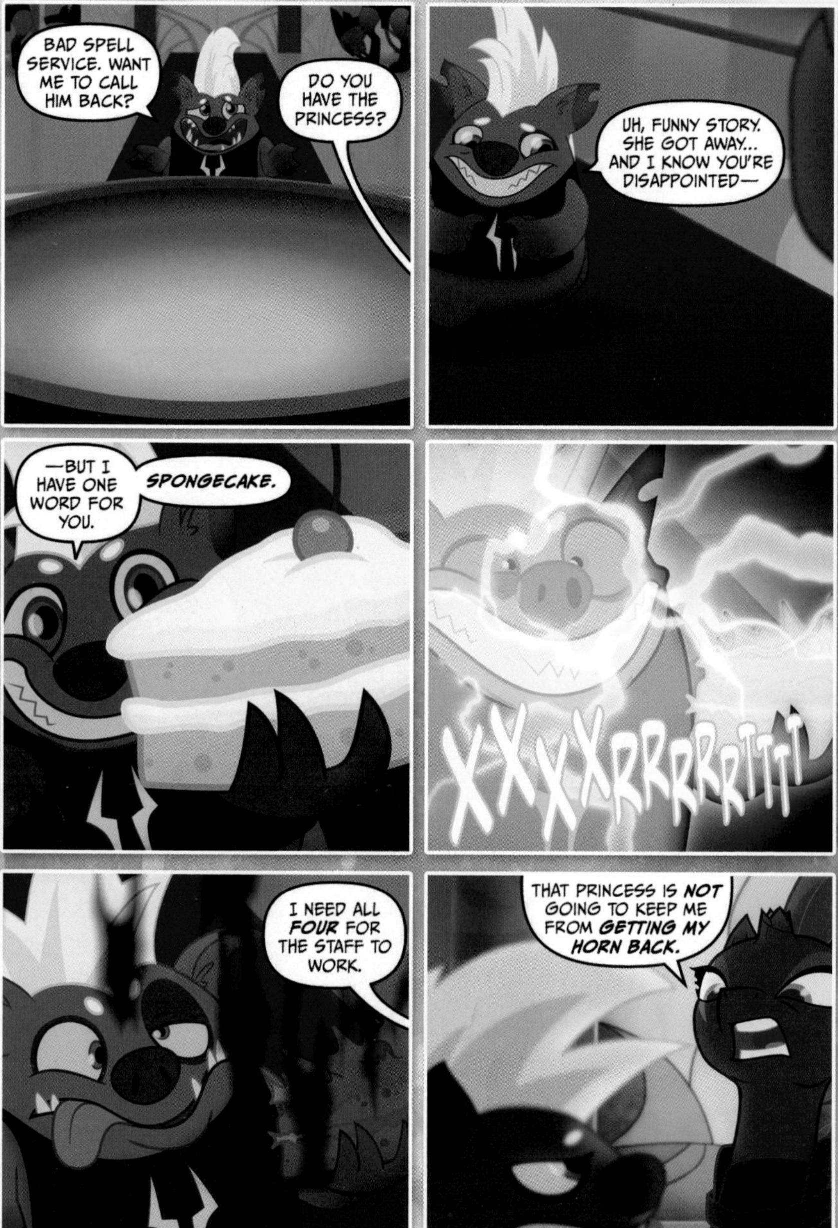
BAD SPELL SERVICE. WANT ME TO CALL HIM BACK?
DO YOU HAVE THE PRINCESS?
UH, FUNNY STORY. SHE GOT AWAY... AND I KNOW YOU'RE DISAPPOINTED—
—BUT I HAVE ONE WORD FOR YOU.
SPONGECAKE.
XXXXRRRRRTTTT
I NEED ALL FOUR FOR THE STAFF TO WORK.
THAT PRINCESS IS NOT GOING TO KEEP ME FROM GETTING MY HORN BACK.

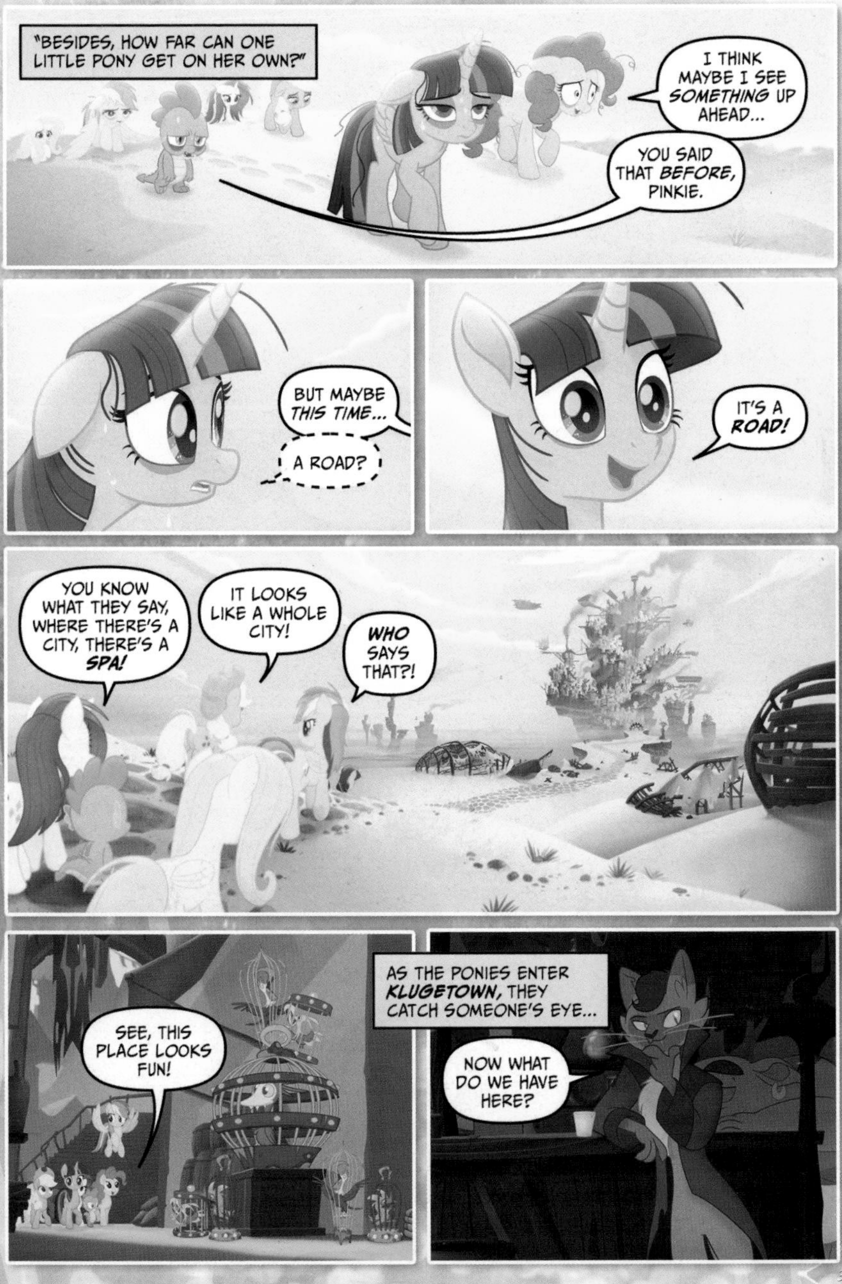
"BESIDES, HOW FAR CAN ONE LITTLE PONY GET ON HER OWN?"
I THINK MAYBE I SEE SOMETHING UP AHEAD...
YOU SAID THAT BEFORE, PINKIE.
BUT MAYBE THIS TIME...
A ROAD?
IT'S A ROAD!
YOU KNOW WHAT THEY SAY, WHERE THERE'S A CITY, THERE'S A SPA!
IT LOOKS LIKE A WHOLE CITY!
WHO SAYS THAT?!
SEE, THIS PLACE LOOKS FUN!
AS THE PONIES ENTER KLUGETOWN, THEY CATCH SOMEONE'S EYE...
NOW WHAT DO WE HAVE HERE?

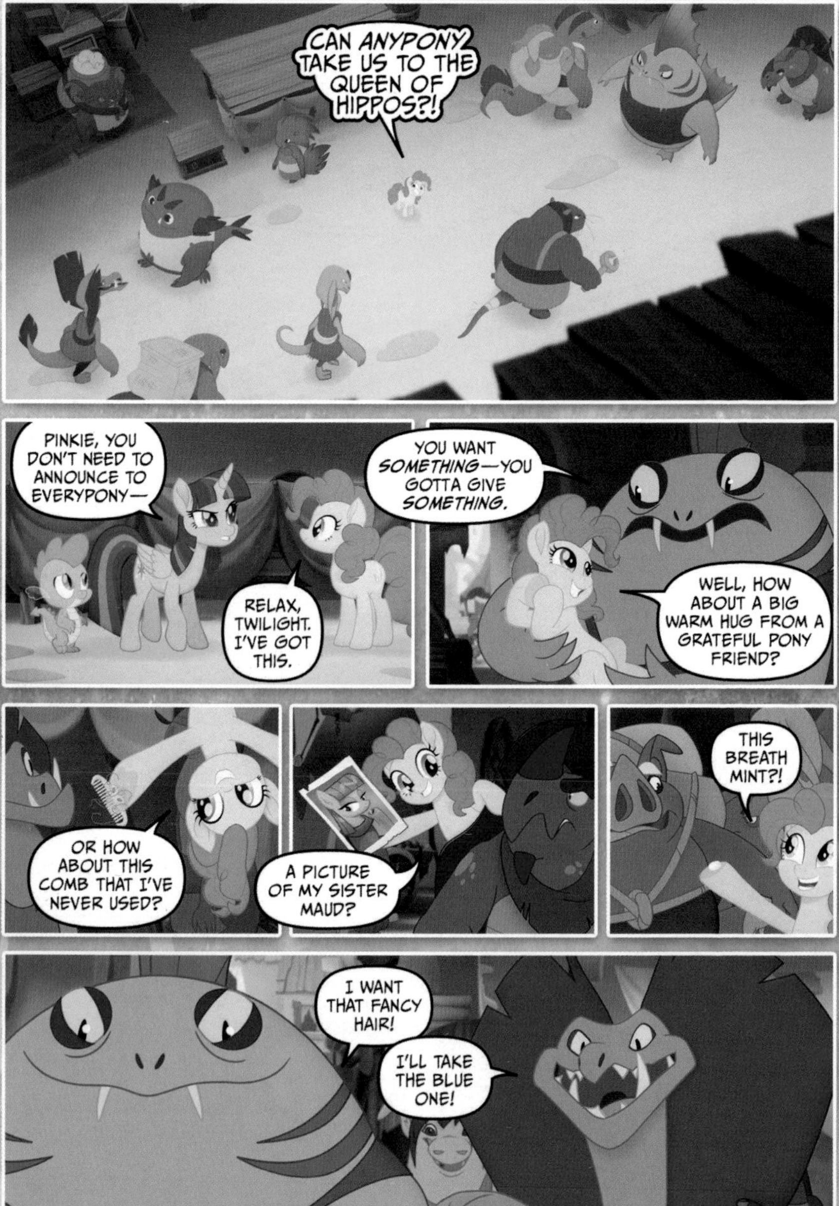
CAN ANYPONY TAKE US TO THE QUEEN OF HIPPOS?!
PINKIE, YOU DON'T NEED TO ANNOUNCE TO EVERYPONY—
RELAX, TWILIGHT. I'VE GOT THIS.
YOU WANT SOMETHING—YOU GOTTA GIVE SOMETHING.
WELL, HOW ABOUT A BIG WARM HUG FROM A GRATEFUL PONY FRIEND?
OR HOW ABOUT THIS COMB THAT I'VE NEVER USED?
A PICTURE OF MY SISTER MAUD?
THIS BREATH MINT?!
I WANT THAT FANCY HAIR!
I'LL TAKE THE BLUE ONE!

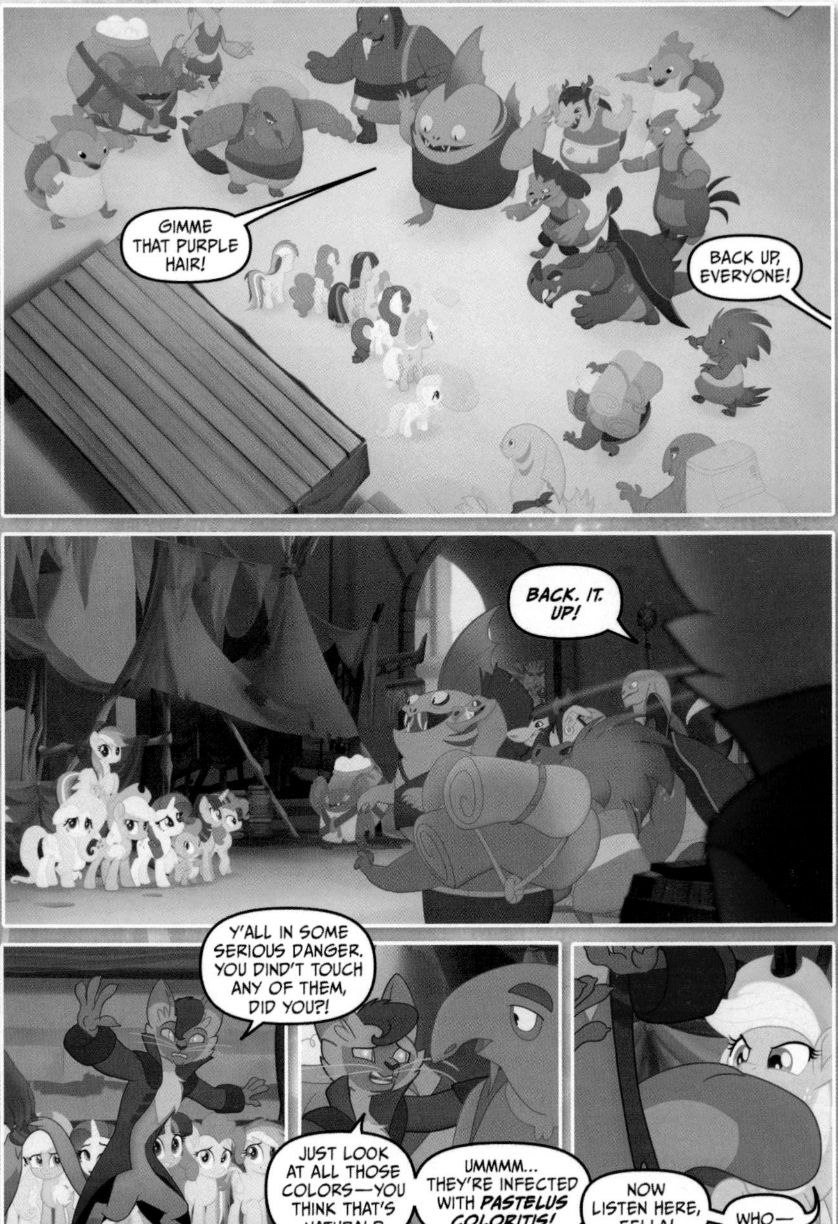
GIMME THAT PURPLE HAIR!
BACK UP, EVERYONE!
BACK. IT. UP!
Y'ALL IN SOME SERIOUS DANGER. YOU DIND'T TOUCH ANY OF THEM, DID YOU?!
JUST LOOK AT ALL THOSE COLORS—YOU THINK THAT'S NATURAL?
UMMMM... THEY'RE INFECTED WITH PASTELUS COLORITIS!
NOW LISTEN HERE, FELLA!
WHO—MPF!

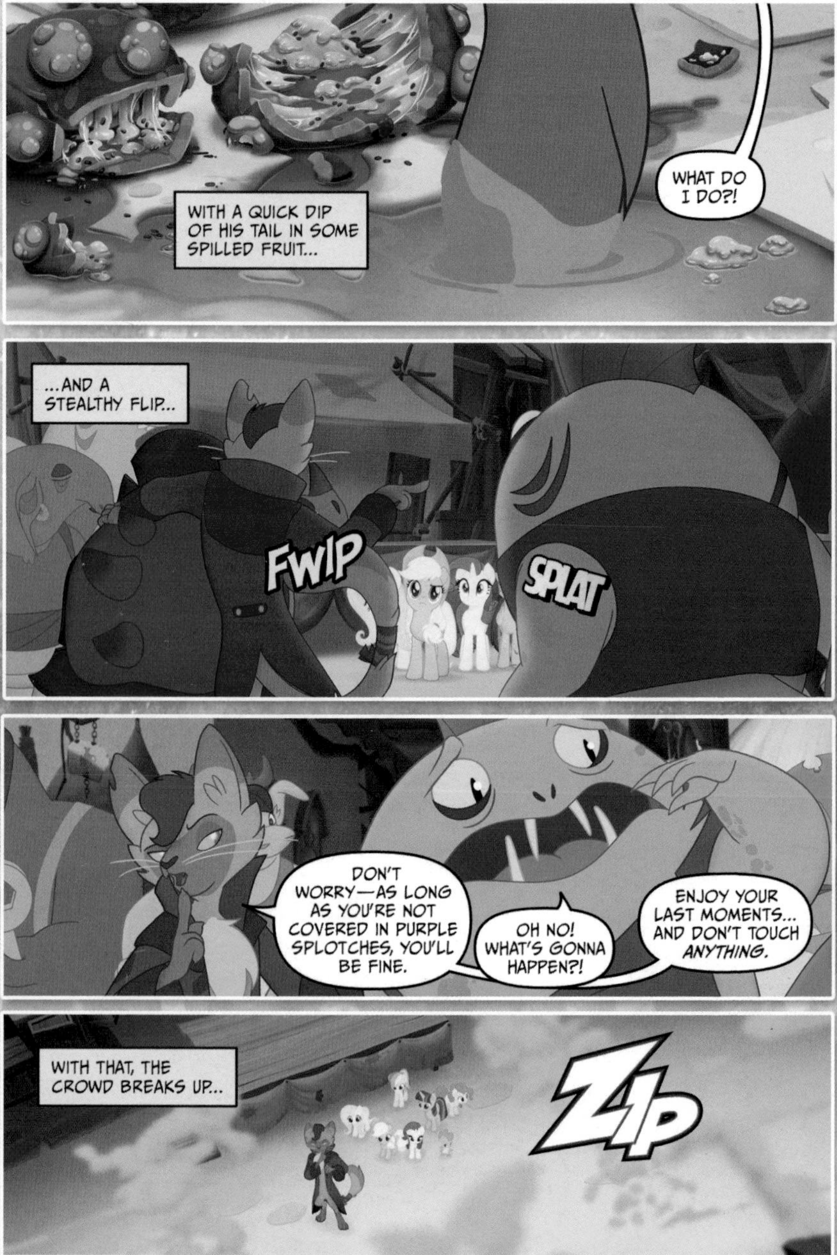
WHAT DO I DO?!
WITH A QUICK DIP OF HIS TAIL IN SOME SPILLED FRUIT...
...AND A STEALTHY FLIP...
FWIP
SPLAT
DON'T WORRY—AS LONG AS YOU'RE NOT COVERED IN PURPLE SPLOTCHES, YOU'LL BE FINE.
OH NO! WHAT'S GONNA HAPPEN?!
ENJOY YOUR LAST MOMENTS... AND DON'T TOUCH *ANYTHING*.
WITH THAT, THE CROWD BREAKS UP...
ZIP

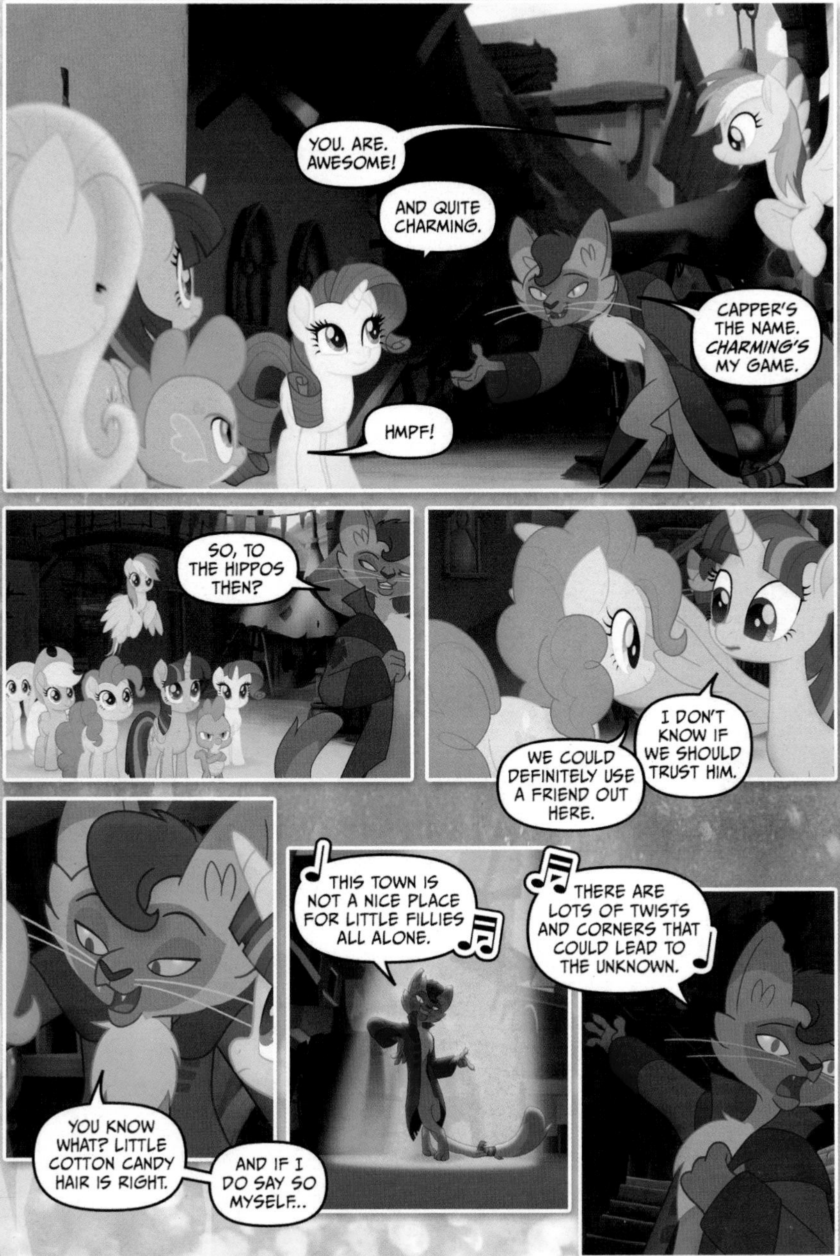
YOU. ARE. AWESOME!
AND QUITE CHARMING.
CAPPER'S THE NAME. *CHARMING'S* MY GAME.
HMPF!
SO, TO THE HIPPOS THEN?
I DON'T KNOW IF WE SHOULD TRUST HIM.
WE COULD DEFINITELY USE A FRIEND OUT HERE.
YOU KNOW WHAT? LITTLE COTTON CANDY HAIR IS RIGHT.
AND IF I DO SAY SO MYSELF...
THIS TOWN IS NOT A NICE PLACE FOR LITTLE FILLIES ALL ALONE.
THERE ARE LOTS OF TWISTS AND CORNERS THAT COULD LEAD TO THE UNKNOWN.

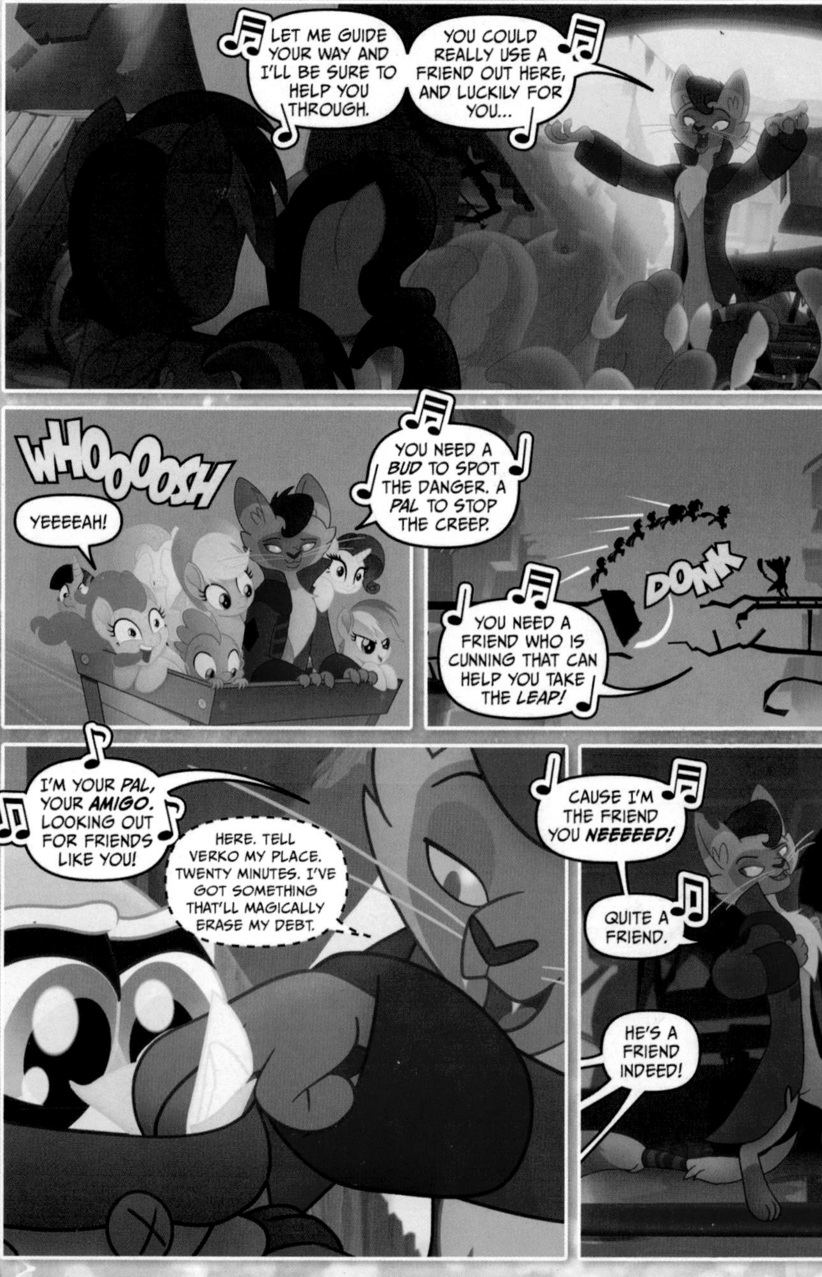
LET ME GUIDE YOUR WAY AND I'LL BE SURE TO HELP YOU THROUGH.
YOU COULD REALLY USE A FRIEND OUT HERE, AND LUCKILY FOR YOU...
WHOOOOOSH
YEEEEAH!
YOU NEED A BUD TO SPOT THE DANGER. A PAL TO STOP THE CREEP.
DONK
YOU NEED A FRIEND WHO IS CUNNING THAT CAN HELP YOU TAKE THE LEAP!
I'M YOUR PAL, YOUR AMIGO. LOOKING OUT FOR FRIENDS LIKE YOU!
HERE. TELL VERKO MY PLACE. TWENTY MINUTES. I'VE GOT SOMETHING THAT'LL MAGICALLY ERASE MY DEBT.
CAUSE I'M THE FRIEND YOU NEEEEED!
QUITE A FRIEND.
HE'S A FRIEND INDEED!

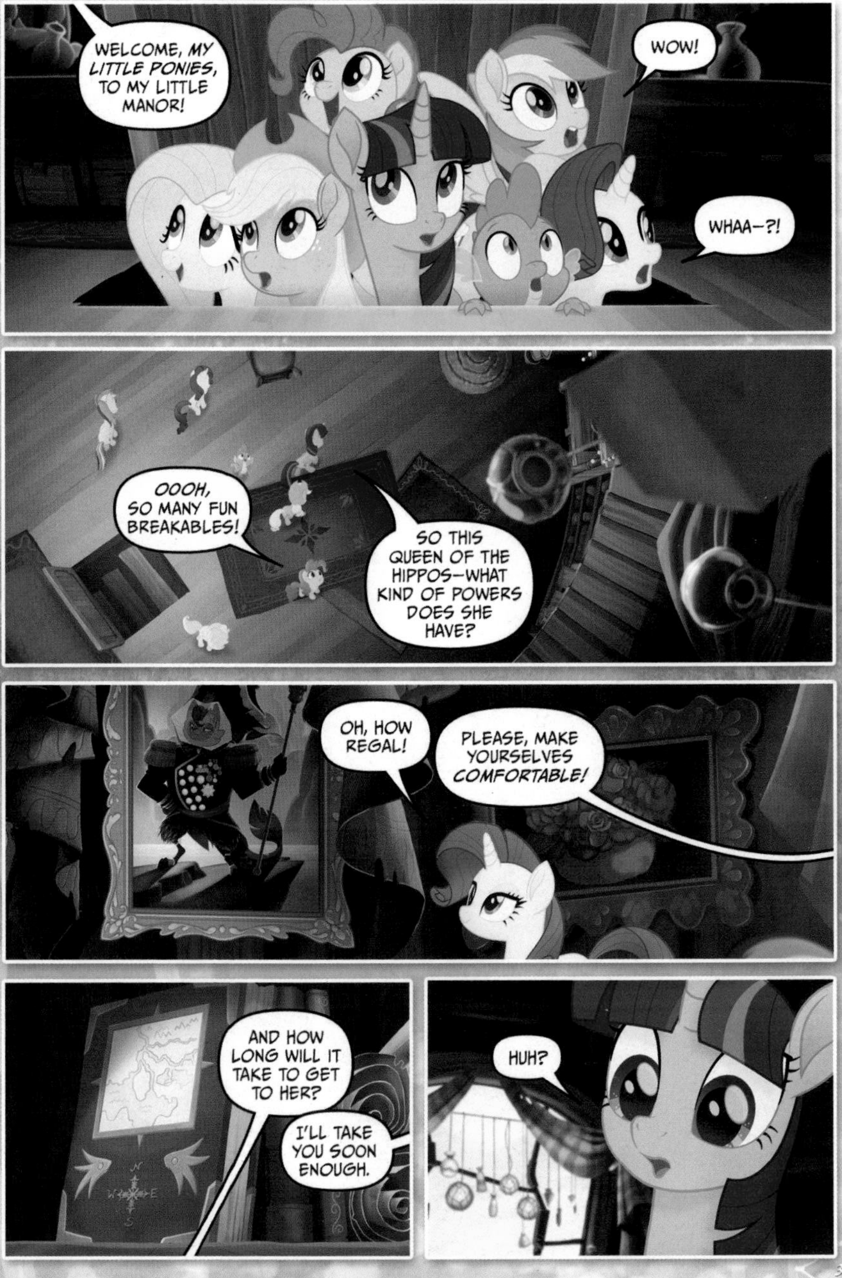
WELCOME, MY LITTLE PONIES, TO MY LITTLE MANOR!
WOW!
WHAA-?!
OOOH, SO MANY FUN BREAKABLES!
SO THIS QUEEN OF THE HIPPOS—WHAT KIND OF POWERS DOES SHE HAVE?
OH, HOW REGAL!
PLEASE, MAKE YOURSELVES COMFORTABLE!
AND HOW LONG WILL IT TAKE TO GET TO HER?
I'LL TAKE YOU SOON ENOUGH.
HUH?

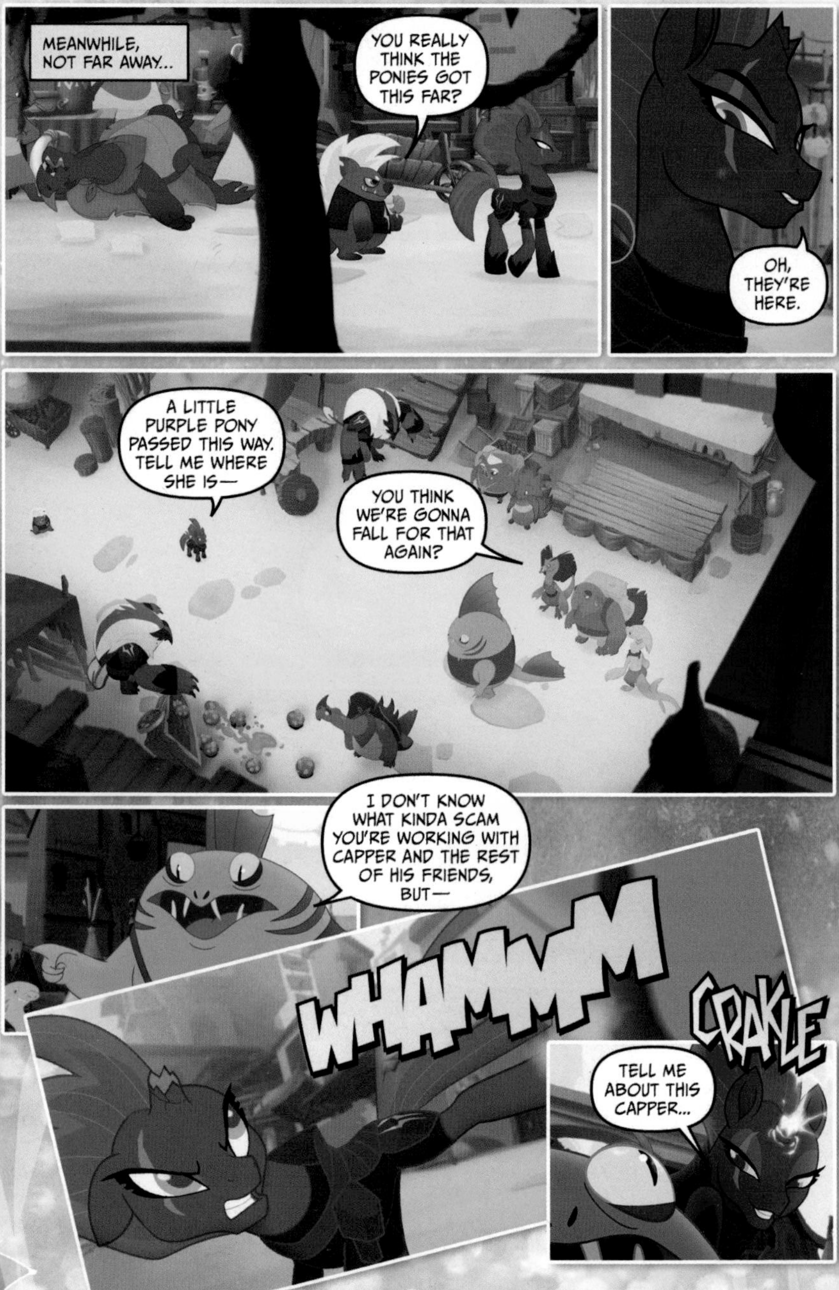
MEANWHILE, NOT FAR AWAY...
YOU REALLY THINK THE PONIES GOT THIS FAR?
OH, THEY'RE HERE.
A LITTLE PURPLE PONY PASSED THIS WAY. TELL ME WHERE SHE IS—
YOU THINK WE'RE GONNA FALL FOR THAT AGAIN?
I DON'T KNOW WHAT KINDA SCAM YOU'RE WORKING WITH CAPPER AND THE REST OF HIS FRIENDS, BUT—
WHAMMMM
CRAKLE
TELL ME ABOUT THIS CAPPER...

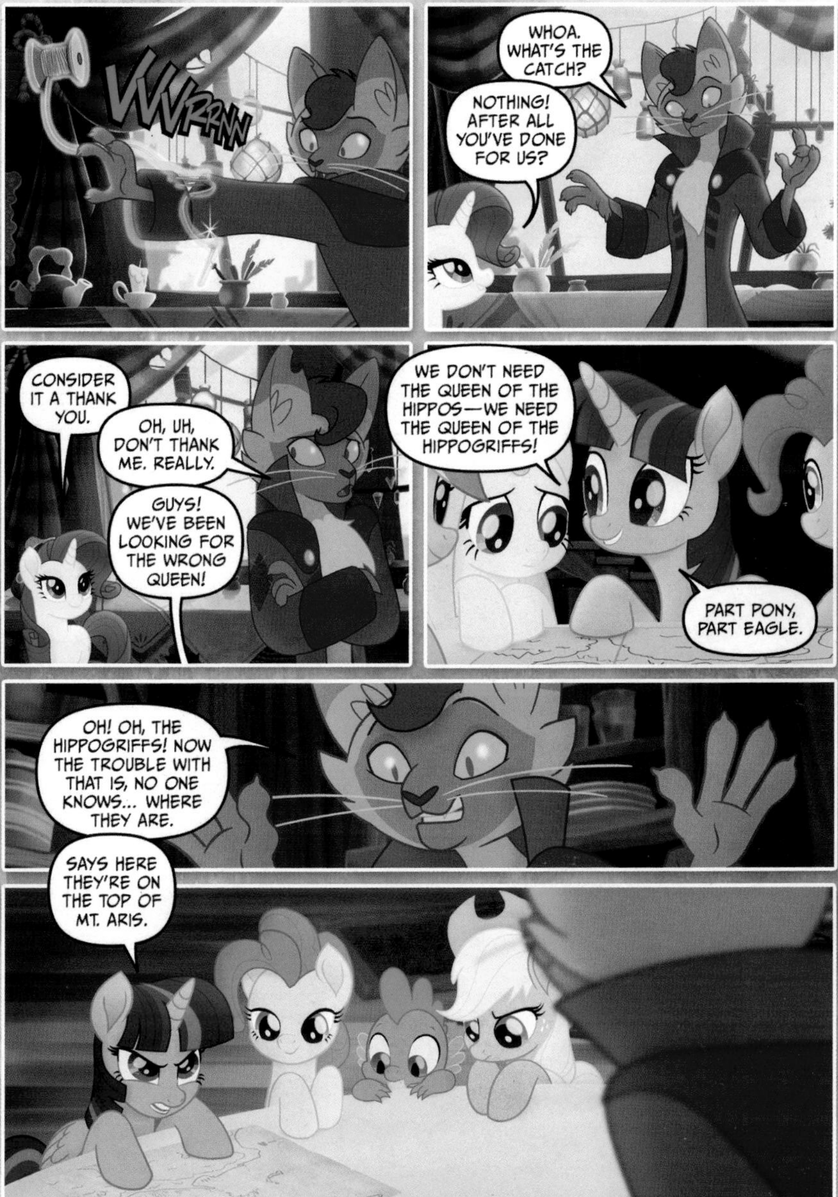
VVVRRNN
WHOA. WHAT'S THE CATCH?
NOTHING! AFTER ALL YOU'VE DONE FOR US?
CONSIDER IT A THANK YOU.
OH, UH, DON'T THANK ME. REALLY.
GUYS! WE'VE BEEN LOOKING FOR THE WRONG QUEEN!
WE DON'T NEED THE QUEEN OF THE HIPPOS—WE NEED THE QUEEN OF THE HIPPOGRIFFS!
PART PONY, PART EAGLE.
OH! OH, THE HIPPOGRIFFS! NOW THE TROUBLE WITH THAT IS, NO ONE KNOWS... WHERE THEY ARE.
SAYS HERE THEY'RE ON THE TOP OF MT. ARIS.

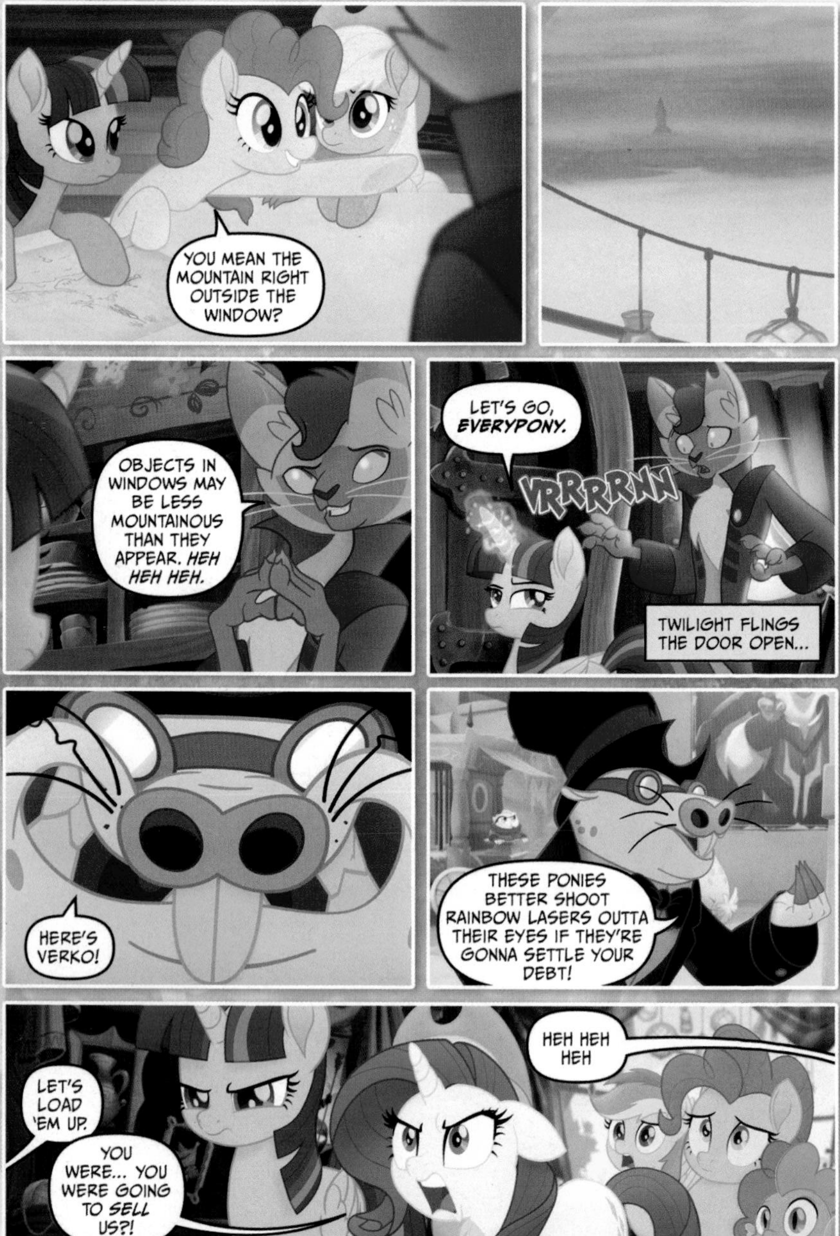
YOU MEAN THE MOUNTAIN RIGHT OUTSIDE THE WINDOW?
OBJECTS IN WINDOWS MAY BE LESS MOUNTAINOUS THAN THEY APPEAR. HEH HEH HEH.
LET'S GO, EVERYPONY.
VRRRRNN
TWILIGHT FLINGS THE DOOR OPEN...
HERE'S VERKO!
THESE PONIES BETTER SHOOT RAINBOW LASERS OUTTA THEIR EYES IF THEY'RE GONNA SETTLE YOUR DEBT!
LET'S LOAD 'EM UP.
HEH HEH HEH
YOU WERE... YOU WERE GOING TO SELL US?!

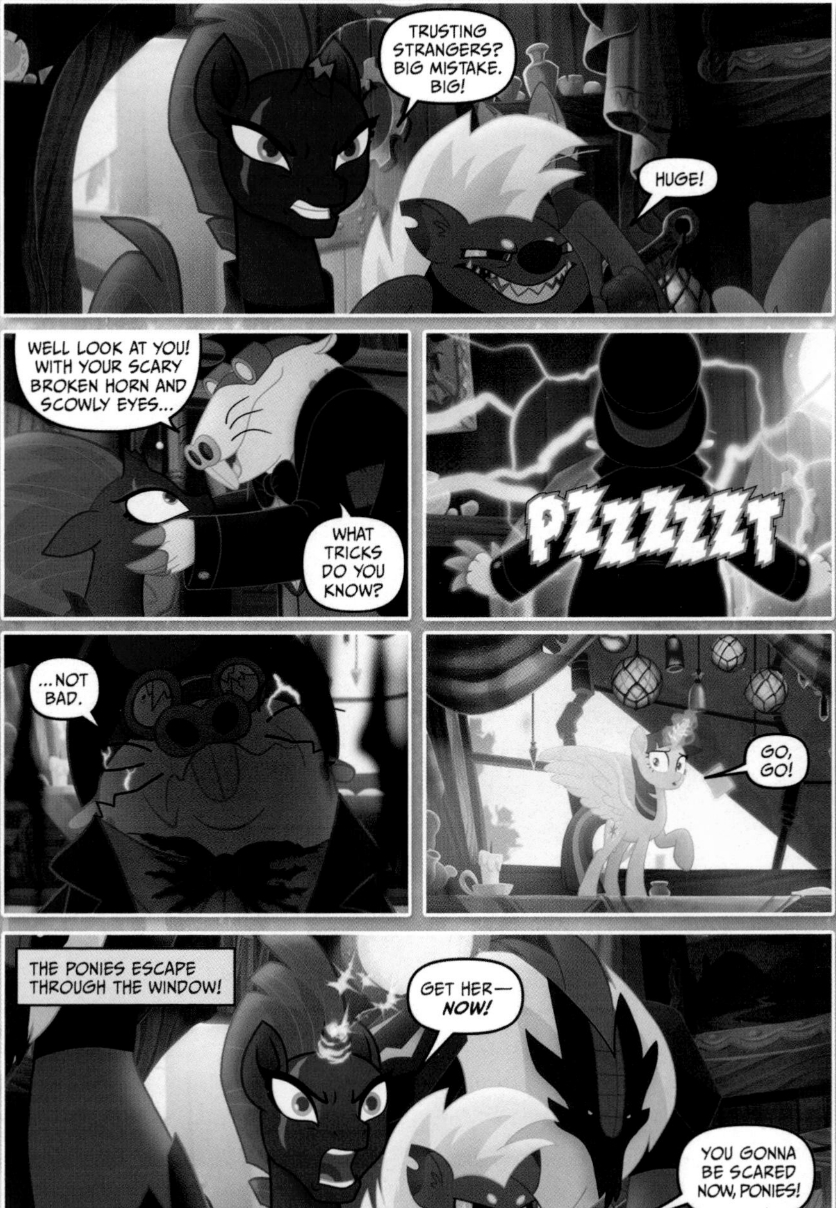
TRUSTING STRANGERS? BIG MISTAKE. BIG!
HUGE!
WELL LOOK AT YOU! WITH YOUR SCARY BROKEN HORN AND SCOWLY EYES...
WHAT TRICKS DO YOU KNOW?
PZZZZZT
...NOT BAD.
GO, GO!
THE PONIES ESCAPE THROUGH THE WINDOW!
GET HER— NOW!
YOU GONNA BE SCARED NOW, PONIES!

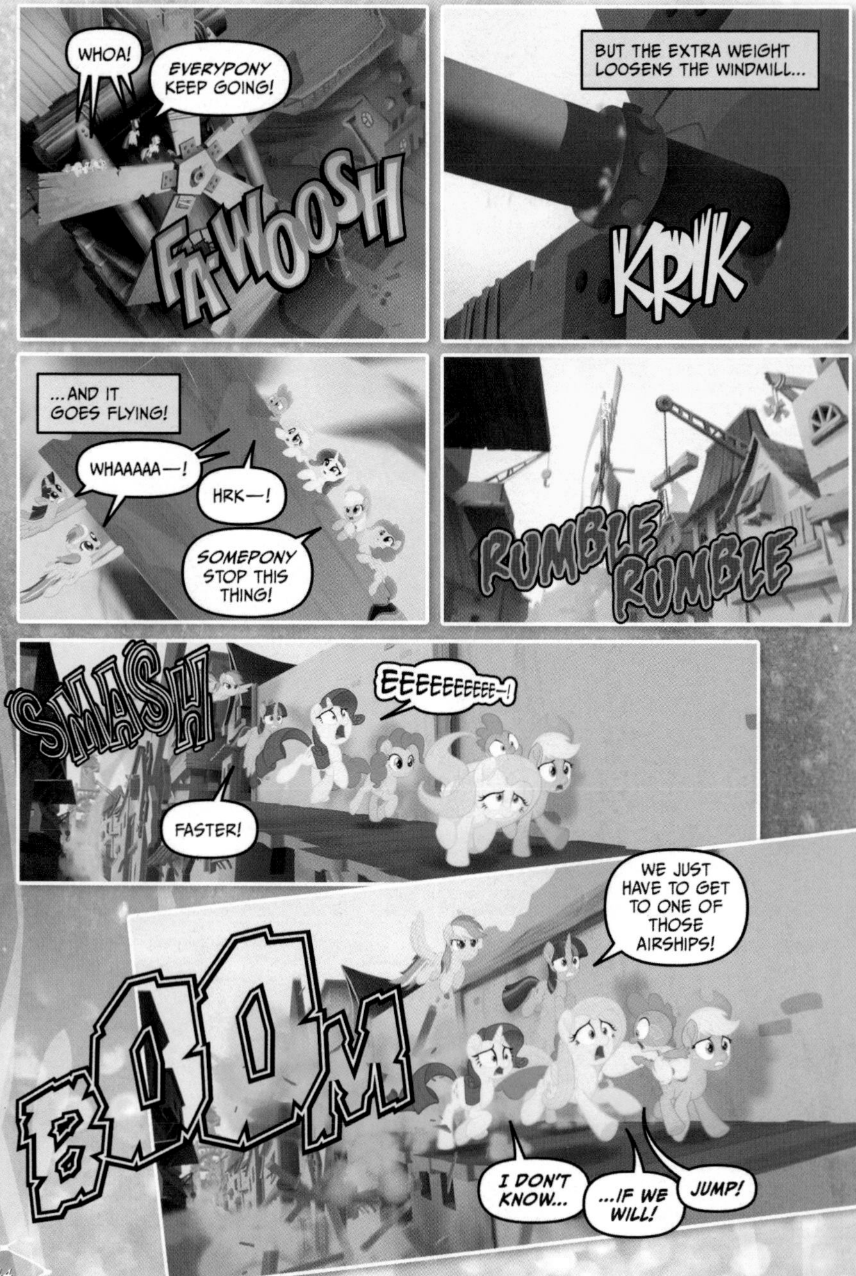
WHOA!
EVERYPONY KEEP GOING!
FA-WOOSH
BUT THE EXTRA WEIGHT LOOSENS THE WINDMILL...
KRIK
...AND IT GOES FLYING!
WHAAAAA—!
HRK—!
SOMEPONY STOP THIS THING!
RUMBLE RUMBLE
SMASH
EEEEEEEEEE—!
FASTER!
WE JUST HAVE TO GET TO ONE OF THOSE AIRSHIPS!
BOOM
I DON'T KNOW...
...IF WE WILL!
JUMP!

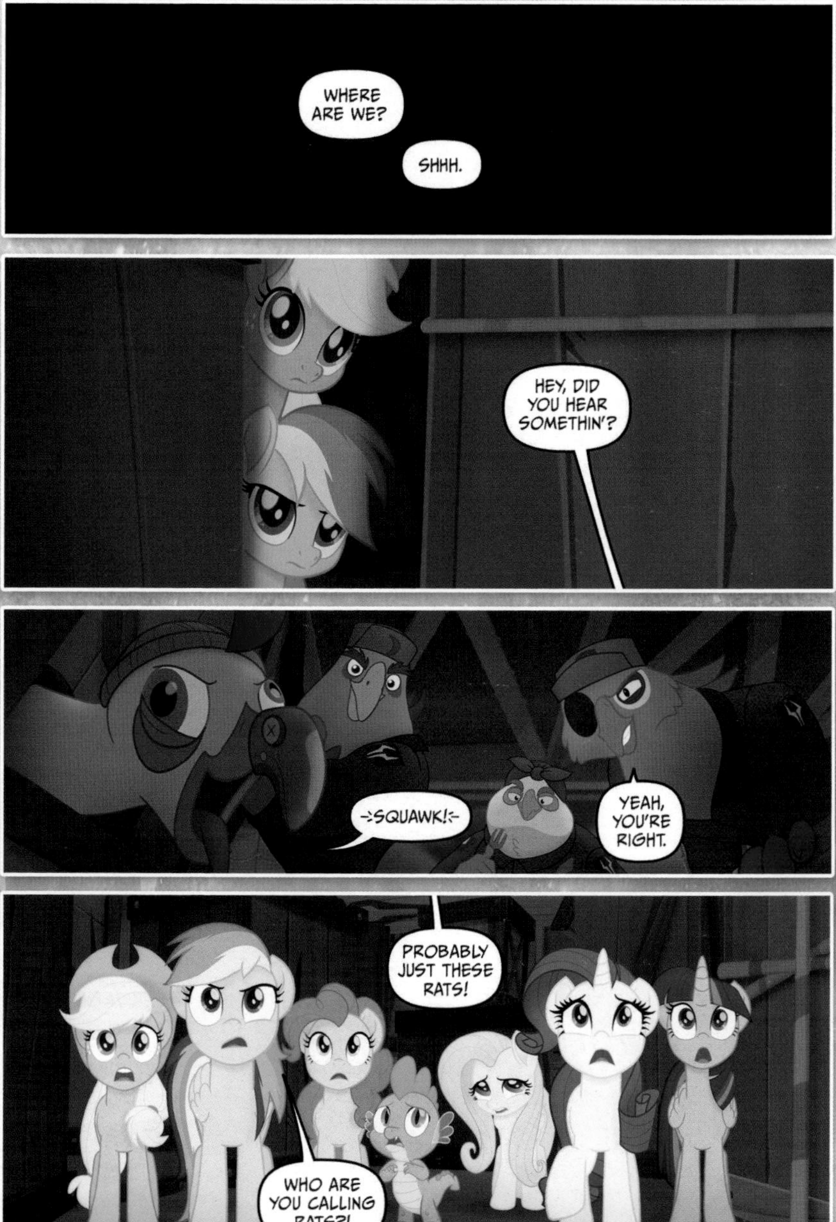
WHERE ARE WE?
SHHH.
HEY, DID YOU HEAR SOMETHIN'?
-SQUAWK!-
YEAH, YOU'RE RIGHT.
PROBABLY JUST THESE RATS!
WHO ARE YOU CALLING RATS?!

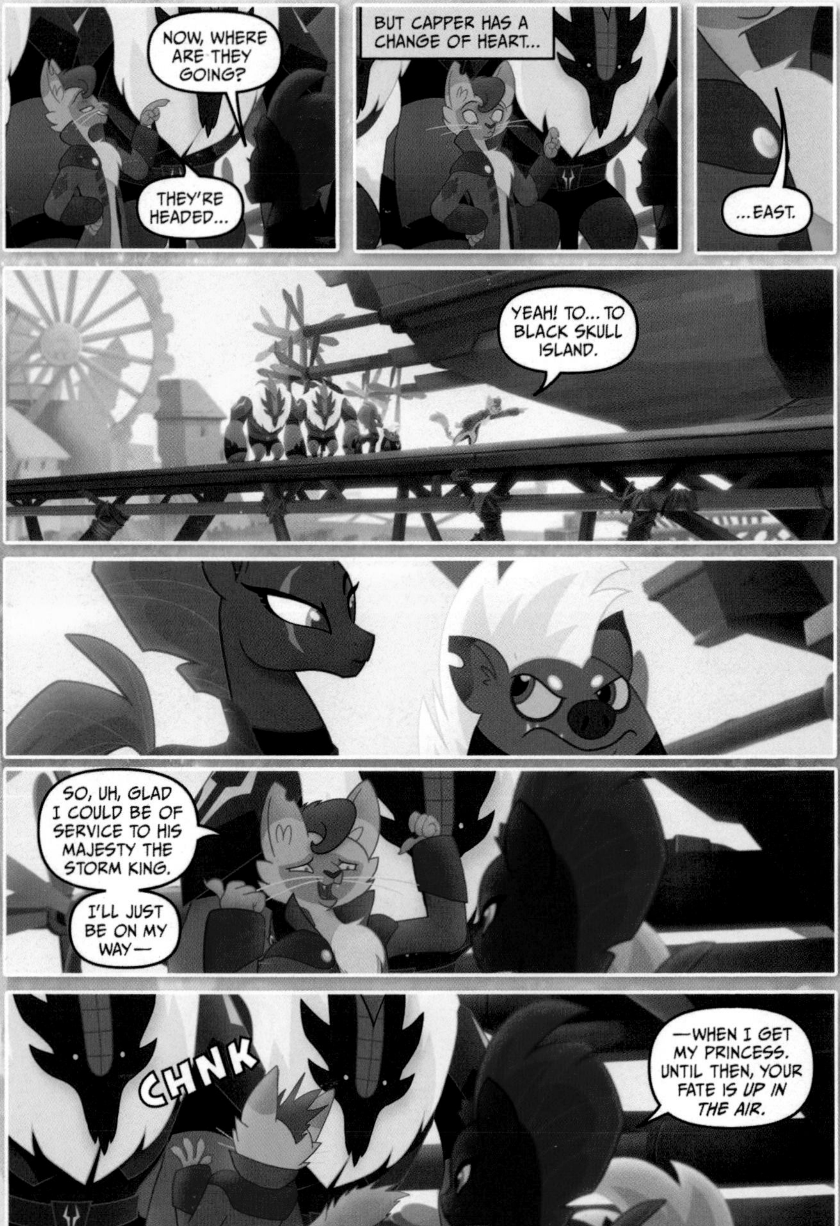
NOW, WHERE ARE THEY GOING?
THEY'RE HEADED...
BUT CAPPER HAS A CHANGE OF HEART...
...EAST.
YEAH! TO... TO BLACK SKULL ISLAND.
SO, UH, GLAD I COULD BE OF SERVICE TO HIS MAJESTY THE STORM KING.
I'LL JUST BE ON MY WAY—
CHNK
—WHEN I GET MY PRINCESS. UNTIL THEN, YOUR FATE IS *UP IN THE AIR.*

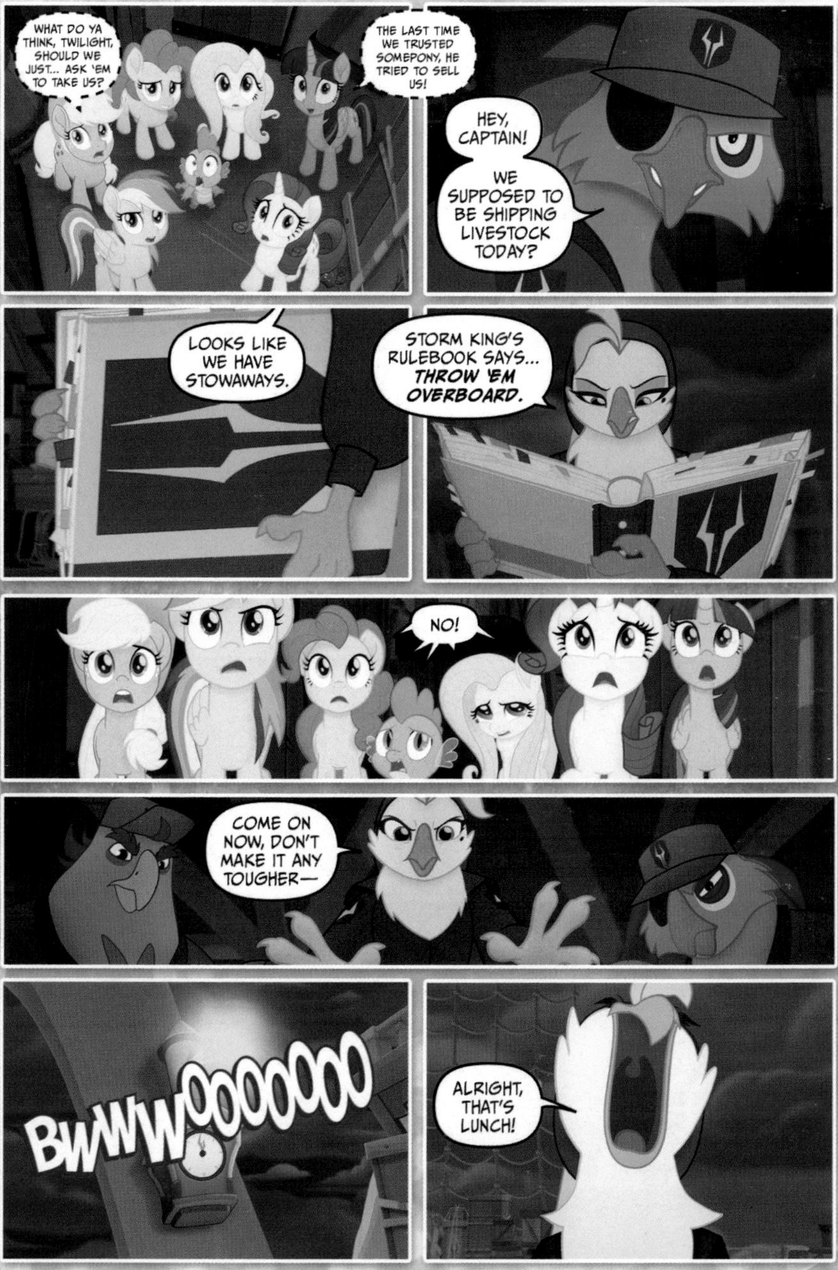
WHAT DO YA THINK, TWILIGHT, SHOULD WE JUST... ASK 'EM TO TAKE US?
THE LAST TIME WE TRUSTED SOMEPONY, HE TRIED TO SELL US!
HEY, CAPTAIN!
WE SUPPOSED TO BE SHIPPING LIVESTOCK TODAY?
LOOKS LIKE WE HAVE STOWAWAYS.
STORM KING'S RULEBOOK SAYS... THROW 'EM OVERBOARD.
NO!
COME ON NOW, DON'T MAKE IT ANY TOUGHER—
BWWWOOOOOOO
ALRIGHT, THAT'S LUNCH!

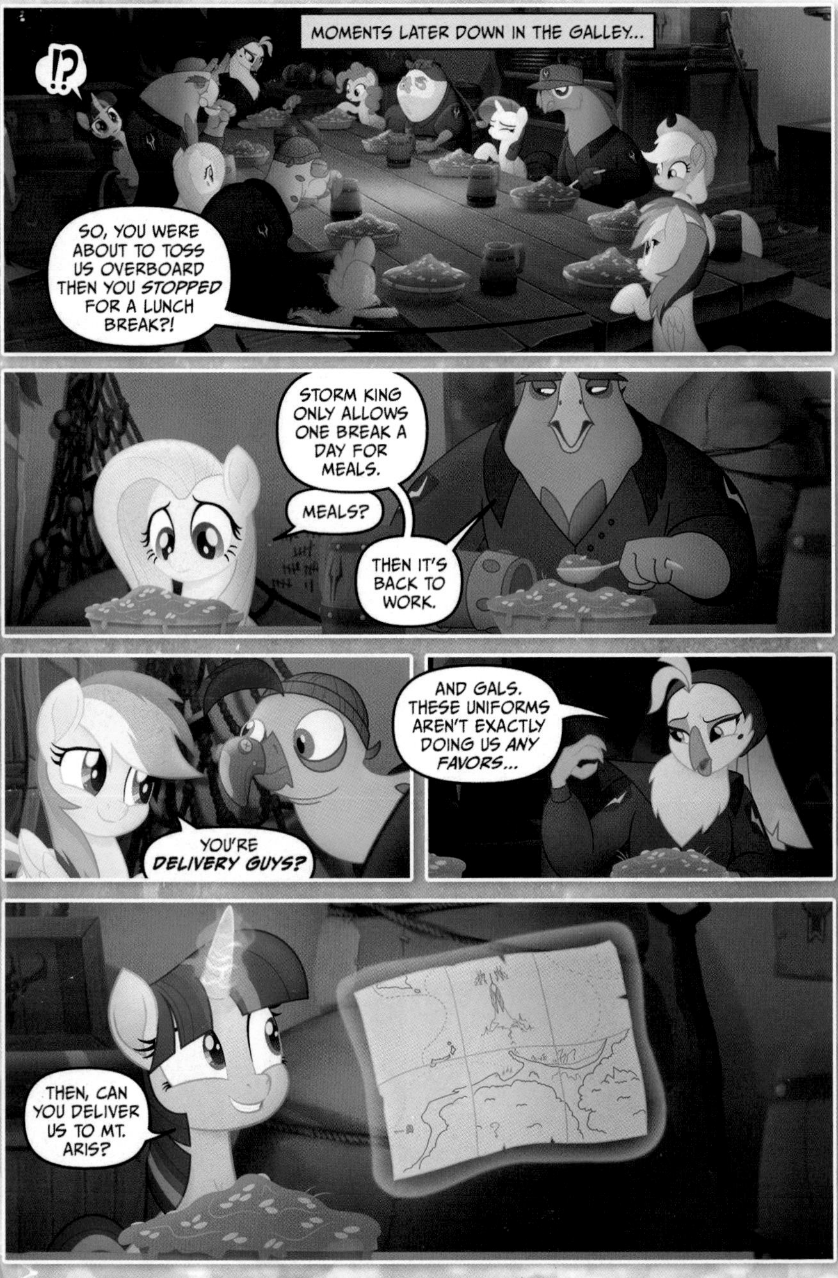
MOMENTS LATER DOWN IN THE GALLEY...
!?
SO, YOU WERE ABOUT TO TOSS US OVERBOARD THEN YOU *STOPPED* FOR A LUNCH BREAK?!
STORM KING ONLY ALLOWS ONE BREAK A DAY FOR MEALS.
MEALS?
THEN IT'S BACK TO WORK.
YOU'RE *DELIVERY GUYS?*
AND GALS. THESE UNIFORMS AREN'T EXACTLY DOING US *ANY FAVORS...*
THEN, CAN YOU DELIVER US TO MT. ARIS?

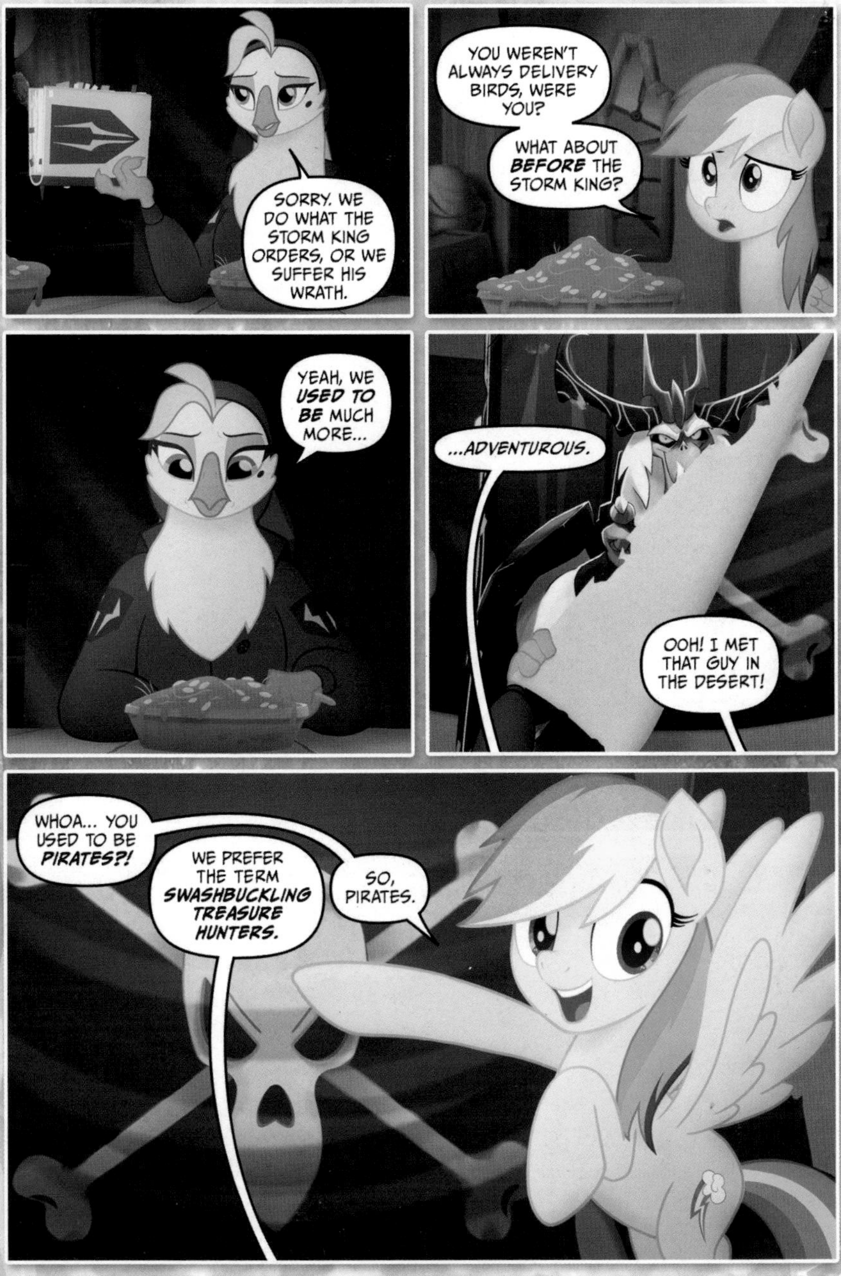
SORRY. WE DO WHAT THE STORM KING ORDERS, OR WE SUFFER HIS WRATH.
YOU WEREN'T ALWAYS DELIVERY BIRDS, WERE YOU?
WHAT ABOUT BEFORE THE STORM KING?
YEAH, WE USED TO BE MUCH MORE...
...ADVENTUROUS.
OOH! I MET THAT GUY IN THE DESERT!
WHOA... YOU USED TO BE PIRATES?!
WE PREFER THE TERM SWASHBUCKLING TREASURE HUNTERS.
SO, PIRATES.

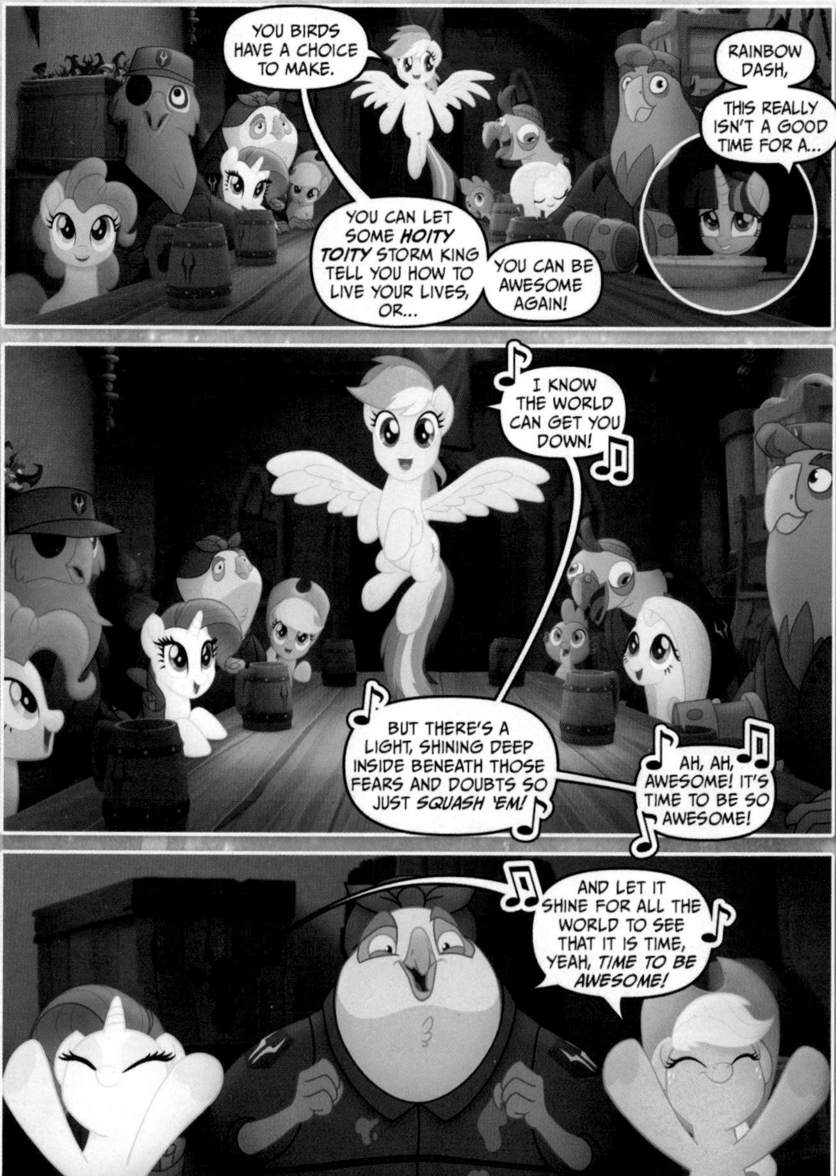

YOU BIRDS HAVE A CHOICE TO MAKE.
YOU CAN LET SOME *HOITY TOITY* STORM KING TELL YOU HOW TO LIVE YOUR LIVES, OR...
YOU CAN BE AWESOME AGAIN!
RAINBOW DASH,
THIS REALLY ISN'T A GOOD TIME FOR A...
I KNOW THE WORLD CAN GET YOU DOWN!
BUT THERE'S A LIGHT, SHINING DEEP INSIDE BENEATH THOSE FEARS AND DOUBTS SO JUST *SQUASH 'EM!*
AH, AH, AWESOME! IT'S TIME TO BE SO AWESOME!
AND LET IT SHINE FOR ALL THE WORLD TO SEE THAT IT IS TIME, YEAH, *TIME TO BE AWESOME!*

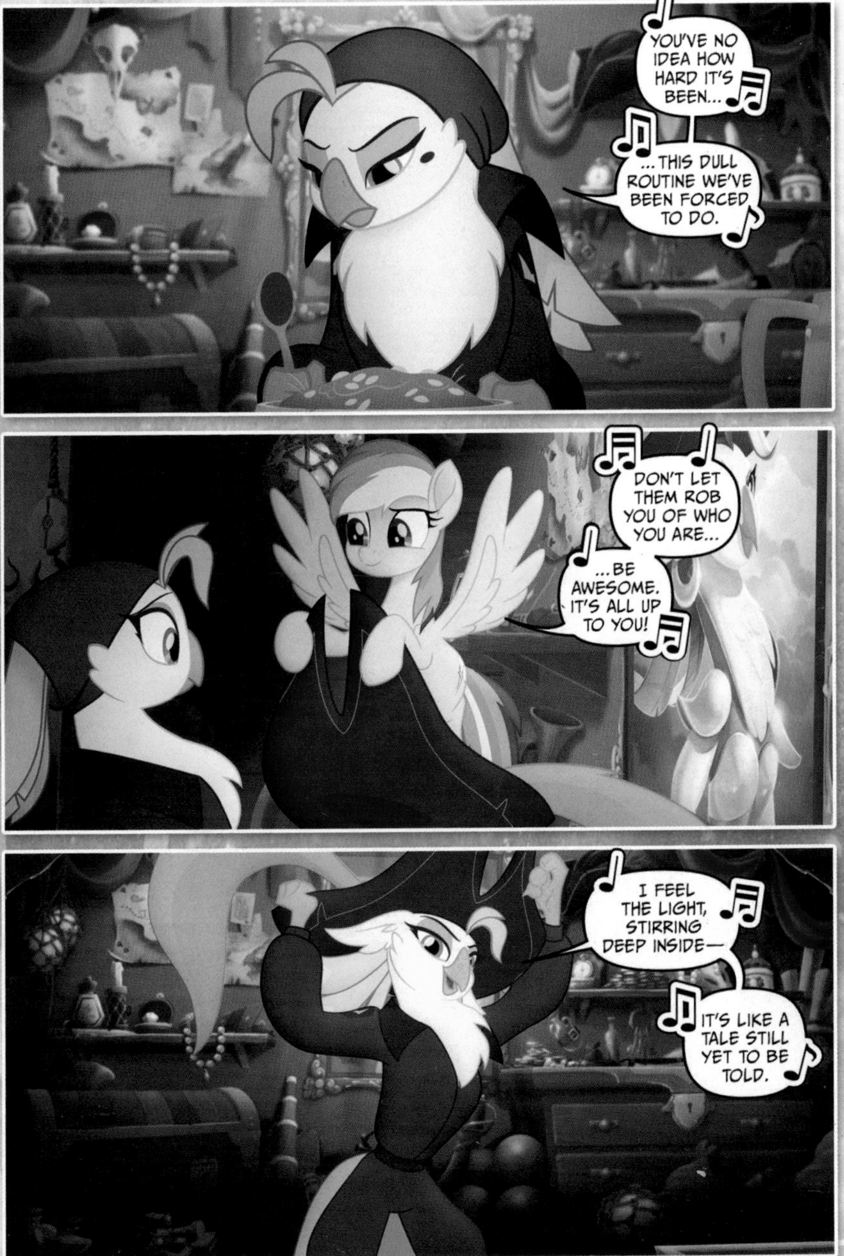
YOU'VE NO IDEA HOW HARD IT'S BEEN...
...THIS DULL ROUTINE WE'VE BEEN FORCED TO DO.
DON'T LET THEM ROB YOU OF WHO YOU ARE...
...BE AWESOME. IT'S ALL UP TO YOU!
I FEEL THE LIGHT, STIRRING DEEP INSIDE—
IT'S LIKE A TALE STILL YET TO BE TOLD.

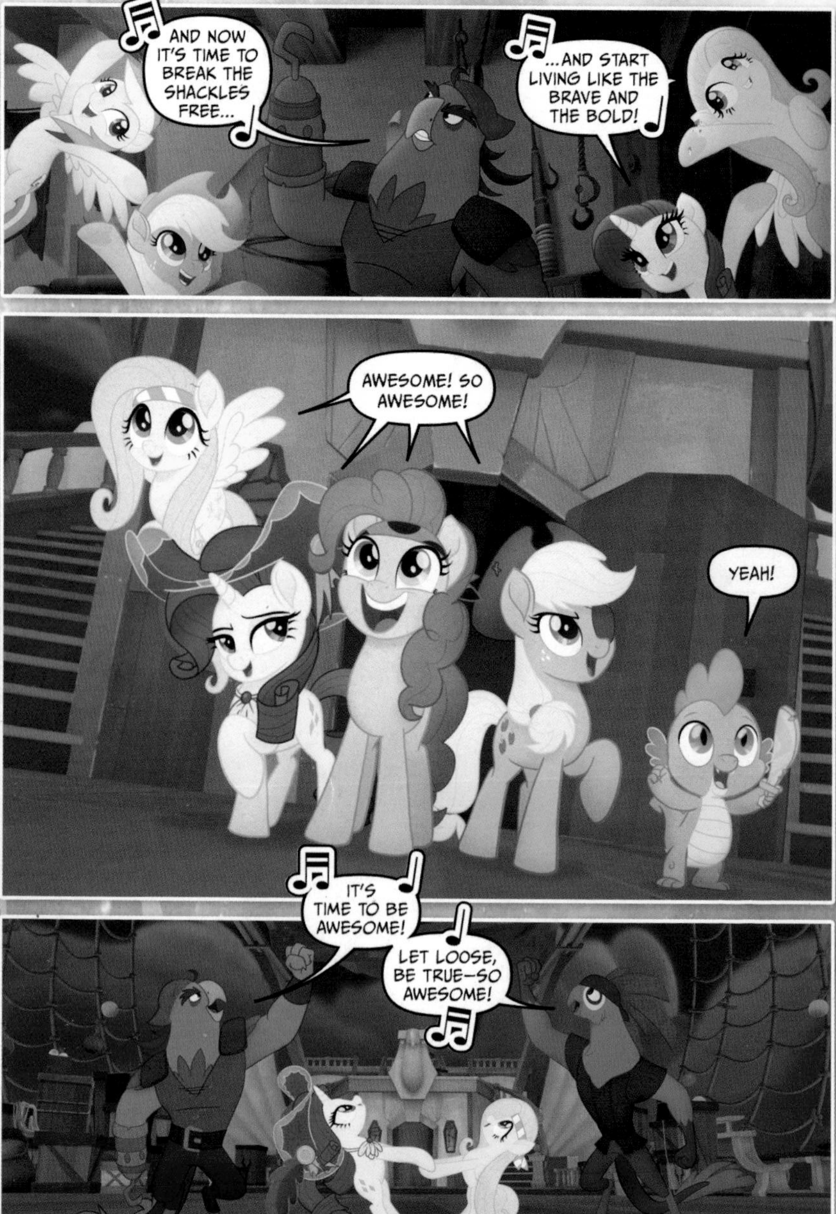
AND NOW IT'S TIME TO BREAK THE SHACKLES FREE...
...AND START LIVING LIKE THE BRAVE AND THE BOLD!
AWESOME! SO AWESOME!
YEAH!
IT'S TIME TO BE AWESOME!
LET LOOSE, BE TRUE—SO AWESOME!

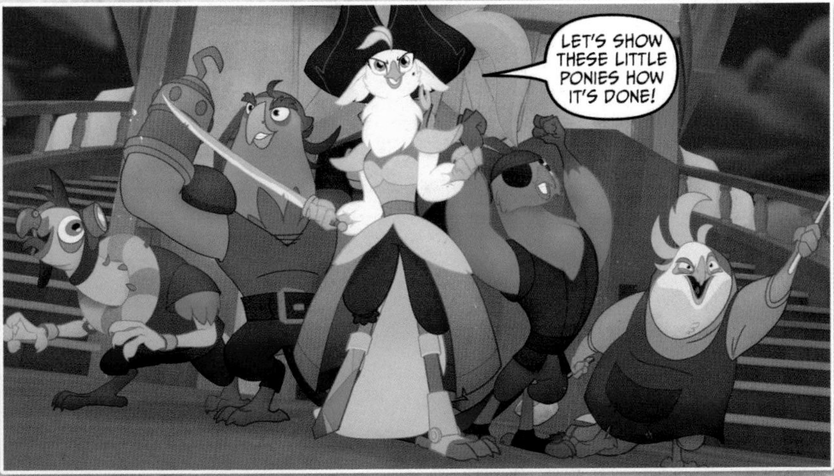
LET'S SHOW THESE LITTLE PONIES HOW IT'S DONE!

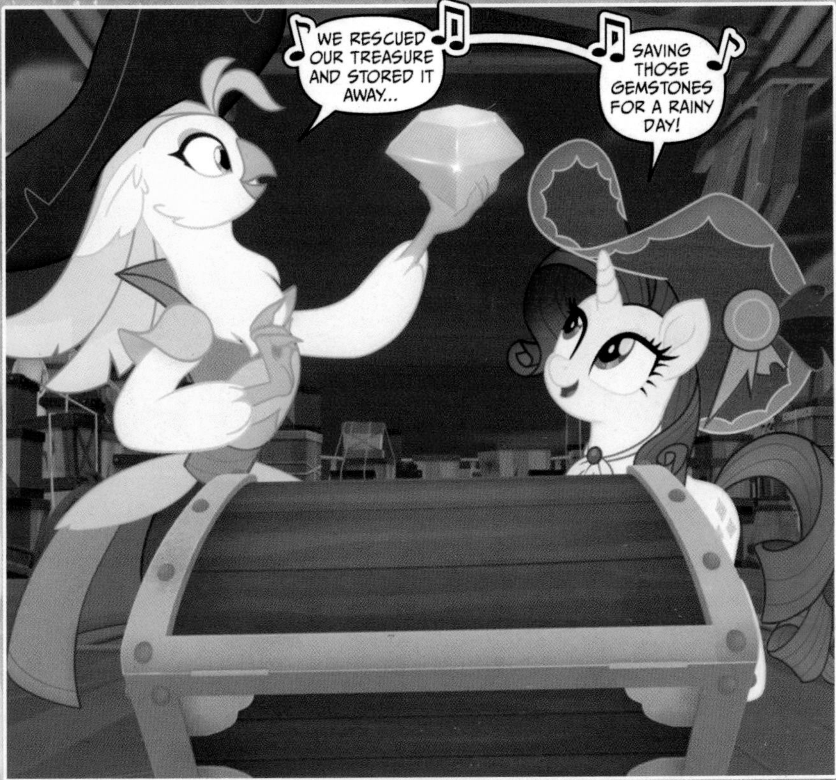
WE RESCUED OUR TREASURE AND STORED IT AWAY...
SAVING THOSE GEMSTONES FOR A RAINY DAY!

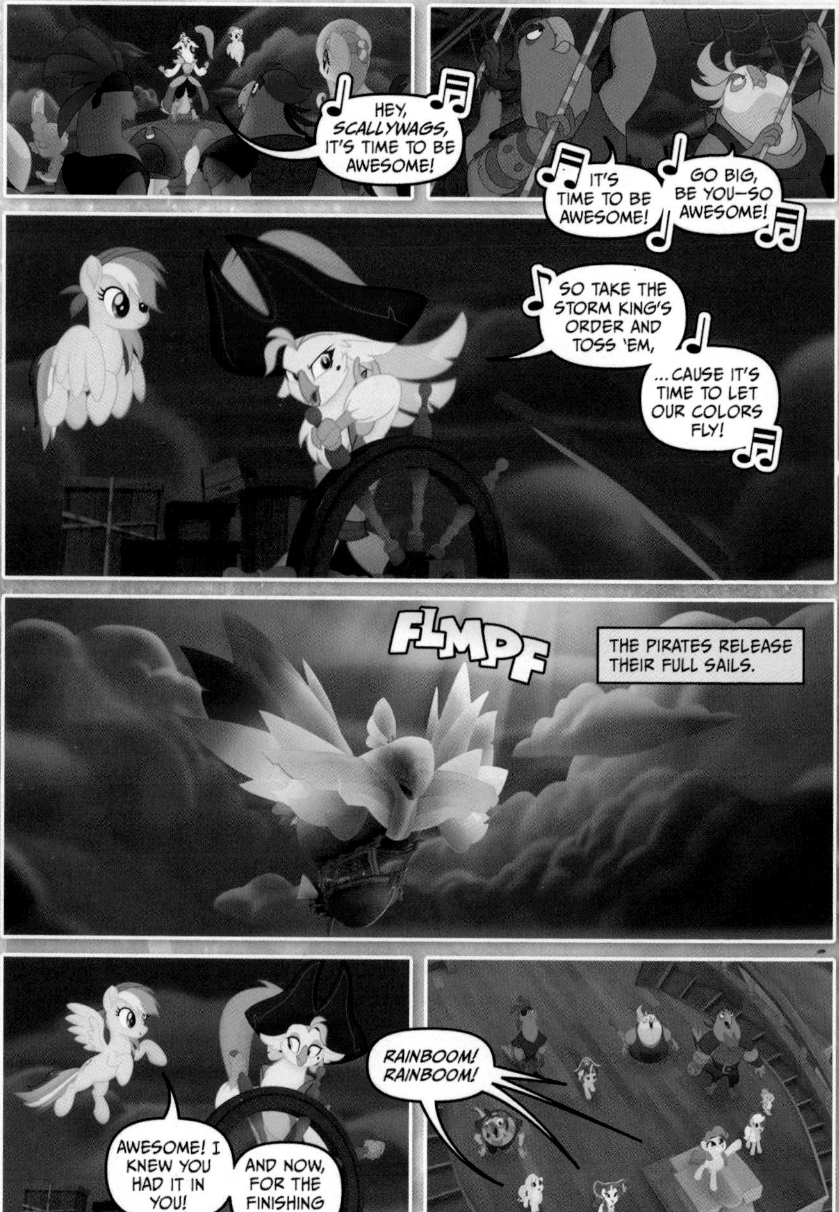
HEY, SCALLYWAGS, IT'S TIME TO BE AWESOME!
IT'S TIME TO BE AWESOME!
GO BIG, BE YOU—SO AWESOME!
SO TAKE THE STORM KING'S ORDER AND TOSS 'EM,
...CAUSE IT'S TIME TO LET OUR COLORS FLY!
FLMPF
THE PIRATES RELEASE THEIR FULL SAILS.
AWESOME! I KNEW YOU HAD IT IN YOU!
AND NOW, FOR THE FINISHING TOUCH!
RAINBOOM! RAINBOOM!

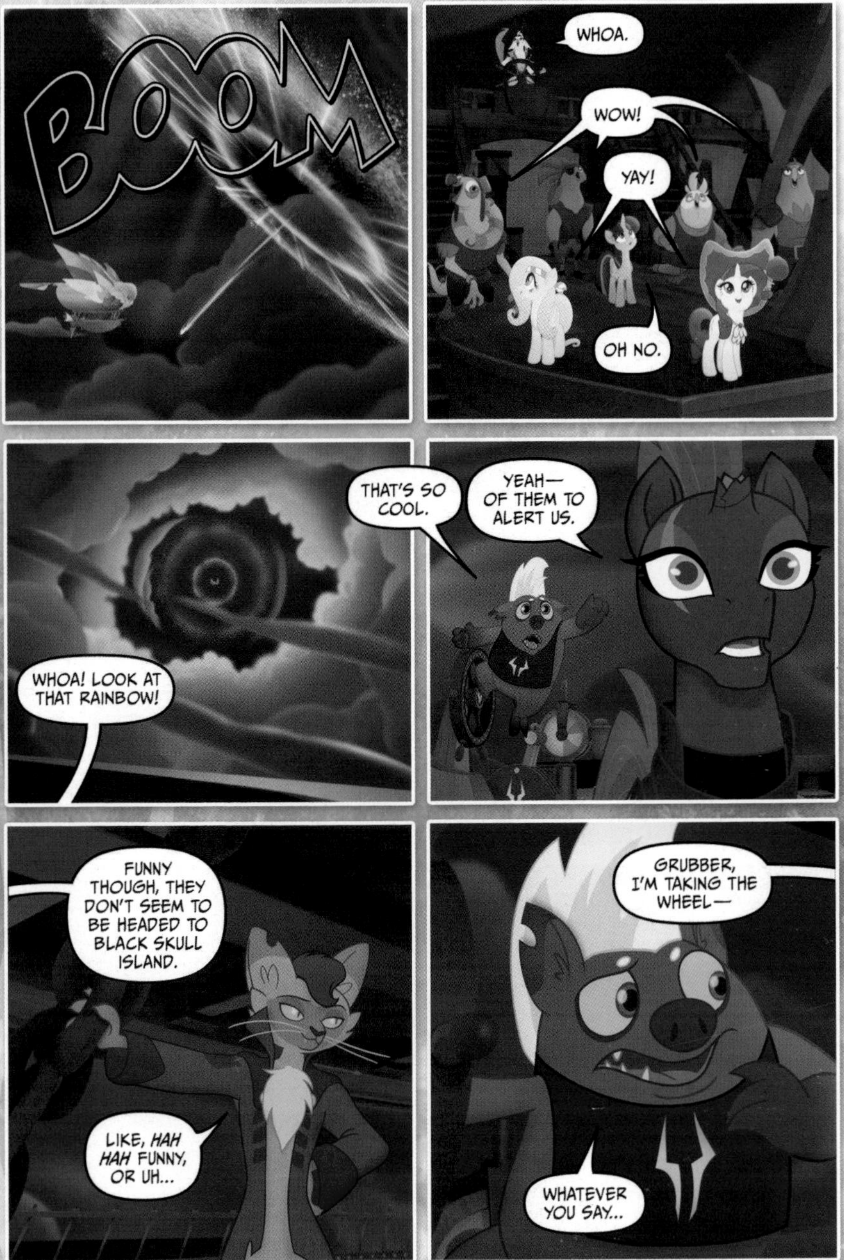
BOOM
WHOA.
WOW!
YAY!
OH NO.
WHOA! LOOK AT THAT RAINBOW!
THAT'S SO COOL.
YEAH— OF THEM TO ALERT US.
FUNNY THOUGH, THEY DON'T SEEM TO BE HEADED TO BLACK SKULL ISLAND.
LIKE, *HAH HAH* FUNNY, OR UH...
GRUBBER, I'M TAKING THE WHEEL—
WHATEVER YOU SAY...

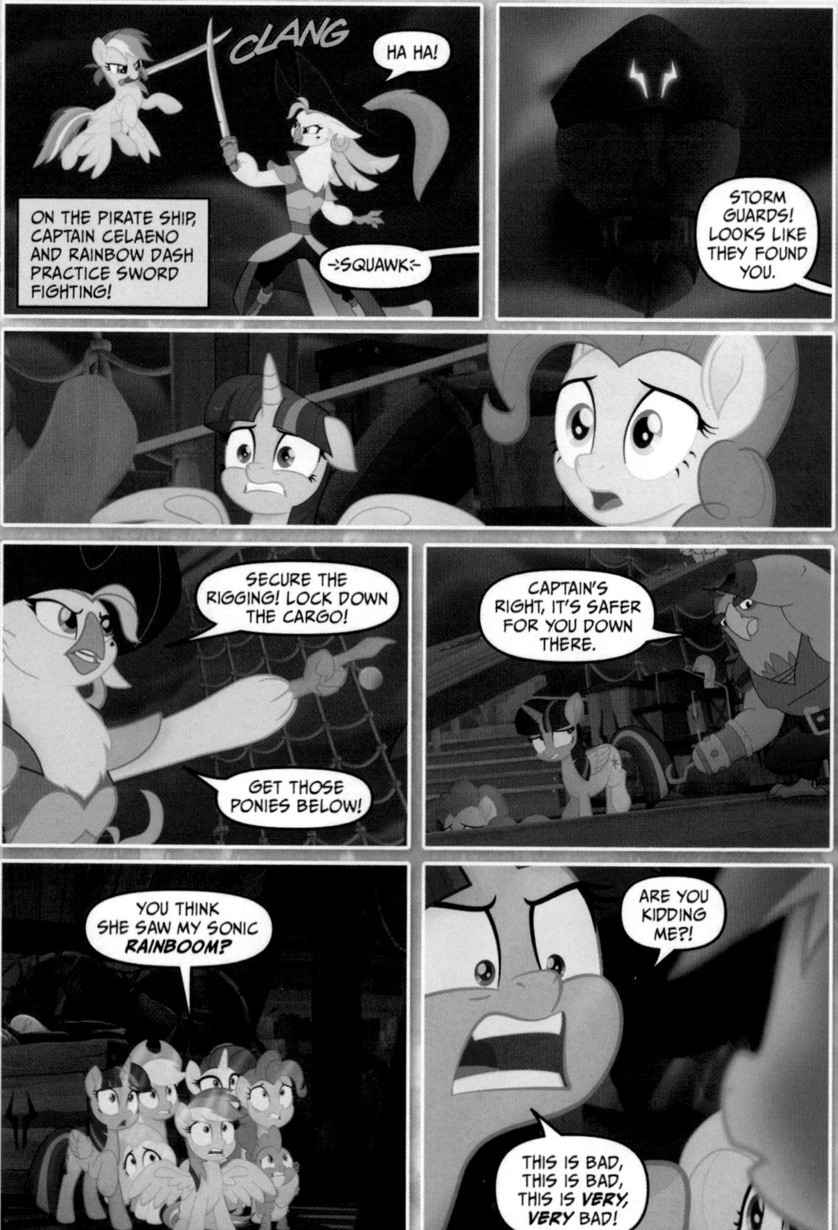

CLANG
HA HA!
ON THE PIRATE SHIP, CAPTAIN CELAENO AND RAINBOW DASH PRACTICE SWORD FIGHTING!
SQUAWK
STORM GUARDS! LOOKS LIKE THEY FOUND YOU.
SECURE THE RIGGING! LOCK DOWN THE CARGO!
GET THOSE PONIES BELOW!
CAPTAIN'S RIGHT, IT'S SAFER FOR YOU DOWN THERE.
YOU THINK SHE SAW MY SONIC ***RAINBOOM?***
ARE YOU KIDDING ME?!
THIS IS BAD, THIS IS BAD, THIS IS ***VERY, VERY*** BAD!

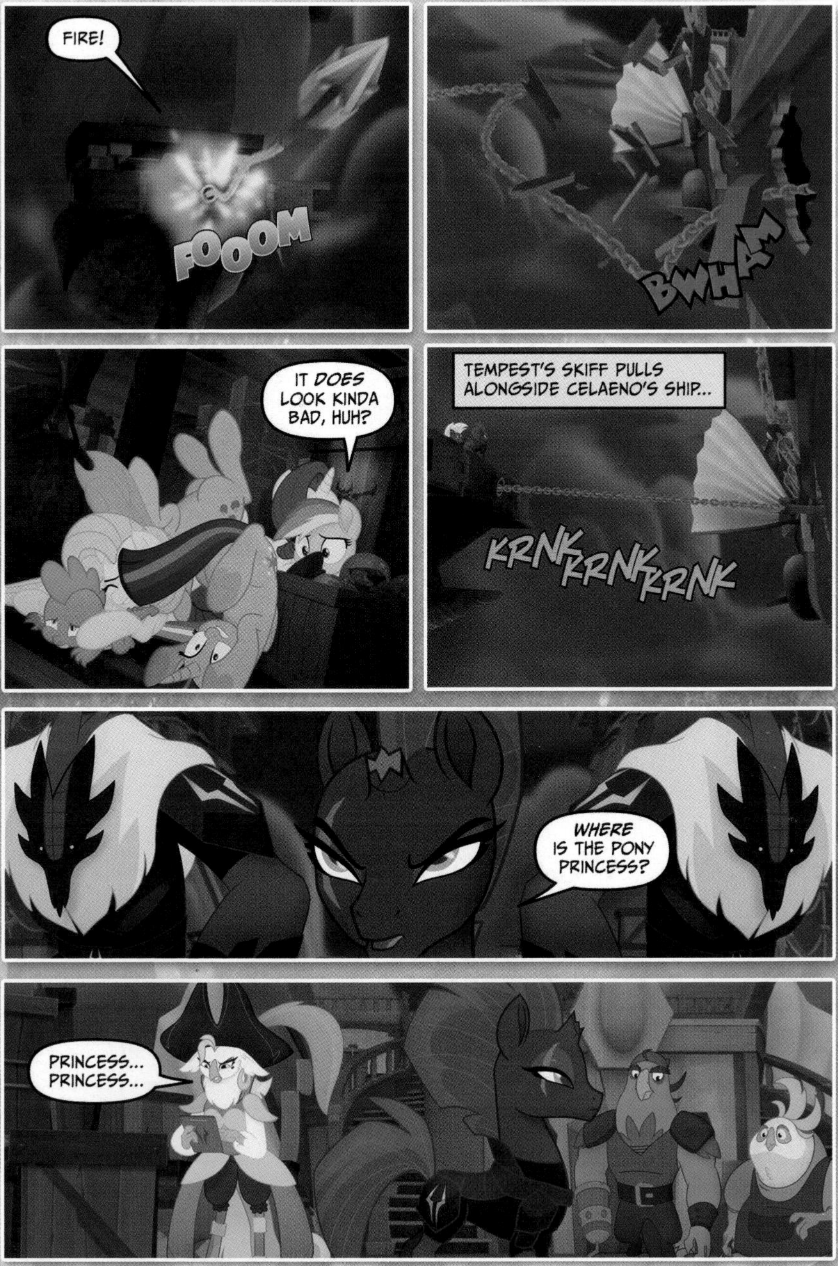
FIRE!
FOOOM
BWHAM
IT DOES LOOK KINDA BAD, HUH?
TEMPEST'S SKIFF PULLS ALONGSIDE CELAENO'S SHIP...
KRNK KRNK KRNK
WHERE IS THE PONY PRINCESS?
PRINCESS... PRINCESS...

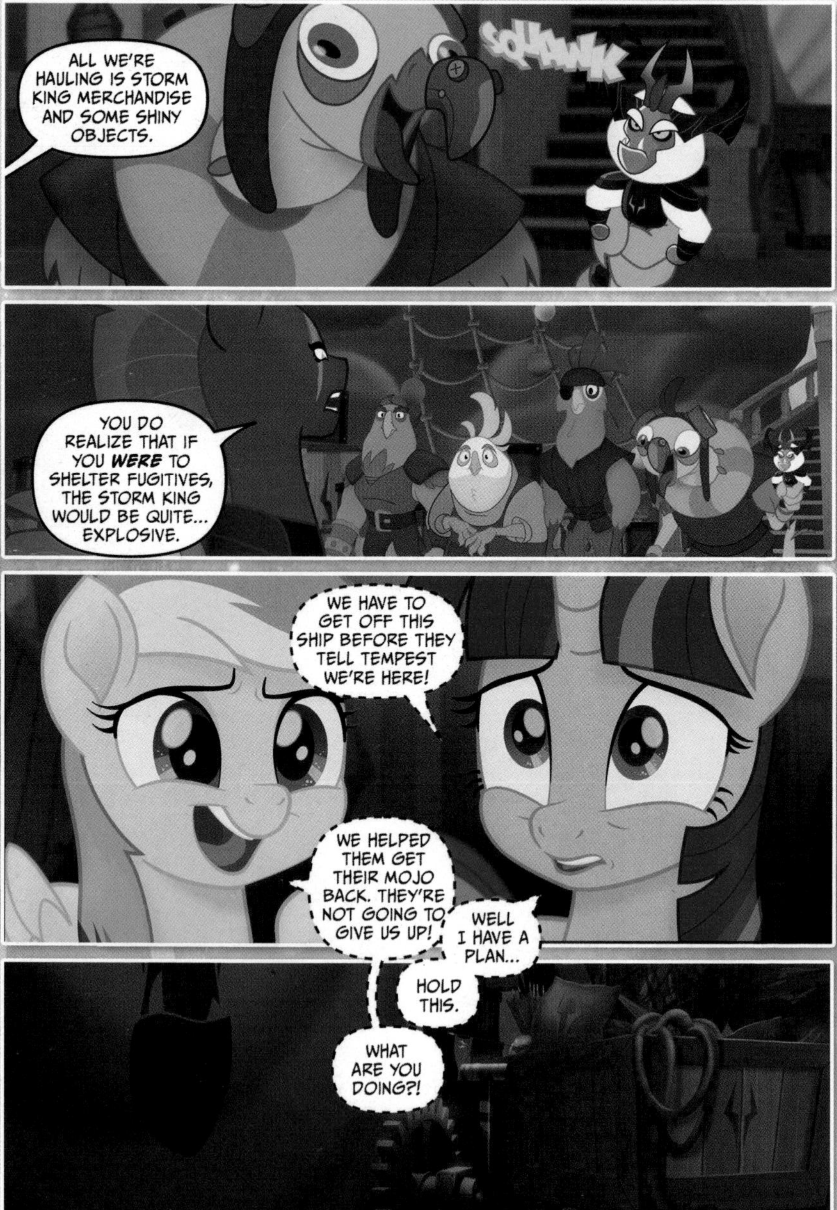
ALL WE'RE HAULING IS STORM KING MERCHANDISE AND SOME SHINY OBJECTS.
SQUAWK
YOU DO REALIZE THAT IF YOU WERE TO SHELTER FUGITIVES, THE STORM KING WOULD BE QUITE... EXPLOSIVE.
WE HAVE TO GET OFF THIS SHIP BEFORE THEY TELL TEMPEST WE'RE HERE!
WE HELPED THEM GET THEIR MOJO BACK. THEY'RE NOT GOING TO GIVE US UP!
WELL I HAVE A PLAN...
HOLD THIS.
WHAT ARE YOU DOING?!

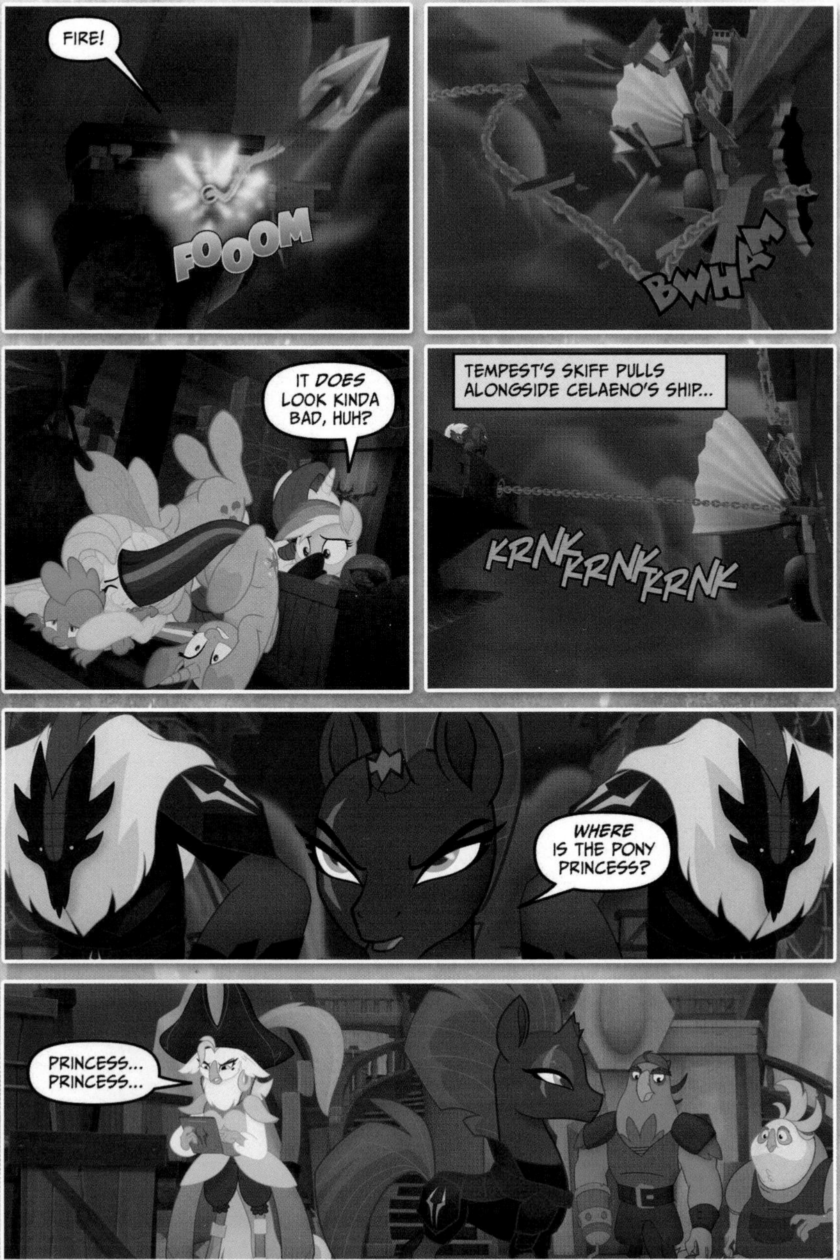
FIRE!
FOOOM
BWHAM
IT DOES LOOK KINDA BAD, HUH?
TEMPEST'S SKIFF PULLS ALONGSIDE CELAENO'S SHIP...
KRNK KRNK KRNK
WHERE IS THE PONY PRINCESS?
PRINCESS... PRINCESS...

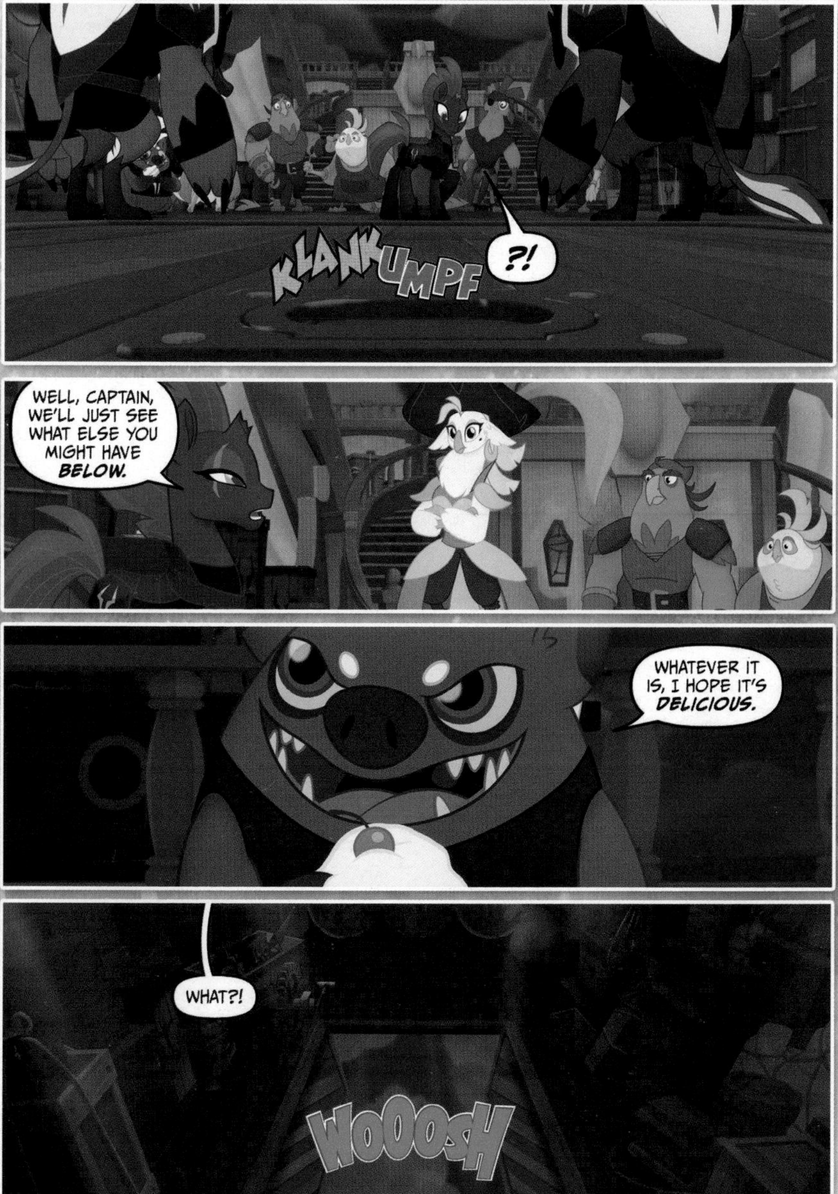
KLANKUMPF
?!
WELL, CAPTAIN, WE'LL JUST SEE WHAT ELSE YOU MIGHT HAVE *BELOW.*
WHATEVER IT IS, I HOPE IT'S *DELICIOUS.*
WHAT?!
WOOOSH

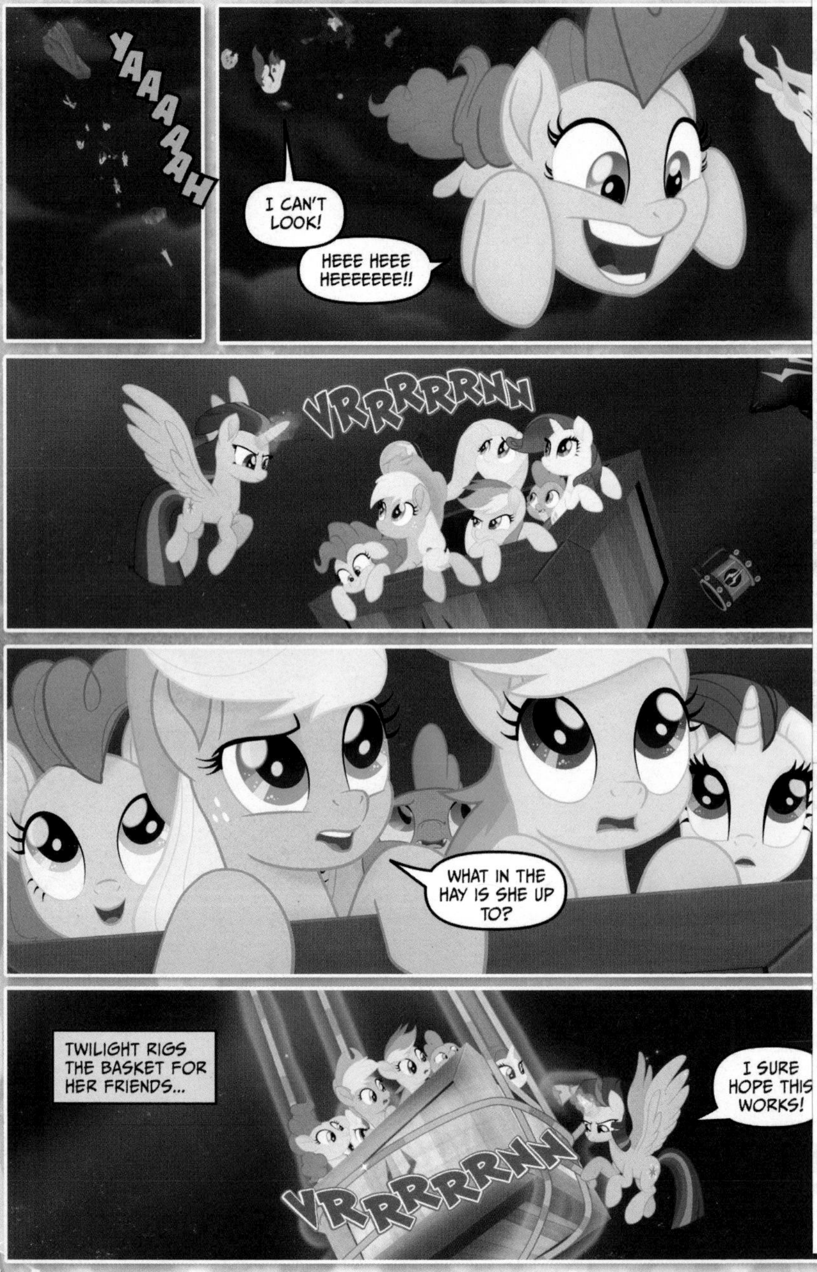
YAAAAAH
I CAN'T LOOK!
HEEE HEEE HEEEEEEE!!
VRRRRRNN
WHAT IN THE HAY IS SHE UP TO?
TWILIGHT RIGS THE BASKET FOR HER FRIENDS...
I SURE HOPE THIS WORKS!
VRRRRRNN

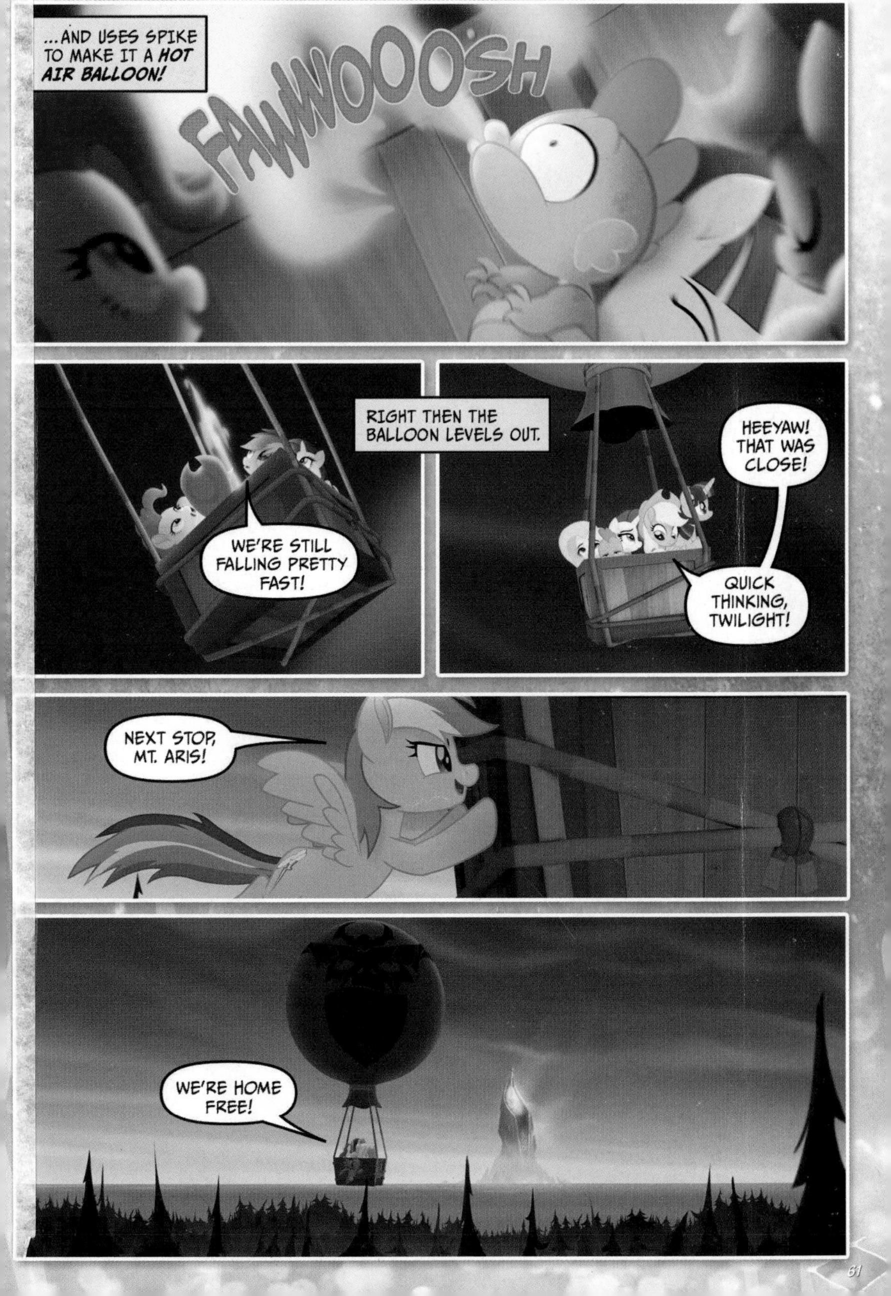
...AND USES SPIKE TO MAKE IT A HOT AIR BALLOON!
FAWWOOOSH
WE'RE STILL FALLING PRETTY FAST!
RIGHT THEN THE BALLOON LEVELS OUT.
HEEYAW! THAT WAS CLOSE!
QUICK THINKING, TWILIGHT!
NEXT STOP, MT. ARIS!
WE'RE HOME FREE!

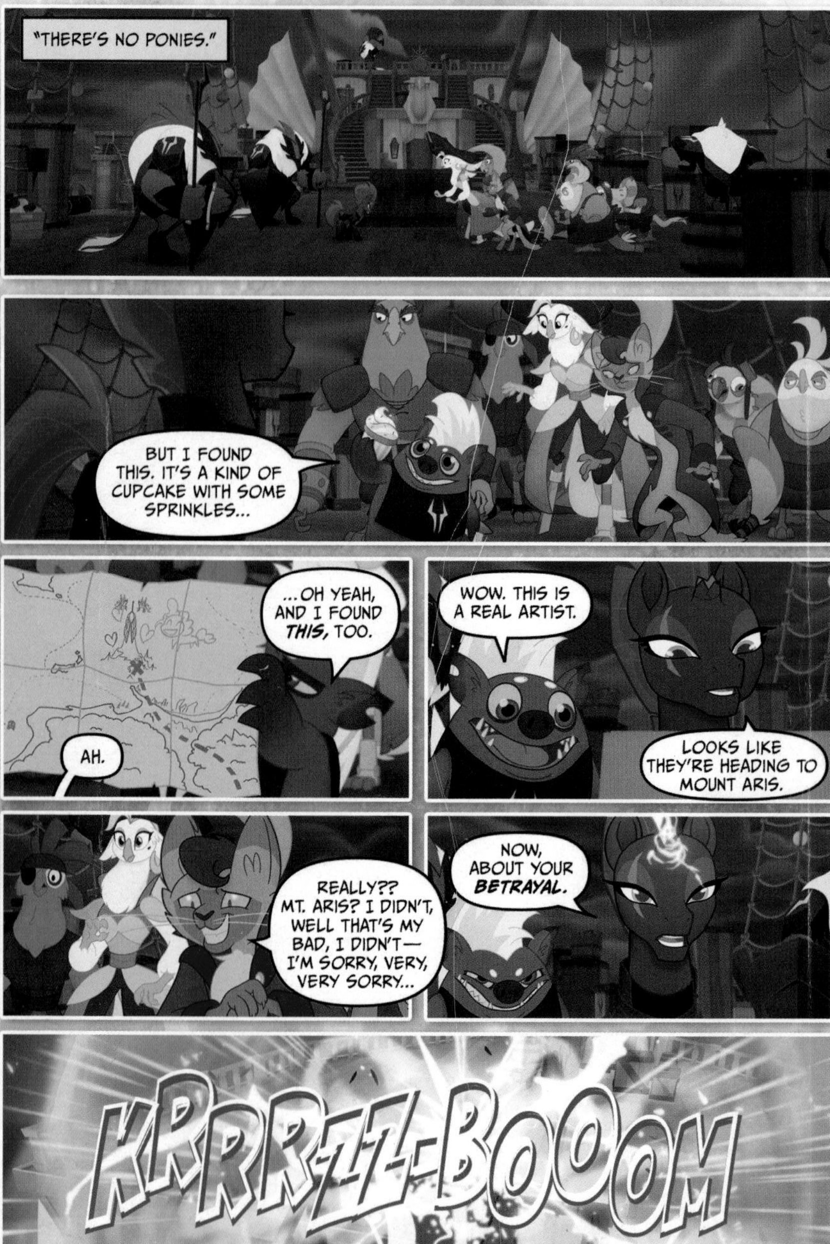
"THERE'S NO PONIES."
BUT I FOUND THIS. IT'S A KIND OF CUPCAKE WITH SOME SPRINKLES...
...OH YEAH, AND I FOUND *THIS,* TOO.
AH.
WOW. THIS IS A REAL ARTIST.
LOOKS LIKE THEY'RE HEADING TO MOUNT ARIS.
REALLY?? MT. ARIS? I DIDN'T, WELL THAT'S MY BAD, I DIDN'T— I'M SORRY, VERY, VERY SORRY...
NOW, ABOUT YOUR ***BETRAYAL.***
KRRRZZ-BOOOOM

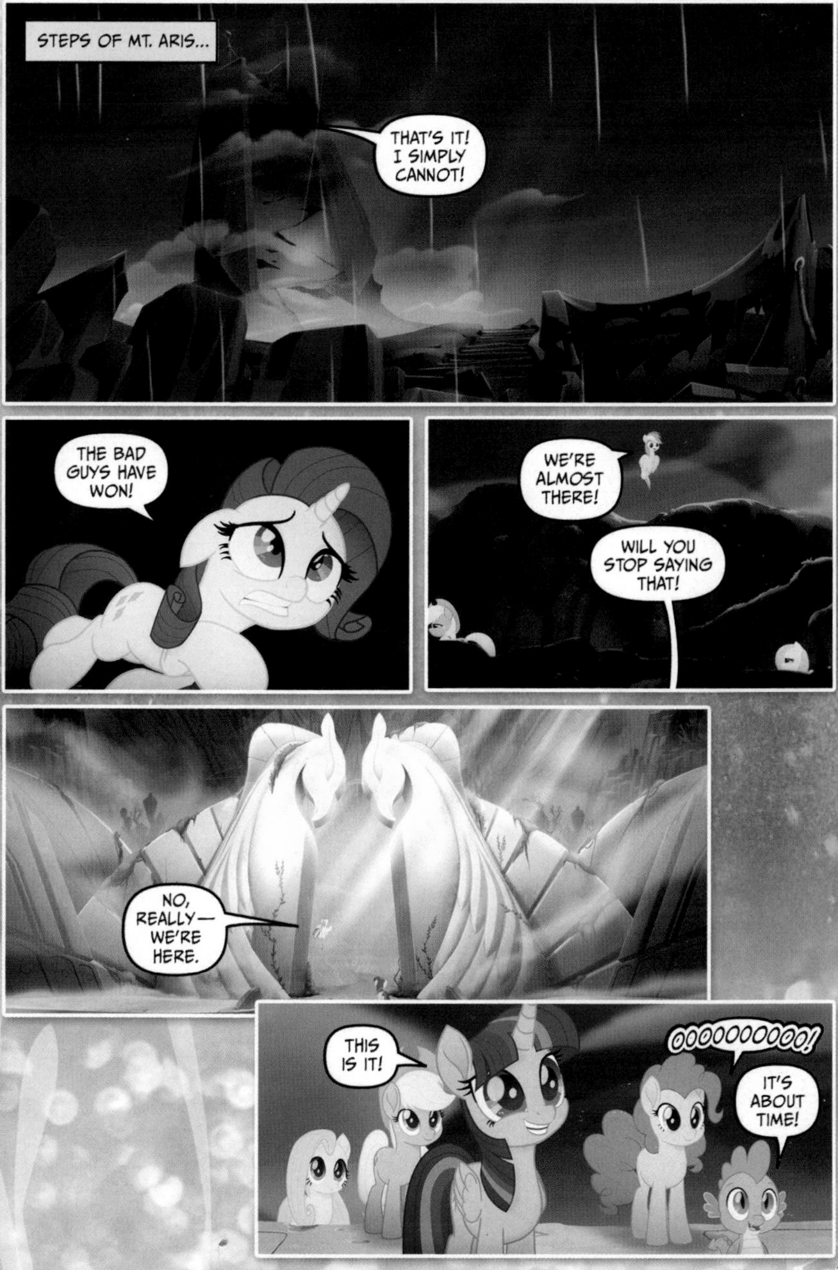
STEPS OF MT. ARIS...
THAT'S IT! I SIMPLY CANNOT!
THE BAD GUYS HAVE WON!
WE'RE ALMOST THERE!
WILL YOU STOP SAYING THAT!
NO, REALLY— WE'RE HERE.
THIS IS IT!
OOOOOOOOOO!
IT'S ABOUT TIME!

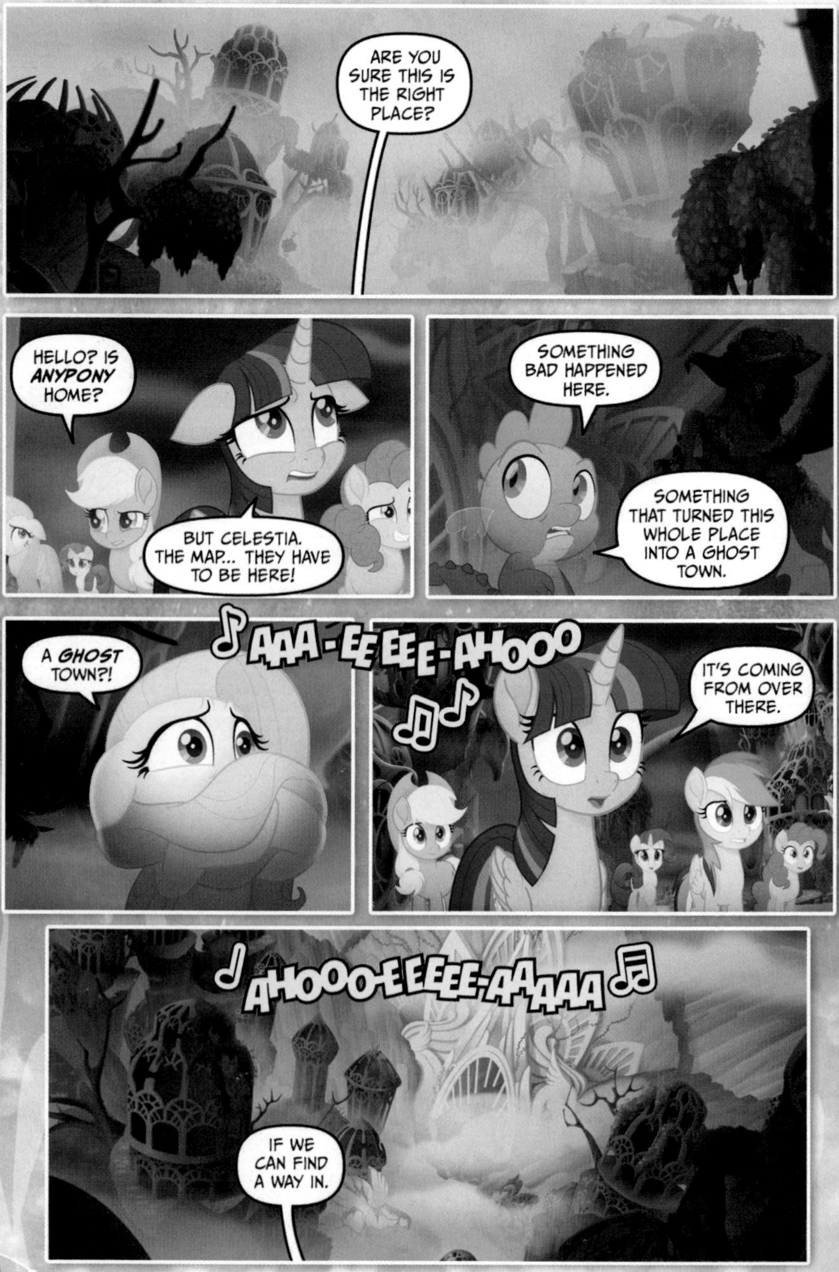

ARE YOU SURE THIS IS THE RIGHT PLACE?
HELLO? IS *ANYPONY* HOME?
BUT CELESTIA. THE MAP... THEY HAVE TO BE HERE!
SOMETHING BAD HAPPENED HERE.
SOMETHING THAT TURNED THIS WHOLE PLACE INTO A GHOST TOWN.
A *GHOST* TOWN?!
AAA-EEEEE-AHOOO
IT'S COMING FROM OVER THERE.
AHOOO-EEEEE-AAAAA
IF WE CAN FIND A WAY IN.

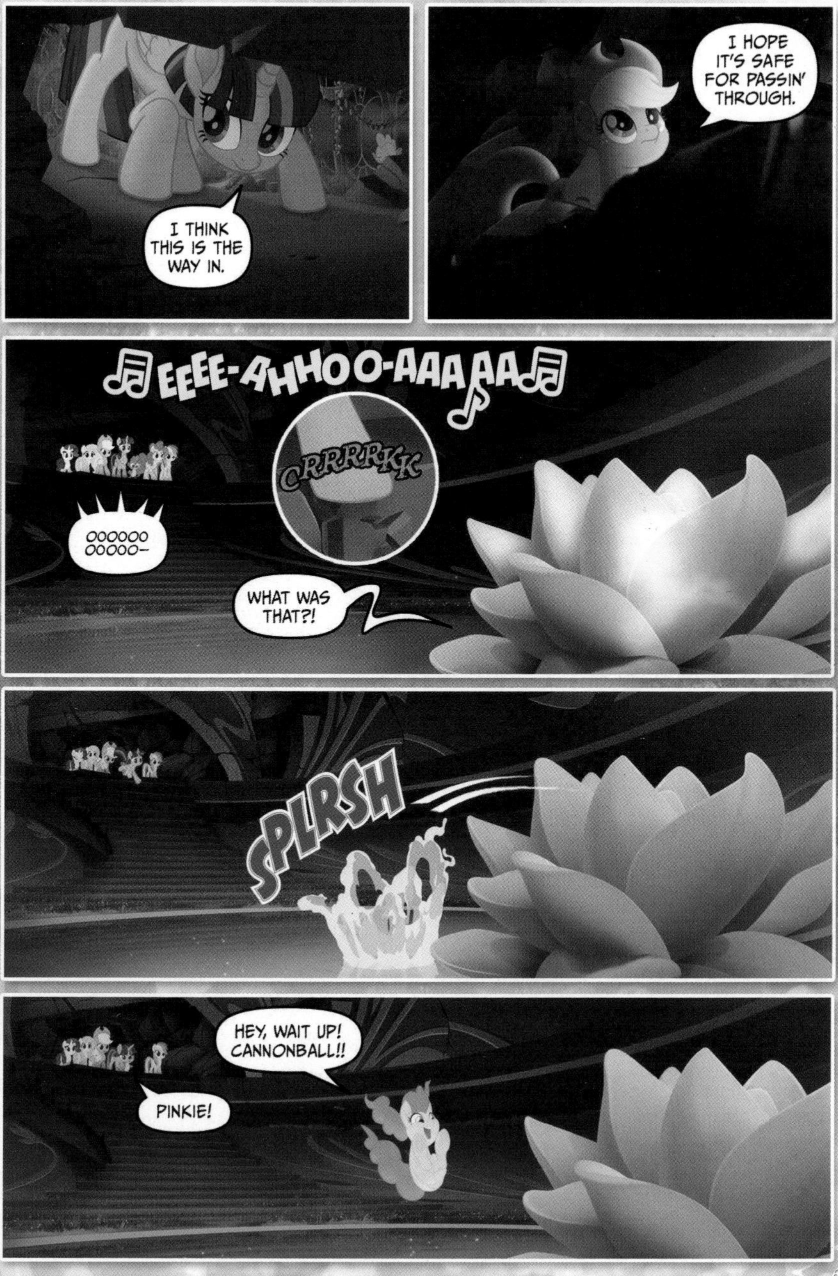
I THINK THIS IS THE WAY IN.
I HOPE IT'S SAFE FOR PASSIN' THROUGH.
EEEE-AHHOO-AAAAAA
CRRRRKK
OOOOOO OOOOO–
WHAT WAS THAT?!
SPLASH
HEY, WAIT UP! CANNONBALL!!
PINKIE!

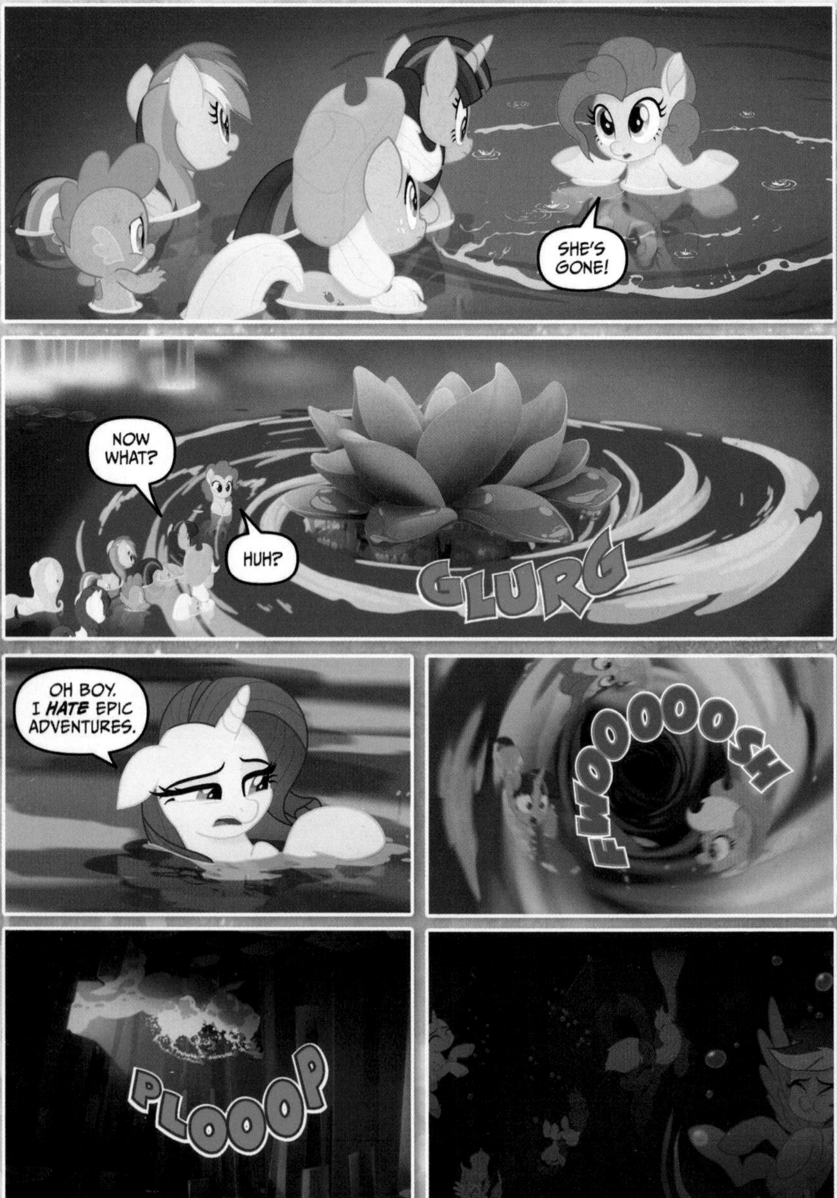
SHE'S GONE!
NOW WHAT?
HUH?
GLURG
OH BOY. I **HATE** EPIC ADVENTURES.
FWOOOOOSH
PLOOOP

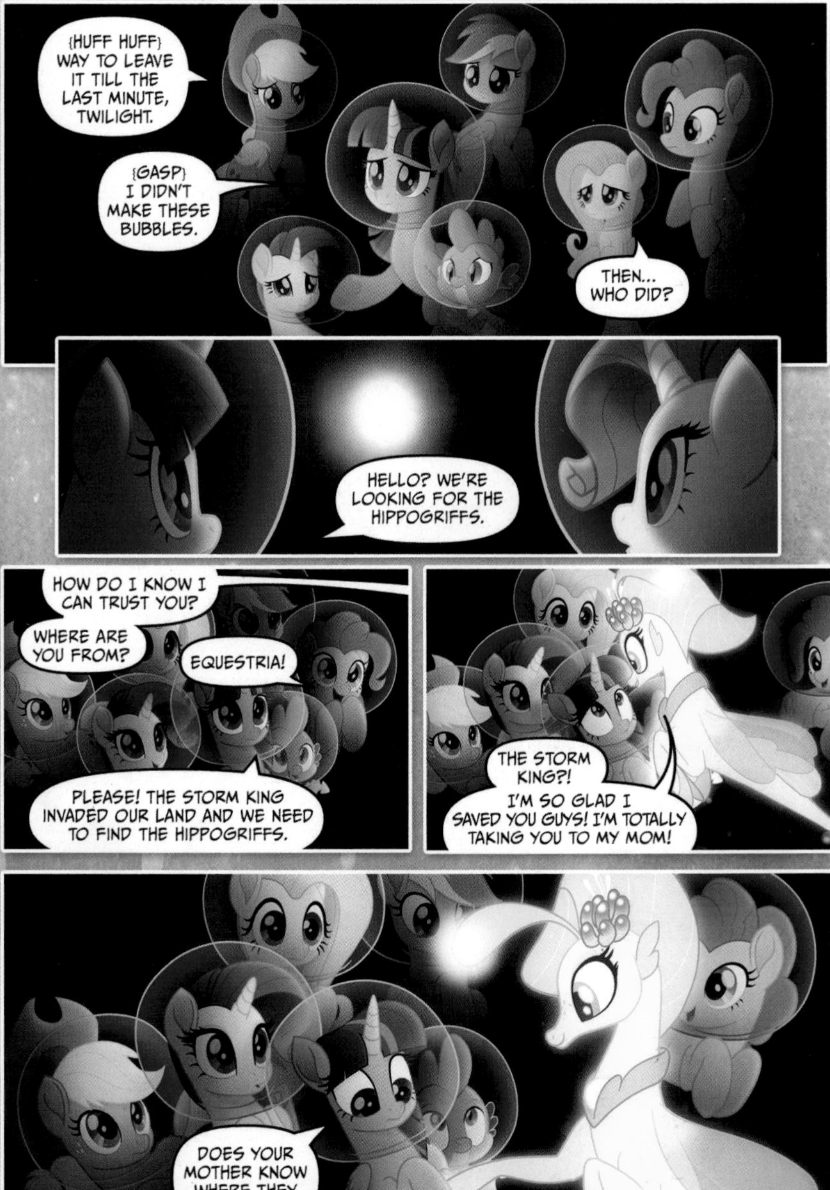
{HUFF HUFF} WAY TO LEAVE IT TILL THE LAST MINUTE, TWILIGHT.
{GASP} I DIDN'T MAKE THESE BUBBLES.
THEN... WHO DID?
HELLO? WE'RE LOOKING FOR THE HIPPOGRIFFS.
HOW DO I KNOW I CAN TRUST YOU?
WHERE ARE YOU FROM?
EQUESTRIA!
PLEASE! THE STORM KING INVADED OUR LAND AND WE NEED TO FIND THE HIPPOGRIFFS.
THE STORM KING?!
I'M SO GLAD I SAVED YOU GUYS! I'M TOTALLY TAKING YOU TO MY MOM!
DOES YOUR MOTHER KNOW WHERE THEY ARE?

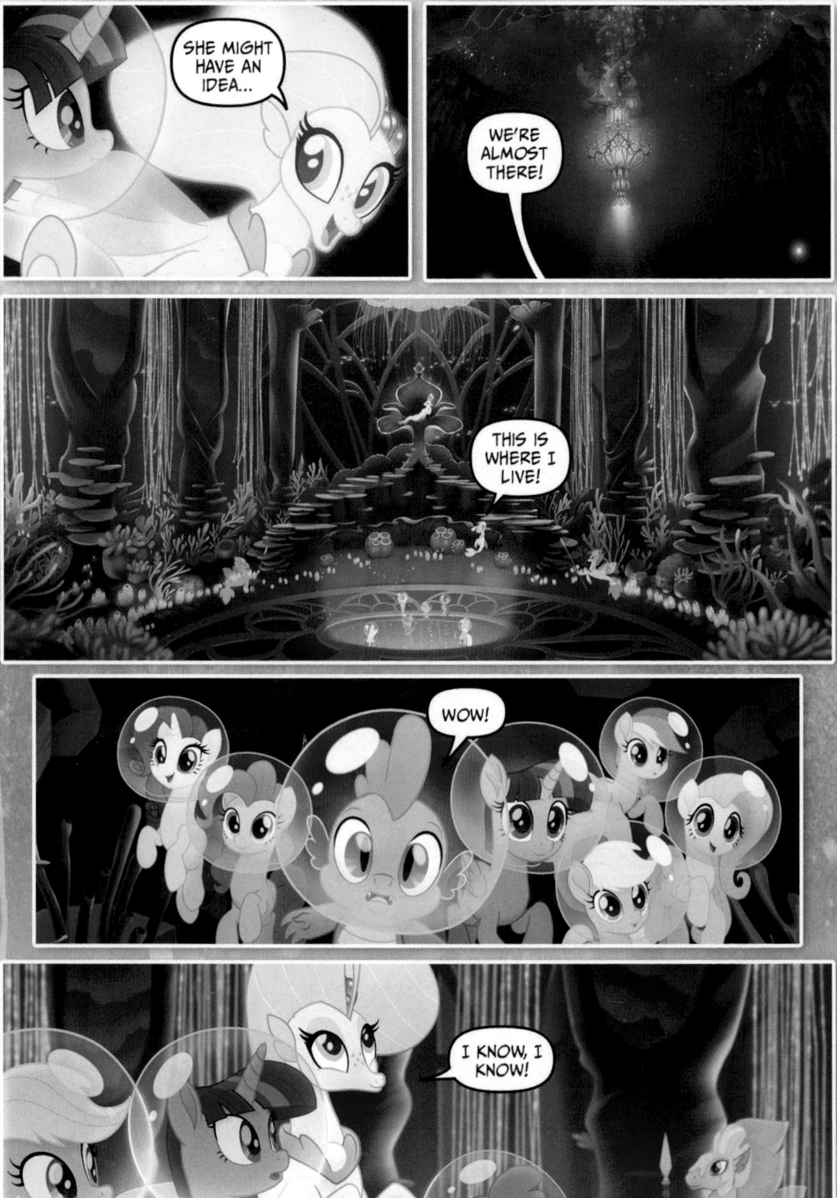
SHE MIGHT HAVE AN IDEA...
WE'RE ALMOST THERE!
THIS IS WHERE I LIVE!
WOW!
I KNOW, I KNOW!

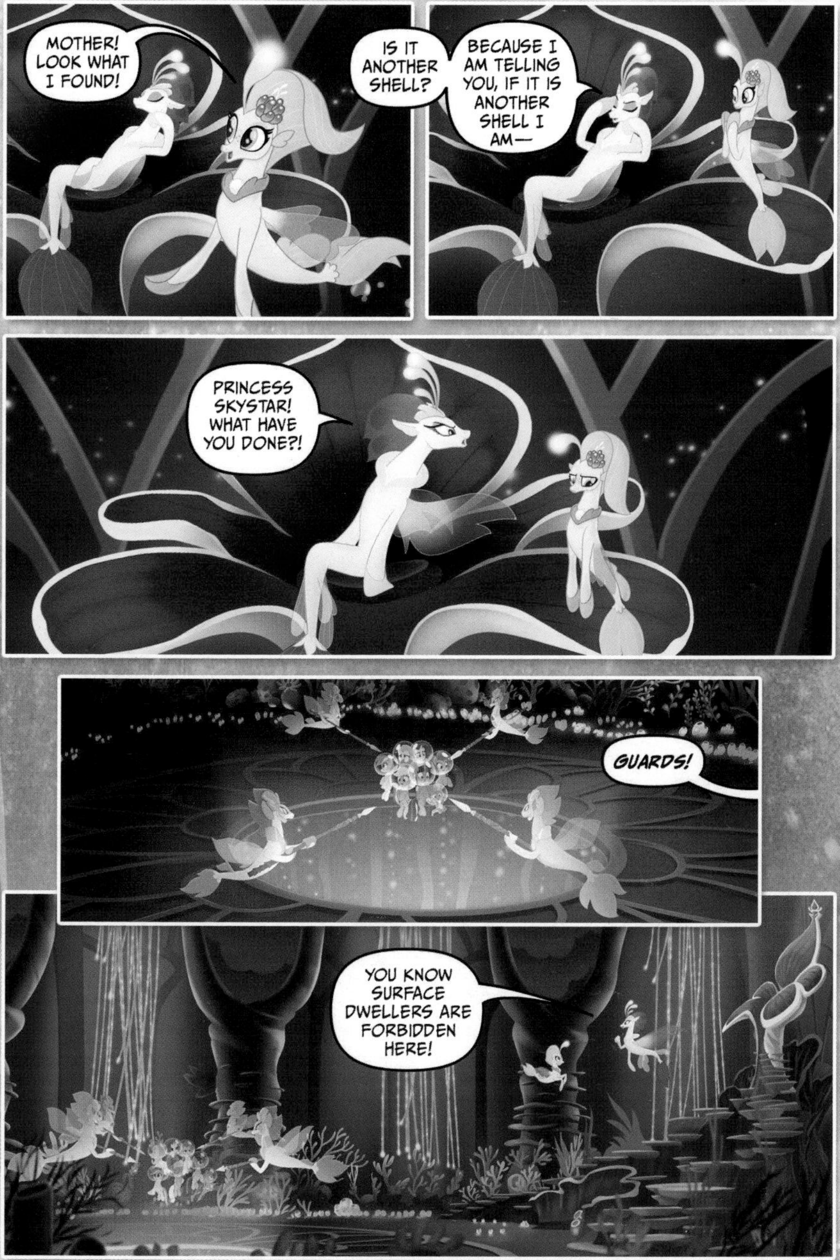
MOTHER! LOOK WHAT I FOUND!
IS IT ANOTHER SHELL?
BECAUSE I AM TELLING YOU, IF IT IS ANOTHER SHELL I AM—
PRINCESS SKYSTAR! WHAT HAVE YOU DONE?!
GUARDS!
YOU KNOW SURFACE DWELLERS ARE FORBIDDEN HERE!

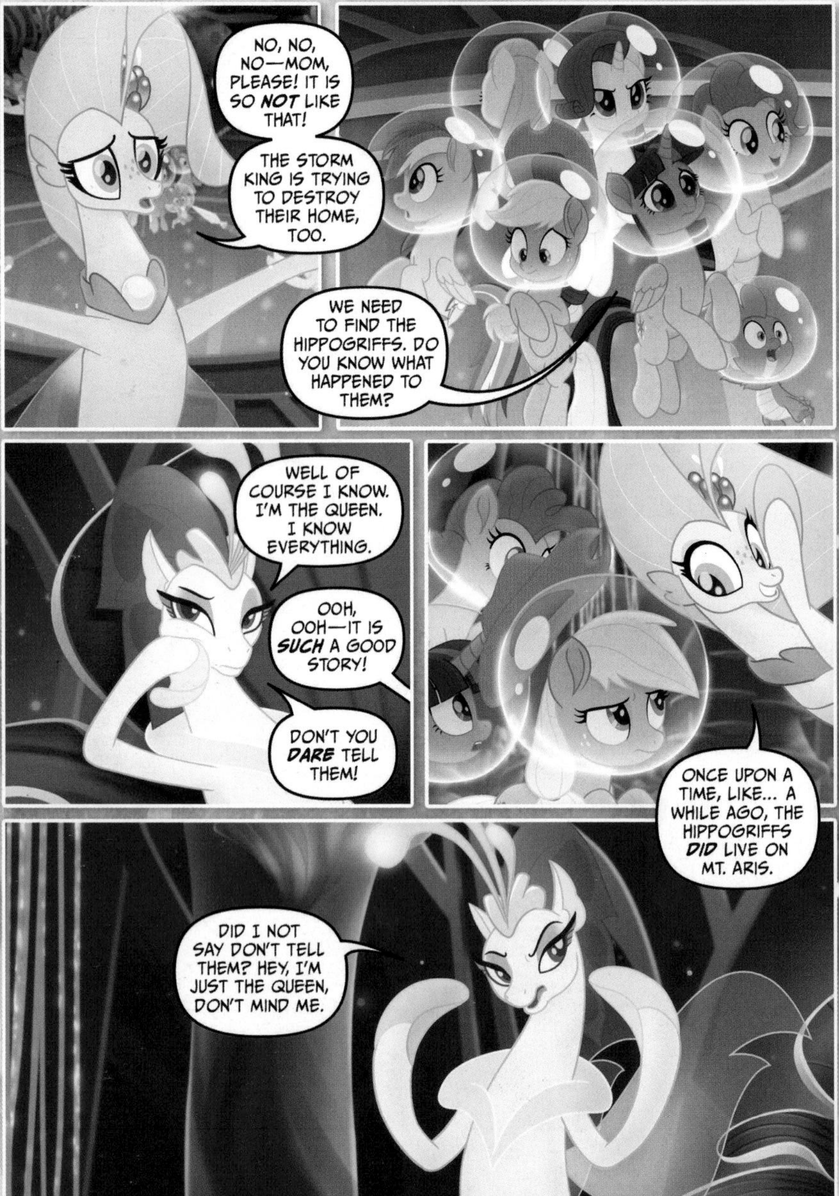
NO, NO, NO—MOM, PLEASE! IT IS SO NOT LIKE THAT!
THE STORM KING IS TRYING TO DESTROY THEIR HOME, TOO.
WE NEED TO FIND THE HIPPOGRIFFS. DO YOU KNOW WHAT HAPPENED TO THEM?
WELL OF COURSE I KNOW. I'M THE QUEEN. I KNOW EVERYTHING.
OOH, OOH—IT IS SUCH A GOOD STORY!
DON'T YOU DARE TELL THEM!
ONCE UPON A TIME, LIKE... A WHILE AGO, THE HIPPOGRIFFS DID LIVE ON MT. ARIS.
DID I NOT SAY DON'T TELL THEM? HEY, I'M JUST THE QUEEN, DON'T MIND ME.

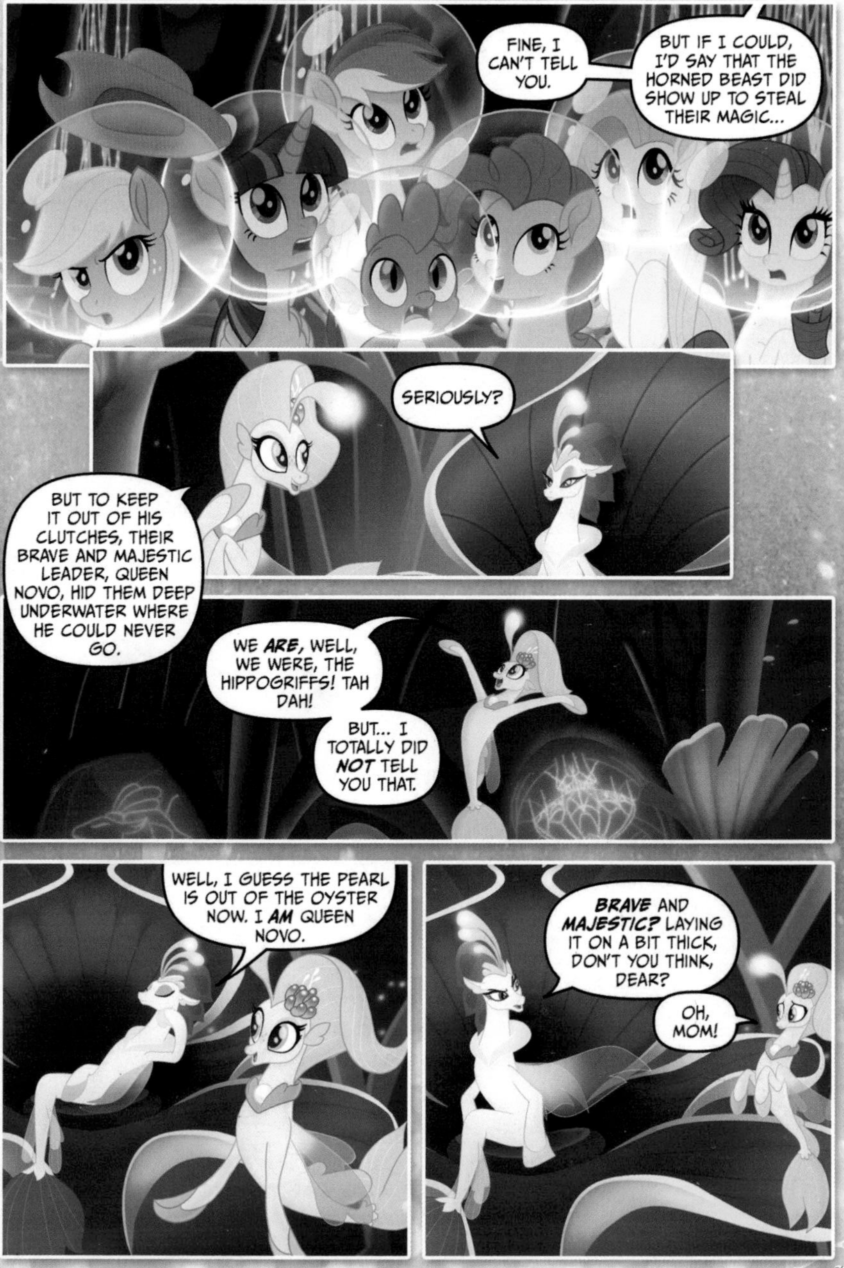

FINE, I CAN'T TELL YOU.
BUT IF I COULD, I'D SAY THAT THE HORNED BEAST DID SHOW UP TO STEAL THEIR MAGIC...
SERIOUSLY?
BUT TO KEEP IT OUT OF HIS CLUTCHES, THEIR BRAVE AND MAJESTIC LEADER, QUEEN NOVO, HID THEM DEEP UNDERWATER WHERE HE COULD NEVER GO.
WE **ARE**, WELL, WE WERE, THE HIPPOGRIFFS! TAH DAH!
BUT... I TOTALLY DID **NOT** TELL YOU THAT.
WELL, I GUESS THE PEARL IS OUT OF THE OYSTER NOW. I **AM** QUEEN NOVO.
BRAVE AND **MAJESTIC?** LAYING IT ON A BIT THICK, DON'T YOU THINK, DEAR?
OH, MOM!

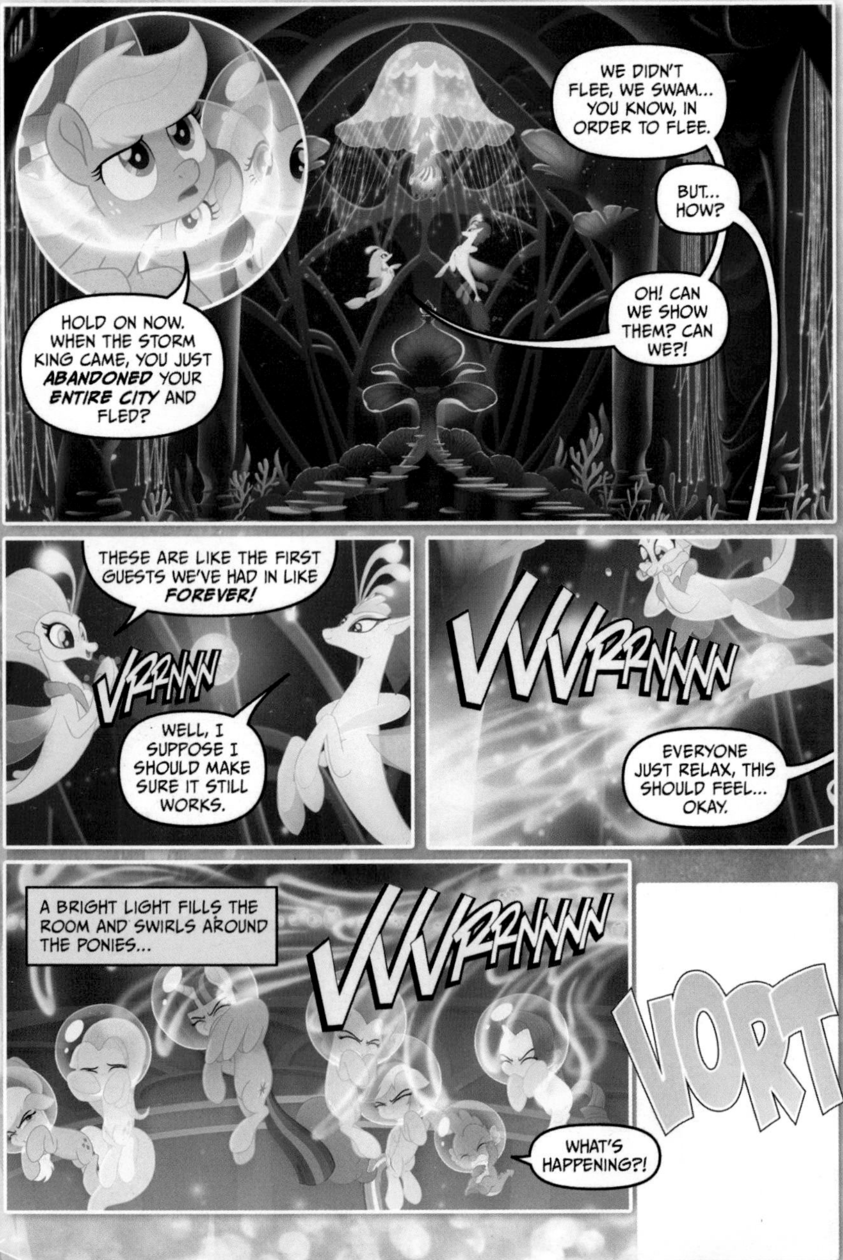
HOLD ON NOW. WHEN THE STORM KING CAME, YOU JUST ABANDONED YOUR ENTIRE CITY AND FLED?
WE DIDN'T FLEE, WE SWAM... YOU KNOW, IN ORDER TO FLEE.
BUT... HOW?
OH! CAN WE SHOW THEM? CAN WE?!
THESE ARE LIKE THE FIRST GUESTS WE'VE HAD IN LIKE FOREVER!
VRRNNN
WELL, I SUPPOSE I SHOULD MAKE SURE IT STILL WORKS.
VVVRRNNNN
EVERYONE JUST RELAX, THIS SHOULD FEEL... OKAY.
A BRIGHT LIGHT FILLS THE ROOM AND SWIRLS AROUND THE PONIES...
VVVRRNNNN
VORT
WHAT'S HAPPENING?!

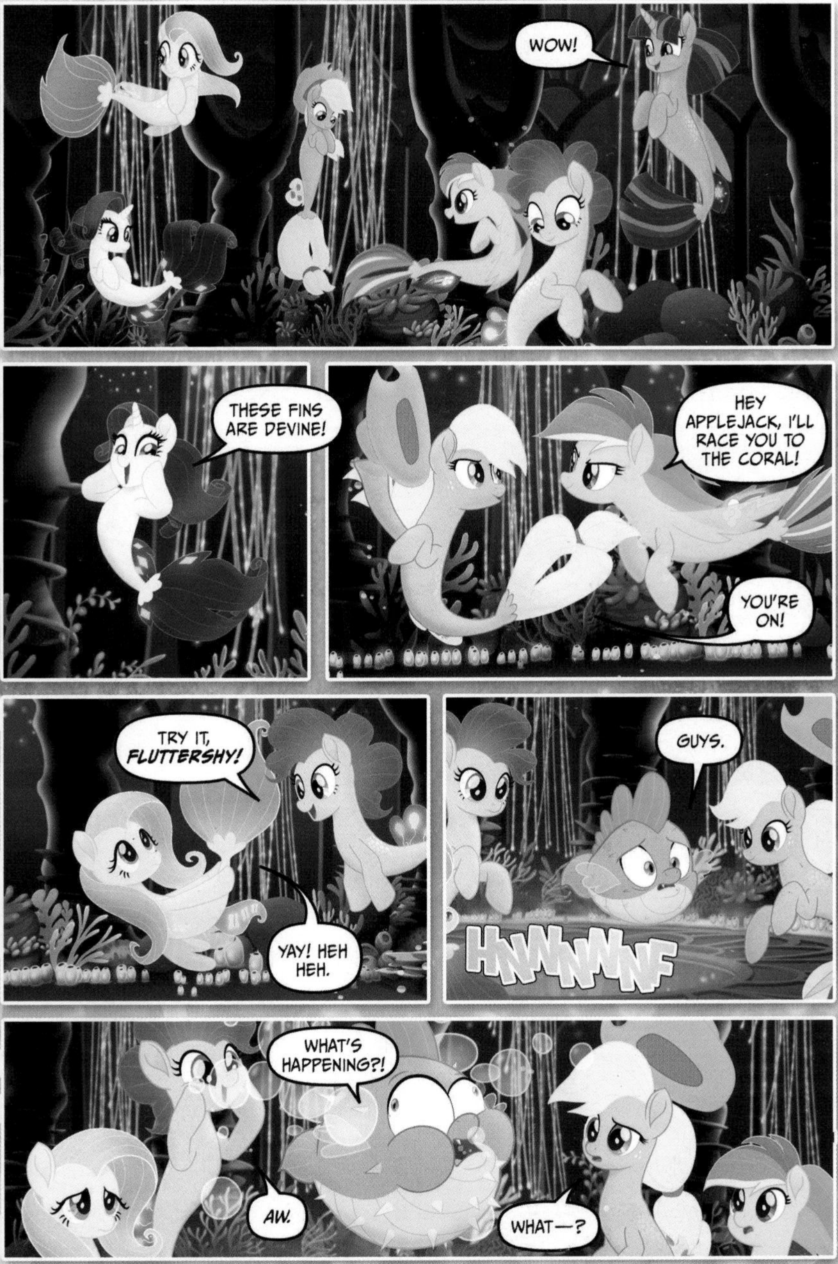
WOW!
THESE FINS ARE DEVINE!
HEY APPLEJACK, I'LL RACE YOU TO THE CORAL!
YOU'RE ON!
TRY IT, *FLUTTERSHY!*
YAY! HEH HEH.
GUYS.
HNNNNNNF
WHAT'S HAPPENING?!
AW.
WHAT—?

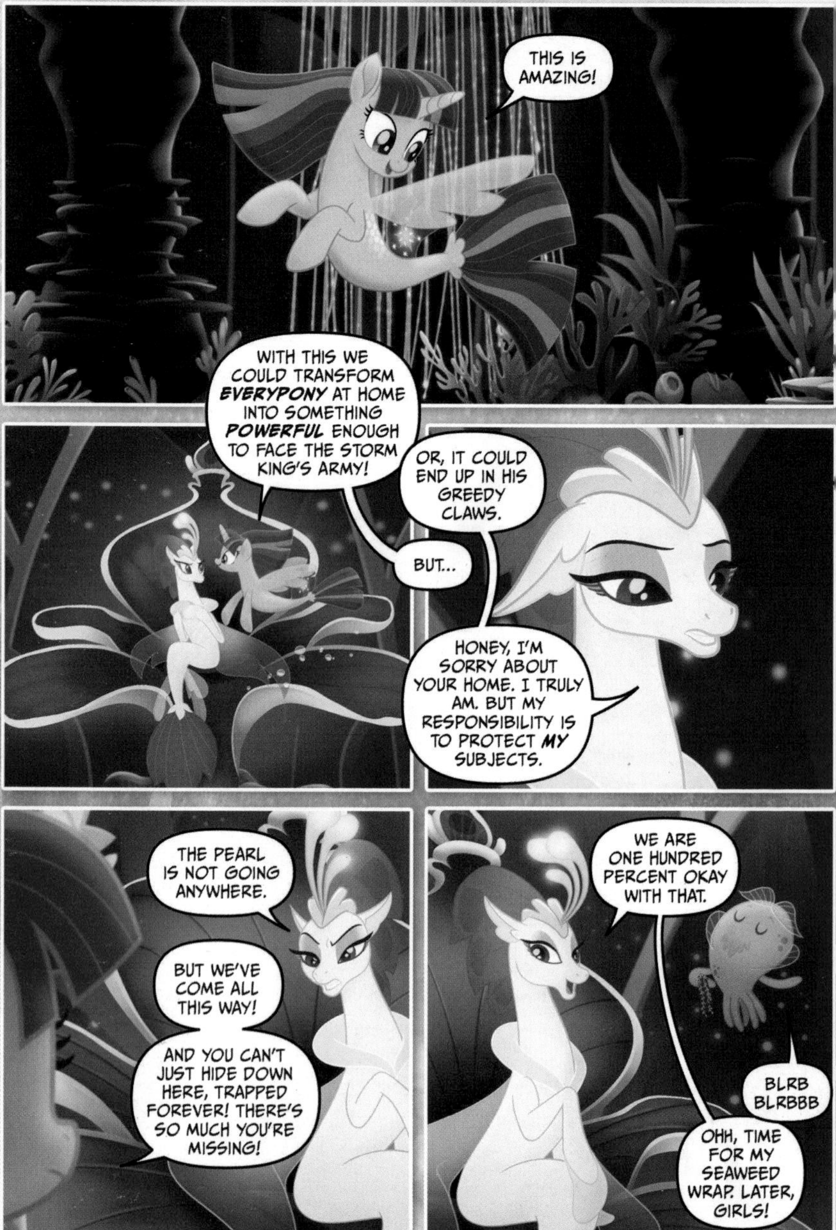
THIS IS AMAZING!
WITH THIS WE COULD TRANSFORM EVERYPONY AT HOME INTO SOMETHING POWERFUL ENOUGH TO FACE THE STORM KING'S ARMY!
OR, IT COULD END UP IN HIS GREEDY CLAWS.
BUT...
HONEY, I'M SORRY ABOUT YOUR HOME. I TRULY AM. BUT MY RESPONSIBILITY IS TO PROTECT MY SUBJECTS.
THE PEARL IS NOT GOING ANYWHERE.
BUT WE'VE COME ALL THIS WAY!
AND YOU CAN'T JUST HIDE DOWN HERE, TRAPPED FOREVER! THERE'S SO MUCH YOU'RE MISSING!
WE ARE ONE HUNDRED PERCENT OKAY WITH THAT.
BLRB BLRBBB
OHH, TIME FOR MY SEAWEED WRAP. LATER, GIRLS!

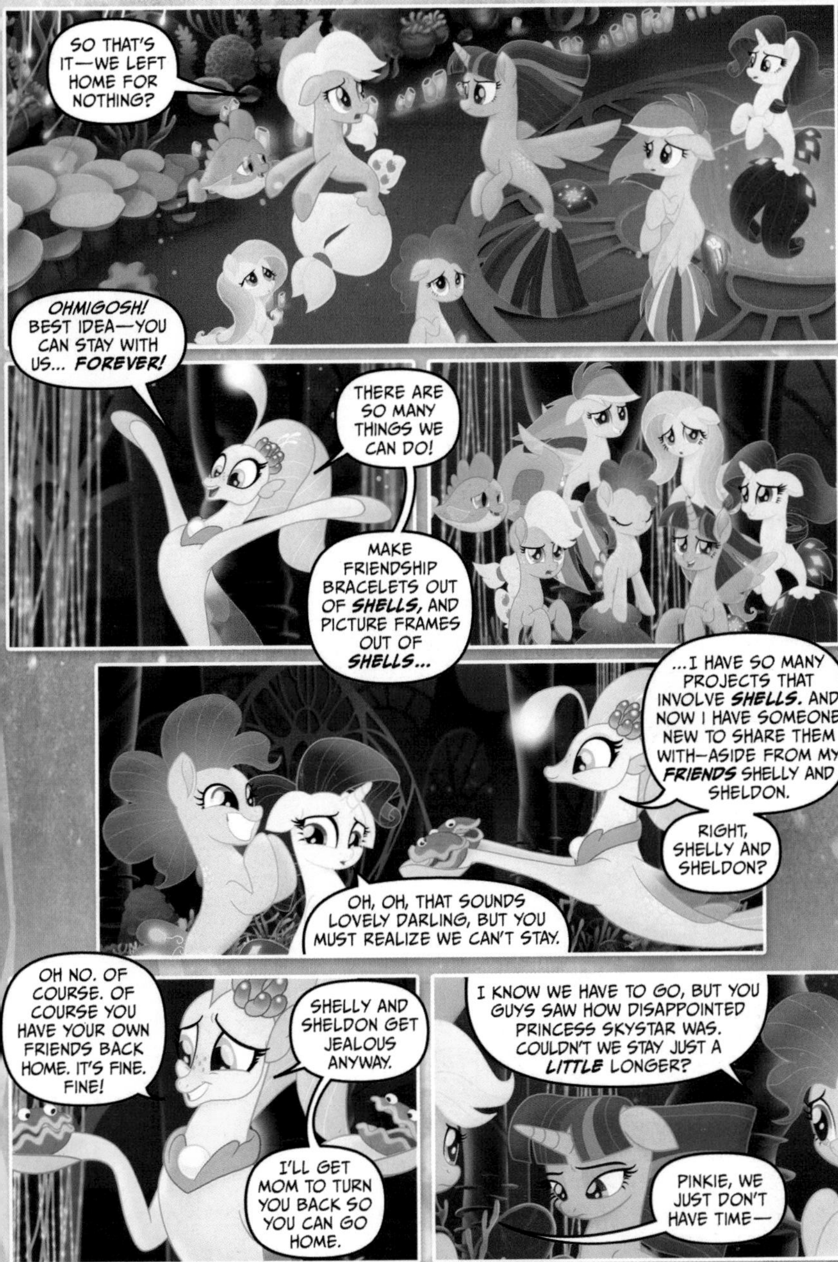
SO THAT'S IT—WE LEFT HOME FOR NOTHING?
OHMIGOSH! BEST IDEA—YOU CAN STAY WITH US... FOREVER!
THERE ARE SO MANY THINGS WE CAN DO!
MAKE FRIENDSHIP BRACELETS OUT OF SHELLS, AND PICTURE FRAMES OUT OF SHELLS...
...I HAVE SO MANY PROJECTS THAT INVOLVE SHELLS. AND NOW I HAVE SOMEONE NEW TO SHARE THEM WITH—ASIDE FROM MY FRIENDS SHELLY AND SHELDON.
RIGHT, SHELLY AND SHELDON?
OH, OH, THAT SOUNDS LOVELY DARLING, BUT YOU MUST REALIZE WE CAN'T STAY.
OH NO. OF COURSE. OF COURSE YOU HAVE YOUR OWN FRIENDS BACK HOME. IT'S FINE. FINE!
SHELLY AND SHELDON GET JEALOUS ANYWAY.
I'LL GET MOM TO TURN YOU BACK SO YOU CAN GO HOME.
I KNOW WE HAVE TO GO, BUT YOU GUYS SAW HOW DISAPPOINTED PRINCESS SKYSTAR WAS. COULDN'T WE STAY JUST A LITTLE LONGER?
PINKIE, WE JUST DON'T HAVE TIME—

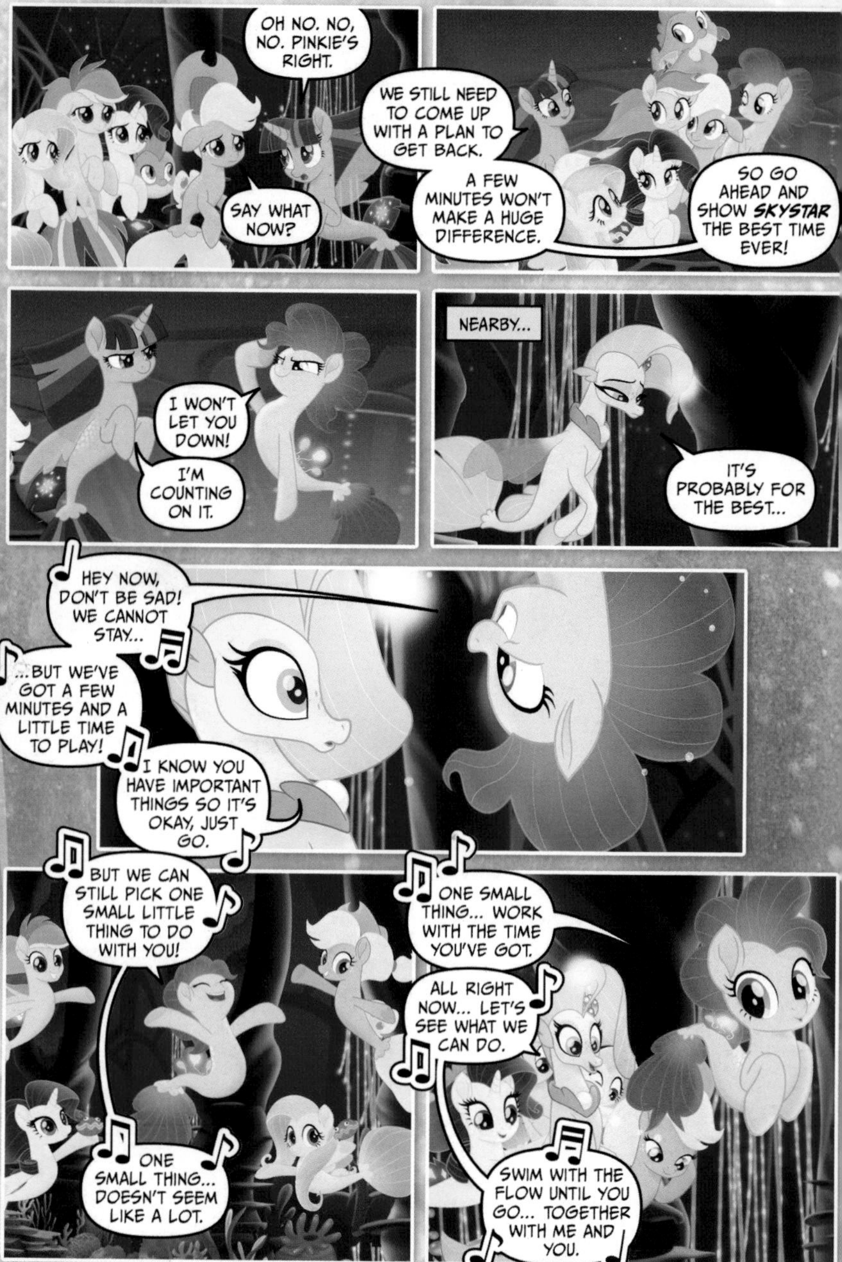
OH NO. NO, NO. PINKIE'S RIGHT.
SAY WHAT NOW?
WE STILL NEED TO COME UP WITH A PLAN TO GET BACK.
A FEW MINUTES WON'T MAKE A HUGE DIFFERENCE.
SO GO AHEAD AND SHOW SKYSTAR THE BEST TIME EVER!
I WON'T LET YOU DOWN!
I'M COUNTING ON IT.
NEARBY...
IT'S PROBABLY FOR THE BEST...
HEY NOW, DON'T BE SAD! WE CANNOT STAY...
...BUT WE'VE GOT A FEW MINUTES AND A LITTLE TIME TO PLAY!
I KNOW YOU HAVE IMPORTANT THINGS SO IT'S OKAY, JUST GO.
BUT WE CAN STILL PICK ONE SMALL LITTLE THING TO DO WITH YOU!
ONE SMALL THING... DOESN'T SEEM LIKE A LOT.
ONE SMALL THING... WORK WITH THE TIME YOU'VE GOT.
ALL RIGHT NOW... LET'S SEE WHAT WE CAN DO.
SWIM WITH THE FLOW UNTIL YOU GO... TOGETHER WITH ME AND YOU.

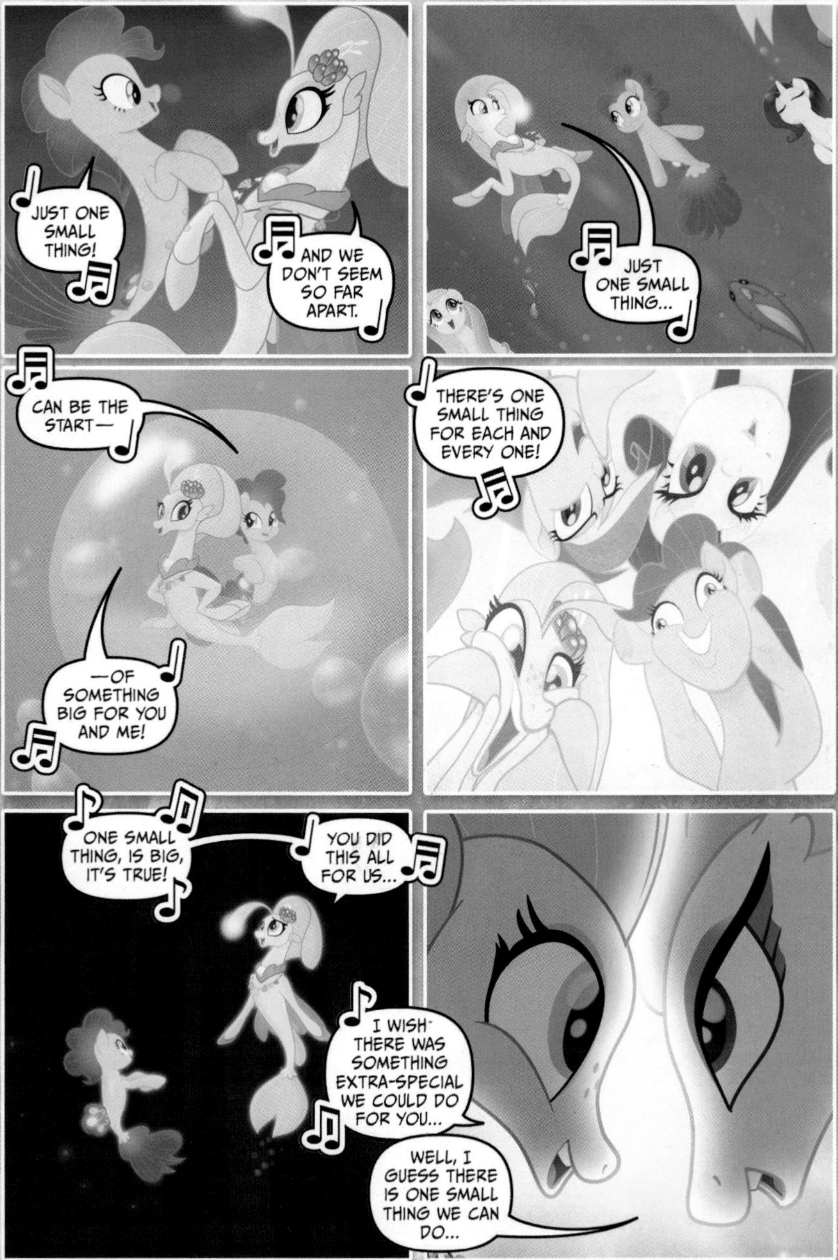
JUST ONE SMALL THING!
AND WE DON'T SEEM SO FAR APART.
JUST ONE SMALL THING...
CAN BE THE START—
—OF SOMETHING BIG FOR YOU AND ME!
THERE'S ONE SMALL THING FOR EACH AND EVERY ONE!
ONE SMALL THING, IS BIG, IT'S TRUE!
YOU DID THIS ALL FOR US...
I WISH THERE WAS SOMETHING EXTRA-SPECIAL WE COULD DO FOR YOU...
WELL, I GUESS THERE IS ONE SMALL THING WE CAN DO...

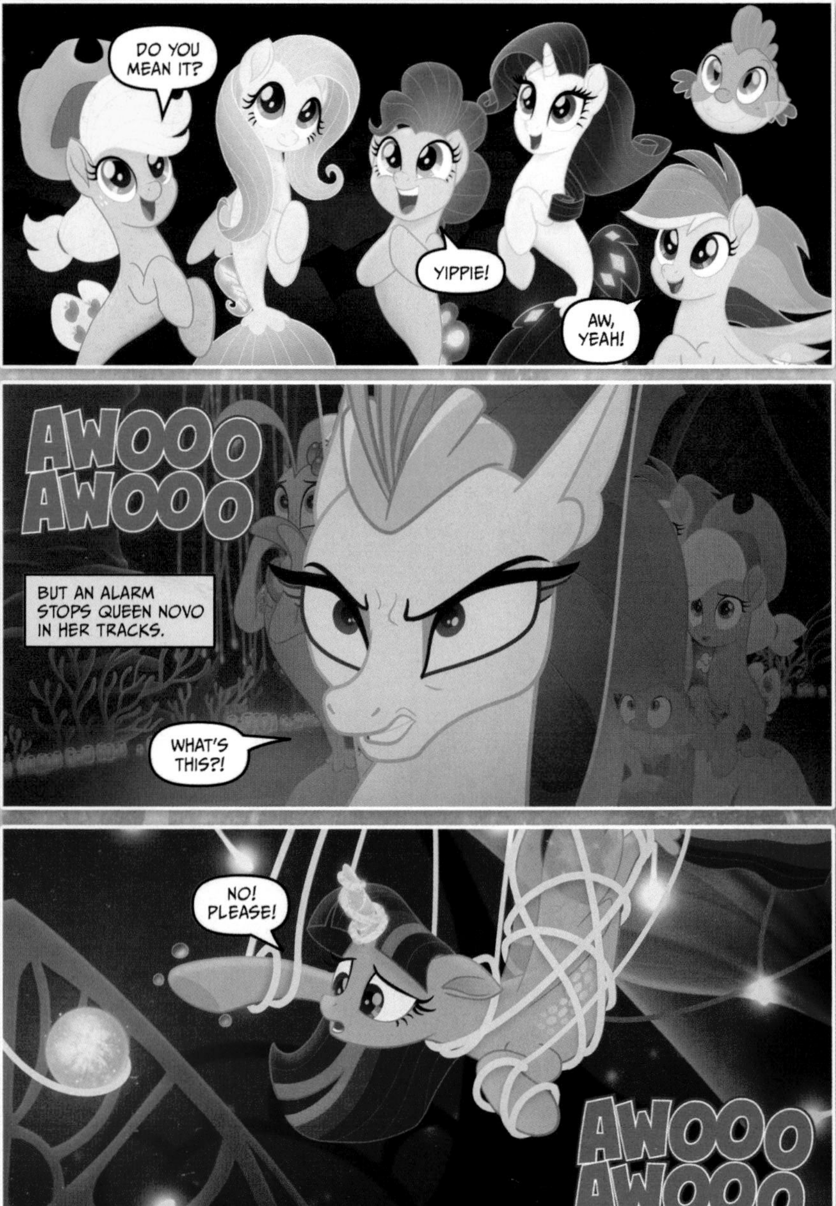
DO YOU MEAN IT?
YIPPIE!
AW, YEAH!
AWOOO AWOOO
BUT AN ALARM STOPS QUEEN NOVO IN HER TRACKS.
WHAT'S THIS?!
NO! PLEASE!
AWOOO AWOOO

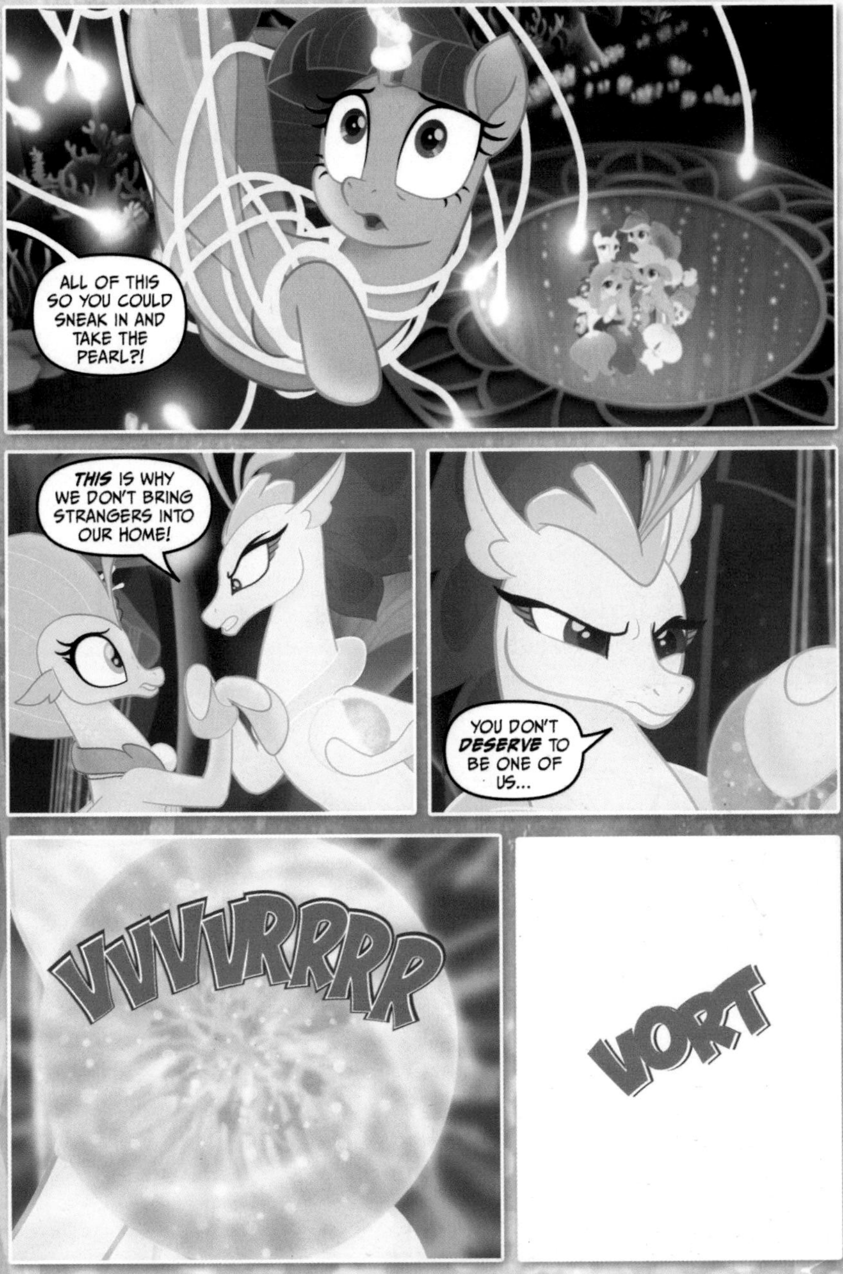

ALL OF THIS SO YOU COULD SNEAK IN AND TAKE THE PEARL?!
THIS IS WHY WE DON'T BRING STRANGERS INTO OUR HOME!
YOU DON'T DESERVE TO BE ONE OF US...
VVVVRRRR
VORT

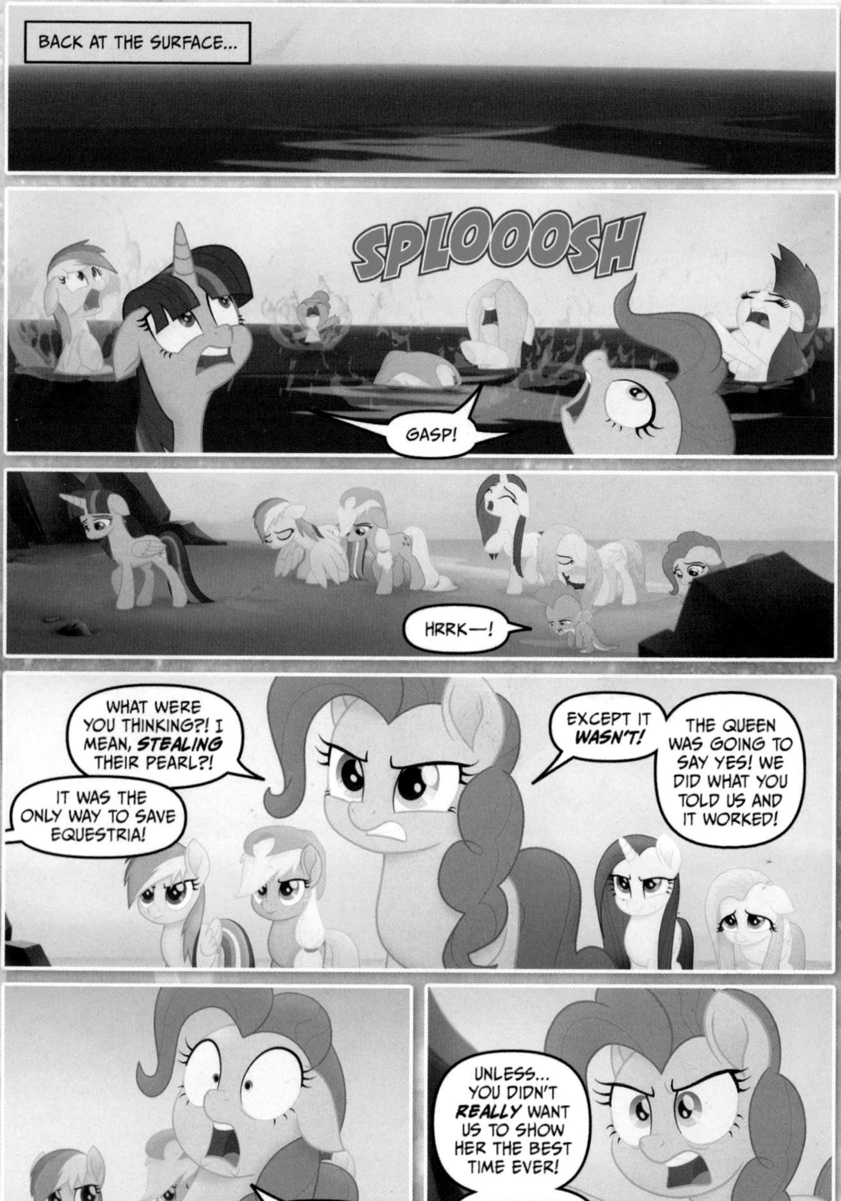
BACK AT THE SURFACE...
SPLOOOSH
GASP!
HRRK—!
WHAT WERE YOU THINKING?! I MEAN, STEALING THEIR PEARL?!
IT WAS THE ONLY WAY TO SAVE EQUESTRIA!
EXCEPT IT WASN'T!
THE QUEEN WAS GOING TO SAY YES! WE DID WHAT YOU TOLD US AND IT WORKED!
GUUUUURP!
UNLESS... YOU DIDN'T REALLY WANT US TO SHOW HER THE BEST TIME EVER!
YOU JUST WANTED US TO DISTRACT HER!

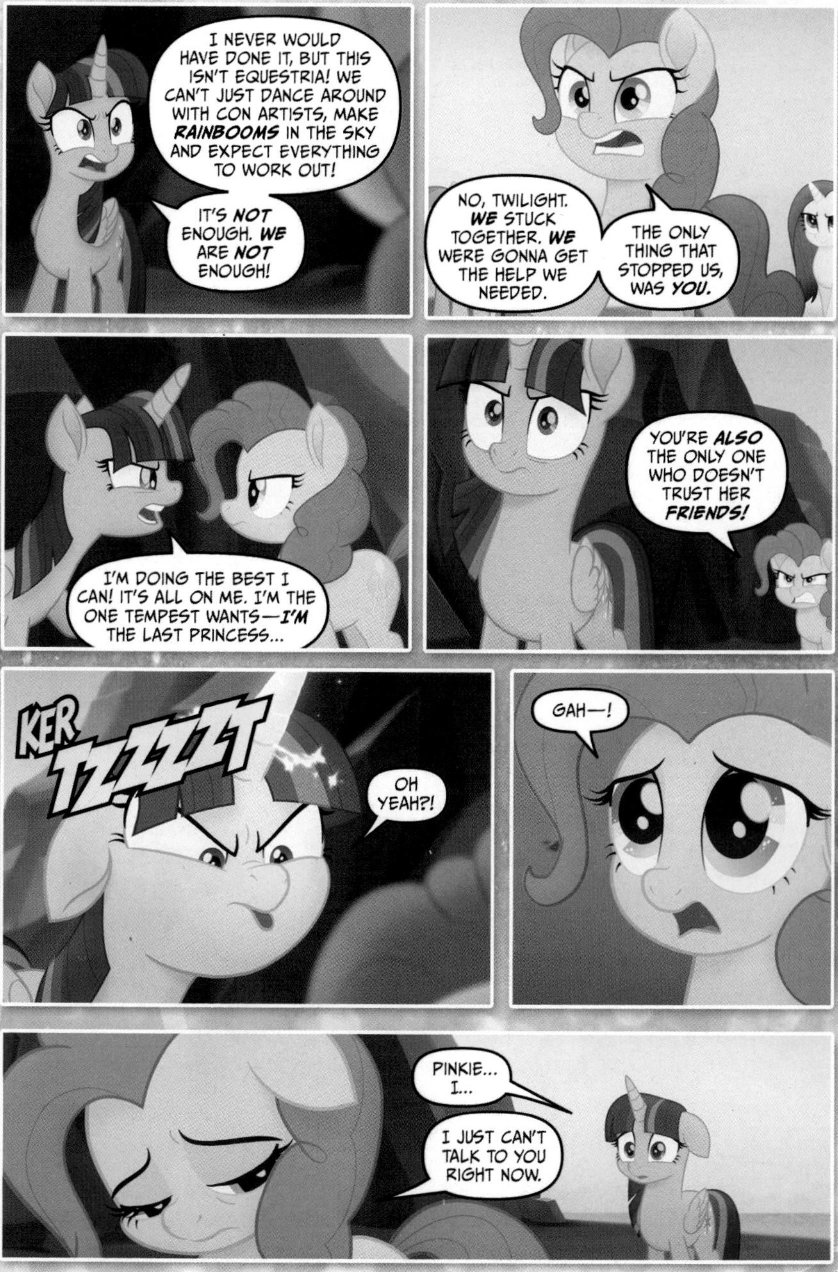
I NEVER WOULD HAVE DONE IT, BUT THIS ISN'T EQUESTRIA! WE CAN'T JUST DANCE AROUND WITH CON ARTISTS, MAKE RAINBOOMS IN THE SKY AND EXPECT EVERYTHING TO WORK OUT!
IT'S NOT ENOUGH. WE ARE NOT ENOUGH!
NO, TWILIGHT. WE STUCK TOGETHER. WE WERE GONNA GET THE HELP WE NEEDED.
THE ONLY THING THAT STOPPED US, WAS YOU.
I'M DOING THE BEST I CAN! IT'S ALL ON ME. I'M THE ONE TEMPEST WANTS—I'M THE LAST PRINCESS...
YOU'RE ALSO THE ONLY ONE WHO DOESN'T TRUST HER FRIENDS!
KER TZZZZT
OH YEAH?!
GAH—!
PINKIE... I...
I JUST CAN'T TALK TO YOU RIGHT NOW.

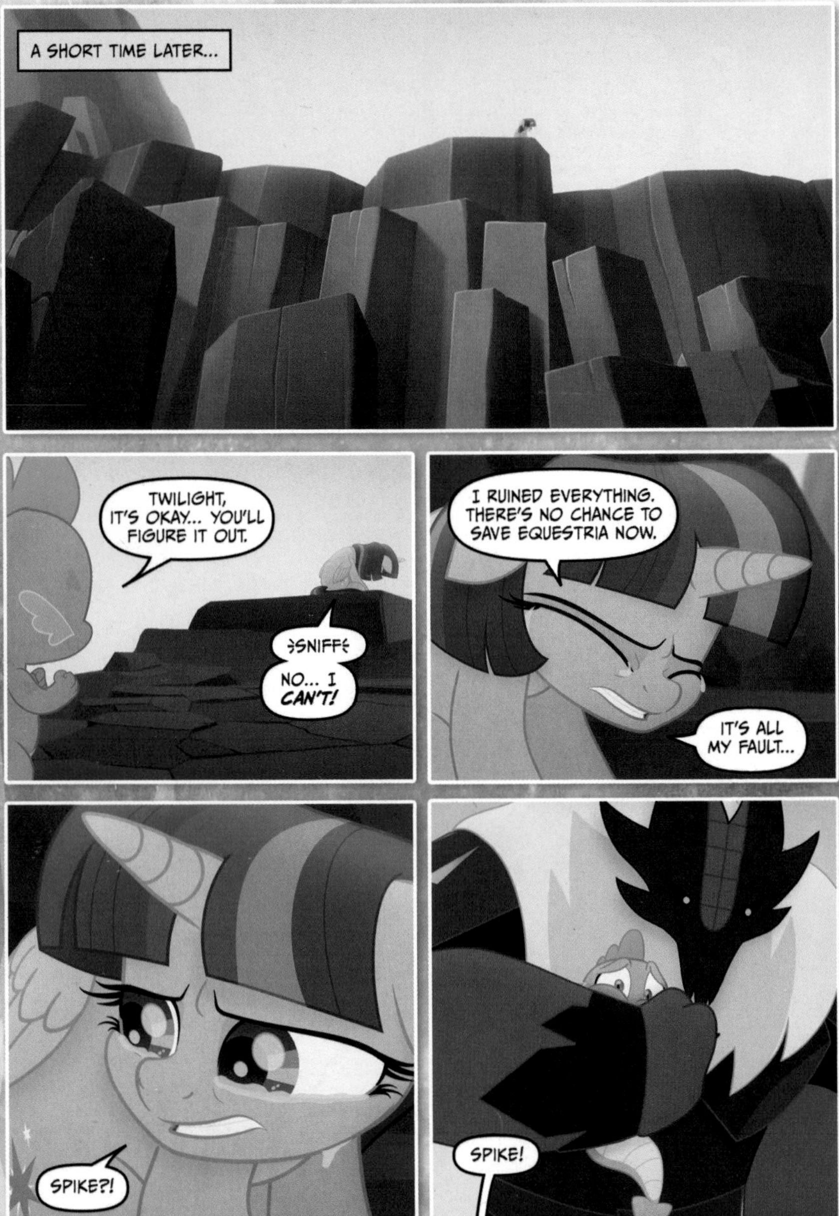

A SHORT TIME LATER...
TWILIGHT, IT'S OKAY... YOU'LL FIGURE IT OUT.
⋟SNIFF⋞
NO... I *CAN'T!*
I RUINED EVERYTHING. THERE'S NO CHANCE TO SAVE EQUESTRIA NOW.
IT'S ALL MY FAULT...
SPIKE?!
SPIKE!

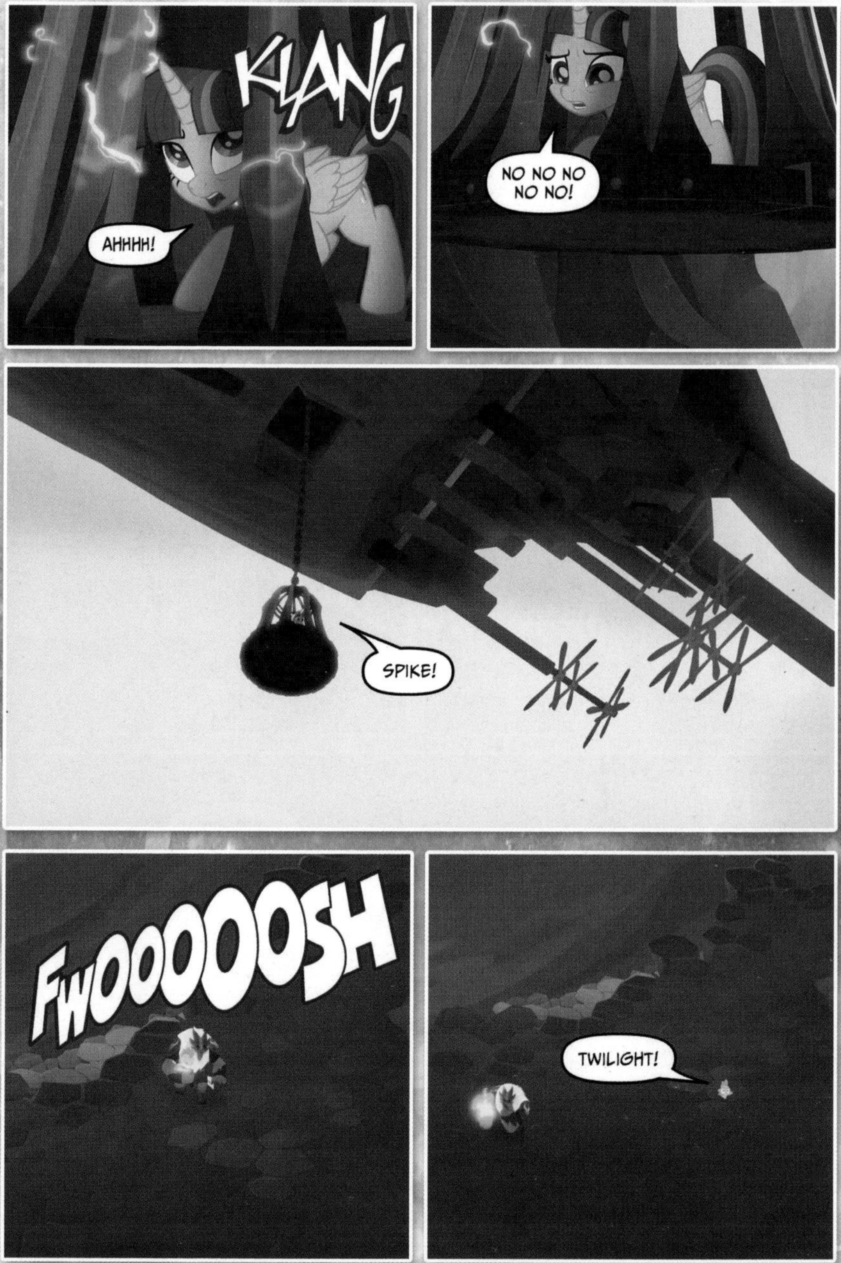
KLANG
AHHHH!
NO NO NO NO NO!
SPIKE!
FWOOOOOSH
TWILIGHT!

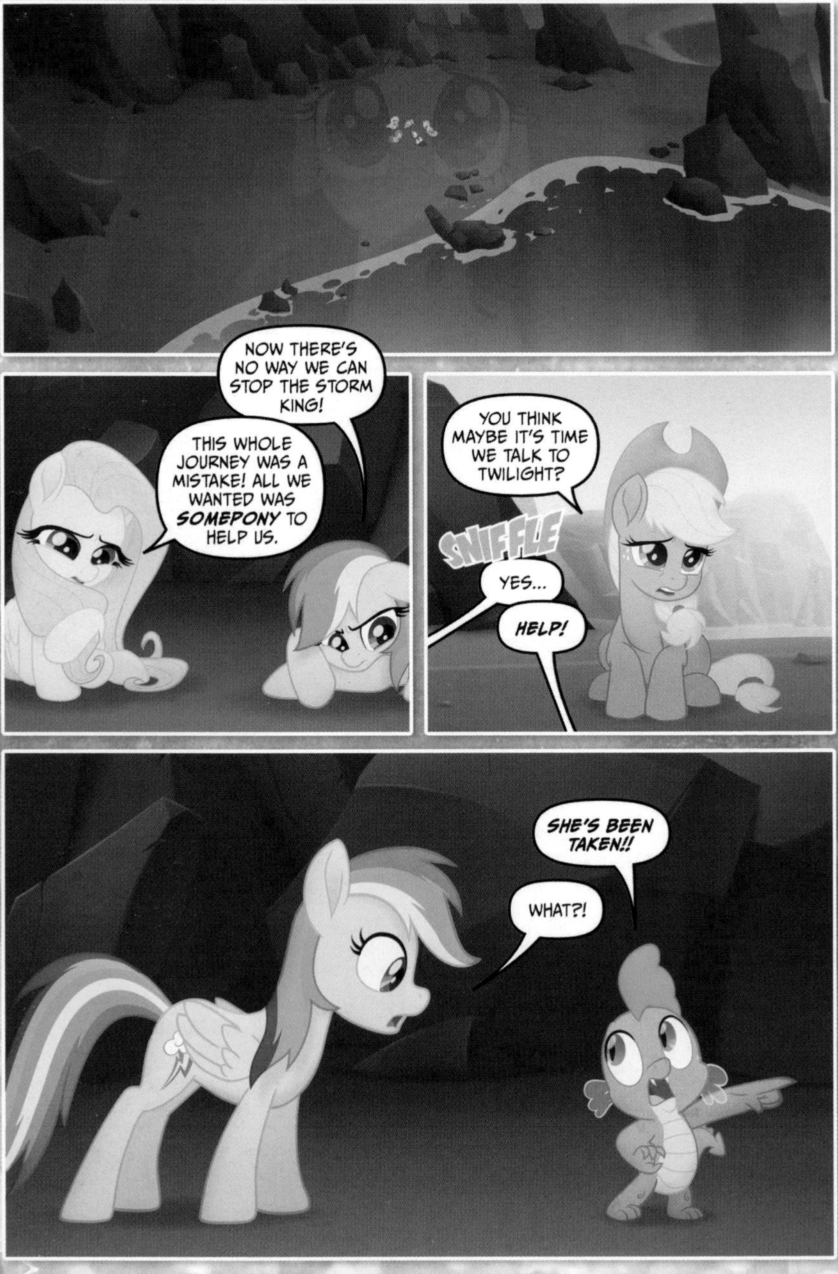
NOW THERE'S NO WAY WE CAN STOP THE STORM KING!
THIS WHOLE JOURNEY WAS A MISTAKE! ALL WE WANTED WAS **SOMEPONY** TO HELP US.
YOU THINK MAYBE IT'S TIME WE TALK TO TWILIGHT?
SNIFFLE
YES...
HELP!
SHE'S BEEN TAKEN!!
WHAT?!

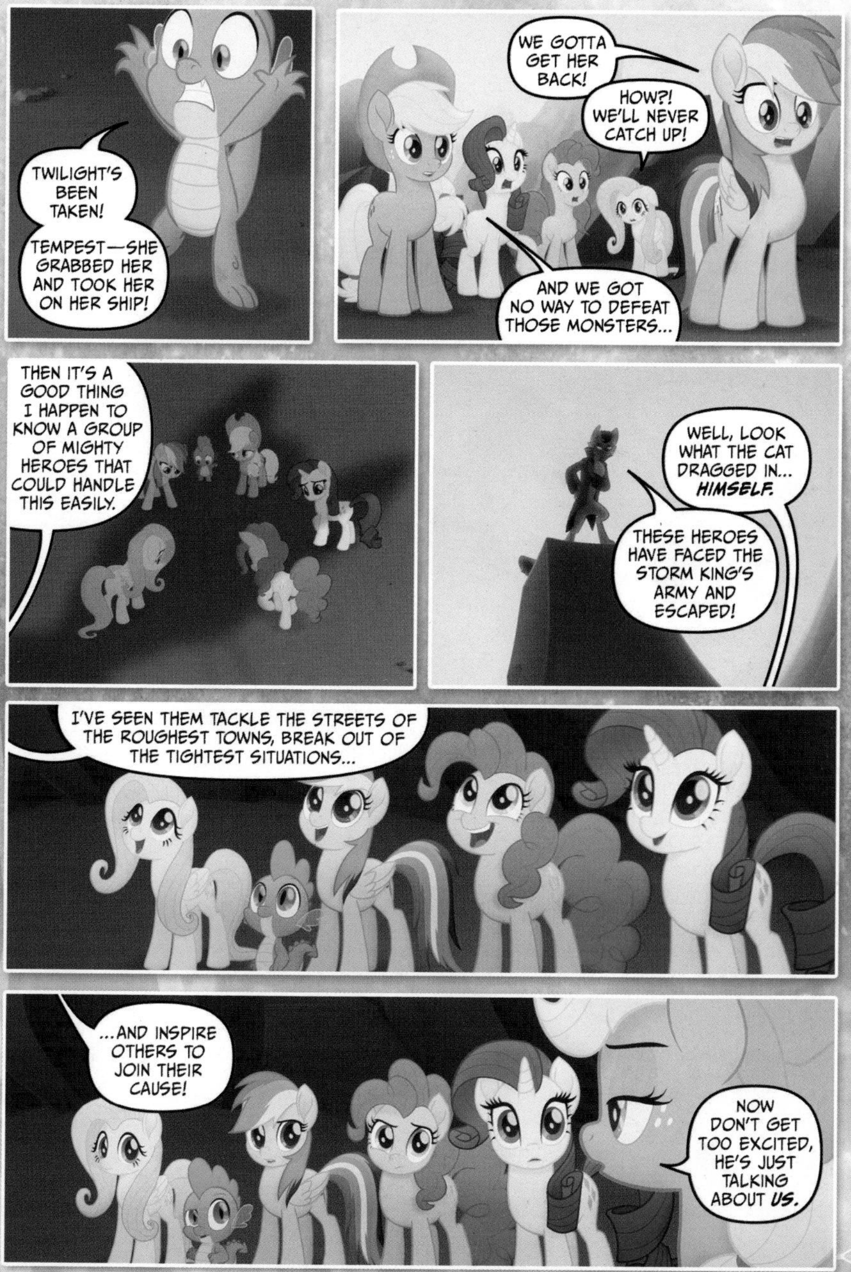
TWILIGHT'S BEEN TAKEN!
TEMPEST—SHE GRABBED HER AND TOOK HER ON HER SHIP!
WE GOTTA GET HER BACK!
HOW?! WE'LL NEVER CATCH UP!
AND WE GOT NO WAY TO DEFEAT THOSE MONSTERS...
THEN IT'S A GOOD THING I HAPPEN TO KNOW A GROUP OF MIGHTY HEROES THAT COULD HANDLE THIS EASILY.
THESE HEROES HAVE FACED THE STORM KING'S ARMY AND ESCAPED!
WELL, LOOK WHAT THE CAT DRAGGED IN... *HIMSELF.*
I'VE SEEN THEM TACKLE THE STREETS OF THE ROUGHEST TOWNS, BREAK OUT OF THE TIGHTEST SITUATIONS...
...AND INSPIRE OTHERS TO JOIN THEIR CAUSE!
NOW DON'T GET TOO EXCITED, HE'S JUST TALKING ABOUT *US.*

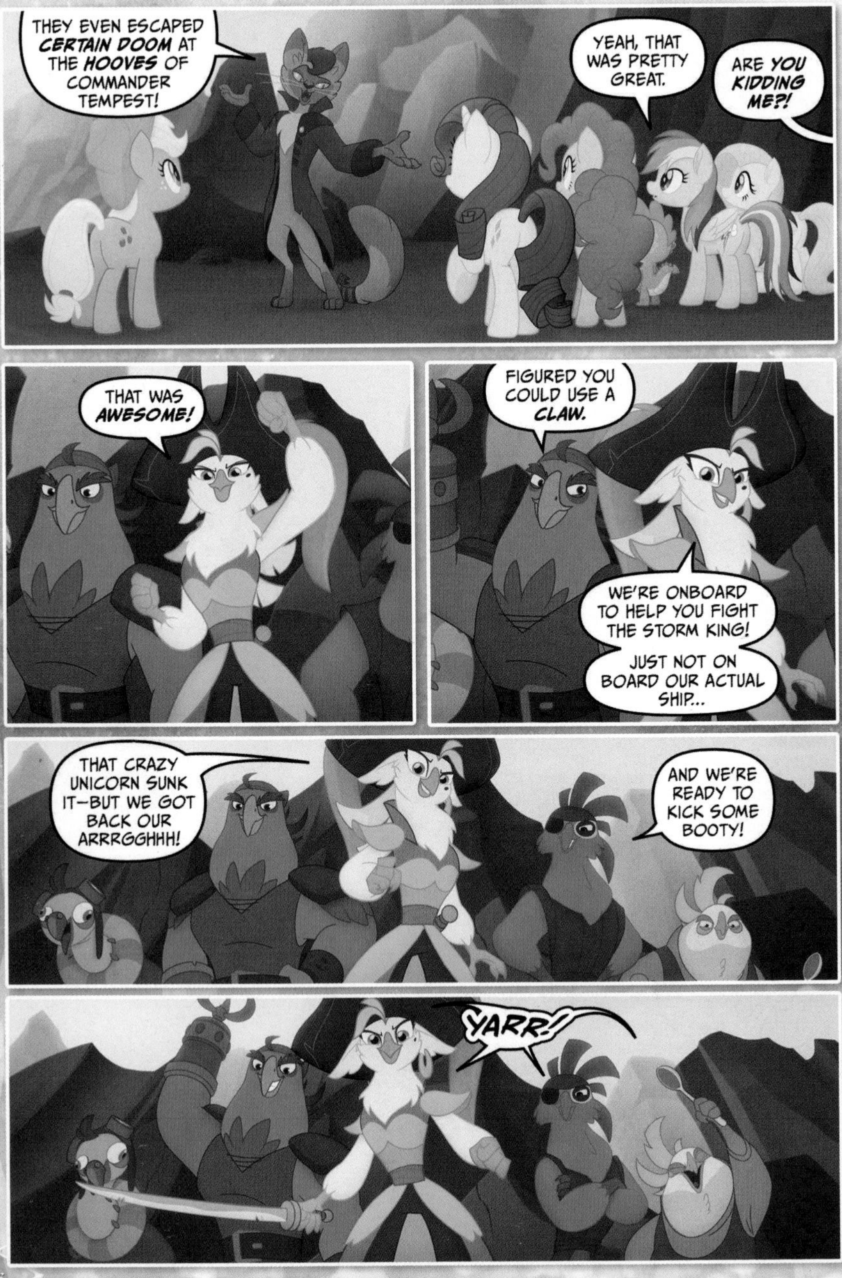
THEY EVEN ESCAPED *CERTAIN DOOM* AT THE *HOOVES* OF COMMANDER TEMPEST!
YEAH, THAT WAS PRETTY GREAT.
ARE *YOU KIDDING ME?!*
THAT WAS *AWESOME!*
FIGURED YOU COULD USE A *CLAW.*
WE'RE ONBOARD TO HELP YOU FIGHT THE STORM KING!
JUST NOT ON BOARD OUR ACTUAL SHIP...
THAT CRAZY UNICORN SUNK IT—BUT WE GOT BACK OUR ARRRGGHHH!
AND WE'RE READY TO KICK SOME BOOTY!
YARR!

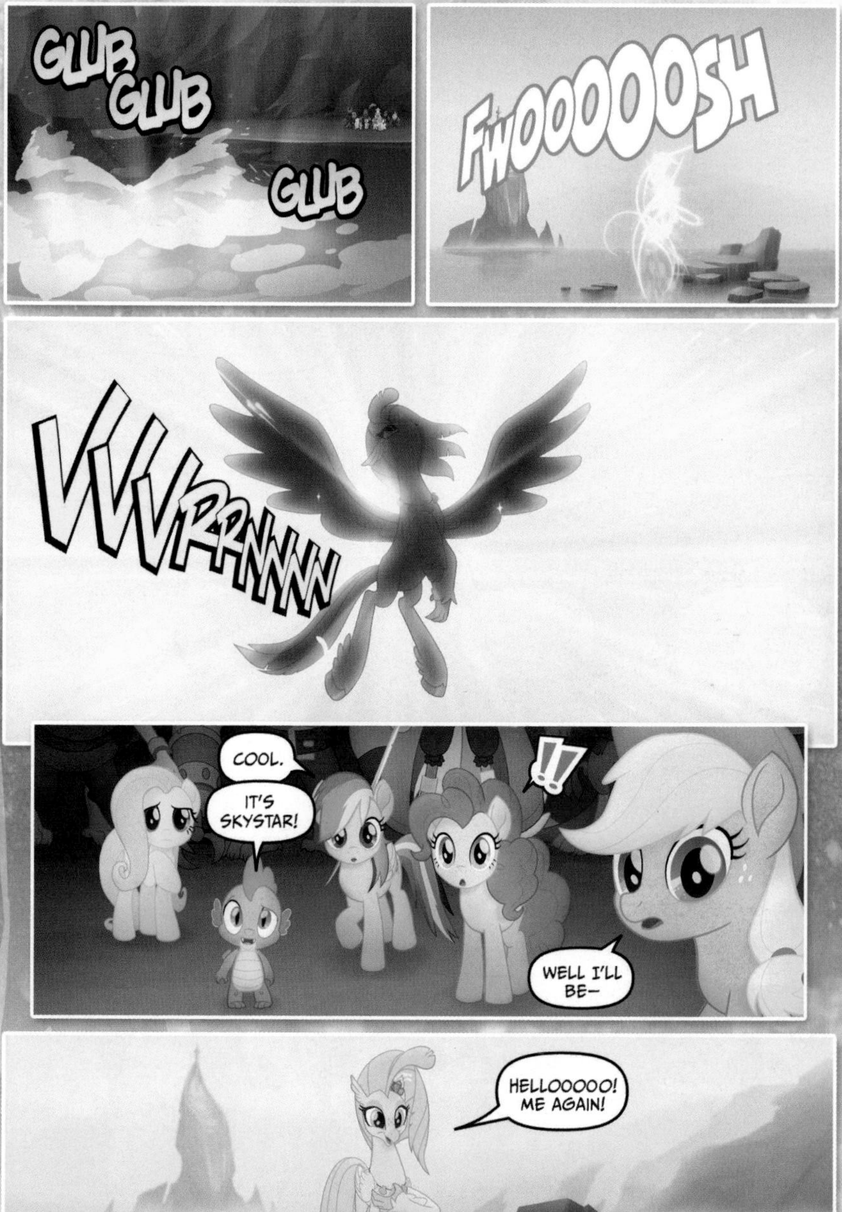
GLUB GLUB
GLUB
FWOOOOOOSH
VVVRRNNNN
COOL.
IT'S SKYSTAR!
!!
WELL I'LL BE—
HELLOOOOO! ME AGAIN!

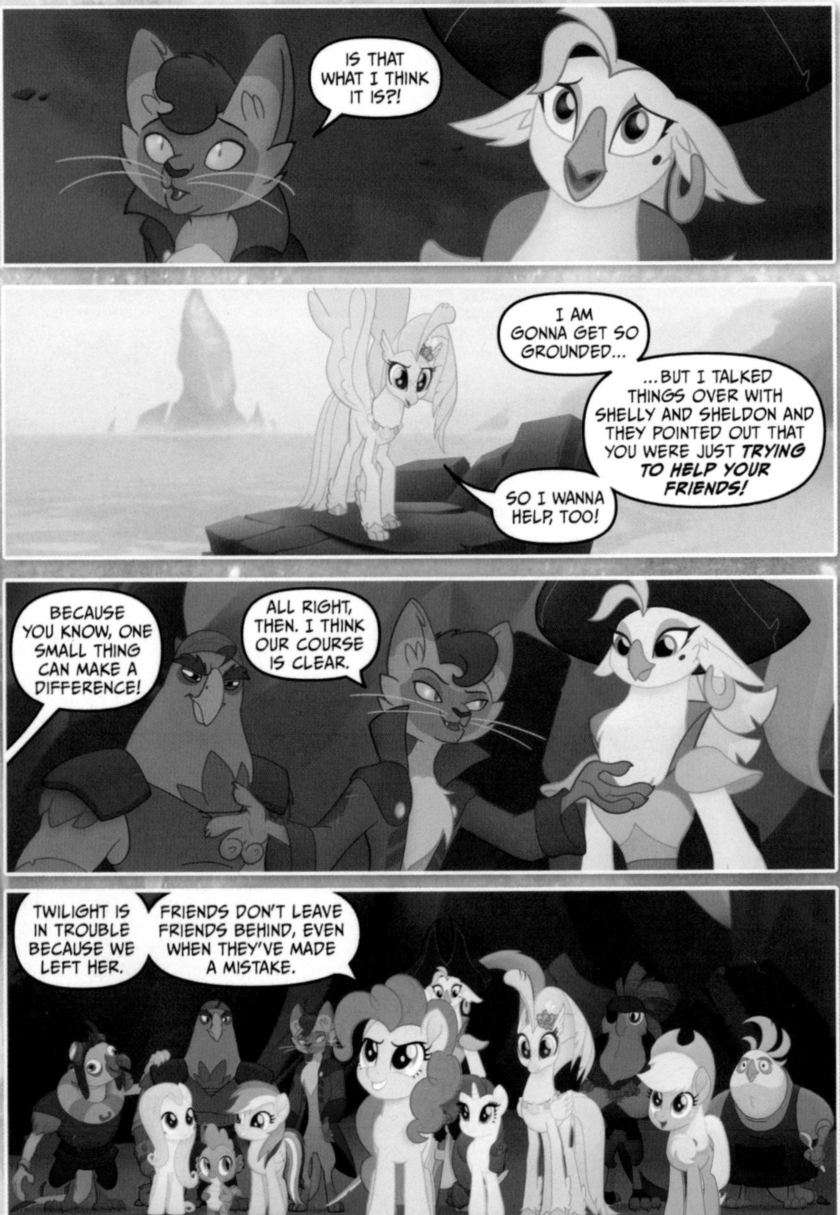
IS THAT WHAT I THINK IT IS?!
I AM GONNA GET SO GROUNDED...
...BUT I TALKED THINGS OVER WITH SHELLY AND SHELDON AND THEY POINTED OUT THAT YOU WERE JUST TRYING TO HELP YOUR FRIENDS!
SO I WANNA HELP, TOO!
BECAUSE YOU KNOW, ONE SMALL THING CAN MAKE A DIFFERENCE!
ALL RIGHT, THEN. I THINK OUR COURSE IS CLEAR.
TWILIGHT IS IN TROUBLE BECAUSE WE LEFT HER.
FRIENDS DON'T LEAVE FRIENDS BEHIND, EVEN WHEN THEY'VE MADE A MISTAKE.

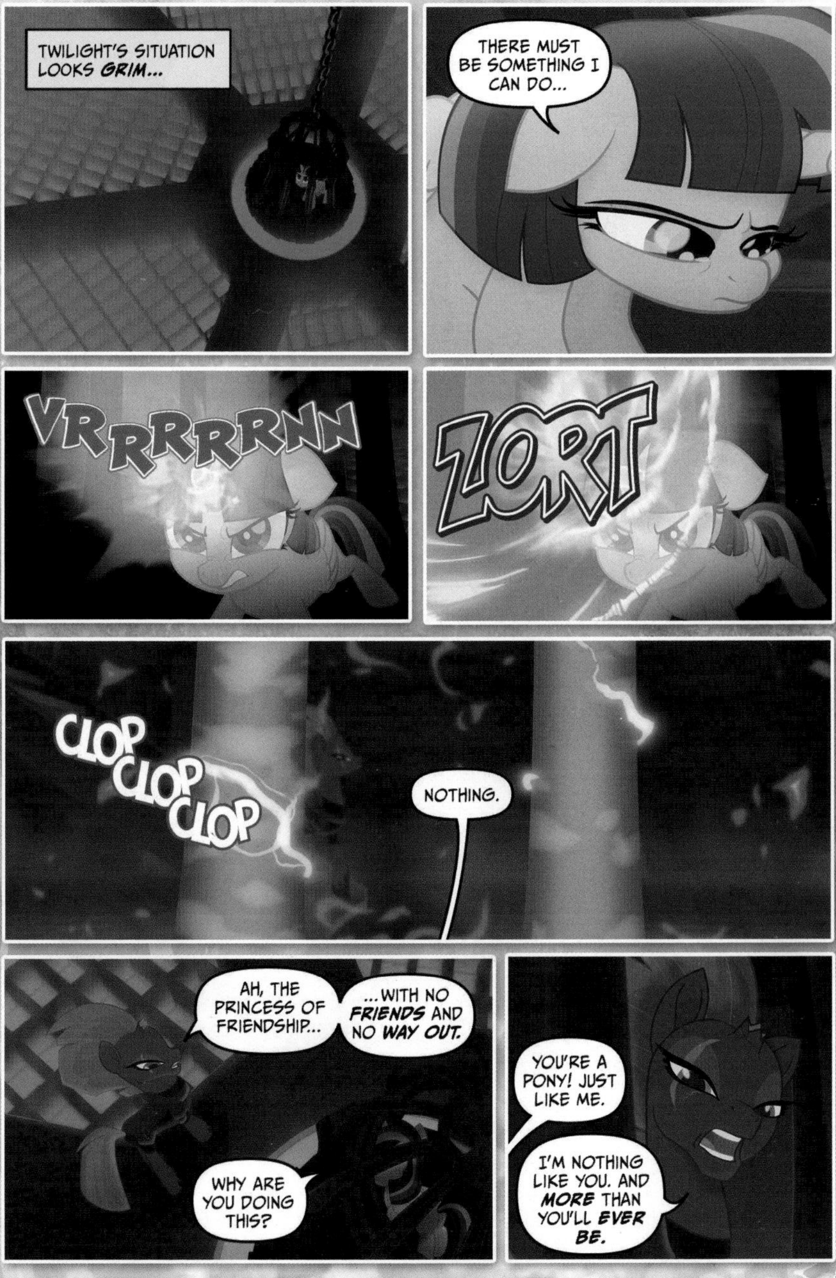
TWILIGHT'S SITUATION LOOKS GRIM...
THERE MUST BE SOMETHING I CAN DO...
VRRRRRRNN
ZORT
CLOP CLOP CLOP
NOTHING.
AH, THE PRINCESS OF FRIENDSHIP...
...WITH NO FRIENDS AND NO WAY OUT.
WHY ARE YOU DOING THIS?
YOU'RE A PONY! JUST LIKE ME.
I'M NOTHING LIKE YOU. AND MORE THAN YOU'LL EVER BE.

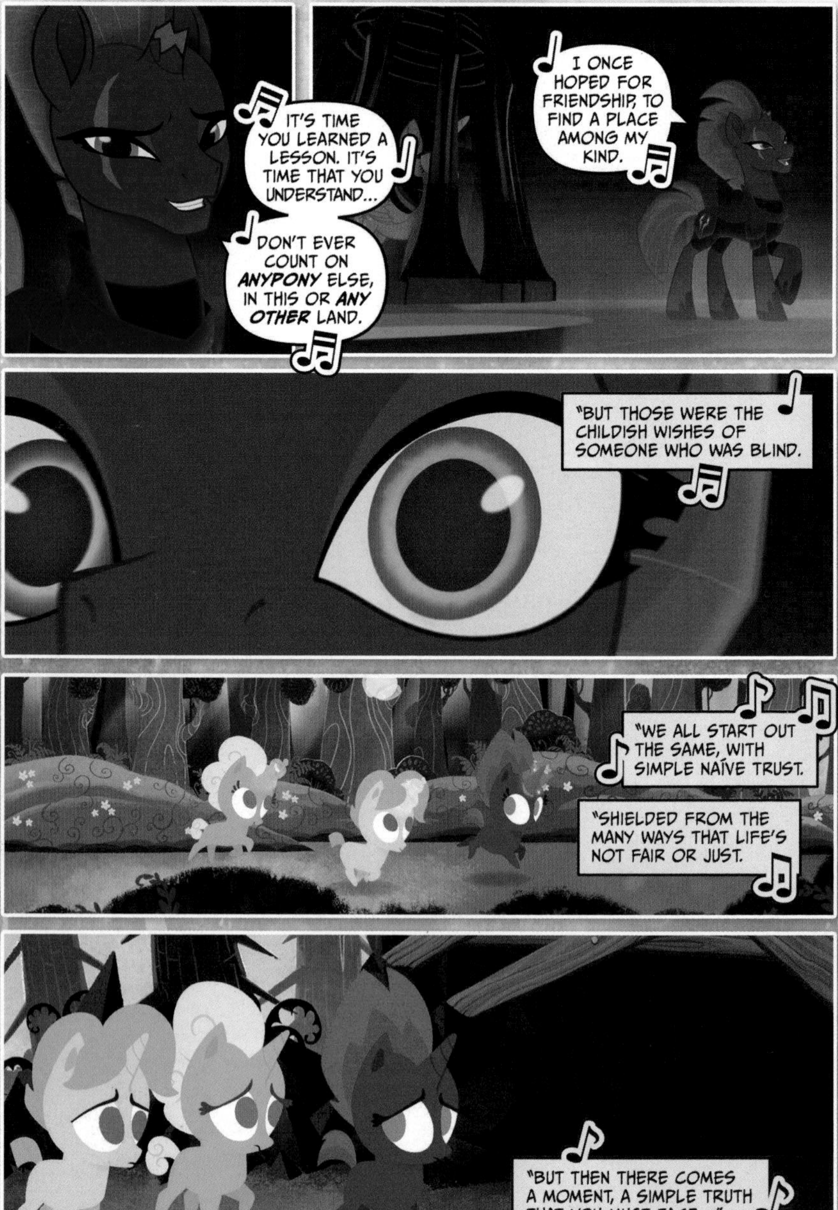
IT'S TIME YOU LEARNED A LESSON. IT'S TIME THAT YOU UNDERSTAND...
DON'T EVER COUNT ON ANYPONY ELSE, IN THIS OR ANY OTHER LAND.
I ONCE HOPED FOR FRIENDSHIP, TO FIND A PLACE AMONG MY KIND.
"BUT THOSE WERE THE CHILDISH WISHES OF SOMEONE WHO WAS BLIND.
"WE ALL START OUT THE SAME, WITH SIMPLE NAÏVE TRUST.
"SHIELDED FROM THE MANY WAYS THAT LIFE'S NOT FAIR OR JUST.
"BUT THEN THERE COMES A MOMENT, A SIMPLE TRUTH THAT YOU MUST FACE..."

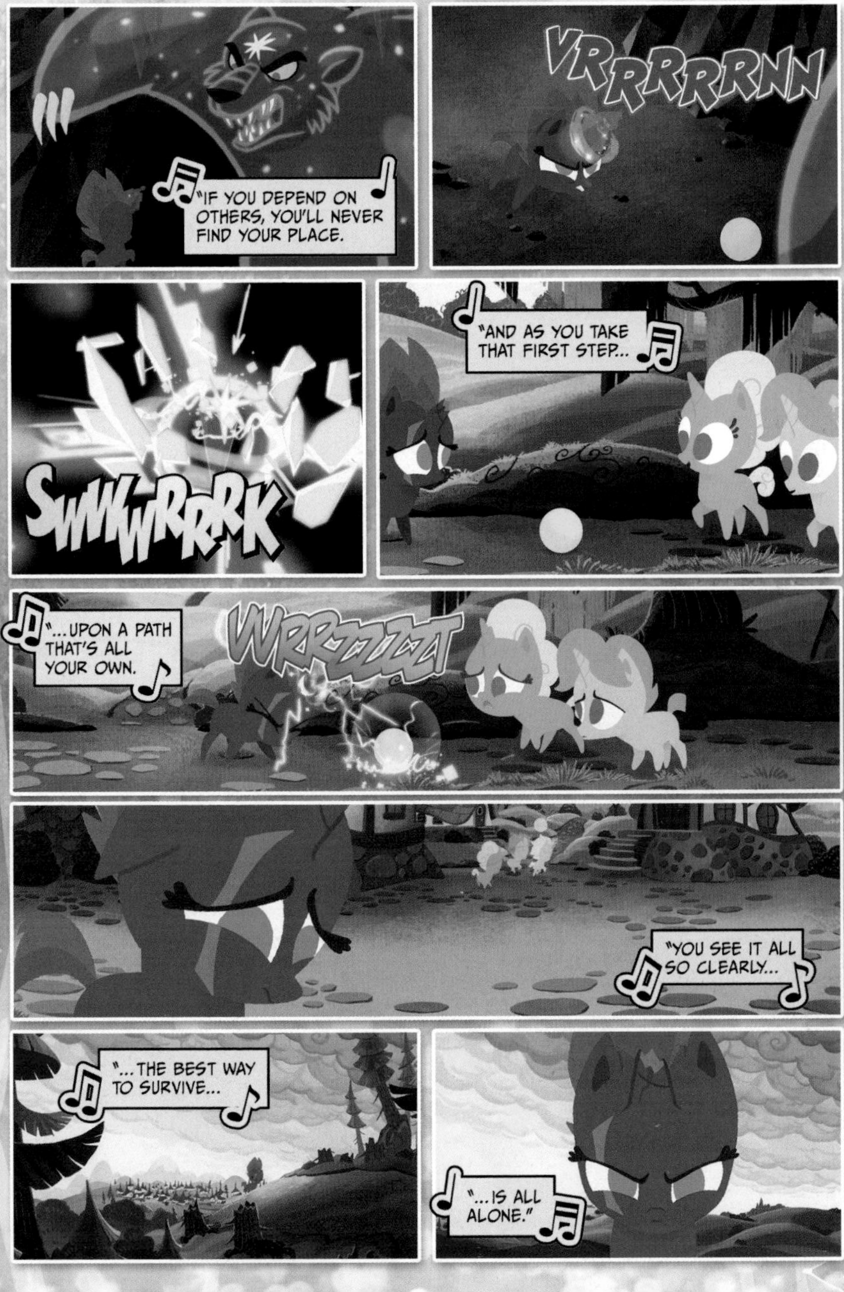
"IF YOU DEPEND ON OTHERS, YOU'LL NEVER FIND YOUR PLACE.
VRRRRRRNN
SWWWRRRK
"AND AS YOU TAKE THAT FIRST STEP...
"...UPON A PATH THAT'S ALL YOUR OWN.
VVRRZZZZT
"YOU SEE IT ALL SO CLEARLY...
"...THE BEST WAY TO SURVIVE...
"...IS ALL ALONE."

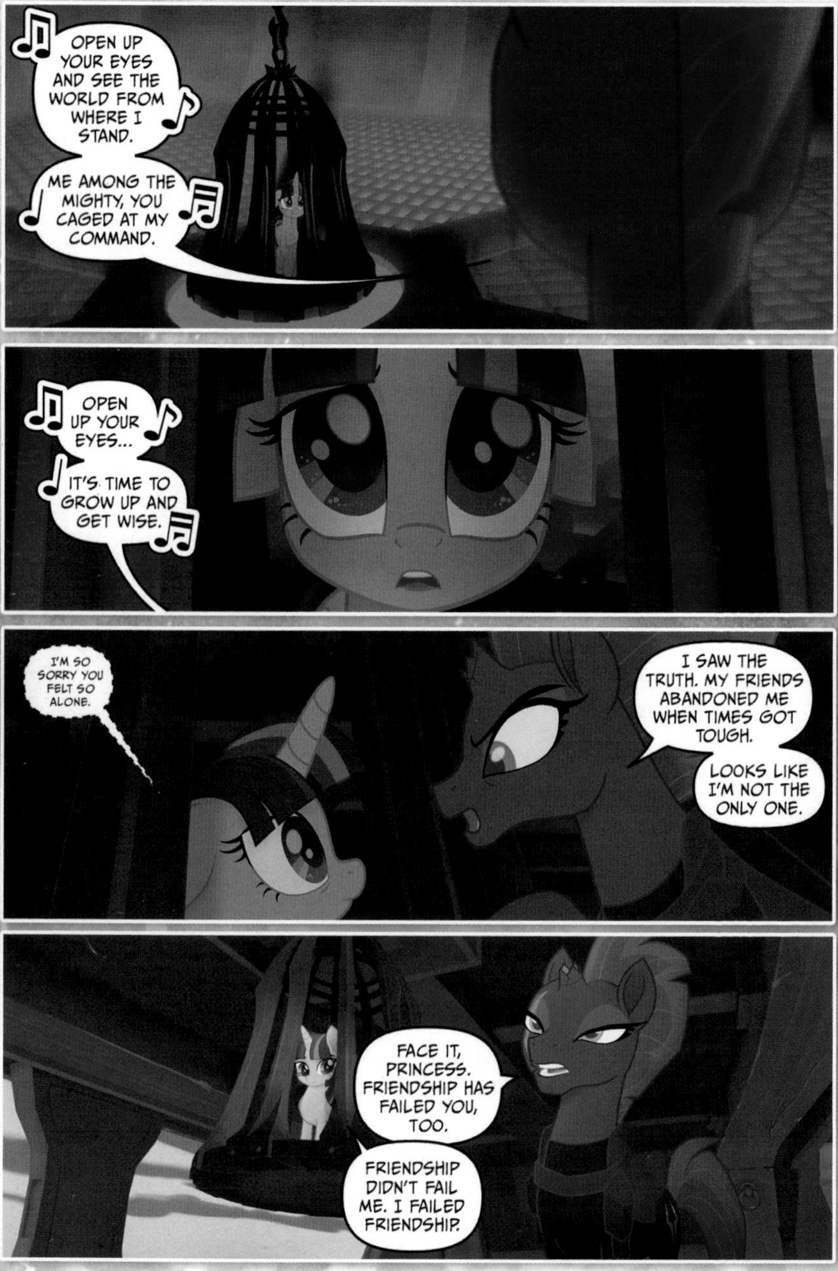
OPEN UP YOUR EYES AND SEE THE WORLD FROM WHERE I STAND.
ME AMONG THE MIGHTY, YOU CAGED AT MY COMMAND.
OPEN UP YOUR EYES...
IT'S TIME TO GROW UP AND GET WISE.
I'M SO SORRY YOU FELT SO ALONE.
I SAW THE TRUTH. MY FRIENDS ABANDONED ME WHEN TIMES GOT TOUGH.
LOOKS LIKE I'M NOT THE ONLY ONE.
FACE IT, PRINCESS. FRIENDSHIP HAS FAILED YOU, TOO.
FRIENDSHIP DIDN'T FAIL ME. I FAILED FRIENDSHIP.

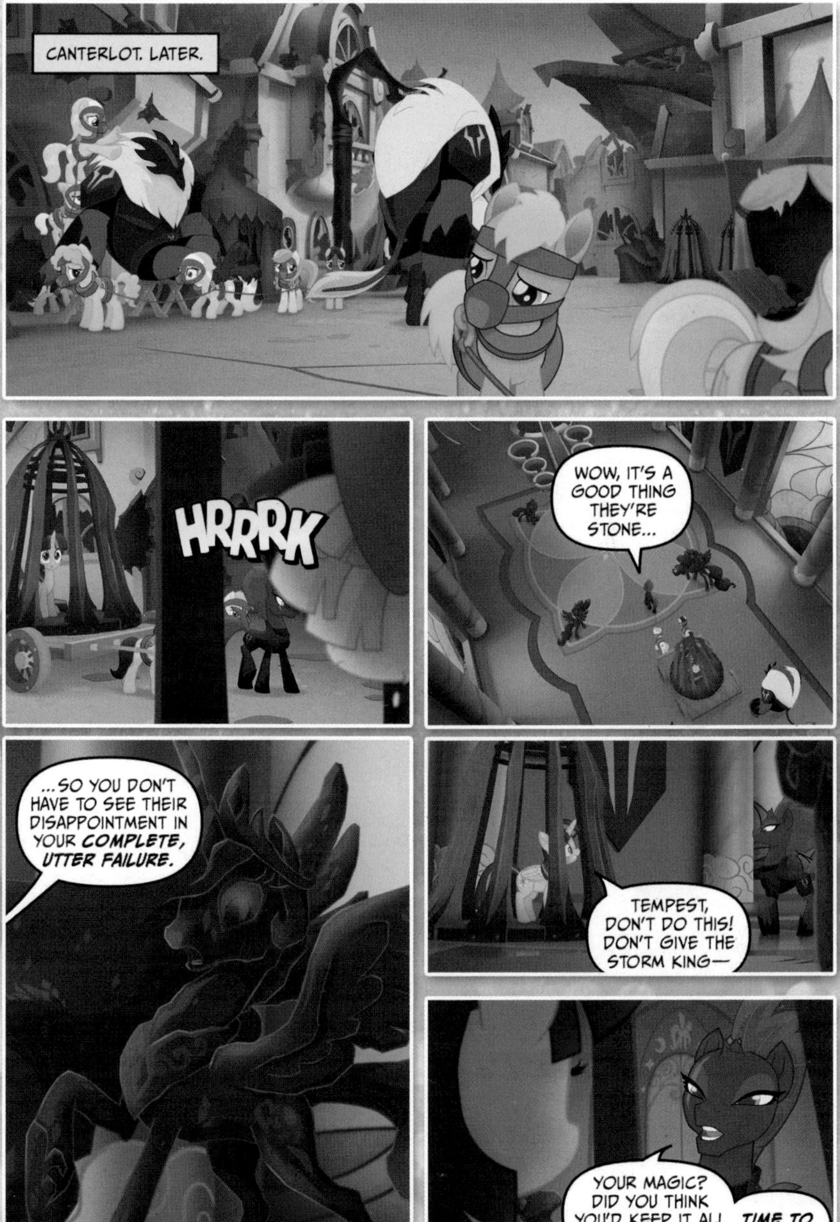
CANTERLOT. LATER.
HRRRK
WOW, IT'S A GOOD THING THEY'RE STONE...
...SO YOU DON'T HAVE TO SEE THEIR DISAPPOINTMENT IN YOUR COMPLETE, UTTER FAILURE.
TEMPEST, DON'T DO THIS! DON'T GIVE THE STORM KING—
YOUR MAGIC? DID YOU THINK YOU'D KEEP IT ALL TO YOURSELF?
TIME TO SHARE.

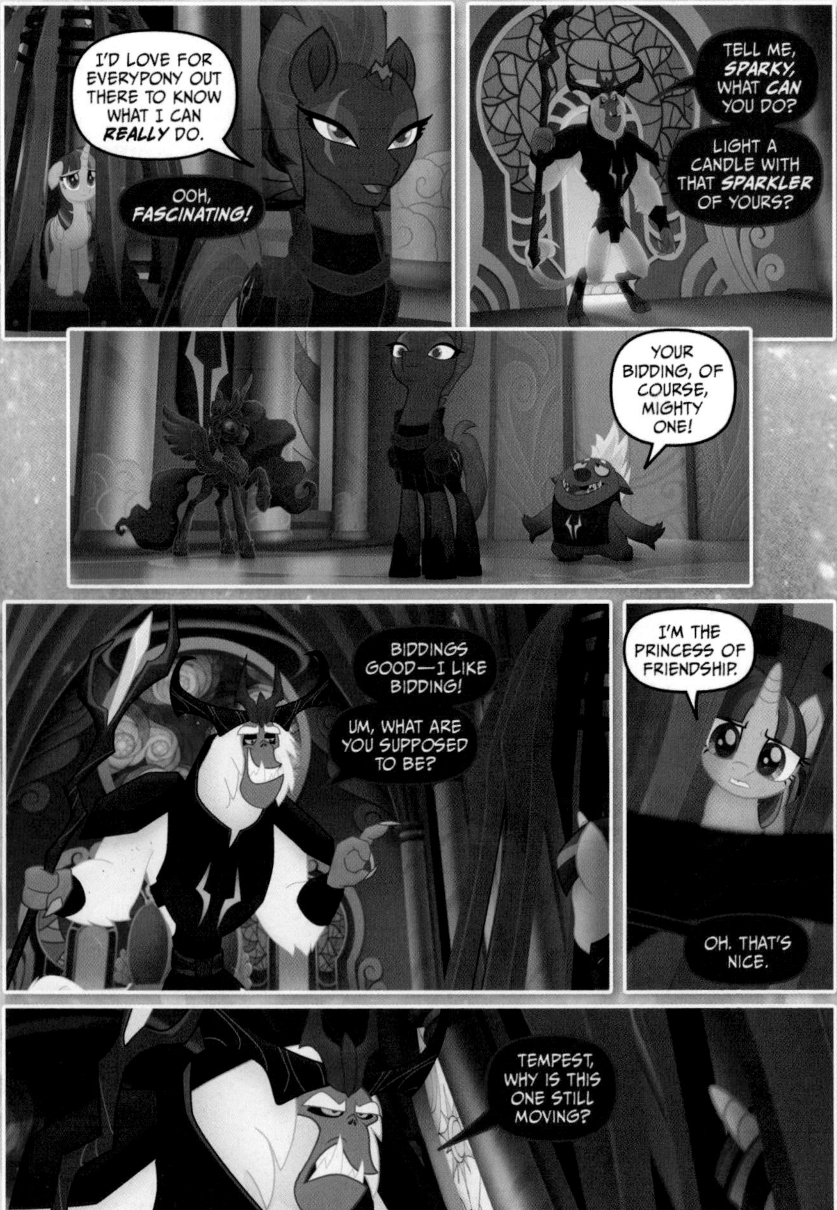
I'D LOVE FOR EVERYPONY OUT THERE TO KNOW WHAT I CAN REALLY DO.
OOH, FASCINATING!
TELL ME, SPARKY, WHAT CAN YOU DO?
LIGHT A CANDLE WITH THAT SPARKLER OF YOURS?
YOUR BIDDING, OF COURSE, MIGHTY ONE!
BIDDINGS GOOD—I LIKE BIDDING!
UM, WHAT ARE YOU SUPPOSED TO BE?
I'M THE PRINCESS OF FRIENDSHIP.
OH. THAT'S NICE.
TEMPEST, WHY IS THIS ONE STILL MOVING?

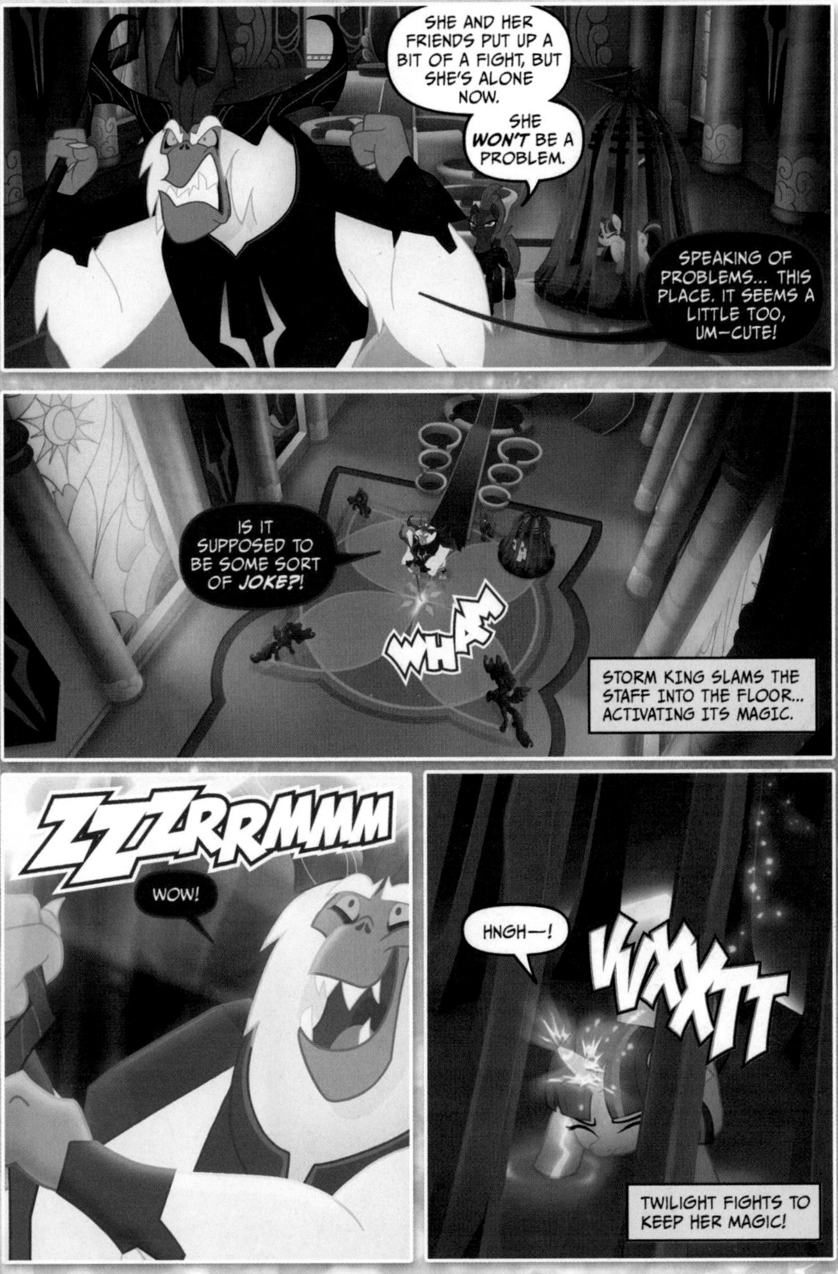
SHE AND HER FRIENDS PUT UP A BIT OF A FIGHT, BUT SHE'S ALONE NOW.
SHE *WON'T* BE A PROBLEM.
SPEAKING OF PROBLEMS... THIS PLACE. IT SEEMS A LITTLE TOO, UM—CUTE!
IS IT SUPPOSED TO BE SOME SORT OF *JOKE?!*
WHAM
STORM KING SLAMS THE STAFF INTO THE FLOOR... ACTIVATING ITS MAGIC.
ZZZRRMMM
WOW!
HNGH—!
VVXXTT
TWILIGHT FIGHTS TO KEEP HER MAGIC!

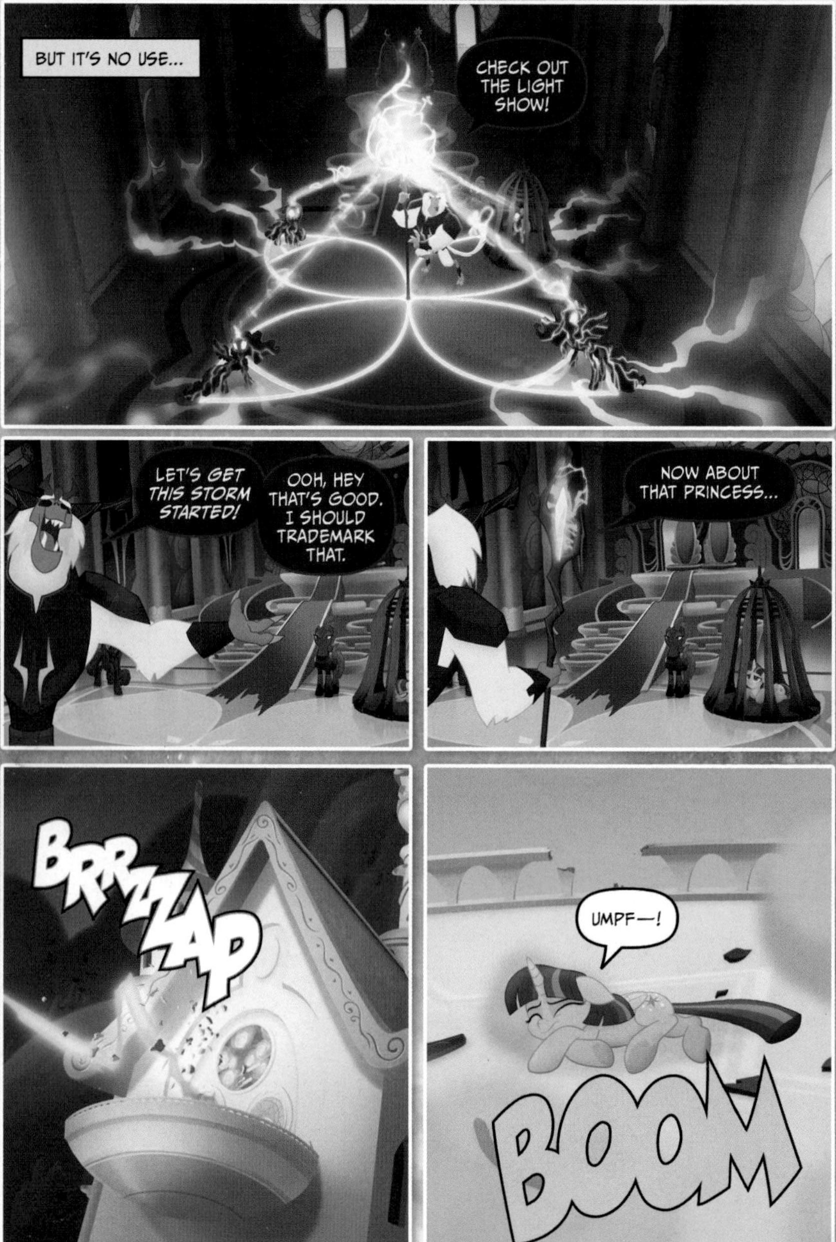
BUT IT'S NO USE...
CHECK OUT THE LIGHT SHOW!
LET'S GET THIS STORM STARTED!
OOH, HEY THAT'S GOOD. I SHOULD TRADEMARK THAT.
NOW ABOUT THAT PRINCESS...
BRRZZZAP
UMPF—!
BOOM

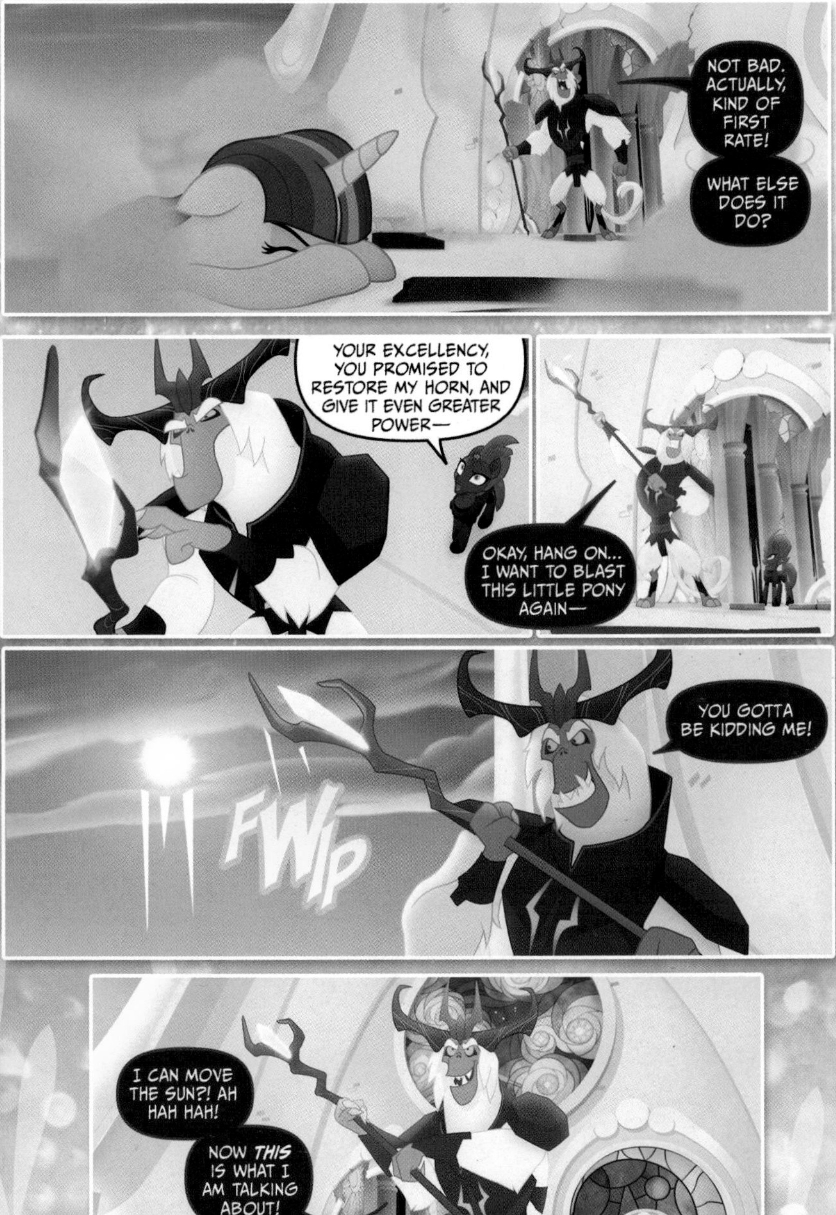
NOT BAD. ACTUALLY, KIND OF FIRST RATE!
WHAT ELSE DOES IT DO?
YOUR EXCELLENCY, YOU PROMISED TO RESTORE MY HORN, AND GIVE IT EVEN GREATER POWER—
OKAY, HANG ON... I WANT TO BLAST THIS LITTLE PONY AGAIN—
FWIP
YOU GOTTA BE KIDDING ME!
I CAN MOVE THE SUN?! AH HAH HAH!
NOW *THIS* IS WHAT I AM TALKING ABOUT!

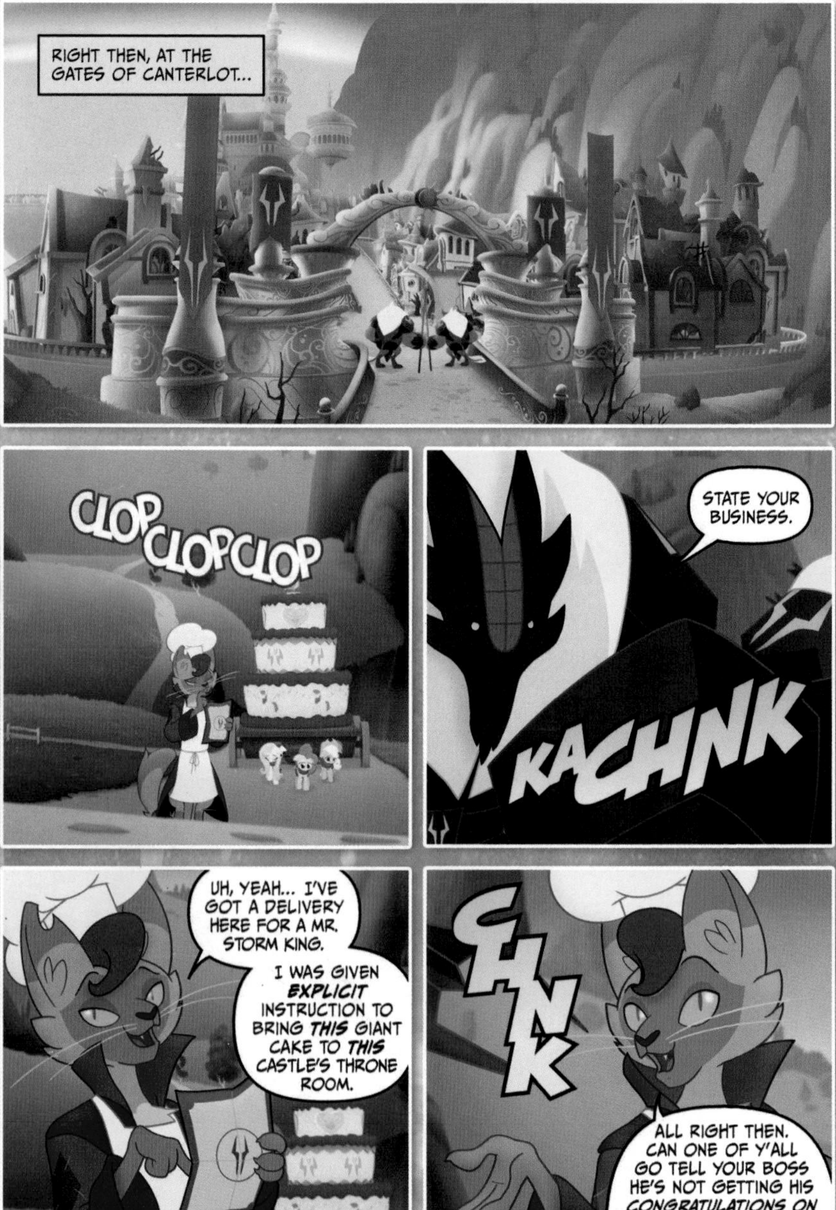
RIGHT THEN, AT THE GATES OF CANTERLOT...
CLOP CLOPCLOP
STATE YOUR BUSINESS.
KACHNK
UH, YEAH... I'VE GOT A DELIVERY HERE FOR A MR. STORM KING.
I WAS GIVEN EXPLICIT INSTRUCTION TO BRING THIS GIANT CAKE TO THIS CASTLE'S THRONE ROOM.
CHNK
ALL RIGHT THEN. CAN ONE OF Y'ALL GO TELL YOUR BOSS HE'S NOT GETTING HIS CONGRATULATIONS ON SUBDUING DEFENSELESS PASTEL PONIES CAKE?

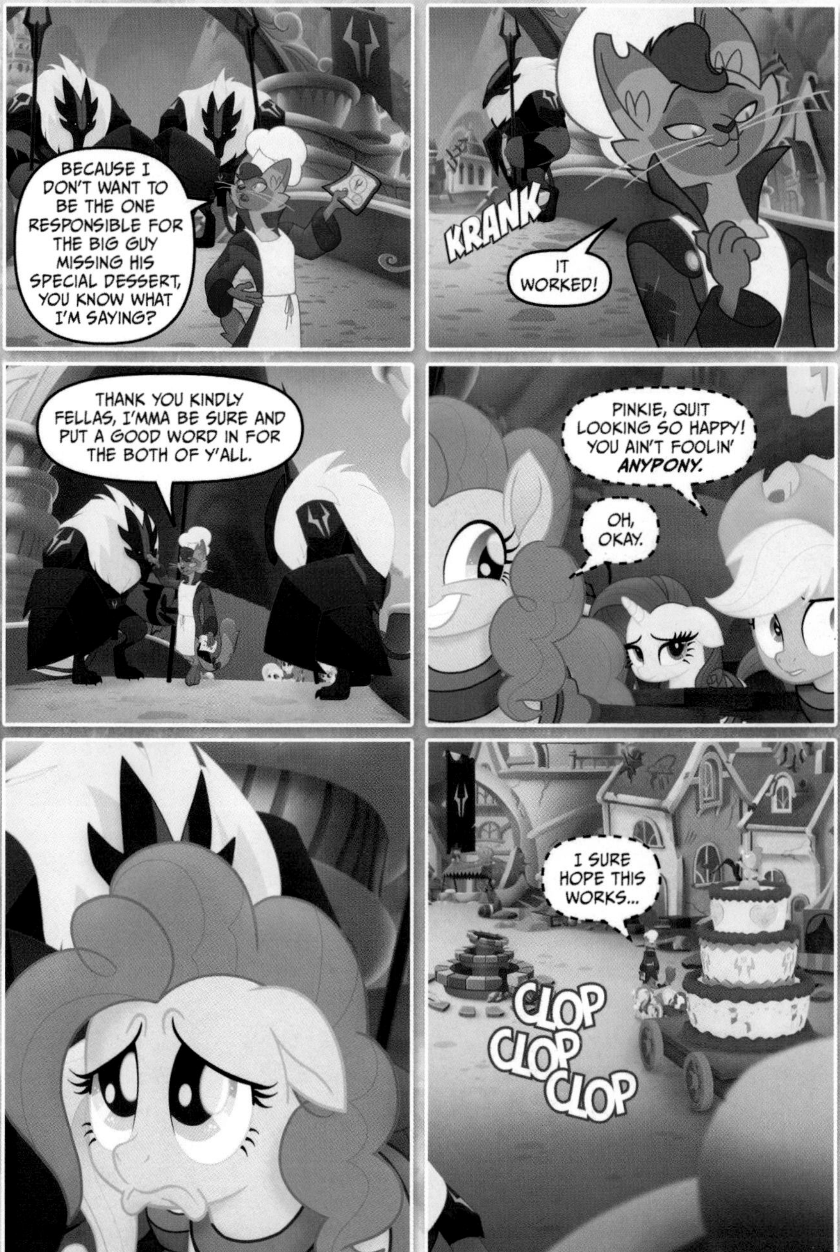
BECAUSE I DON'T WANT TO BE THE ONE RESPONSIBLE FOR THE BIG GUY MISSING HIS SPECIAL DESSERT, YOU KNOW WHAT I'M SAYING?
KRANK
IT WORKED!
THANK YOU KINDLY FELLAS, I'MMA BE SURE AND PUT A GOOD WORD IN FOR THE BOTH OF Y'ALL.
PINKIE, QUIT LOOKING SO HAPPY! YOU AIN'T FOOLIN' ANYPONY.
OH, OKAY.
I SURE HOPE THIS WORKS...
CLOP
CLOP
CLOP

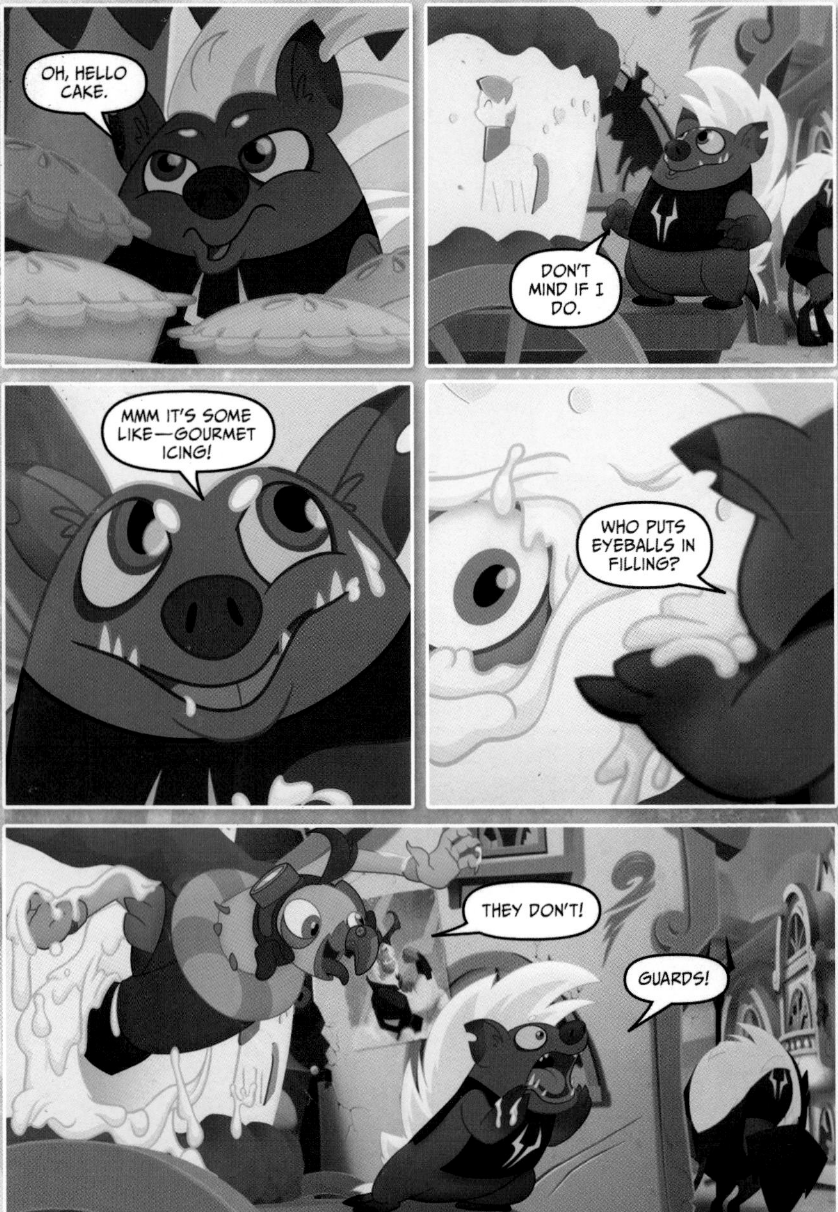
OH, HELLO CAKE.
DON'T MIND IF I DO.
MMM IT'S SOME LIKE—GOURMET ICING!
WHO PUTS EYEBALLS IN FILLING?
THEY DON'T!
GUARDS!

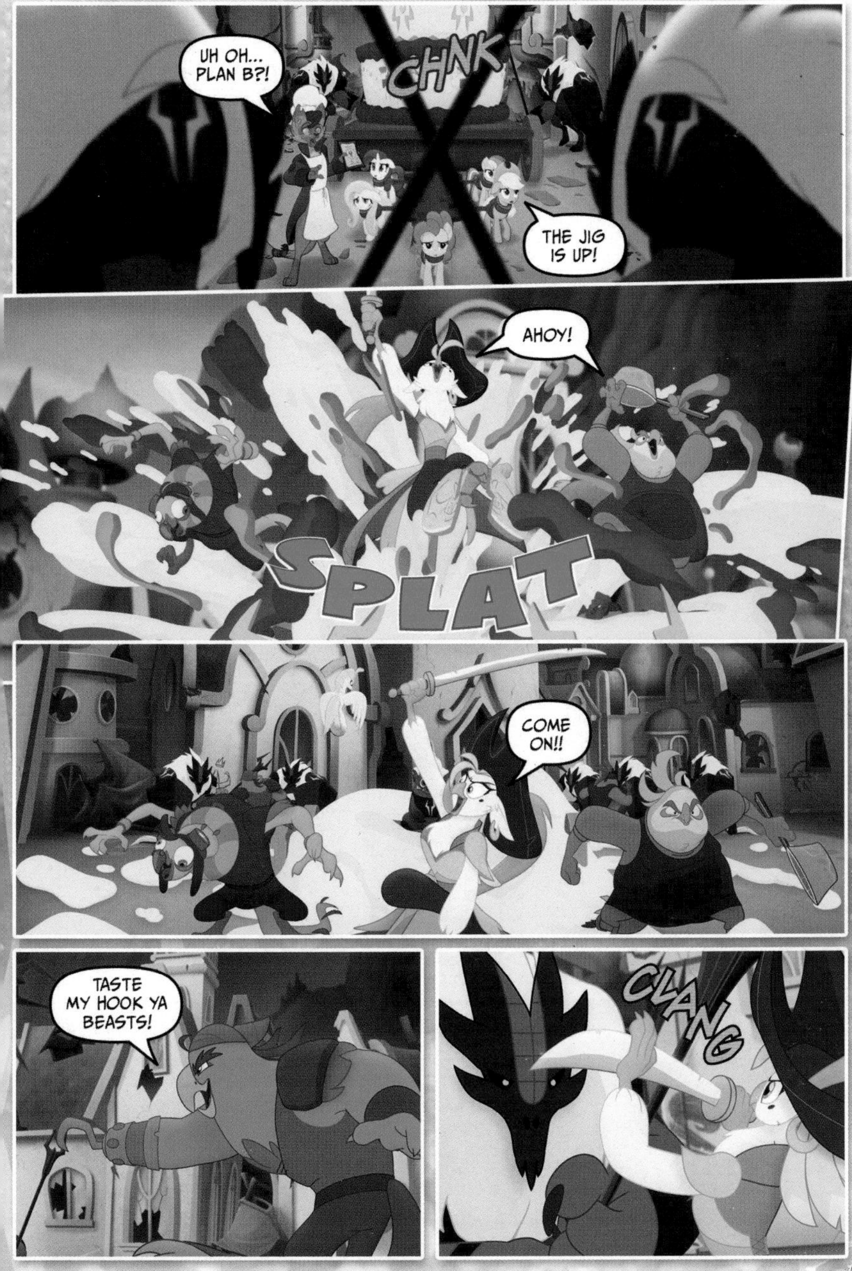
UH OH... PLAN B?!
CHNK
THE JIG IS UP!
AHOY!
SPLAT
COME ON!!
TASTE MY HOOK YA BEASTS!
CLANG

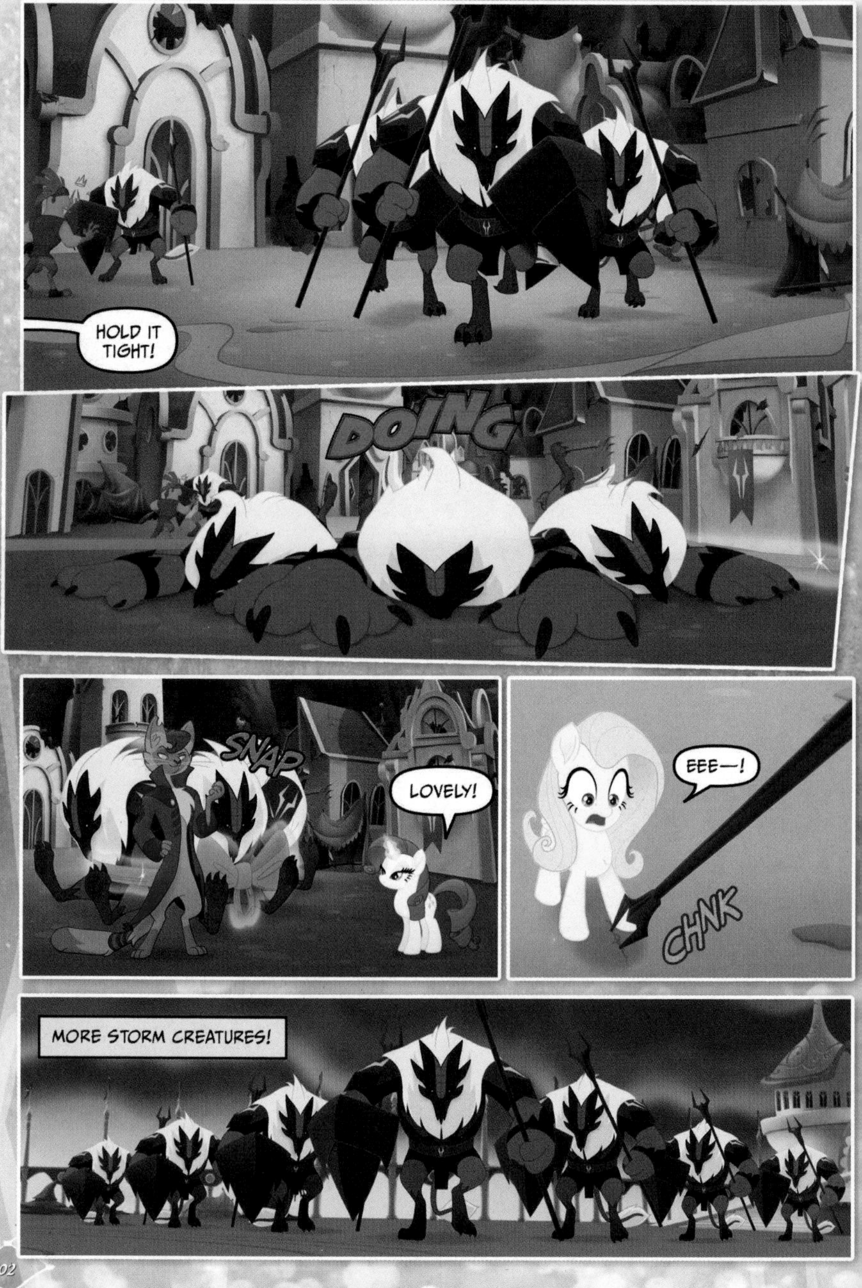
HOLD IT TIGHT!
DOING
SNAP
LOVELY!
EEE—!
CHNK
MORE STORM CREATURES!

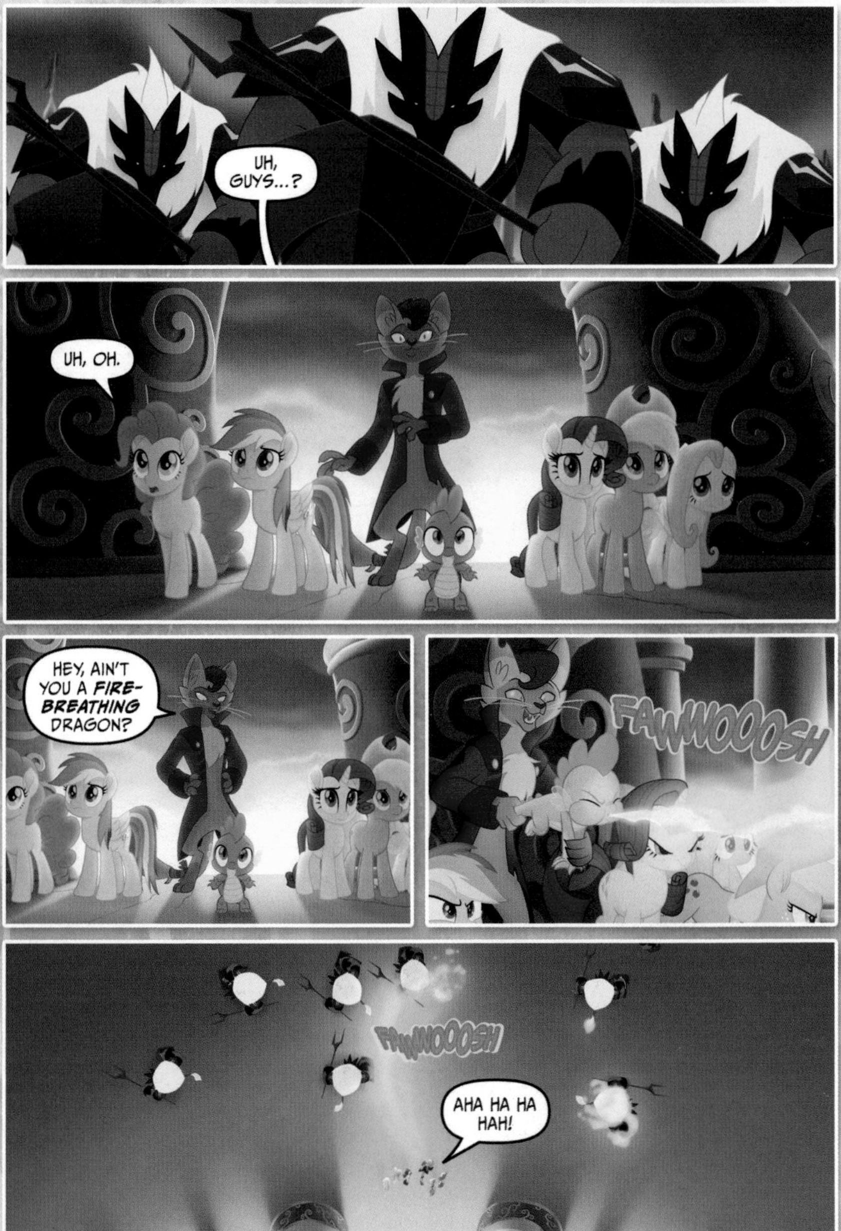
UH, GUYS...?
UH, OH.
HEY, AIN'T YOU A *FIRE-BREATHING* DRAGON?
FAWWOOOSH
FAWWOOOSH
AHA HA HA HAH!

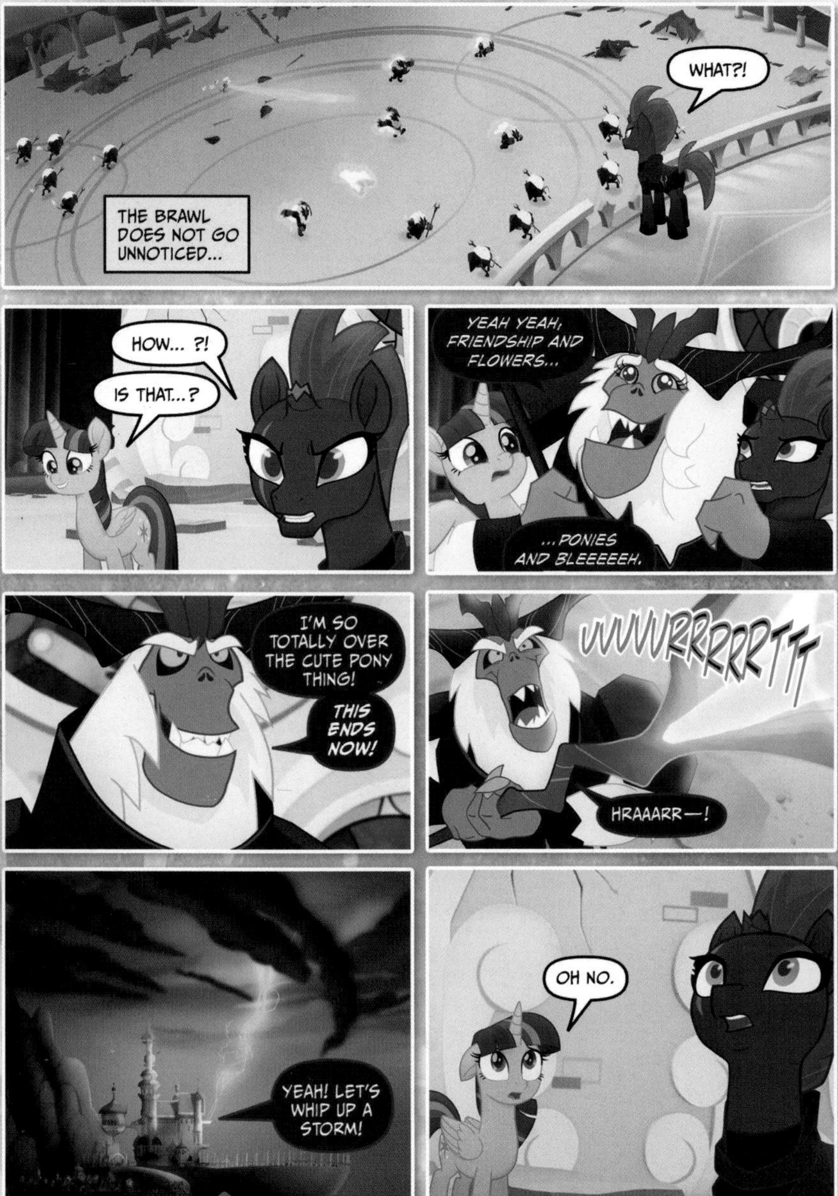
THE BRAWL DOES NOT GO UNNOTICED...
WHAT?!
HOW... ?!
IS THAT...?
YEAH YEAH, FRIENDSHIP AND FLOWERS...
...PONIES AND BLEEEEEH.
I'M SO TOTALLY OVER THE CUTE PONY THING!
THIS ENDS NOW!
VVVVVRRRRRRTTT
HRAAARR—!
YEAH! LET'S WHIP UP A STORM!
OH NO.

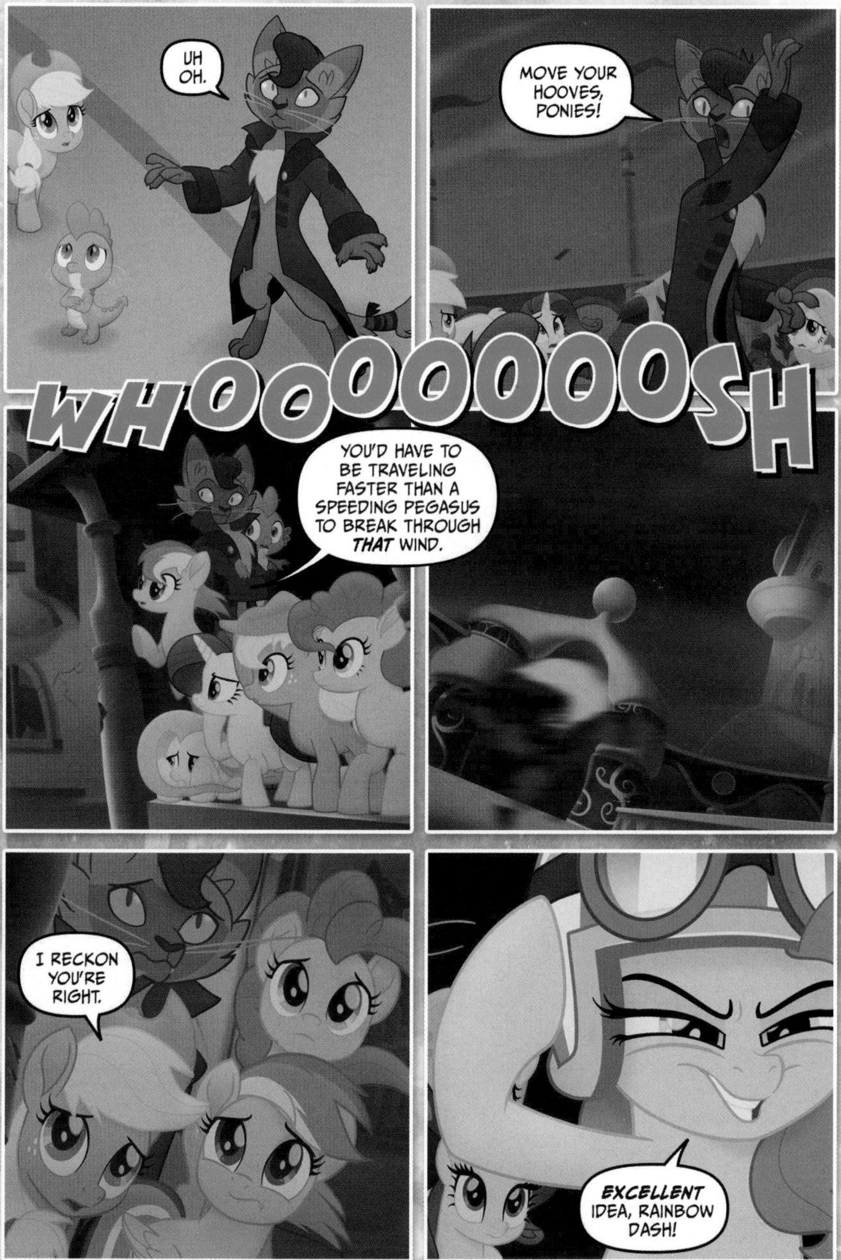
UH OH.
MOVE YOUR HOOVES, PONIES!
WHOOOOOOOOSH
YOU'D HAVE TO BE TRAVELING FASTER THAN A SPEEDING PEGASUS TO BREAK THROUGH THAT WIND.
I RECKON YOU'RE RIGHT.
EXCELLENT IDEA, RAINBOW DASH!

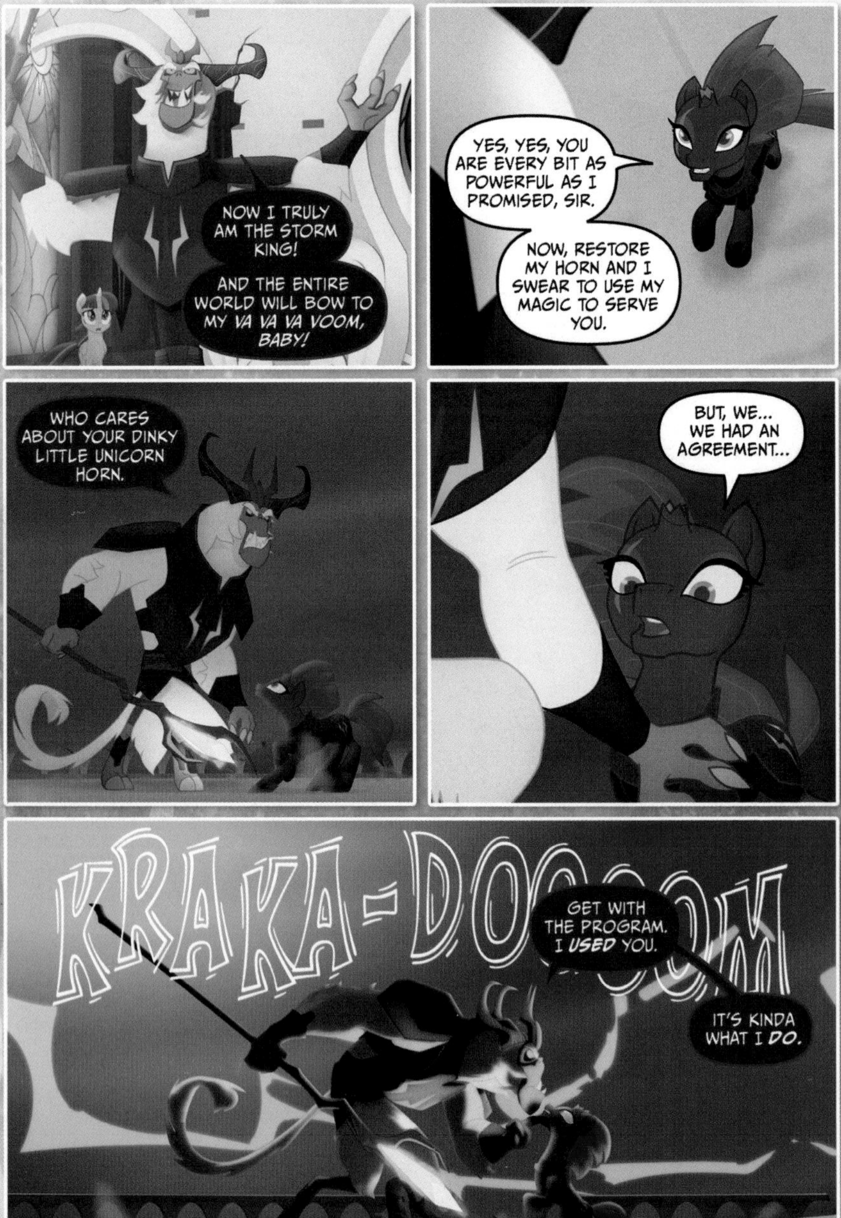
NOW I TRULY AM THE STORM KING!
AND THE ENTIRE WORLD WILL BOW TO MY VA VA VA VOOM, BABY!
YES, YES, YOU ARE EVERY BIT AS POWERFUL AS I PROMISED, SIR.
NOW, RESTORE MY HORN AND I SWEAR TO USE MY MAGIC TO SERVE YOU.
WHO CARES ABOUT YOUR DINKY LITTLE UNICORN HORN.
BUT, WE... WE HAD AN AGREEMENT...
KRAKA-DOOOOOM
GET WITH THE PROGRAM. I USED YOU.
IT'S KINDA WHAT I DO.

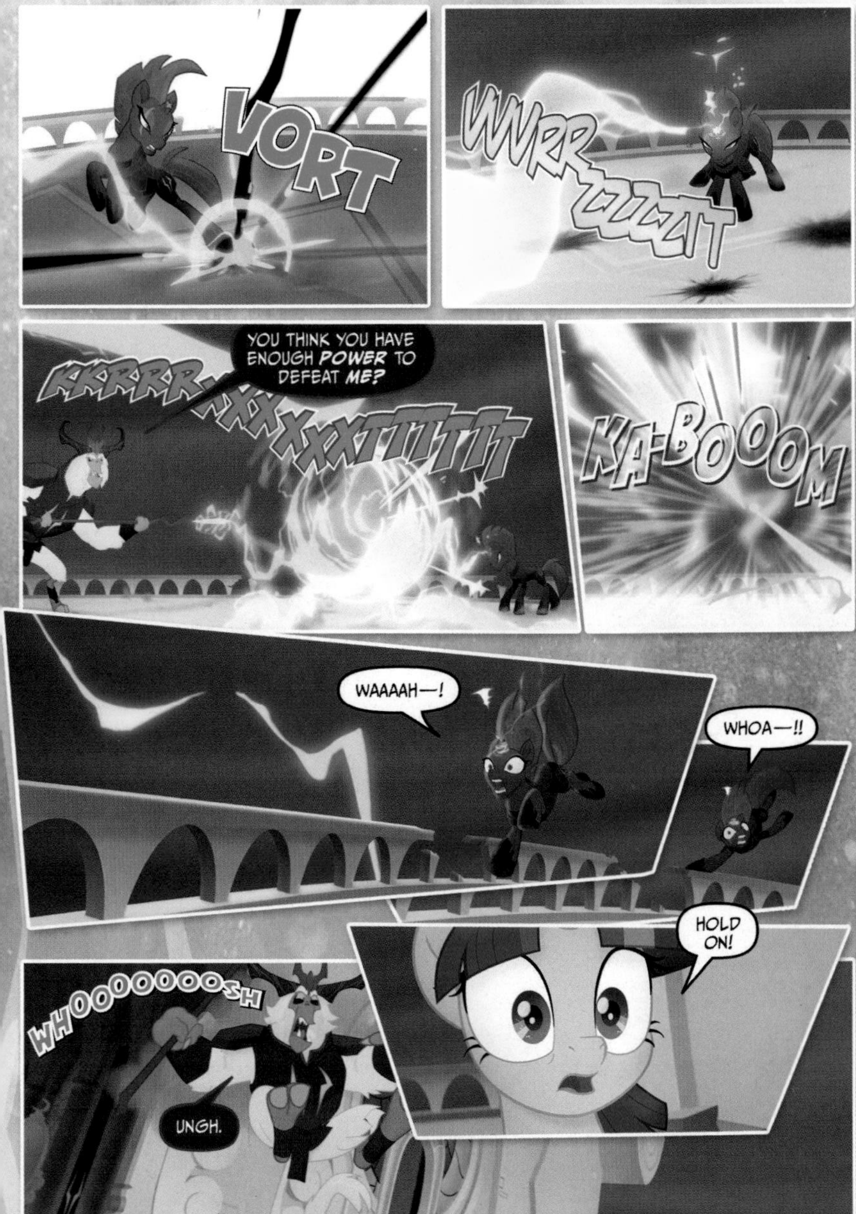
VORT
VVVRR ZZZZTT
KKRRRRRXXXXXXTTTTTTT
YOU THINK YOU HAVE ENOUGH POWER TO DEFEAT ME?
KA-BOOOOM
WAAAAH—!
WHOA—!!
HOLD ON!
WHOOOOOOOOSH
UNGH.

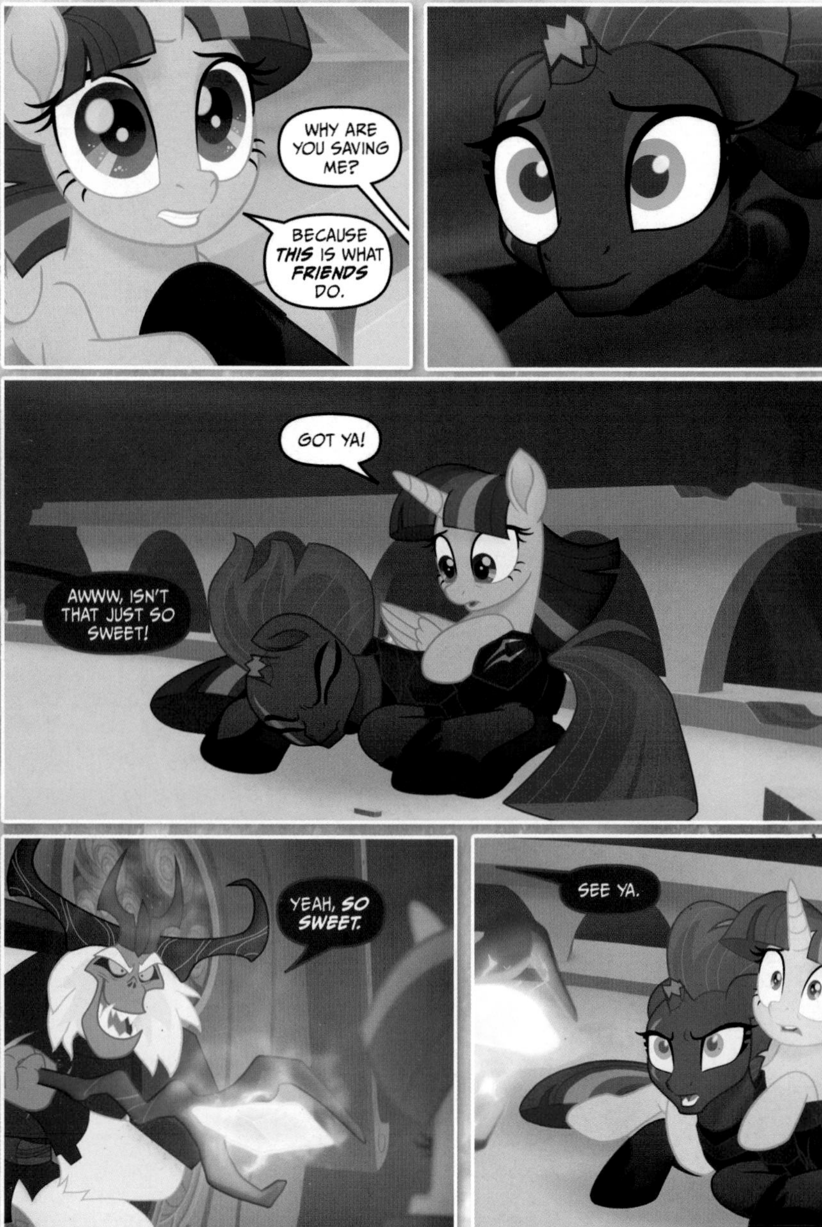
WHY ARE YOU SAVING ME?
BECAUSE THIS IS WHAT FRIENDS DO.
GOT YA!
AWWW, ISN'T THAT JUST SO SWEET!
YEAH, SO SWEET.
SEE YA.

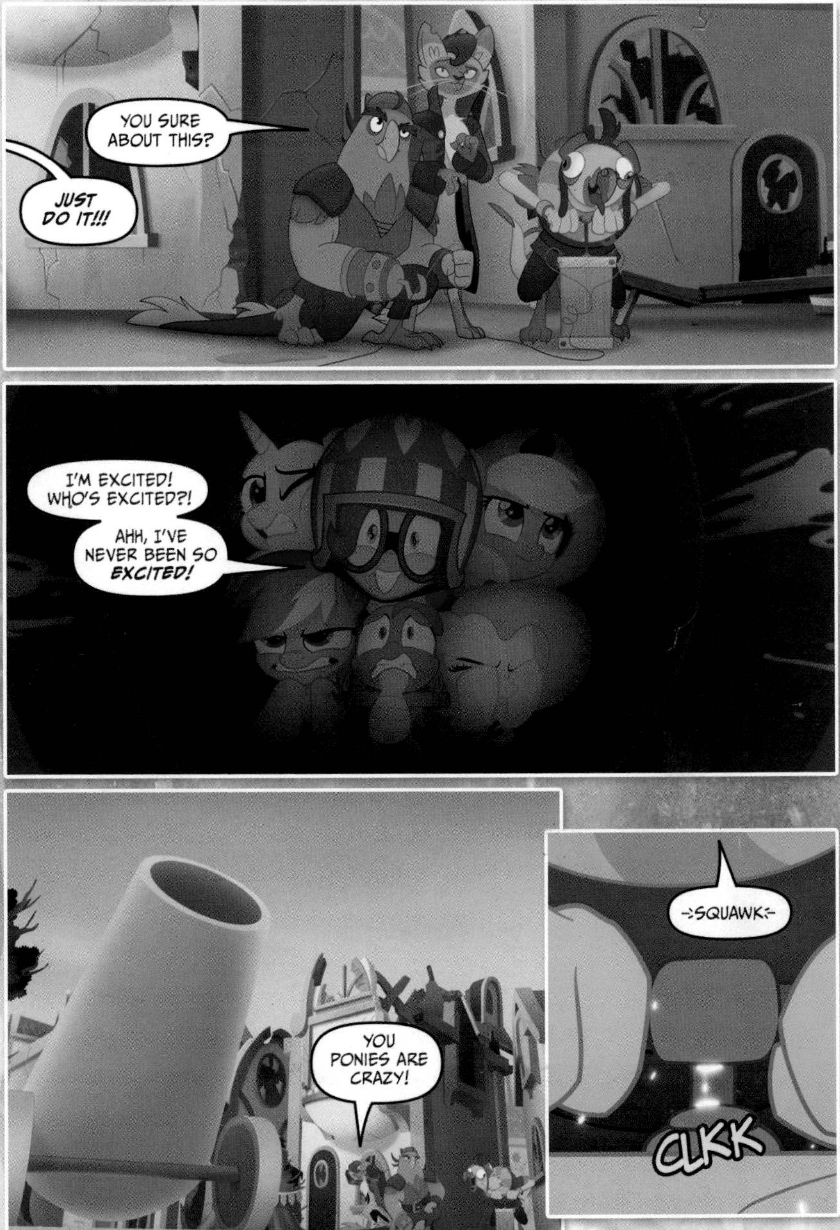
YOU SURE ABOUT THIS?
JUST DO IT!!!
I'M EXCITED! WHO'S EXCITED?!
AHH, I'VE NEVER BEEN SO EXCITED!
YOU PONIES ARE CRAZY!
-SQUAWK-
CLKK

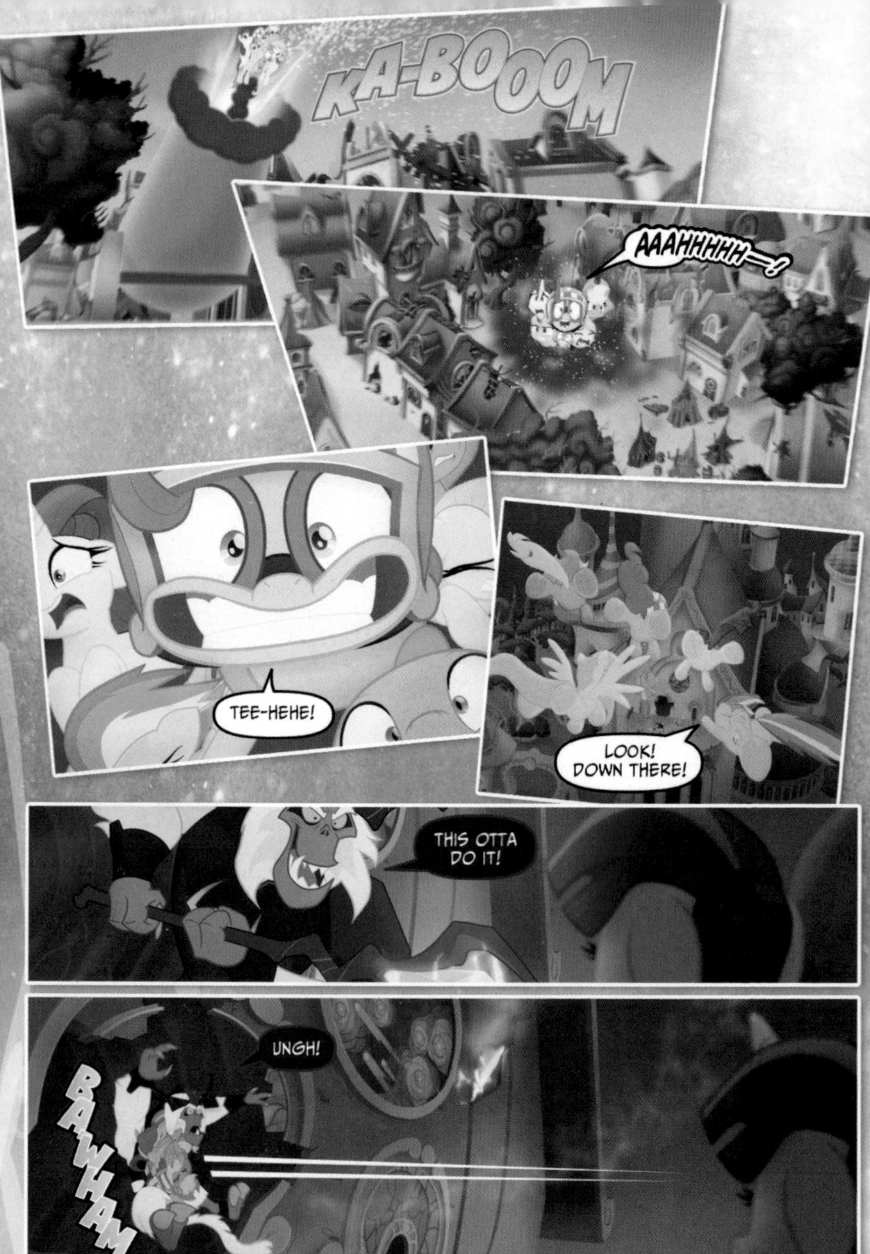
KA-BOOOOM
AAAHHHHH—!
TEE-HEHE!
LOOK! DOWN THERE!
THIS OTTA DO IT!
UNGH!
BAWHAM

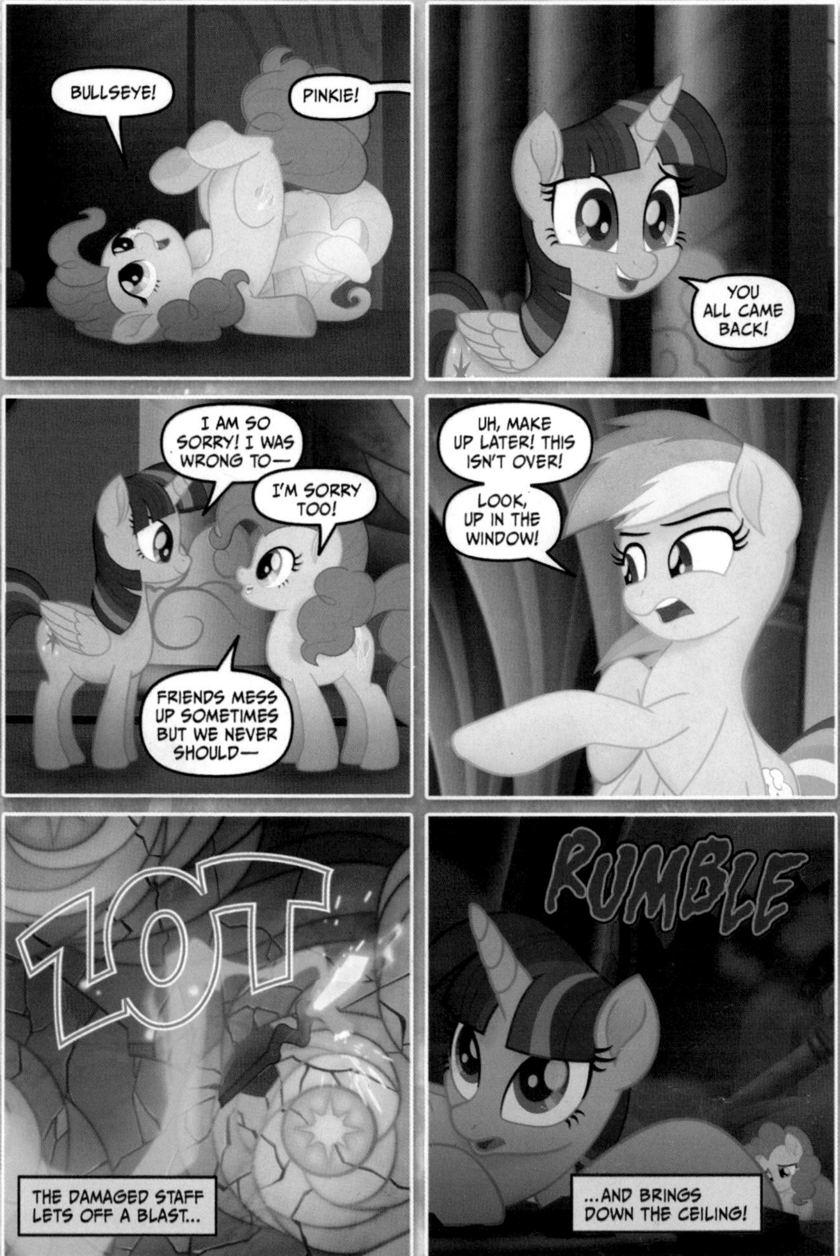
BULLSEYE!
PINKIE!
YOU ALL CAME BACK!
I AM SO SORRY! I WAS WRONG TO—
I'M SORRY TOO!
FRIENDS MESS UP SOMETIMES BUT WE NEVER SHOULD—
UH, MAKE UP LATER! THIS ISN'T OVER!
LOOK, UP IN THE WINDOW!
ZOT
THE DAMAGED STAFF LETS OFF A BLAST...
RUMBLE
...AND BRINGS DOWN THE CEILING!

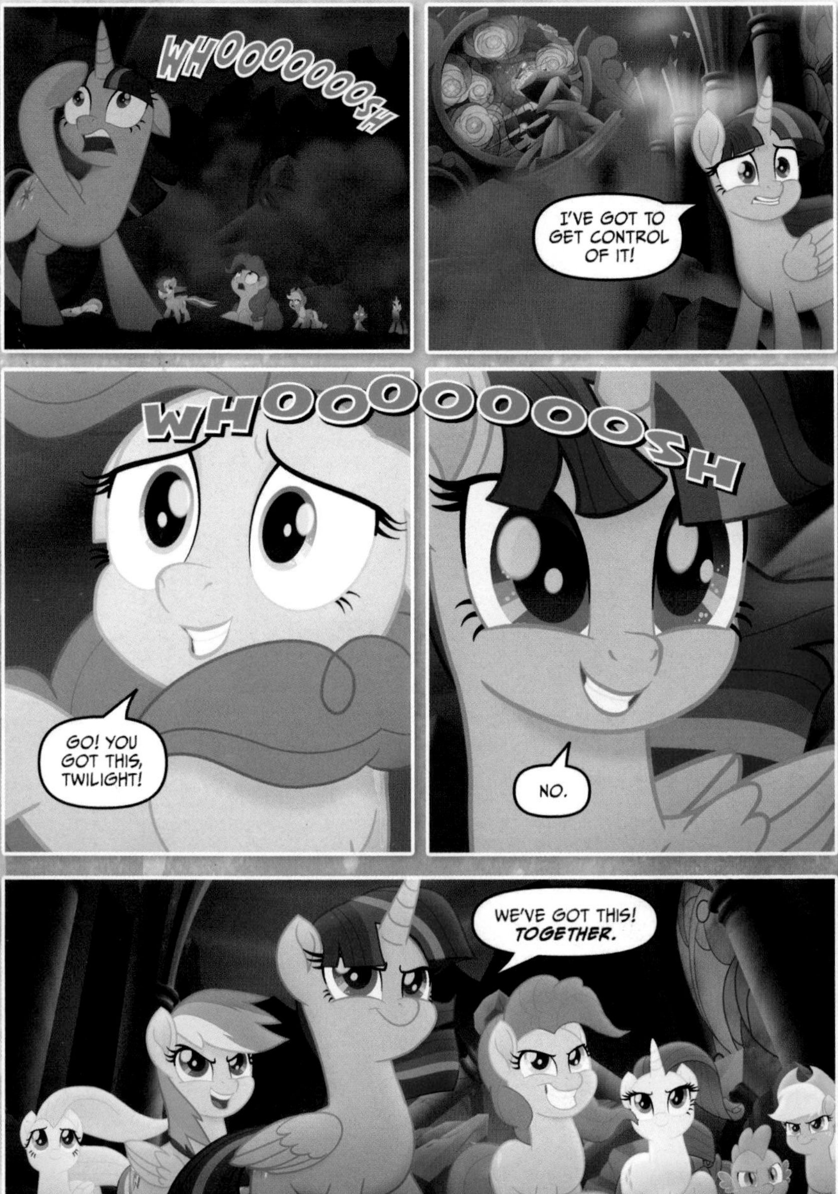
WHOOOOOOOOSH
I'VE GOT TO GET CONTROL OF IT!
WHOOOOOOOOOOSH
GO! YOU GOT THIS, TWILIGHT!
NO.
WE'VE GOT THIS! *TOGETHER.*

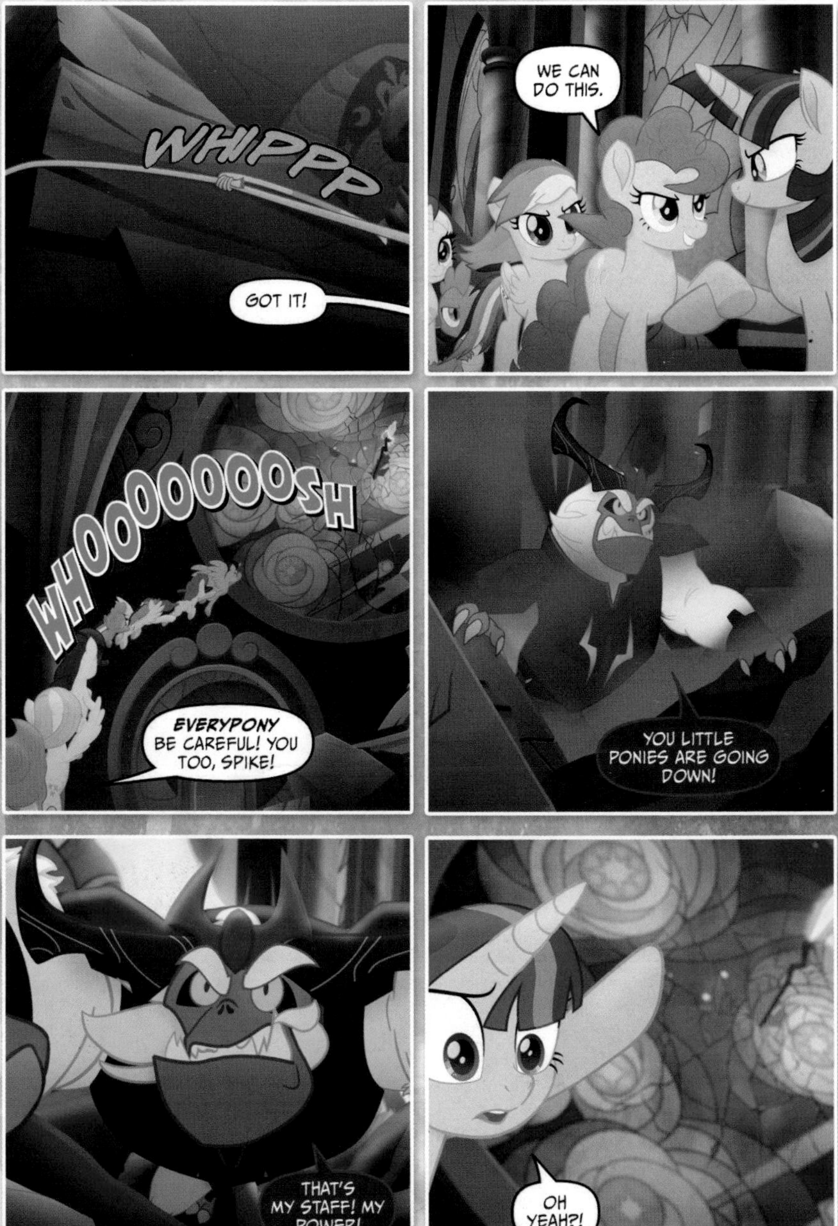
WHIPPP
GOT IT!
WE CAN DO THIS.
WHOOOOOOOOSH
EVERYPONY BE CAREFUL! YOU TOO, SPIKE!
YOU LITTLE PONIES ARE GOING DOWN!
THAT'S MY STAFF! MY POWER!
OH YEAH?!

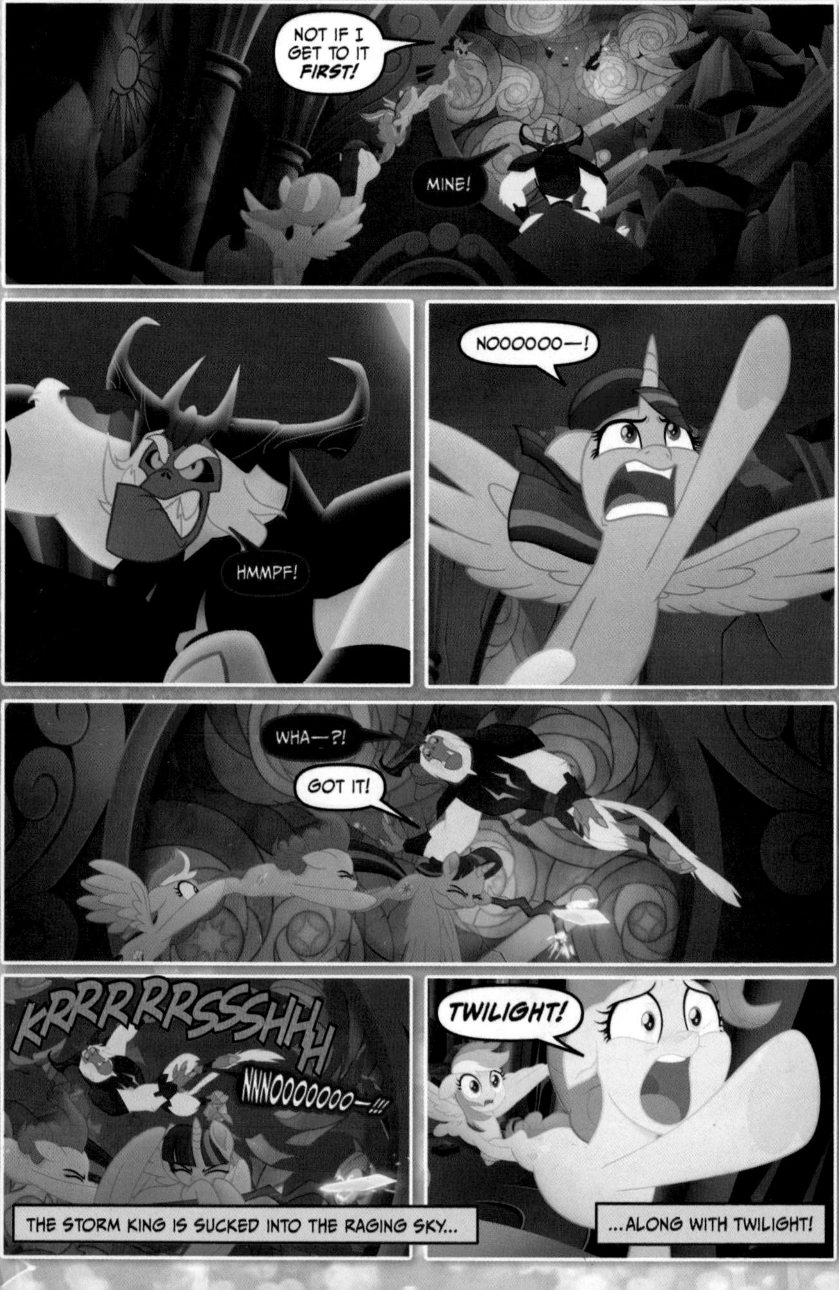
NOT IF I GET TO IT FIRST!
MINE!
HMMPF!
NOOOOOO—!
WHA—?!
GOT IT!
KRRRRRSSSHHHH
NNNOOOOOOOO—!!!
THE STORM KING IS SUCKED INTO THE RAGING SKY...
TWILIGHT!
...ALONG WITH TWILIGHT!

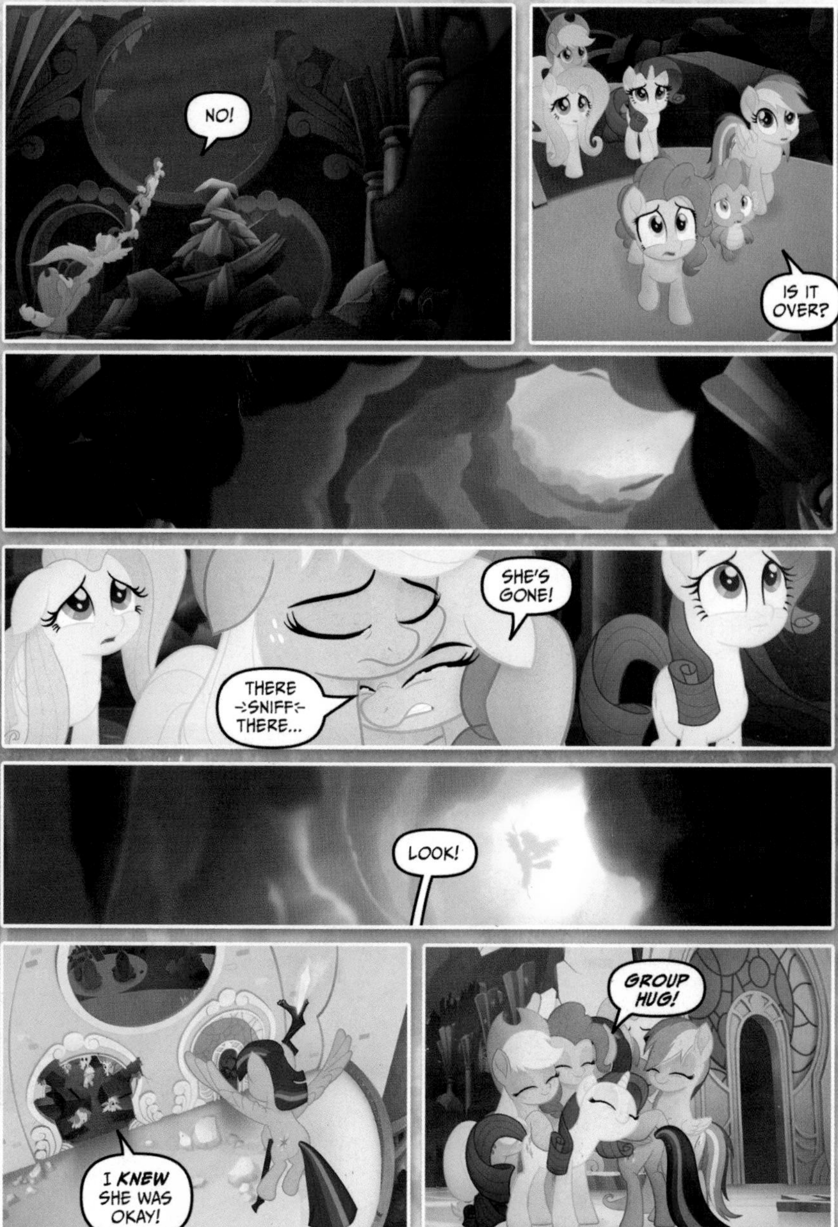
NO!
IS IT OVER?
SHE'S GONE!
THERE -SNIFF- THERE...
LOOK!
I KNEW SHE WAS OKAY!
GROUP HUG!

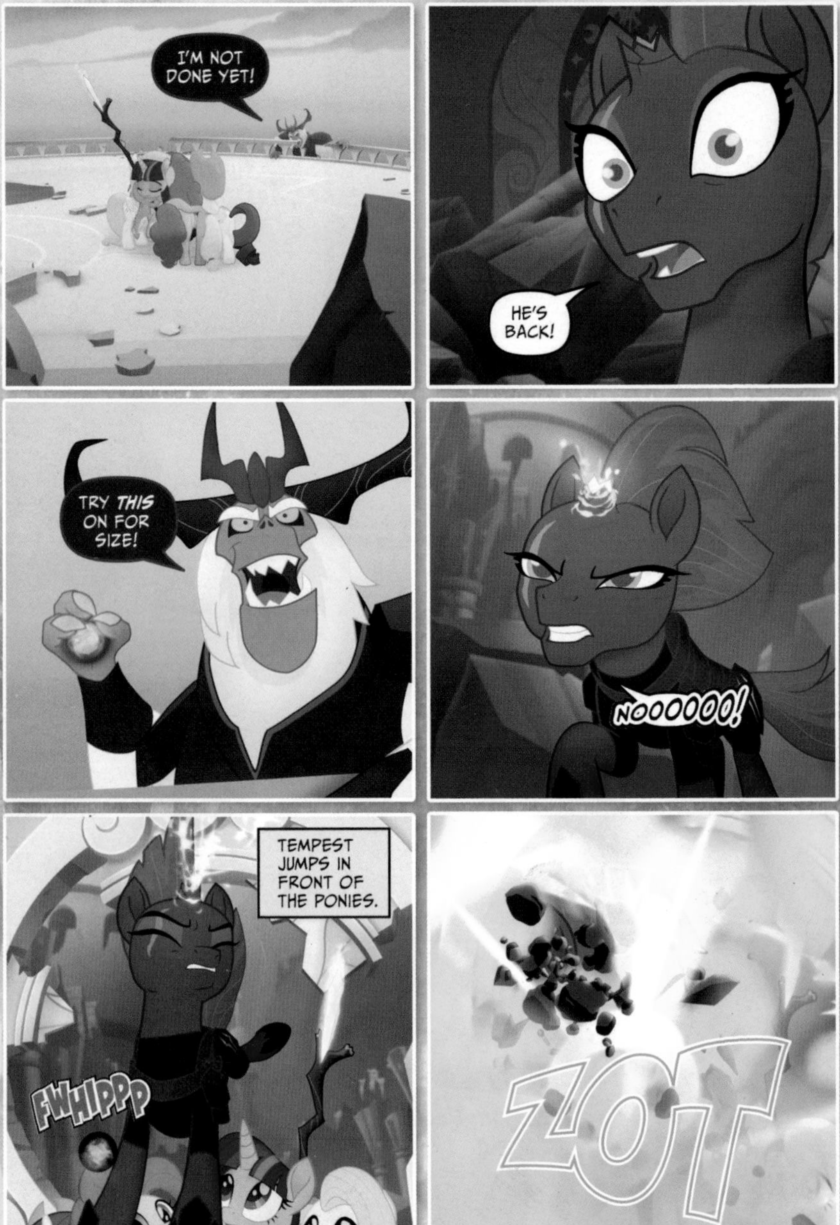

I'M NOT DONE YET!
HE'S BACK!
TRY THIS ON FOR SIZE!
NOOOOOO!
TEMPEST JUMPS IN FRONT OF THE PONIES.
FWHIPPP
ZOT

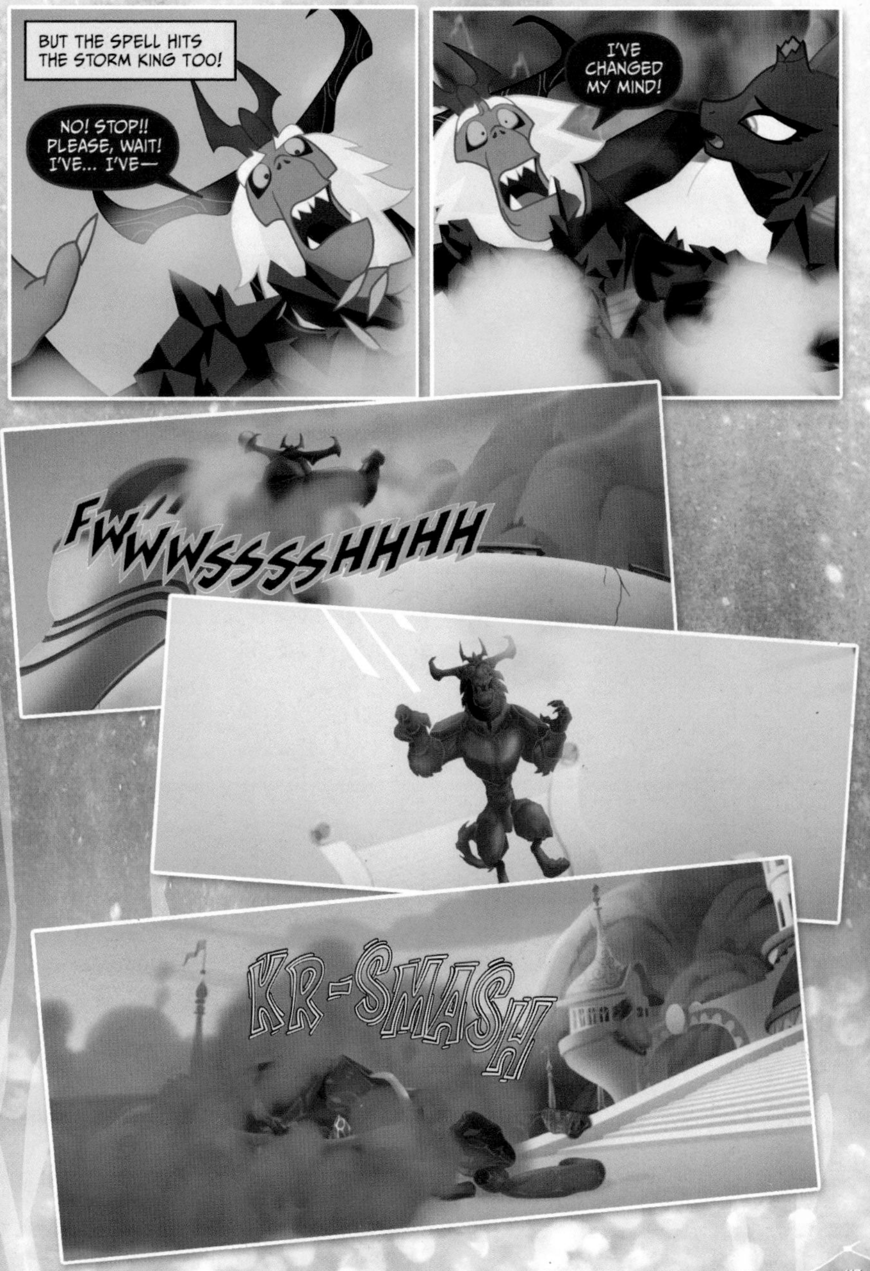
BUT THE SPELL HITS THE STORM KING TOO!
NO! STOP!! PLEASE, WAIT! I'VE... I'VE—
I'VE CHANGED MY MIND!
FWWWSSSSHHHH
KR-SMASH

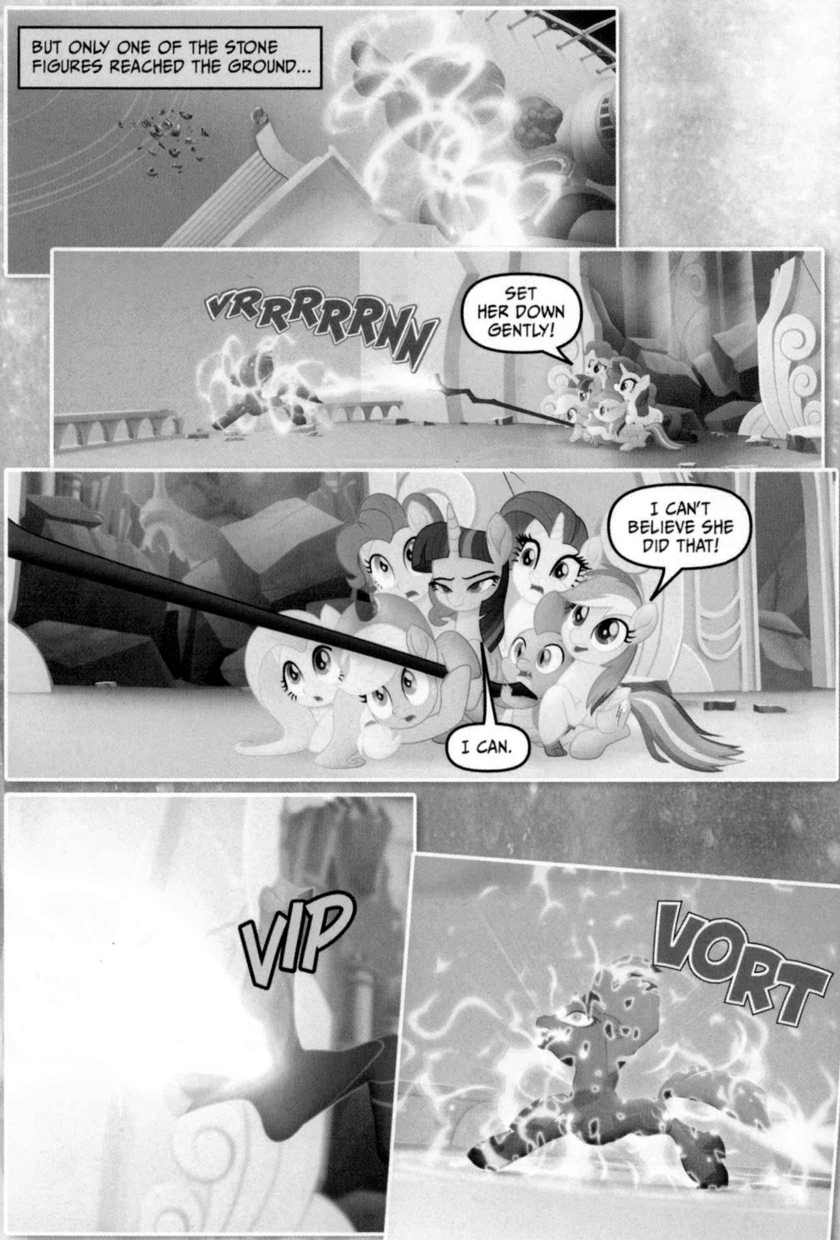

BUT ONLY ONE OF THE STONE FIGURES REACHED THE GROUND...
VRRRRRNN
SET HER DOWN GENTLY!
I CAN'T BELIEVE SHE DID THAT!
I CAN.
VIP
VORT

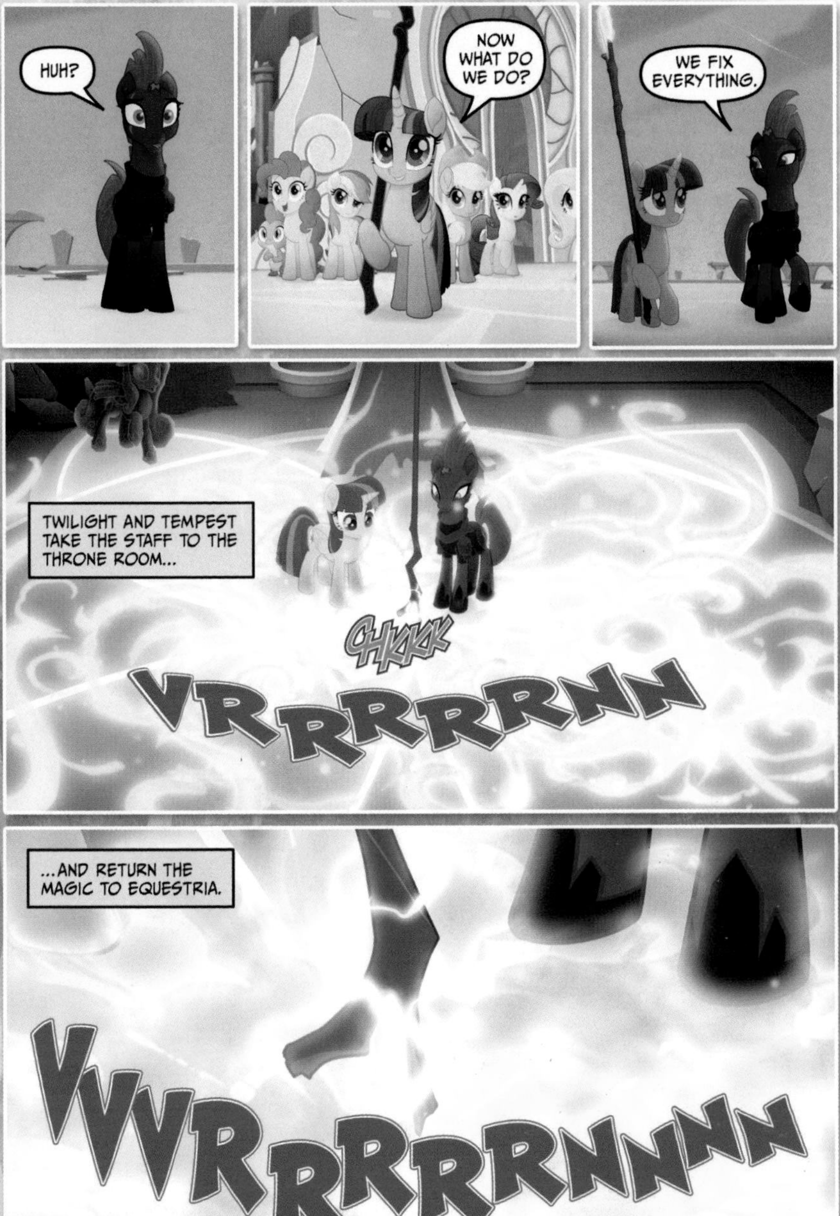
HUH?
NOW WHAT DO WE DO?
WE FIX EVERYTHING.
TWILIGHT AND TEMPEST TAKE THE STAFF TO THE THRONE ROOM...
CHKKK
VRRRRRNN
...AND RETURN THE MAGIC TO EQUESTRIA.
VVVRRRRRNNNN

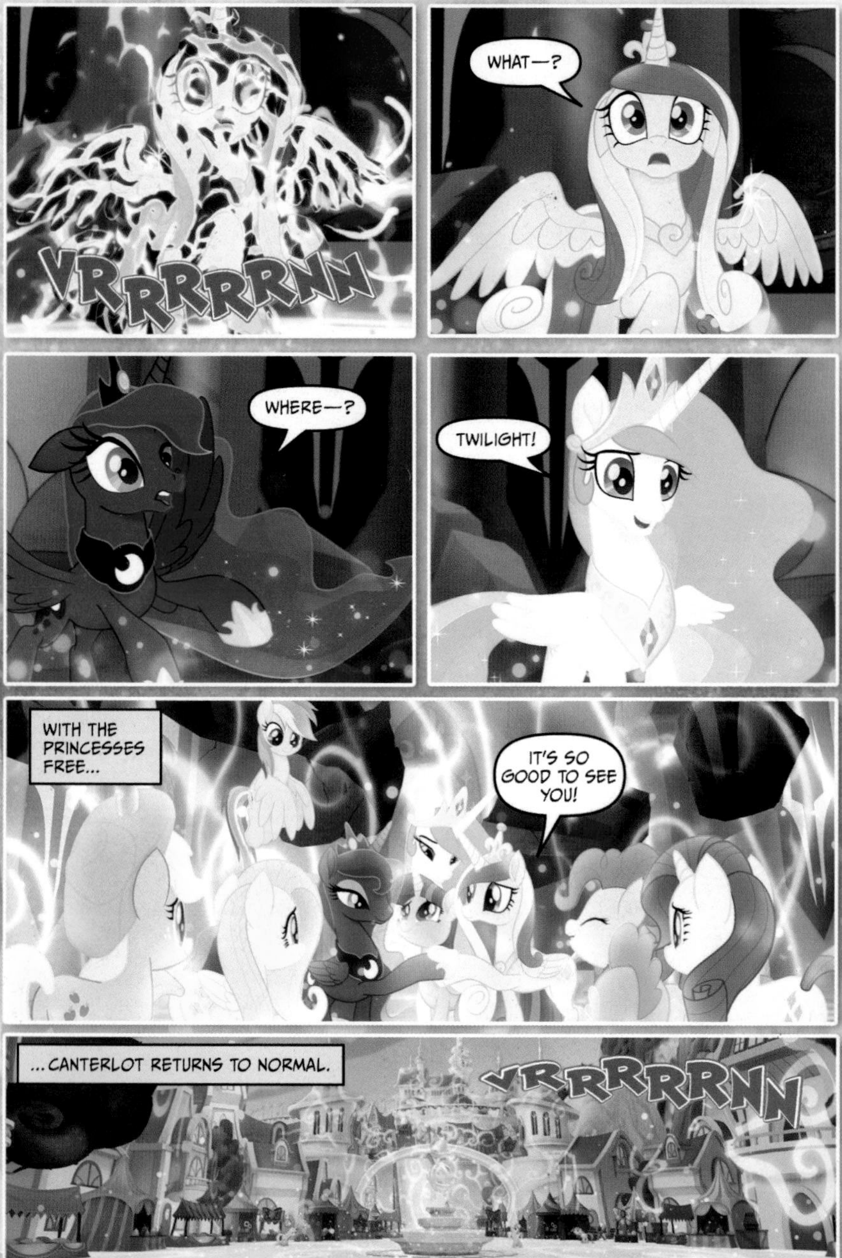
VRRRRRRNN
WHAT—?
WHERE—?
TWILIGHT!
WITH THE PRINCESSES FREE...
IT'S SO GOOD TO SEE YOU!
...CANTERLOT RETURNS TO NORMAL.
VRRRRRRNN

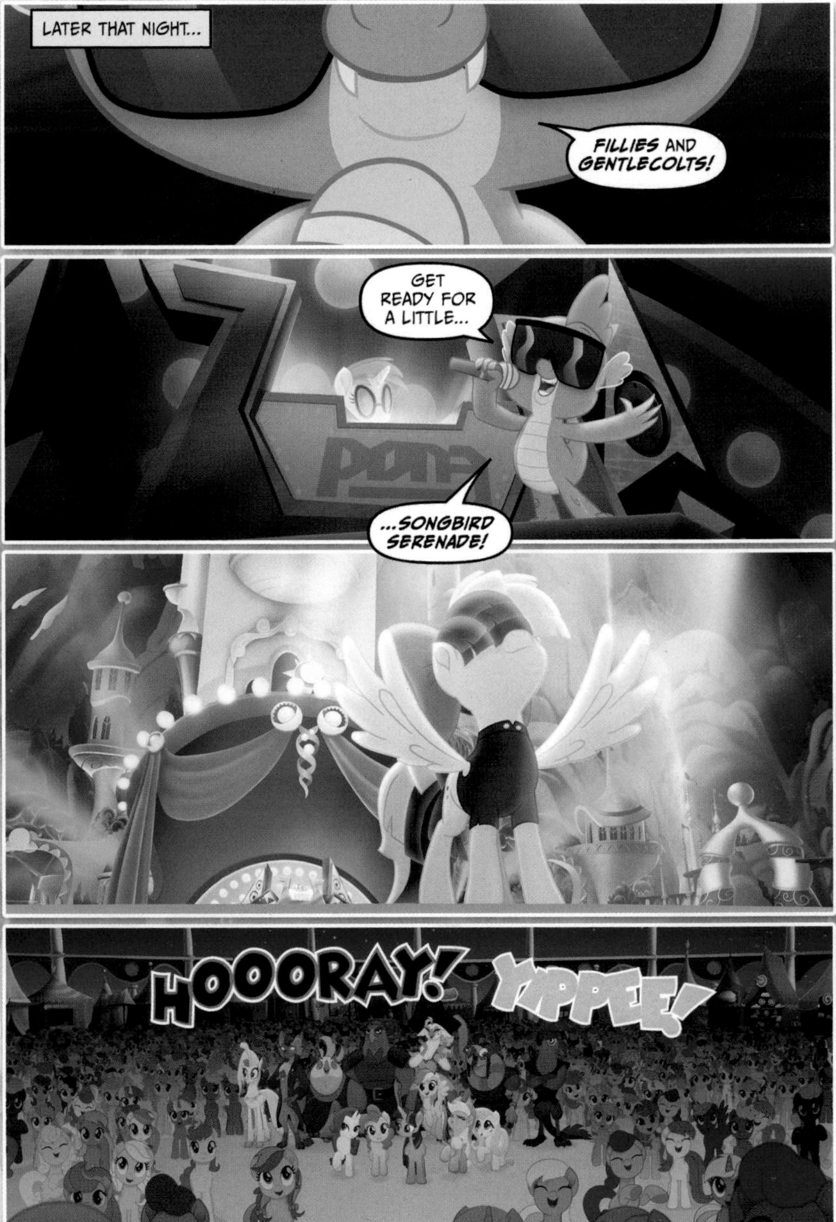
LATER THAT NIGHT...
FILLIES AND GENTLECOLTS!
GET READY FOR A LITTLE...
...SONGBIRD SERENADE!
HOOORAY!
YIPPEE!

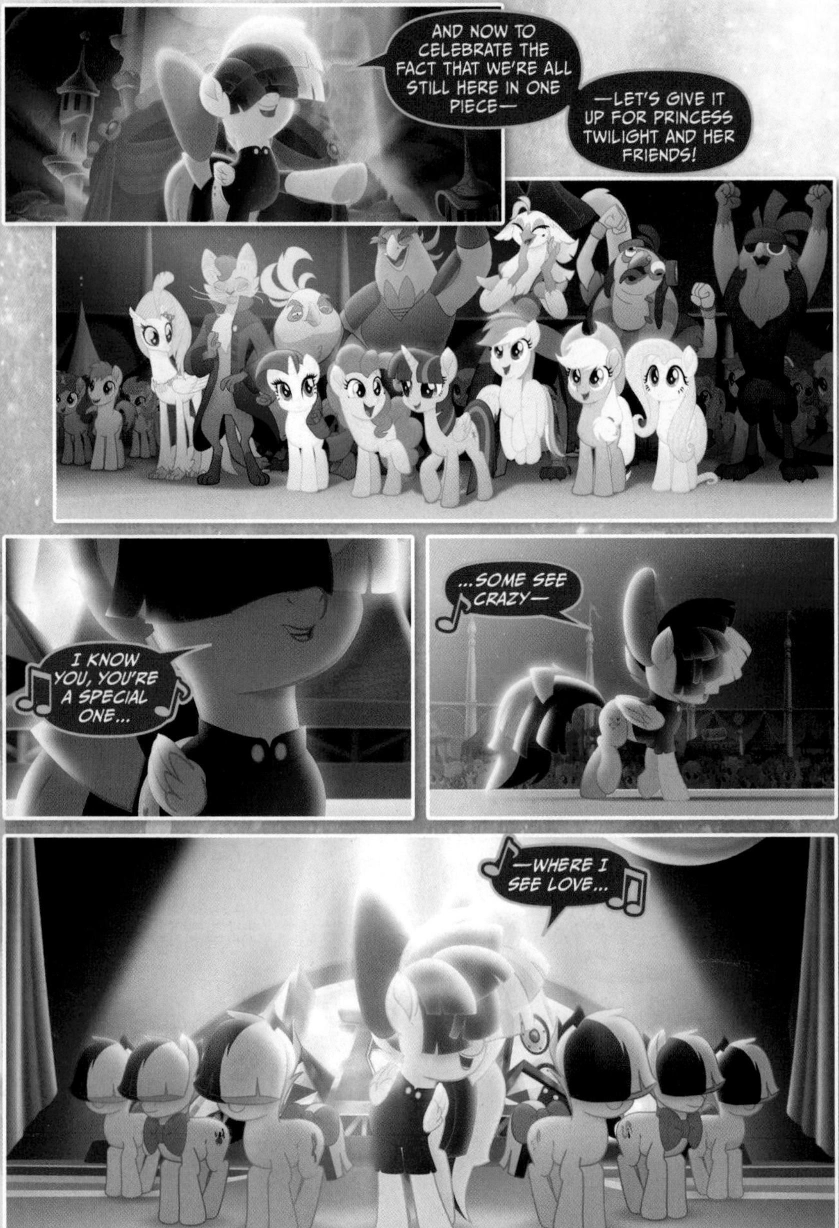
AND NOW TO CELEBRATE THE FACT THAT WE'RE ALL STILL HERE IN ONE PIECE—
—LET'S GIVE IT UP FOR PRINCESS TWILIGHT AND HER FRIENDS!
I KNOW YOU, YOU'RE A SPECIAL ONE...
...SOME SEE CRAZY—
—WHERE I SEE LOVE...

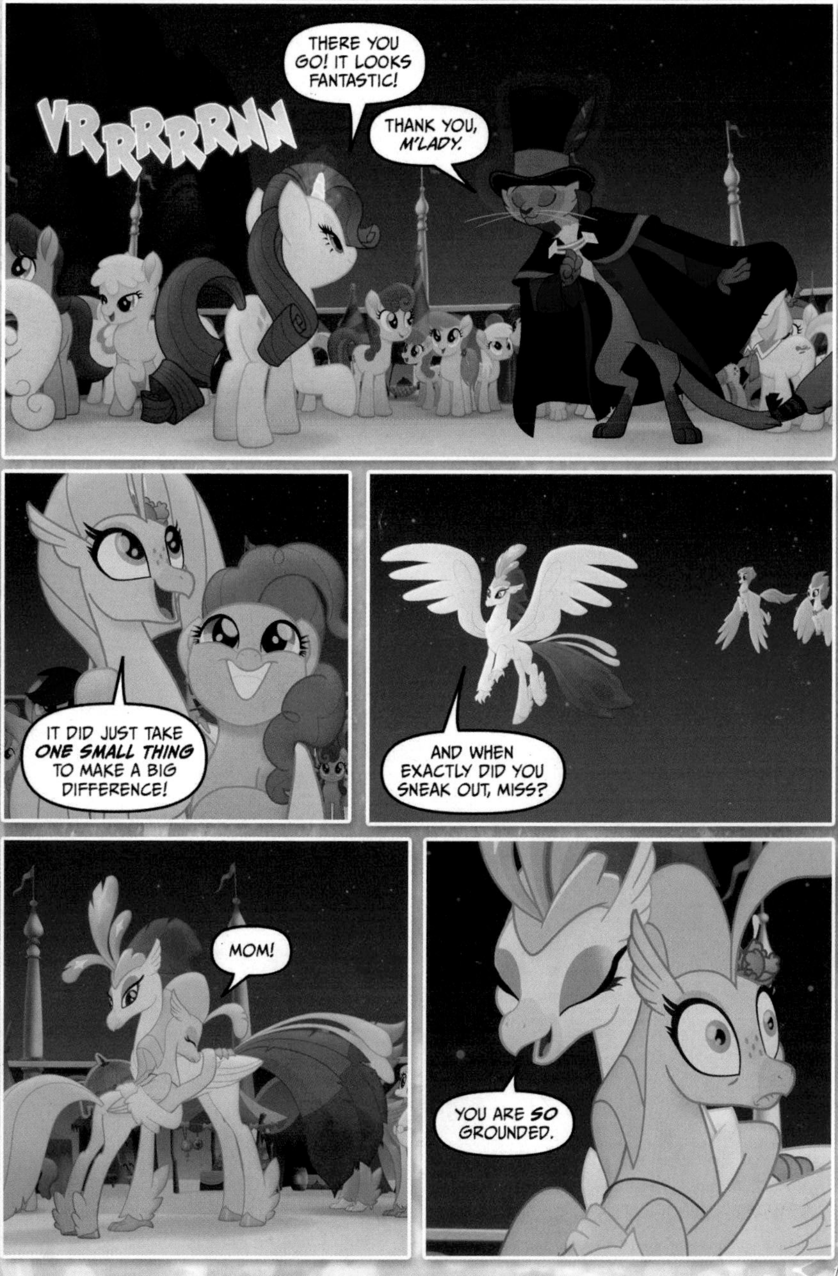
VRRRRRRNN
THERE YOU GO! IT LOOKS FANTASTIC!
THANK YOU, *M'LADY.*
IT DID JUST TAKE ***ONE SMALL THING*** TO MAKE A BIG DIFFERENCE!
AND WHEN EXACTLY DID YOU SNEAK OUT, MISS?
MOM!
YOU ARE ***SO*** GROUNDED.

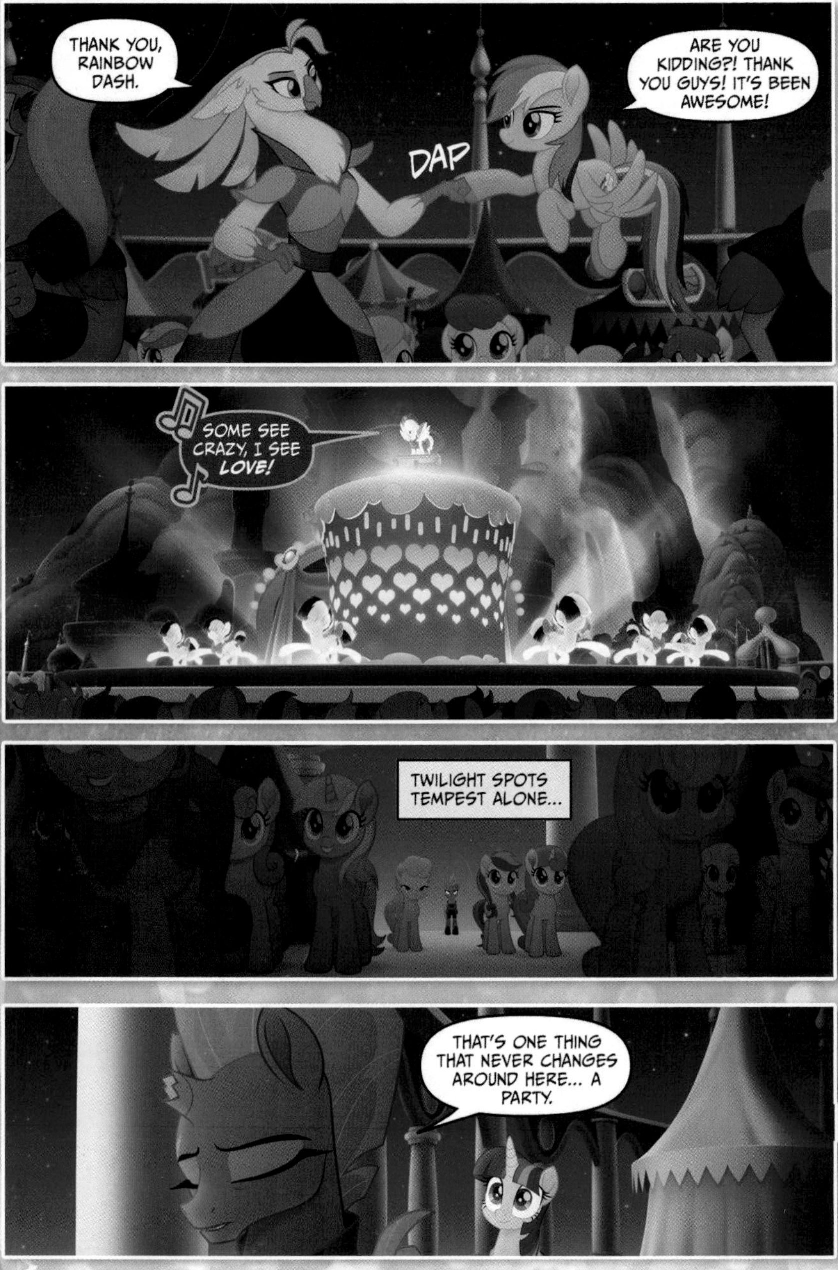
THANK YOU, RAINBOW DASH.
ARE YOU KIDDING?! THANK YOU GUYS! IT'S BEEN AWESOME!
DAP
SOME SEE CRAZY, I SEE LOVE!
TWILIGHT SPOTS TEMPEST ALONE...
THAT'S ONE THING THAT NEVER CHANGES AROUND HERE... A PARTY.

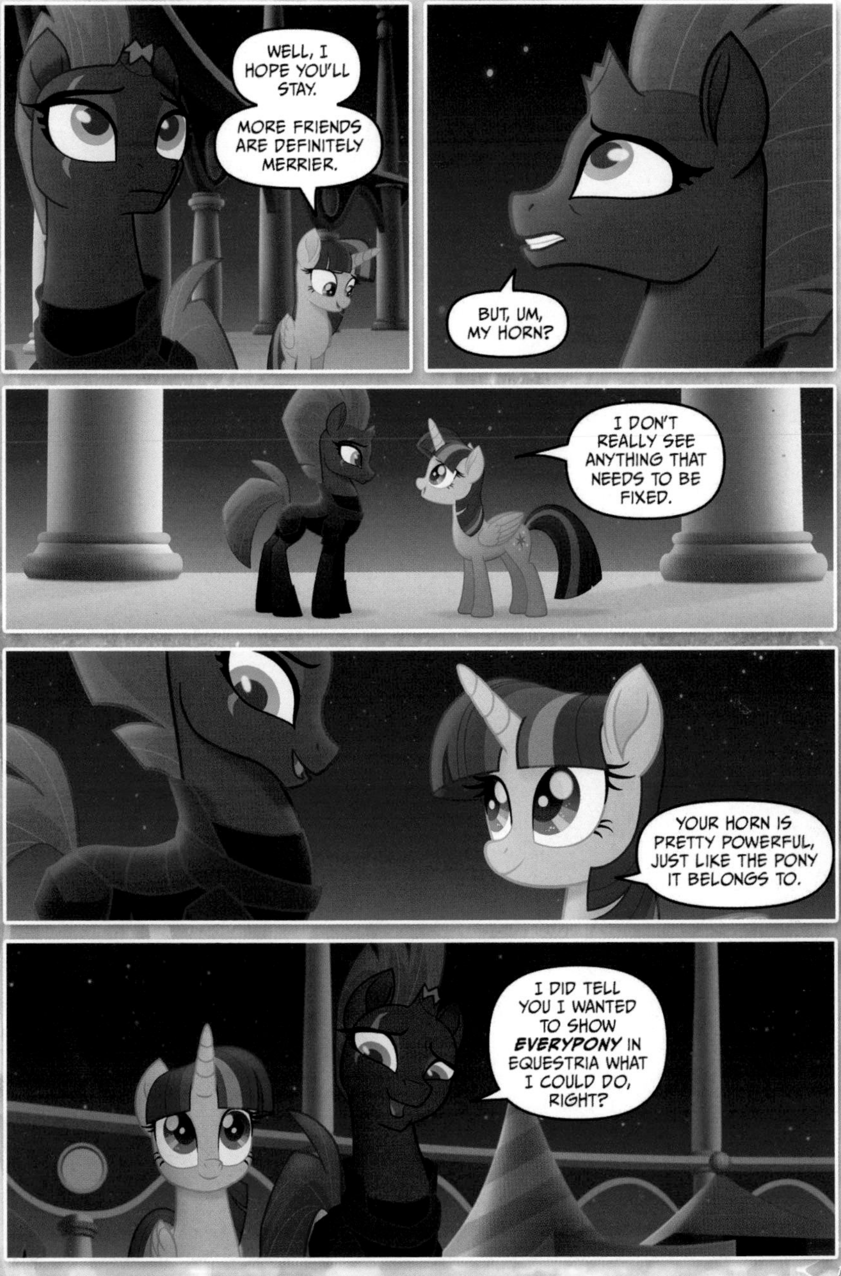
WELL, I HOPE YOU'LL STAY.
MORE FRIENDS ARE DEFINITELY MERRIER.
BUT, UM, MY HORN?
I DON'T REALLY SEE ANYTHING THAT NEEDS TO BE FIXED.
YOUR HORN IS PRETTY POWERFUL, JUST LIKE THE PONY IT BELONGS TO.
I DID TELL YOU I WANTED TO SHOW ***EVERYPONY*** IN EQUESTRIA WHAT I COULD DO, RIGHT?

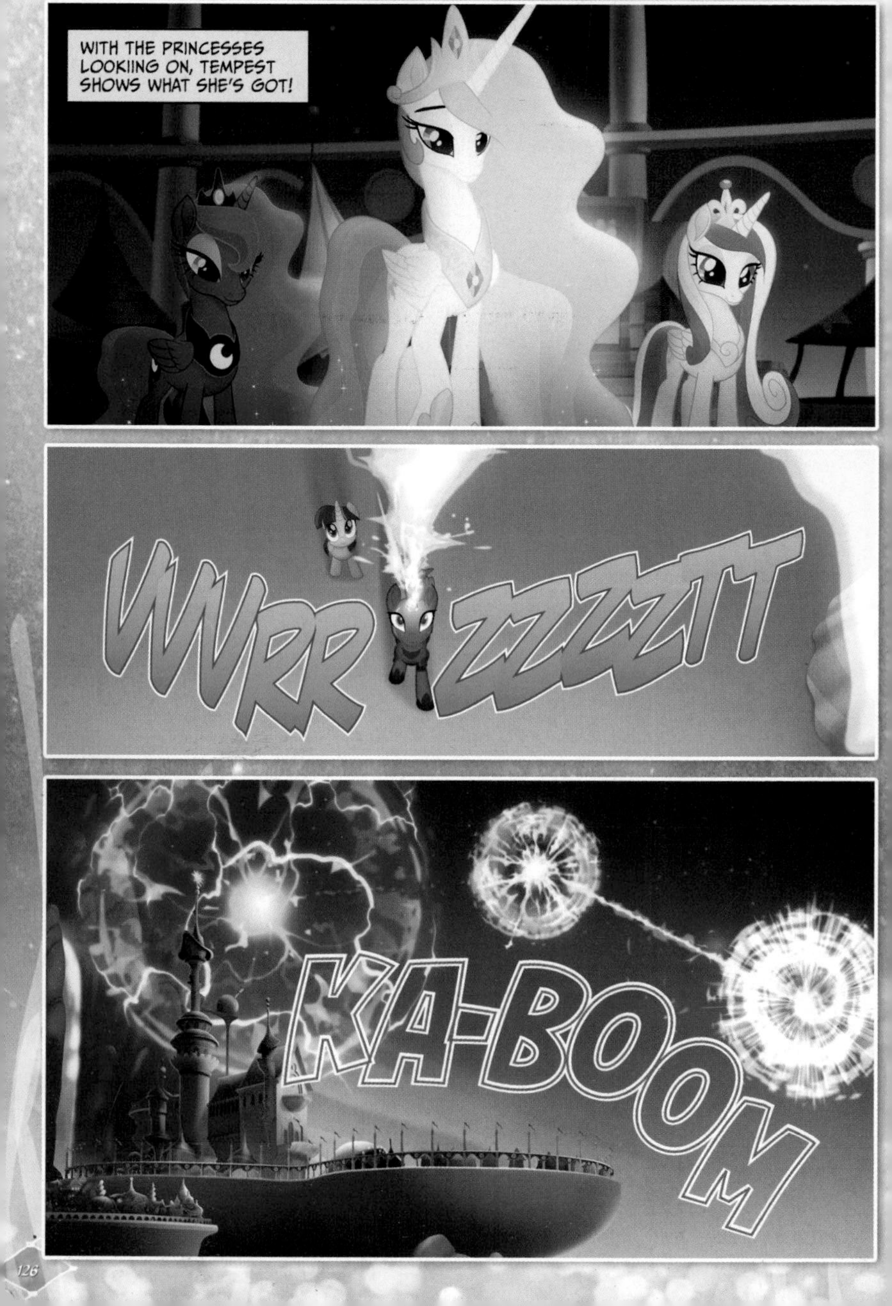
WITH THE PRINCESSES LOOKIING ON, TEMPEST SHOWS WHAT SHE'S GOT!
WRRZZZZTT
KA-BOOOM

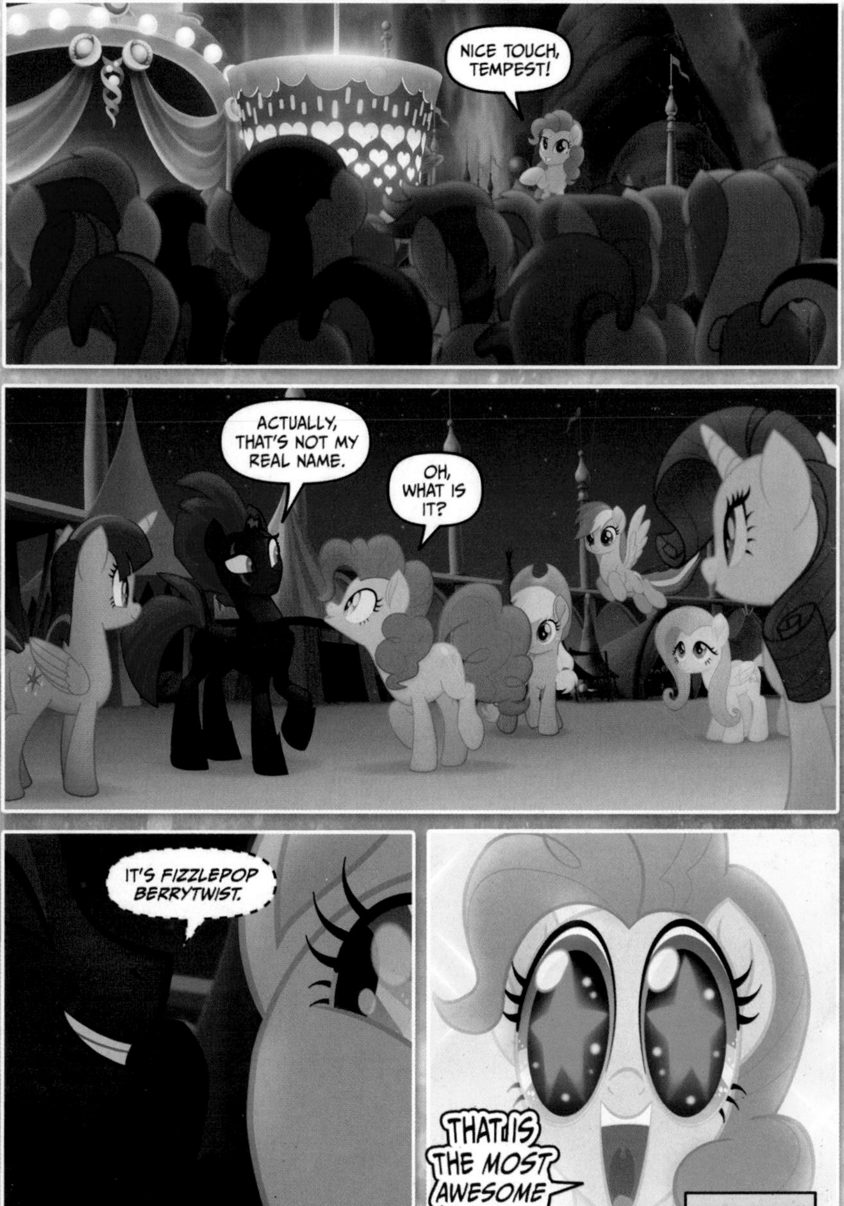
NICE TOUCH, TEMPEST!
ACTUALLY, THAT'S NOT MY REAL NAME.
OH, WHAT IS IT?
IT'S FIZZLEPOP BERRYTWIST.
THAT IS THE MOST AWESOME NAME EVER!!!
THE END!

my LITTLE PONY The MOVIE

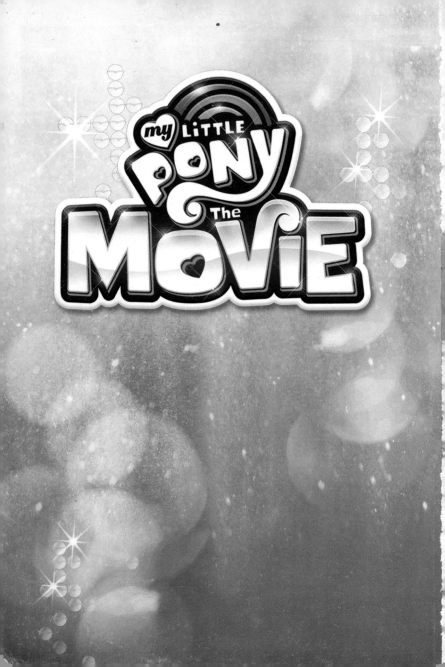